courtesy of the author

MAI JIA, who spent many years in the Chinese military, is one of China's bestselling and most famous writers. He is the author of seven novels, three of which have been turned into television series and films. Mai has won almost every major book prize in China, including its highest literary honor, the Mao Dun Literature Prize. *Decoded* has been translated into eighteen languages and published in thirty-five countries.

Additional Praise for *Decoded*

"A mixture of Kafka and Agatha Christie . . . An utterly fascinating read."   —Edward Wilson, *The Independent* (London)

"The book's subtle ambiguity is extended to its own conclusion, the decoding of which the reader is compelled to take part in."
                                        —*The Wall Street Journal*

"Subtle and psychologically focused . . . The central story is a gripping one. . . . It leaves you eager to read more of Mai's work."
                                        —*The Observer* (London)

"Riveting . . . at once heartbreaking and thought-provoking . . . [Mai is] a Chinese literary treasure."   —*Booklist* (starred review)

"An intricate and carefully presented story that will draw readers in and hold their attention right until the end."   —*Bustle*

"Between the thrills of pulp fiction and those novels which come to be considered classics, there are boundaries and lines which, for many writers, are difficult to cross, and may take a lifetime (if ever) to realize. Mai Jia's achievement is that he has overcome that barrier with steady and assured strides. The footprints he has left behind form an ingenious, secretive literary treasure map."
                        —Wong Kar-wai, director of *The Grandmaster*

"When I say that [*Decoded*] is excellent, I am referring both to its remarkable literary qualities and to the fact that it demands to be read in a single sitting."
                        —Alai, Mao Dun Literature Prize–winning
                        author of *Red Poppies*

DECODED

Mai Jia

Translated from the Chinese by
Olivia Milburn and Christopher Payne

Picador   Farrar, Straus and Giroux   New York

www.picadorusa.com
www.twitter.com/picadorusa • www.facebook.com/picadorusa
picadorbookroom.tumblr.com

Picador® is a U.S. registered trademark and is used by Farrar, Straus and Giroux under license from Pan Books Limited.

For book club information, please visit www.facebook.com/picadorbookclub or e-mail marketing@picadorusa.com.

The Library of Congress has cataloged the Farrar, Straus and Giroux edition as follows:

Mai, Jia 1963–
    [Jie mi. English]
    Decoded / Mai Jia ; Translated from the Chinese by Olivia Milburn and
    Christopher Payne. — First American edition.
        pages   cm
    Originally published in Chinese in 2002 by China Youth Publishing Group,
    Beijing entitled Jie mi.
    ISBN 978-0-374-13580-5 (hardcover)
    ISBN 978-0-374-71084-2 (e-book)
        I. Milburn, Olivia, translator.   II. Payne, Christopher, 1976– translator.
    III. Title.
    PL2882.I28 J5513 2014
    895.13'52—dc23

                                                                        2013039911

Picador Paperback ISBN 978-1-250-06235-2

Picador books may be purchased for educational, business, or promotional use.
For information on bulk purchases, please contact the Macmillan Corporate and Premium Sales
Department at 1-800-221-7945, extension 5442, or write to specialmarkets@macmillan.com.

Originally published in China by China Youth Publishing Group, Beijing
English translation originally published in Great Britain by Allen Lane, an imprint of Penguin Books UK

First published in the United States by Farrar, Straus and Giroux

First Picador Edition: March 2015

10 9 8 7 6 5 4 3 2 1

In the Beginning

I.

The man who left Tongzhen on the little black ferry in 1873 with a view to studying abroad was the youngest member of the seventh generation of that famous family of salt merchants: the Rongs of Jiangnan. When he left, he was called Rong Zilai, but by the time he returned he was called John Lillie. Going by what people said later on, he was the first person in the Rong family to break from their mercantile heritage and become an academic, not to mention a great patriot. Of course, this development was inextricably linked with the many years that he spent abroad. However, when the Rong family originally picked him to be the one to go overseas, it was not because they wanted him to bring about this fundamental change in the clan's fortunes, but because they were hoping that it might help Grandmother Rong live for a little bit longer.

As a young woman, Grandmother Rong had proved an excellent mother, giving birth to nine sons and seven daughters over the course of two decades; what is more, all of them lived to be adults. It was these children who laid the foundations of the Rong family fortune, making her position at the very top of the clan hierarchy unassailable. Thanks to the assiduous attentions of her children and grandchildren she lived much longer than she might otherwise have done, but she was not a happy woman. She was afflicted by all sorts of distressing and complex dreams, to the point where she often woke up screaming; even in broad daylight she would still be suffering from the lingering terrors of the night. When these nightmares tormented her, her numerous progeny, not to mention the vast wealth of the family, came to seem a crushing burden. The flames licking the incense in the brazier often flickered uncertainly with the force of her high-pitched shrieks. Every morning, a couple of local scholars would be invited to come to the Rong mansion to interpret the old lady's dreams, but as time went by it became clear that none of them were much use.

Of all the many people called in to interpret her dreams, Grandmother Rong was the most impressed by a young man who had recently washed up in Tongzhen from somewhere overseas. Not only did he make no mistakes in explaining the inner meanings of the old lady's dreams, but sometimes he even seemed to display clairvoyance in interpreting the significance of individuals who would appear in the future. It was only his youth that led people to imagine that his abilities in this direction were superficial – or to use Grandmother Rong's own words, 'nothing good ever came of employing people still wet behind the ears'. He was very good at explaining dreams but his divination skills were much poorer. It seemed that if he started off on the wrong foot, he simply could not right himself again. To tell the truth, he was very good at dealing with the old lady's dreams from the first part of the night, but he was completely unable to cope with those that she had towards dawn, or the dreams within dreams. By his own account, he had never formally studied this kind of divination technique, but had managed to learn a little simply by following his grandfather around and listening in. Having only dabbled in this kind of thing before, he could hardly be classed as an expert.

Grandmother Rong moved aside a sliding panel in the wall and showed him the silver ingots stacked within, begging him to bring his grandfather to China. The only answer that she received was that it was impossible. There were two reasons for this. First, his grandfather was already very wealthy and had lost all interest in making more money a long time ago. Furthermore, his grandfather was a very old man and the thought of having to travel across the ocean at his time of life might very well scare him to death. On the other hand the young man did come up with one practical suggestion for the old lady: send someone overseas to study.

If Mohammed won't go to the mountain, then the mountain will have to come to Mohammed.

The next task was to find a suitable person to go from among the old lady's myriad descendants. There were two crucial criteria for selection. It would have to be someone with an unusual sense of filial duty to Grandmother Rong, who would be prepared to suffer for her sake. What is more, it would have to be someone intelligent and interested in study, who could learn the complicated techniques of dream interpretation and divination in the shortest possible time and to a very high level. After a careful process of triage, a twenty-year-old grandson named Rong Zilai was selected for the task. Thus, Rong Zilai, armed with a letter of recommendation from the foreign young man and burdened with the task of finding a way to prolong his wretched grandmother's life, set out to cross the ocean in search of learning. One month later, on a stormy night, just as Rong Zilai's steamer was forging its way through the ocean swell, his grandmother dreamed that a typhoon swallowed up the ship and sank it, sending her grandson to feed the fishes. Caught up in her dream, the old lady was so horrified that she ceased breathing. The trauma of her dream resulted in cardiac arrest; the old lady died in her sleep. Thanks to the length and difficulty of his journey, by the time that Rong Zilai stood in front of his would-be tutor and reverently presented his letter of introduction, the old man handed him another letter in return which announced the news of his grandmother's death. Information always travels much faster than people do. As we know from personal experience, it is the fastest runner that gets to the tape first.

The old man looked at this young man who had come from so far away with a sharp glance, so keen that it could have been used to shoot down a flying bird. It seemed as though he was genuinely interested in taking on this foreign student, who had come to him in his twilight years. Thinking it over afterwards, however, since Grandmother Rong had died, there was no point in studying this esoteric skill and so, while he appreciated the old man's offer, Rong Zilai decided to go back home. However, while he was waiting for his passage, he got to know another Chinese man at the college. This man took him to attend a couple of classes, after which he had no intention of leaving because he had discovered that there was a lot here that he needed to know. He stayed with the other Chinese man – during the day, the two of them attended classes in mathematics and geometry with students from Bosnia and Turkey. At night, he would attend concerts with a senior student from Prague. He enjoyed himself so much that he did not realize how quickly time was passing; when he finally decided that it was time to return, seven years had gone by. In the autumn of 1880, Rong Zilai got on a boat together with a couple of dozen barrels of new wine and began retracing his steps on the long journey home. By the time he arrived back, in the depths of winter, the wine was already perfectly drinkable.

To quote the inhabitants of Tongzhen on the subject: the Rong family had not changed at all during these seven years – the Rong clan was still the Rong clan, the salt merchants were still salt merchants, a flourishing family continued to flourish and the money came rolling in just like before. The only thing that was different was the young man who had gone abroad – he wasn't so young any more, and he had acquired a really peculiar name: Lillie. John Lillie. Furthermore, he was now afflicted by all sorts of strange habits: he didn't have a queue, he wore a short jacket rather than a long silk gown, he liked to drink wine that was the colour of blood, he larded his speech with words that sounded like the chirping of a bird, and so on. The strangest thing of all was that he simply could not stand the smell of salt – when he went down to the harbour or to the shop and the stinging scent of the salt assaulted his nostrils, he would begin to retch or sometimes even to vomit bile. It seemed particularly dreadful that the son of a salt merchant would be unable to tolerate the smell of salt; people treated him almost as if he had contracted an unmentionable disease. Later on, Rong Zilai explained what had happened – when he was on the boat sailing across the ocean, he had accidentally fallen in, swallowing so much briny water that he very nearly died. The horror of this event had etched itself into the very marrow of his bones. After that he had kept a tea leaf in his mouth at all times when on the boat, otherwise he simply would not have been able to endure it. Of course, explaining what had happened was one thing, getting people to accept the news was something else entirely. If he could not stand the smell of salt, how on earth was he supposed to work in the family business? You can't have the boss going round with a mouth full of tea leaves all the time.

This was a very thorny problem.

Fortunately, before he left for foreign parts, Grandmother Rong had put it in writing that when he came back from his studies he was to have all the silver behind the sliding panel in her room as a reward for his filial piety. Later on, he used that money well, for it paid for him to open a school in the provincial capital, C City, which he called Lillie's Academy of Mathematics.

That was the predecessor of the famous N University.

2.

N University started to become famous when it was still just Lillie's Academy of Mathematics.

The first person to make the academy famous was John Lillie himself. In spite of all opposition, he shocked everyone by insisting that the academy should be opened to women students. For the first few years of its existence, the academy was treated somewhat like a peepshow. Anyone who had business taking them to the provincial capital would make time to visit the academy and have a look, to enjoy the spectacle. They behaved just as if they were talking a walk through a red-light district. With the feudal attitudes that people had in those days, the mere fact that the academy took women students ought to have been enough to get it closed by the authorities. There were a lot of explanations offered for why it was able to survive – of which that given in the official genealogy of the Rong family is perhaps the most reliable. According to the genealogy, all the early women students at the academy were members of the principal branch of the Rong family. They might as well have come right out and said: if we want to ruin our own daughters what is that to do with you? Keeping it all in the family turned out to be a very good idea. It was the only reason that gossip was never able to bring about the closure of Lillie's Academy of Mathematics. In somewhat the same way as the growth of children is accompanied by a lot of howling, the furore surrounding Lillie's Academy of Mathematics simply helped it to become more famous.

The second person to bring the academy to public recognition was also a member of the Rong family – the child born when John Lillie's older brother (then already past sixty years of age) took a concubine. The child was a daughter and she was John Lillie's niece. She was born with a large, round head, but there was absolutely nothing else wrong with her; in fact, she was a remarkably intelligent girl. At a very early age it became apparent that she was unusually clever, particularly at anything involving mathematics or calculation. She first attended the academy at the age of eleven, and when she was twelve she took part in a competition with an expert abacist. No one could believe their eyes when they saw how fast she was; she could multiply two four-figure numbers in the time it took a man to spit. The kind of mathematical problem that other people had to wrack their brains over unravelled at her touch, but this seemed to disappoint the people who challenged her to answer and they wondered out loud whether she might not have cheated by finding out the question in advance.

A blind man who made his living by telling people's fortunes from the shape of their heads once told her that she was the kind of genius that only came along once every thousand years.

The year that she turned seventeen, she set off halfway around the world with her cousin, who was going to study at Cambridge University. As the boat plunged into the thick fog that hung over the London docks, her cousin (who enjoyed composing little poems) was inspired by the scene to write something –

> Thanks to the power of the ocean wave,
> I have come to Great Britain.
> Great Britain,
> Great Britain,
> The fogs cannot conceal your magnificence . . .

Having been woken up by her cousin reciting this ditty aloud, she turned bleary-eyed to look at her golden watch. She said, 'We have been travelling for thirty-nine days and seven hours.'

Immediately the pair of them went into a well-practised question and answer routine:

'Thirty-nine days and seven hours is . . . ?'

'Nine hundred and forty-three hours.'

'Nine hundred and forty-three hours is . . . ?'

'Fifty-six thousand, five hundred and eighty minutes.'

'Fifty-six thousand, five hundred and eighty minutes is . . . ?'

'Three million, three hundred and ninety-four thousand and eight hundred seconds.'

This kind of game had become part of her life – people treated her like a human abacus, expecting her to perform calculations like that at the drop of a hat. The constant exercise of her unusual abilities resulted in them becoming even more pronounced. It got to the stage where people changed her name: everyone called her 'Abacus'. Because her head was unusually large, some people even called her 'Abacus Head'. The fact is that she was better than any abacist. It seemed as though all the mathematical skills built up by generations of the Rong family in the course of their business had become concentrated in her; as if quantitative experience had finally brought about a qualitative change.

When she got to Cambridge, while keeping all her old mathematical skill, it turned out that she also had another – hitherto unsuspected – talent for learning languages. Where other people just have to grit their teeth and get on with it, she seemed to pick up languages really easily from her foreign room-mates, and she just got quicker and quicker at it. She found a new room-mate every term and by the time the term was over, she seemed to be able to speak a new language, with a remarkable verve and grasp of idiom. Of course, there is nothing special in this method of language-learning – it is a perfectly standard method that seems to work for pretty much everyone who tries it. The amazing thing was the results that she obtained. It enabled her to learn seven languages within the space of a couple of years, and what is more this was not just a matter of speaking them: she could also read and write them. One day, she happened to meet a dark-haired young woman in the college grounds and tried to talk to her. When she could not communicate, she tried each of the seven languages that she had learned in turn, but with no result. It turned out that this girl had just arrived from Milan and spoke only Italian. Once she had discovered this, she immediately invited her to become her room-mate. It was that term that she also started work on the design of Newton's Mathematical Bridge.

Newton's Mathematical Bridge is one of the sights of Cambridge University. The bridge is composed from 7,177 timbers, all of a different size. In total there are 10,299 tangent planes, so if you were going to nail each of the tangent planes together, then at the very least you would need 10,299 nails. However, Newton threw all the nails into the Cam and built his bridge to be held together by gravity alone – that is what makes it a mathematical marvel. For many years, students at the mathematics department at Cambridge University dreamed of cracking the secret of the Mathematical Bridge – or rather, you could say that what they wanted to do was to make an exact replica of the Mathematical Bridge on paper. No one succeeded. A number of people worked out a way of replicating the bridge that required more than 1,000 nails, but only a handful were able to design a version that required fewer than a thousand. The person who got the closest was an Icelander, with a design that required only 561 nails. The famous mathematician Professor Sir Joseph Larmor (at that time the President of the Newtonian Mathematical Society) then promised that anyone who could come up with a design that used fewer nails, even if it were only one less than that number, would receive a doctorate in mathematics from Cambridge University. That was how 'Abacus Head' received a university certificate for a doctoral degree from Cambridge, because her model of the Mathematical Bridge required only 388 nails. After the award ceremony, she ended up chatting with one of the dons in Italian, demonstrating that she had mastered yet another language.

This happened in her fifth year at Cambridge, when she was twenty-two years old.

The following year, a pair of brothers who hoped to take the human race into the air came to Cambridge to visit her; their vision and bravery impressed her so much that she went to America with them. Two years later, in North Carolina, the first ever airplane successfully took off over the sand dunes and soared into the sky. Underneath the belly of the airplane, there was a legend in silver letters, recording the names of the most important people involved in the design and construction of the machine. In the fourth line it said:

Wing designer: Rong 'Abacus' Lillie, from C City, China.

Rong 'Abacus' Lillie was the name that she used when she was in the West, but in the genealogy of the Rong clan, her name is given as Rong Youying, a descendant in the eighth generation of the family.

And the pair that took her away from Cambridge University were the pioneers of heavier-than-air human flight: the Wright brothers.

If the Wrights' Flyer took her name into the sky, she took the reputation of Lillie's Academy of Mathematics into the stratosphere. After the Xinhai Revolution, she realized that the nation's fate was trembling in the balance, so breaking her longstanding engagement to her fiancé, she returned to her alma mater to take up the position of Head of the Department of Mathematics. By this time Lillie's Academy of Mathematics had already changed its name to N University. In the summer of 1913, the President of the Newtonian Mathematical Society, Professor Sir Joseph Larmor, visited China, bringing with him a model of her design for the Mathematical Bridge using only 388 nails, which was then constructed in the grounds of the university. This event served only to make N University even more famous; you could say that Professor Sir Joseph Larmor was the third person to really bring the place to prominence.

In October 1943, Japanese bombing burnt N University to the ground. The remarkable gift that Professor Sir Joseph Larmor had given them — the 1:250 model of Newton's Mathematical Bridge — was destroyed in that fire. But by that time the woman who designed it had already been dead for twenty-nine years. She passed away the year after Larmor's visit to N University, before she was even forty years old.

3

Rong Youying, otherwise known as Rong 'Abacus' Lillie or 'Abacus Head', died in childbirth.

It all happened so long ago that everyone who saw her suffer and die is now dead themselves, but the story of the terrible agony that she endured has been passed down from one generation to the next, as the tale of an appalling battle might have been. As it was told and retold, the story became more refined and more classic in its details, until it became almost like an event in the sagas. As you might imagine, her sufferings in childbirth were horrific – by all accounts her screams resounded constantly for two days and two nights, as the stench of blood pervaded first her room at the hospital, then the corridor, before finally making its way out onto the main road. The doctor tried the most advanced techniques of the time, and the most stupid of birthing methods, to try to help the baby to be born, but the head still would not emerge from the womb. To begin with the corridor outside the delivery room was crammed with members of the Rong family – and the paternal Lin clan – waiting for the baby to be born, but as time went on they gradually dispersed until there were only a couple of female servants left. Even the toughest were appalled by the length and difficulty of the labour; it became clear that even the joy of welcoming the new arrival would not be able to make up for the horror of the death of his mother. Sometimes her death seemed imminent, at other times it appeared as if she might pull through, as time marched inexorably on towards its merciless decision.

Old Mr Lillie was the last to arrive in the corridor, but he was also the last to leave. Before he left, he said: 'Either this baby is going to be a genius, or a devil.'

'There is an eighty to ninety per cent chance that this baby is never going to be born,' the doctor said.

'She will have the baby.'

'No she won't.'

'You don't understand, she is a really remarkable woman.'

'But I do understand women and if she has this baby, it is going to be a miracle.'

'She is the kind of person that miracles happen to!'

Old Lillie wanted to leave once he had said his piece.

The doctor prevented him from going. 'This is a hospital and you need to listen to what I have to say. What do you want me to do if she really can't give birth to this baby?'

Old Lillie was silent for a moment.

The doctor persevered: 'Do you want me to save the adult or the baby?'

Old Lillie said without a moment's hesitation: 'Of course you save the adult!'

Of course, in the face of all-powerful destiny and fate, how could old Mr Lillie's wish be taken into account? At dawn, the woman in labour found her strength totally exhausted after yet another night of struggle, and she slipped into unconsciousness. The doctor roused her by dousing her with ice-cold water and injecting a double dose of stimulant, preparing for the final push. The doctor explained it quite clearly: if this last attempt did not work, they were going to have to abandon the baby in order to save the mother's life. Things did not go at all according to plan; it was the mother who suffered organ failure as she made that final attempt to give birth. In the end, the baby's life was saved by an emergency Caesarean section.

This baby was born at the cost of his own mother's life, from which you can see how much she suffered in the process. After the baby was finally born, everyone was shocked to see how massive his head was. Compared to her son, her head was nothing! To have a first baby with such an enormous head, not to mention the fact that she was almost forty at the time, was pretty much guaranteed to kill the wretched woman. There are times when the workings of fate seem really mysterious: a woman who could send a couple of tons of metal up into the sky ended up as the victim of one of Nature's practical jokes.

After the baby was born, even though the Lin family chose all sorts of names for him – nicknames, style names, formal names and what have you – they quickly discovered that it was all a wasted effort – his huge head and the horrible story of how he had come into this world ensured that everyone called him 'Killer Head'.

'Killer Head!'

'Killer Head!'

It was a name that no one ever got tired of.

'Killer Head!'

'Killer Head!'

His friends called him that.

Everyone called him that.

It is hard to believe, but nevertheless it is a fact that eventually everyone called him 'Killer', and he deserved the name, for he did some truly terrible things. The Lin family was the richest family in the provincial capital and the shops they owned filled both sides of a two-kilometre-long stretch of one of the big boulevards. However, once the Killer grew up, their vast holdings started to shrink rapidly as they had to pay off his gambling debts or get him out of other kinds of trouble. If it hadn't been for the whore who picked up a knife and stabbed him to death, the Lin family would have lost their house along with everything else. The story goes that the Killer first got involved in criminal activities when he was twelve, and he was twenty-two when he died. During that decade he had participated in a dozen or more murders and had seduced and abandoned countless women. At the same time, he gambled away a mountain of money and a whole street's worth of shops. It was very shocking to people that such a remarkable woman, a genius such as comes along maybe once every thousand years, could produce such a wicked son.

The Lin family breathed a sigh of relief when the Killer died; only to find themselves being pestered by a mysterious woman. She arrived from somewhere outside the province and demanded to see the head of the Lin family. Once he admitted her, she just got down on her knees without another word and started to cry. Pointing to her protruding belly, she said: 'This is young Mr Lin's baby!' The Lin family knew that if you wanted to put all the women that the Killer had seduced out to sea, you would have enough to pack out half a dozen boats; but so far none of them had turned up at the house claiming to be pregnant. What is more, this woman came from another province, so they were suspicious as well as angry. They literally had her kicked out of the door. The woman thought that the kicking would result in a miscarriage, a prospect that did not particularly bother her. However, in spite of the bruising and the pain that she had suffered, the baby stayed put. She balled up her fist and punched herself hard in the stomach a couple of times, which also had no effect. She was so upset that she sat down in the middle of the road and started bawling. She ended up being surrounded by a circle of onlookers, one of whom felt sorry for her and suggested that she go to N University to try her luck there. After all, they were the Killer's family too. The woman staggered off to the university, to kneel in front of old John Lillie. Old Mr Lillie was a very upright and highly principled man who was deeply upset at any evidence that other people had behaved badly. He was very sympathetic to anyone who had suffered an injustice, so he took the woman in. The following day, he ordered his son, Rong Xiaolai – the one that people called Young Lillie – to take her to his old home town of Tongzhen.

The Rong mansion at Tongzhen occupied half the village. The roofs of the different buildings were still as closely packed together as the scales on a fish, though they were starting to get old. Flaked-off bald patches had appeared on the paintwork of the pillars and eaves, making it clear that times were changing. After Old Lillie set up his academy in the provincial capital, many members of the Rong family moved there to study with him, which began the decline of the mansion from its glory days. One of the reasons for this precipitate decline was that very few of the young people who had left were interested in returning to carry on the family business. Furthermore, things were looking very bleak anyway – after the government introduced the state monopoly on salt, the Rong family were deprived of their chief source of income. The attitudes of many of the members of the Rong family who studied with Old Lillie were deeply affected by these developments: they had become interested in scientific method and upholding the truth; they were not at all interested in making money and living in the lap of luxury. Isolated in their ivory tower, the collapse of the family business and the concomitant decline in their fortunes did not seem to affect them in the slightest. Within a decade, the Rong family lost virtually all that they had once owned, though they did not like to talk openly about how this came about. In fact, everyone could see the reason hanging up over the main gate to the mansion. It was a placard with five huge words picked out in gold: 'Supporter of the Northern Expedition'. There was a story behind this. Apparently, when the National Revolutionary Army reached C City, Old Lillie saw all the students out in the streets collecting money for the cause, and he was so moved that he went back to Tongzhen that very night to sell the docks and half the shops that represented the business empire the Rong family had built up over the generations. He used the money to buy a boatload of ammunition for the Northern Expedition, for which he was rewarded with this placard. Because of this, the Rong family came to be regarded as great patriots. Unfortunately, not long afterwards, the famous general who wrote the calligraphy for the inscription became a wanted criminal, on the run from the KMT government, which significantly dimmed its lustre. Later on, the government had a new placard made with exactly the same wording and identical gilding, but with different calligraphy. They asked the Rong family for permission to exchange it for the old one, but Old Lillie simply refused. From that moment on, the Rong family seemed to get into endless trouble with the government, so their business was guaranteed to suffer. Old Lillie didn't mind the business suffering, but he did want the placard to stay. He went so far as to say that the placard would be taken down only over his dead body.

The Rong family had to accept that they were getting poorer all the time.

The Rong mansion, which had once been bustling with life as masters and servants went about their business, was now desolate and quiet. When you did see people about, it quickly became apparent that many of them were old and that there were far more women than men, far more servants than masters. The place was obviously falling into ruin, as things went from bad to worse. As fewer and fewer people lived there, particularly young lively people, the house seemed even larger than normal and much more silent. Birds built their nests in the trees, spiders spun their webs in front of the doors, the paths between buildings became lost in the weeds as they wound their way into the darkness, the pet birds flew off into the sky, the artificial mountain became a real one, the flower garden became a wilderness and the rear courtyards turned into a maze. If you say that in the past the Rong family mansion had been like a beautiful, elegant and brightly coloured painting, you could say that now, although the traces of the original pigment still remained, the lines of the earlier sketches had reappeared, blurring the purity of the finished work. If you wanted to hide an anonymous and mysterious woman with an unsatisfactory background, you could not have found a better place.

Young Lillie really wracked his brains over how to make Mr and Mrs Rong accept this woman. All the members of the seventh generation of the Rong family were now dead, with the exception of Old Lillie living far away at the provincial capital. That made Mr and Mrs Rong the undisputed heads of the Rong clan in Tongzhen. Mr Rong was now well on in years and had had a stroke, which had destroyed his faculties and forced him to spend all his time in bed. He was reduced to the status of a cipher; all real power had long ago slipped into Mrs Rong's hands. If it was indeed the Killer that had got this woman pregnant, then Mr and Mrs Rong were indisputably the baby's aunt and uncle, but that didn't mean that they were going to like it. Remembering that Mrs Rong was a devout Buddhist, Young Lillie started to feel the beginnings of a plan germinating in his mind. He took the woman straight into Mrs Rong's prayer chamber and there, wreathed in incense and accompanied by the sound of her tapping a wooden fish, Young Lillie and Mrs Rong began their discussion. Mrs Rong said, 'Who is she?'

'A woman.'

'Whatever it is that you want, you had better make it quick, because I want to get on with reciting my sutras.'

'She's pregnant.'

'I am not a doctor, what do you want me to do about it?'

'She is a very devout Buddhist and grew up in a nunnery. She isn't married, but last year she went to Putuo Mountain to pray to the Buddhist statue there. When she got back, she discovered that she was pregnant. Do you believe her?'

'Does it matter whether I believe her?'

'If you believe her, then will you take her in?'

'What happens if I don't believe her?'

'If you don't believe her, I will throw her out onto the street.'

Mrs Rong spent a sleepless night, and the Buddha was no help at all in making up her mind. However, at noon, just as Young Lillie was pretending that he was getting ready to throw the woman out of the house, she suddenly made her decision. She said, 'She can stay. Amitabha Buddha, bless his holy name.'

Taking Up the Burden

I.

I spent every holiday for two years on the railways of southern China, travelling the country to interview the fifty-one middle-aged or elderly eyewitnesses to these events; it was only after having compiled thousands of pages of notes that I finally felt able to sit down and write this book. It was my experiences of travelling round the region that meant that I came to understand why the south is different. In my own personal experience, after arriving in the south, I would feel as though each one of my pores was tingling with life – breathing deeply, enjoying every minute, my skin became smoother, even my hair seemed to become more glossy and black. It is not difficult to understand why I decided to write my book in the south – what is harder to understand is why, having moved there, my writing style also changed. I could clearly sense that the soft air of the south was giving me courage and patience in my writing – a task which I normally find extremely troublesome; at the same time, my story began striking out in new tangents, just like the lush growth of a southern tree. The main protagonist of my story still has not appeared yet, though he will soon arrive. In one sense, you could say that he is already here, it is just that you have not seen him; in the same way that when a seed begins to sprout, the first shoots are invisible below the surface of the well-watered soil.

Twenty-three years earlier, the brilliant Rong Youying had gone through appalling suffering to give birth to the Killer; everyone must have hoped that such a thing would not happen again. However, a few months after the mysterious woman went to live with the Rongs, history repeated itself. Because she was so much younger, the mysterious woman's screams had a redoubled power, like a knife shrieking against the grinder. Her screams floated through the darkened mansion, making the flames of the lamps flicker and dance, making even the flesh of the crippled and dazed Mr Rong creep. First one midwife came and went and then another, sometimes they emerged to swap one cloth for a fresh one, but each one left the room with the heavy stench of blood clinging to her body and splashes of blood everywhere, like butchers. The blood dripped from the bed down onto the floor, only to spread across and out over the doorsill. Once out of the room it continued to seep into the cracks between the dark stones set into the path, and on until it reached the roots of a couple of old plum trees growing amid the mud and the weeds. Everyone thought that those blackened plum trees in the overgrown garden were dead, but that winter they suddenly burst into flower – people said that this was because they had supped on human blood. But by the time that the plum blossoms bloomed in January, the mysterious woman was long dead and her soul had flown off to become a hungry ghost haunting some desolate stretch of hillside.

Those who were there at the time said it was a miracle that the mysterious woman was able to give birth to the baby at all; some of them also said that having given birth to the baby, for the mother to survive would be adding one miracle on top of the other. That didn't happen here – the baby was born, but the mysterious woman suffered a haemorrhage and died. It is not that easy to have one miracle happening right after the other. That was not the real problem though – the real problem was that when the midwife cleaned the baby of blood and slime, everyone was shocked to discover that he looked just like the Killer: the thick mat of dark hair, the huge head, right down to the shape of the Mongolian spot above his buttocks: the two were the same. Young Lillie's innocent little deception stood revealed now as a nasty trick; the mysterious baby born after his mother's pilgrimage turned in the blink of an eye into the illegitimate brat of a murderer foisted on his long-suffering relations. If it had not been for the fact that Mrs Rong found some resemblance in the baby to his grandmother, the sainted Miss Lillie, even she would have steeled herself to abandoning him in some uninhabited stretch of wilderness. In fact, it seems that when the question of simply getting rid of the baby was seriously mooted, it was his connection to his grandmother that saved his life and ensured that he was brought up in the Rong mansion.

The baby survived, but this certainly wasn't a matter of congratulation for the Rongs – they did not even recognize him as a member of the family. For the longest time, anyone who wanted to talk about him called him the 'Grim Reaper'. One day, Mr Auslander happened to walk past the front door of the old servant couple who were tasked with looking after the baby and they politely invited him in, hoping that he could choose a new name for the child. They were both pretty elderly by this time and found it most unpleasant to speak to the baby like that, as if he had come there to kill them. They had been thinking about changing his name for a while. To begin with they had tried to come up with a name themselves – the kind of baby-name that other children in the village had – but they couldn't find anything that really seemed to stick; they used it, but no one else did. Hearing their neighbours call him the 'Grim Reaper' all the time gave both of the old people the willies and they found themselves often having nightmares. That is why, for want of any better suggestion, they were forced to ask Mr Auslander to think of something, something that would appeal to everyone.

Mr Auslander was the foreigner who all those years before had been invited to the house to interpret Grandmother Rong's dreams. Grandmother Rong adored him, but he was certainly not every rich man's cup of tea. There was the time when, down at the docks, he interpreted the dream of a tea merchant from another province: that earned him a crippling beating. Both his arms and legs were broken, but that was not the half of it: one of his bright blue eyes was put out. He crawled back to the Rong family mansion and they took him in, thinking of it as a good deed that would help the old lady to rest in peace. Once he had entered their household he never left again. Eventually he found himself a job to do which suited him right down to the ground – as befitted such a wealthy and prominent family, the Rongs decided that they needed a genealogy compiled. As the years went by, he came to know the various different branches of the family better than anyone. He knew the history of the clan, the men and the women, the main branches and the illegitimate offspring, which ones were flourishing and which had failed, who had gone where and done what: everything was sitting in his notes. So when it came to this baby, other people might be completely in the dark, but Mr Auslander knew exactly which branch of the family he came from and what scandals surrounded his birth. And it was because he knew exactly who the baby was that picking the right name for him was such a ticklish issue.

Mr Auslander thought about the matter and decided that before choosing a proper name for the baby, they would have to deal with the issue of a surname. What was the baby's surname? Of course, he ought to be called Lin, but to put it mildly that surname now had unfortunate connotations for everyone. He could take the surname Rong, but it would be most unusual for someone to take their grandmother's maiden name – it didn't really seem suitable. It would of course be perfectly acceptable for him to take his mother's surname, but what was the mystery woman's name? Even if they knew it, it would hardly be appropriate to use it: that would be rattling the skeletons in the family closet with a vengeance! Thinking about it carefully, Mr Auslander decided to put the issue of choosing a proper name for the baby to one side for the moment and concentrate on finding a suitable baby-name for him. Mr Auslander thought about the baby's huge head and the suffering that he would face having lost both his parents so young, how he would have to make his way without any help from his family, and suddenly an idea flashed into his mind. He decided to call the baby 'Duckling'.

When this was reported to Mrs Rong in her prayer chamber, she sniffed the incense meditatively while she spoke: 'Although people called his father horrible names too, in the case of the Killer, he was actually responsible for the death of his mother, a truly wonderful woman and a great credit to the Rong family. You could not find a better name for him if you searched for a month of Sundays. On the other hand, this baby was responsible for the death of a shameless whore. That woman dared to blaspheme against the Buddha, a crime for which she deserves a thousand deaths! Killing her doesn't count as a crime: it's a work of merit. Calling the poor little thing the Grim Reaper does seem a little unfair. In the future we can call him Duckling, though it is hardly likely that he is going to grow into a swan.'

'Duckling!'

'Duckling!'

No one cared where he came from or who his parents were.

'Duckling!'

'Duckling!'

No one cared whether he lived or died.

In all that great mansion, the only person who treated Duckling like another human being – who treated him as he would any other child – was Mr Auslander, who had drifted there from the other side of the ocean. Every day after he had completed his morning tasks and had his midday siesta, he would walk along the dark little pebble path overhung with flowers to where the old servant couple lived. He would sit down next to the wooden crate in which Duckling was playing and smoke a cigarette, talking in his own language about the dream that he had had the night before. It seemed as though he were talking to Duckling but in fact he was talking to himself, because Duckling was still too little to understand. Every so often he would bring the baby a rattle or a little pottery toy, and bit by bit Duckling came to adore the old man. Later on, when Duckling learned to walk, or to be precise when he learned to crawl, the very first place he went on his own was to Mr Auslander's office in the Pear Garden.

The Pear Garden, as the name suggests, was named after its pear trees: two-hundred-year-old pear trees. There was a little wooden house in the middle of the garden, the attics of which had been used by the Rong family for storing their supply of opium and medicinal herbs. One year, a female servant disappeared in mysterious circumstances – to begin with they imagined that she had eloped with some man; later on they discovered her body, already badly decomposed, inside this building. The woman's death was impossible to cover up: soon every single member of the Rong family and their entire staff knew all about it. Subsequently the Pear Garden became the subject of ghost stories and people were scared to go there; people would change colour when its name was mentioned and if children were being tiresome, their parents would threaten them, 'If you don't stop that immediately, we'll leave you in the Pear Garden!' Mr Auslander took advantage of other people's fear of the place to live quietly and without interference. Every year when the pear trees flowered, Mr

Auslander would look at the misty sprays of blossom and smell their intensely sweet fragrance with the feeling that this place was exactly what he had been looking for all these years. When the pear flowers fell, he would sweep up the fallen petals and dry them in the sun, before placing them in the building that he might enjoy the fragrance of the blossoms all the year round – a kind of eternal spring. When he wasn't feeling well, he would make tea with the flowers. He found it very settling for his stomach; it made him feel a lot better.

After the first time that Duckling came, he came every day. He would not say anything, but he would stand underneath the pear trees and watch Mr Auslander in silence, timidly, like a frightened fawn. Since he had practised standing up in his wooden crate from a very young age, he walked a little bit earlier than most other children. On the other hand he was much slower at learning to talk. At past two years of age, when other children of the same age were stringing together their first sentences, he could only make one sound – *jia . . . jia*. This made people wonder whether he might not prove to be mute. However, one day when Mr Auslander was taking his lunchtime siesta on a rattan chaise longue, he suddenly heard someone call out to him in a desolate voice:

'Dad . . . dy!'
'Dad . . . dy!'
'Dad . . . dy!'

Mr Auslander realized that someone was trying to call him 'Daddy'. He opened his eyes and saw that Duckling was standing next to him, tugging at his jacket with his little hand, his eyes wet with tears. This was the first time in his life that Duckling had ever called out to anyone, and he thought of Mr Auslander as his father. Since his father had seemed to him to be dead, he started crying, and when he cried, he brought his father back to life. That very day, the foreign gentleman took little Duckling into the Pear Garden to live with him. A couple of days later, the eighty-year-old Mr Auslander climbed up into one of the pear trees to hang a swing, to be little Duckling's present on the occasion of his third birthday.

Duckling grew up surrounded by pear flowers.

Eight years later, just as the pear flowers were beginning their annual dance off the trees, Mr Auslander looked up at the flurries of petals whirling through the sky. Moving along with tottering steps, he carefully mulled over every word he planned to use. Every evening, he wrote out the lines that he had composed during the day. Within a couple of days he had formulated the letter which he sent to Young Lillie – the son of Old Lillie – at the provincial capital. That letter resided in a drawer for more than a year, but when the old man realized that he did not have much longer to live, he took it out again, telling Duckling to put it in the post. Due to the war, Young Lillie had no fixed abode and often moved around, so the letter did not reach him for a couple of months.

The letter said:

To: The Vice-Chancellor of the University

Dear Sir,

I do not know if writing this letter to you will be the last mistake I ever make. It is because I think I might be making a mistake, and because I would like to spend more time with Duckling, that I will not immediately put this letter in the post. By the time this letter reaches you, I will be dying; in which case – even if it is a mistake – I will no longer care. I can use the special powers granted to those who are about to die to refuse to carry any further the burdens life has placed upon me. These burdens have been, if I may say so, quite sufficiently numerous and heavy. However, I am also planning to use the all-seeing eyes supposed to be granted to the dead to check up on how seriously you take the points raised in my letter and what you propose to do about them. In many ways, you could say that this is my last will and testament. I have lived on this difficult and dangerous planet for a long time – almost a century. I know how well you treat the dead in this country, not to mention how badly you treat the living. The first is entirely praiseworthy; the latter is not. It is for this very reason that I am certain you will not disobey my final instructions.

I have only one regret and that is Duckling. I have been his guardian for many years, *faute de mieux*, but now I can hear the bell tolling for me and it is clear that I have only a few days left. It is time for someone else to take care of him. I beg you to take over as his guardian. There are three reasons that you would be the perfect choice.

1. It is thanks to your bravery and generosity – you and your father (Old Lillie) – that he was ever born at all.
2. Whether you admit it or not, he is a member of the Rong family and his grandmother was the person that your father loved and admired more than anyone else in the world.
3. This child is very clever. These last few years, he has been my new-found-land. At every step, I have found myself amazed and impressed by his truly remarkable intelligence. Do not be misled by his somewhat misanthropic and cold personality; I believe that he is just as clever as his grandmother was, not to mention the fact that the two of them are as alike in appearance as two peas in a pod. She was exceptionally clever, extremely creative; an amazingly forceful personality. Archimedes said, 'Give me a place to stand and I will move the earth.' I believe that he is that kind of person. However, right now he needs you, because he isn't quite twelve years old.

Believe what I tell you and take the child away from here. Bring him up in your home because he needs you, needs your love, and needs an education. Perhaps more than anything else, he needs you to give him a name.

I beg you!

I beg you!

This is the first and last time I have ever begged anyone for anything.

The dying R. J.
Tongzhen, 8 June 1944

2

1944 was the worst year that the people of the provincial capital, C City – and N University at its heart – had ever experienced. First they suffered in the front line of battle; then they were ground under the heel of the Nanjing puppet government. This brought about an enormous change not only to the appearance of the city, but also to the hearts of its people. When Young Lillie received Mr Auslander's letter, the worst of the fighting was already over, but the chaos unleashed by the bad faith of the temporary government had reached the point of no return. By this time Old Lillie had been dead for many years and Young Lillie's position at N University had been adversely affected by the collapse in his father's fortunes, not to mention the intransigent attitude of the puppet government. Nevertheless, the puppet government thought very highly of Young Lillie. First of all he was famous, which meant that he was useful to them in a way that an ordinary man wouldn't have been; secondly the Rong family had suffered a great deal at the hands of the KMT government, so they were hoping that he would prove amenable. So when the puppet government was first established, they generously offered Young Lillie (at that time just acting vice-chancellor of the university) the job of chancellor, imagining that this would be all that it took to buy him. They were not expecting that he would tear up the brevet in front of everyone and proclaim in a stentorian voice: 'We Rongs would rather die than betray our country!'

As you might imagine, Young Lillie's answer was very popular, but it guaranteed that he was not going to find himself with an official position. He had already been thinking for some time of avoiding the repulsive overtures of the puppet government (and the associated ferocious infighting in the university) by going into hiding in Tong-zhen, but Mr Auslander's letter unquestionably speeded his departure. Still mulling over the letter, he stepped off the paddle-steamer. At a glance he picked out the steward of the Rong mansion from the crowd huddled together against the rain and wind. The steward asked him politely if he had had a good journey. Instead of responding, he asked abruptly, 'How is Mr Auslander?'

'Mr Auslander is dead,' the steward said. 'He passed away some weeks ago.'

Young Lillie felt his heart thump in his chest. Then he asked: 'Where is the child?'

'Who do you mean?'

'Duckling.'

'He is still at the Pear Garden.'

He was living in the Pear Garden, that was right enough, but no one seemed to know what he was doing in there, since he hardly ever came out and very few people bothered to go in. Everyone knew that he was living in the mansion, but he seemed to move from place to place like a lost soul, with hardly anyone even catching a glimpse of him. According to the steward, Duckling was the next best thing to a mute.

'I don't understand a thing that he says to me,' the steward said. 'He doesn't often speak, and when he does, he might as well not bother, because no one can understand it.'

The steward also said that according to the servants in the main mansion, it was only because the old foreign gentleman got down on his hands and knees and kowtowed three times to the Third Master that he agreed to allow Duckling to carry on living at the Pear Garden after his death. Otherwise they would have thrown him out onto the street. He went on to say that Mr Auslander had left his savings of many decades to Duckling and that was what he was living on, since the Rong family couldn't possibly afford to pay for his food.

It was lunchtime the next day when Young Lillie walked into the Pear Garden. The rain had stopped by then, but having fallen continuously for several days, it had washed the buildings clean while creating a thick squelchy layer of mud underfoot. His footsteps left deep prints in the mud and in some places it was deep enough to cover his galoshes. As far as Young Lillie could see, there were no other footprints to be seen – the spiderwebs in the trees were empty, the spiders having retreated under the eaves to get out of the rain. Some of them were now busily occupied spinning a new web in front of the door. If it were not for the smoke rising from the chimney and the sound of something being chopped on a block, he would have believed the place to be deserted.

Duckling was chopping up a sweet potato. There was boiling water in the pot on the stove, in which a few grains of rice were bobbing about. He did not seem alarmed at Young Lillie's intrusion, nor was he angry. He just looked at him for a moment and then went back to his work, as if it was his grandfather who had come in after a short absence – his grandfather or perhaps a dog? He was smaller than Young Lillie had been expecting, and his head was not as large as people said. His skull was dolichocephalic and oddly pointed on top; almost as if he were wearing a homburg hat – perhaps it was because of this that his head did not appear abnormally huge. Young Lillie did not find anything at all remarkable in his appearance; however, his cold, calm manner made a very deep impression; he was like a little old man. The only nice pieces of furniture in the room were the medicine chest (left over from the original use of the building), a table and a director's chair. There was a large volume lying open on the table, a musty smell emanating from its leaves. Young Lillie closed the book so that he could read the title on the spine: it was an English book – one volume of the *Encyclopaedia Britannica*. Young Lillie put the book down and looked questioningly at the child. Then he asked, 'Are you reading this?'

Duckling nodded.

'Can you understand it?'

Duckling nodded again.

'Did Mr Auslander teach you?'

He nodded again.

'You don't say anything: is this because you are mute?' As Young Lillie spoke, he realized that his tone of voice was more aggressive than he had intended, as if he were blaming the child. 'If you are, then nod your head twice. If you are not, then say so.' Because he was afraid that the child might not understand Chinese, Young Lillie repeated what he had said in English.

Duckling walked over to the stove, put the sweet potato that he had just finished chopping into the water and replied in English that he was not a mute.

Young Lillie asked him again if he could speak Chinese and Duckling replied – in Chinese – that he could.

Young Lillie laughed and said, 'Your Chinese is as bad as my English. Did you learn it from Mr Auslander?'

Duckling nodded again.

Young Lillie said, 'Don't nod.'

Duckling said, 'Fine.'

Young Lillie said, 'It is many years since I last used my English and it is terribly rusty. In the future we had better speak Chinese together.'

Duckling said in Chinese, 'Fine.'

Young Lillie walked over to the table, sat down in the director's chair and lit a cigarette. He asked, 'How old are you?'

'Twelve.'

'Apart from getting you to read these books, did Mr Auslander teach you anything else?'

'No.'

'You mean that Mr Auslander never taught you how to interpret dreams? He was famous for that.'

'He taught me that.'

'Are you any good?'

'Yes.'

'I had a dream last night. Would you interpret it for me?'

'No.'

'Why not?'

'Because I only interpret my own dreams.'

'Well, why don't you tell me what kind of things you dream about . . .'

'I dream about all sorts of things.'

'Have you seen me in your dreams?'

'I have.'

'Do you know who I am?'

'Yes.'

'Who?'

'You are a member of the eighth generation of the Rong family to live here and you were born in 1883. You are the twenty-first in your generation. Your name is Rong Xiaolai and your style name is Dong-qian, and your soubriquet is Zeshi. People call you "Young Lillie". You are the son of the founder of N University, Old Lillie. You graduated from the mathematics department at N University in 1906; in 1912 you went to the United States to study, and obtained a Master's degree from MIT. In 1926 you returned to your alma mater to teach and you have been there ever since. You are now the vice-chancellor of N University and a full professor in the department of mathematics.'

'You know a lot about me.'

'I know a lot about all the members of the Rong family.'

'Did Mr Auslander teach you?'

'Yes.'

'Did he teach you anything else?'

'No.'

'Do you go to school?'

'No.'

'Would you like to go to school?'

'I don't know; I have never really thought about it.'

The water in the pot had now come to the boil again and filled the room with its warmth – that and the smell of cooking. The old man stood up with the intention of going out into the garden. The child thought that he was leaving and called out to him to wait a moment. He said that Mr Auslander had left something for him. As he spoke, he walked in the direction of the bed. He pulled a paper parcel out from underneath the bed and handed it to him with the words: 'Daddy told me that when you came I was to give this to you.'

'Daddy?' The old man thought for a moment. 'You mean Mr Auslander?'

'Yes.'

'What is this?' The old man picked up the parcel.

'When you open it, sir, you will see.'

Whatever was inside had been wrapped up in a couple of layers of brown paper and looked pretty large. This however turned out to be a mistaken impression, for when all the paper wrappings had been removed, they revealed a statuette of the Bodhisattva Guanyin that you could hold in the palm of your hand. It had been carved from mutton-fat jade and had a single dark sapphire set between its eyes as the *urna*, the Buddhist 'Third Eye'. Holding it delicately in his hand the old man scrutinized it carefully; immediately he sensed a kind of icy pure aura spreading from his palm to the rest of his body – a testament to the high quality of the jade. The workmanship was also excellent; the combination of these two factors suggested that this statuette had a long and complex history. He was sure that such a remarkable treasure must be worth a very great deal of money. The old man thought the matter over, looking at the child. Then he said with a sigh, 'I hardly knew Mr Auslander. Why should he leave me any bequest at all?'

'I don't know.'

'You know, this statuette is worth a lot of money. You should keep it.'

'No.'

'Mr Auslander took you in when you were only a baby and he loved you as if you were his own son; you ought to take it.'

'No.'

'You need it more than I do.'

'No.'

'Or is it that Mr Auslander was worried that you would be cheated if you tried to sell it yourself and wanted me to do it for you?'

'No.'

While he was speaking, the old man's eyes happened to fall on the outer wrapping paper and he noticed that it was covered in figures, line after line of calculations, as if someone were working out a very difficult sum. When he spread out all the papers and looked at them, he realized that they were all the same, covered in line after line of mathematical calculations. Changing the subject completely, the old man now asked: 'Did Mr Auslander teach you mathematics?'

'No.'

'Who wrote this then?'

'I did.'

'Why?'

'I was trying to work out how many days Daddy lived for . . .'

3

The disease that finally killed Mr Auslander first manifested itself in his throat. Maybe this was some kind of karmic revenge for all those years he had spent interpreting other people's dreams – everything that he had gained in life had come to him thanks to his elegant turn of speech; likewise all the harm he had suffered was brought about by others taking umbrage at his choice of words. Even before he started composing his last letter to Young Lillie, he had already pretty much lost the ability to speak. It was this that made him feel that death was coming and that he needed to start making some plans for Duckling's future. Every morning during those silent days, Duckling would put a cup of pear blossom steeped in water by the old man's bed and he would be woken by the faint breath of its perfume; as he watched the pale dried flowers would uncurl in the warm liquid. It made him feel calm and relaxed. These pear blossoms seemed to alleviate the pain he felt from his badly set bones; he came to think of them as the one thing that had enabled him to live to this great age. When he had first begun collecting these flowers, it was simply because he was bored. After a time, he began to appreciate the startling clarity of their colour, not to mention their delicate texture. He would collect the flowers and sun them under the eaves. When they were completely dry, he would put them in his pillow or on top of his desk. Every time he smelled their fragrance, it seemed as if he were prolonging their flowering season by keeping them by him.

Since he had only one eye and his legs had never recovered properly after they were broken, he found it difficult to get around. As a result, he spent much of his life sitting in his chair. As time went on, he gradually became sick with constipation; at its worst he felt that there was no point in him being alive. One year, at the beginning of winter, his constipation returned. He used all his regular methods: every morning when he first woke up he would down a large bowl of cold water, then he would continue drinking more in the hope of giving himself a stomach-ache. This time the constipation proved particularly obdurate – for a couple of days he downed cup after cup of water, but with no sign of the slightest reaction from his guts. He had only succeeded in making himself even more sick; he felt terribly unwell and hopeless. One evening he came back from the town having picked up his medicine – fumbling round in the dark he picked up the bowl of cold water waiting for him by the front door and drained it to the dregs. Because he drank it so quickly, it was only afterwards that he realized there had been a strange flavour to the water – at the same time he felt that something or other soft had gone down his throat with the liquid – a horrifying experience. When he lit his oil lamp, he discovered that the bowl was full of sodden dried pear petals. Maybe they had been blown there by the wind, or maybe they had been disturbed by a rat. He had never heard that pear blossom could be used to make a drink and so he waited uneasily to find out what happened next – he was even ready to discover that they were going to kill him. But before he had managed to finish brewing up his medicine, he felt a pain deep in his guts. Soon, he realized that this was the pain he had been hoping for day and night. He knew that he would be okay. After a long and resonant fart he headed off to the lavatory. When he returned, he was completely relaxed.

On previous occasions, any relief from constipation had been followed by a period of serious stomach inflammation. Thus his stoppage of the bowels would normally be followed by dreadful diarrhoea, as if he had to proceed through these two extremes to recover. This time, however, he seemed to have escaped from this vicious circle – his constipation relieved, he made a complete recovery without any other symptoms or problems. He now started to become seriously interested in the medicinal properties of pear-blossom water. What had begun as a pure accident now struck him as the inner workings of divine providence. From this time onwards, he would brew himself a cup of pear blossoms the way that other people make themselves a cup of tea – the more he drank, the more he enjoyed it. Every year when the pear trees flowered, he would feel an incomparable joy and sense of satisfaction. Picking these fragrant and delicate blossoms, he would feel as if he were slowly recovering his long-lost health. Under the stress of long-term pain, he had dreamed every night of the pear flowers bursting open in the sunlight, floating through the wind and the rain. It was a sign that he hoped that God would let him die, would let him leave with the pear blossoms.

Early one morning, the old man called Duckling to his bedside and gestured that he wanted a piece of paper and a pen. He wrote down the following message: 'When I am dead, I want you to put pear flowers in my coffin.' That evening, he called Duckling back to his bedside and again demanded paper and pen, so that he could give more detailed instructions: 'I am eighty-nine years old and I would like eighty-nine pear flowers to be buried with me.' The next morning he called Duckling to his bedside again and, once supplied with paper and pen, he made his wishes even more precise: 'Work out how many days there are in eighty-nine years and then bury me with that number of pear flowers.' Perhaps the old man was confused and fearful in the face of his oncoming death, for at the moment that he wrote these increasingly complex instructions, he seemed to forget completely that he had never taught Duckling any mathematics.

Although he had never formally been taught any mathematics, Duckling was quite capable of this kind of simple addition. It is part of life, everyday stuff: a moderately intelligent child, even if you don't formally teach them this kind of skill, will still be able to manage it. If you look at it from that point of view, then Duckling had already received as much instruction in addition and subtraction as he needed, since every year when the pear blossoms began to fall from the trees, Mr Auslander would collect them and afterwards get Duckling to count them. When he had come up with the correct number, it would be noted on the wall. Later on, Mr Auslander might well get him to count them again and the total was written up a second time on the wall. That way, by the time that the flowers had all fallen, Duckling's addition and subtraction had had a thorough work-out, not to mention his understanding of numbers and decimal places. However, that was all that he had learned. Now he was going to have to rely on this strictly limited experience to calculate how many days his daddy had been alive, based on the information that old Mr Auslander had prepared for his tombstone, including the time and place of his birth. Because he had such limited mathematical experience, the calculation took ages – it was a whole day before he got a result. Dusk was falling when Duckling walked up to the bed and showed the result of his lengthy calculation to his daddy, who by that time no longer even had the strength to nod his head. He touched the boy's hand gently and then closed his eyes for the last time. It was for this reason that Duckling had no idea whether the answer he had obtained was right or not. When he realized that Young Lillie was looking at his workings out, for the very first time he began to understand that this relationship might be very important to him, so he began to feel nervous and uncomfortable.

Duckling had used three sheets of paper for working out his calculations. Even though they were not numbered, when Young Lillie looked at the uppermost page, he realized immediately that it was also the first page. The first page began like this:

One year: 365 days.
Two years: 365 + 365 = 730 days.
Three years: 730 + 365 = 1,095 days.
Four years: 1,095 + 365 = 1,460 days.
Five years: 1,490 + 365 = 1,855 days.

Having got this far, Young Lillie realized that Duckling didn't know how to do multiplication. Since he did not know multiplication, he had no choice but to use this cumbersome method. Having added up year by year until he reached the total for eighty-nine years, he worked out the figure of 32,485 days. From this figure he had deducted 253 days, leaving a final total of 32,232 days.

Duckling asked, 'Am I right?'

Young Lillie realized that Duckling was wrong, because of course not every year consists of 365 days. According to the solar calendar, every four years you have a leap year, which consists of 366 days. On the other hand he also realized that it cannot have been easy for a child of twelve to work through such a long and tiresome calculation without making any mistakes. He didn't want to upset him, so he said that the answer was correct and praised him for all the trouble that he had gone to:

'You are absolutely right about one thing. By basing your calculations on the number of days in a whole year, starting from the day of his birth, you saved yourself a lot of trouble. If you think about it, if you had started your count on the first of January, it would have left you with two incomplete years at the beginning and end of Mr Auslander's life to include in your final count, whereas this way you only have to think about the number of days that he lived past his birthday. That really has saved you a lot of effort.'

'But now I have worked out a much easier way of doing it,' Duckling said.

'How?'

'I don't know what it is called, but look at this.'

As he spoke, Duckling fished another couple of pages out from under his bed for the old man to look at.

These pieces of paper were of a completely different size and texture from the previous ones, and Duckling's handwriting was also somewhat altered, indicating that it must have been written at some other time. Duckling said that he wrote it after Daddy's funeral. Young Lillie looked at it and realized that the left-hand column contained addition as before, while the right-hand column contained the method of calculation that he did not know the name for:

$$\text{One year: 365 days.} \quad 365 . 1 = 365.$$
$$\text{Two years: } 365 + 365 = 730 \text{ days.} \quad 365 . 2 = 730.$$
$$\text{Three years: } 730 + 365 = 1{,}095 \text{ days} \quad 365 . 3 = 1{,}095.$$

As I am sure you will have realized, Duckling was using a dot to indicate multiplication – he did not know the proper sign and hence had to invent one of his own. Using this dual method of calculation, he had worked out a total for the first twenty years. But from the twenty-first year, he swapped the order of the two methods, giving his dot multiplication first and the addition second:

$$\text{Twenty-one years: } 365 . 21 = 7{,}665 \text{ days.}$$
$$7{,}300 + 365 = 7{,}665 \text{ days.}$$

At this stage, Young Lillie noticed that the figure of 7,665 obtained by multiplication had been corrected; the original answer had been something like 6,565. After that the total for every year was worked out the same way. The dot method came first and the addition came second; furthermore the result obtained by multiplication sometimes showed signs of having been corrected, to fit with the figure obtained by addition. However, the figure obtained by multiplication for the first twenty years of old Mr Auslander's life did not seem to have been corrected. That meant two things:

1. For calculating the first twenty years, Duckling was using addition as his primary method, while his dot principle was just a kind of decoration, which he seemed to regard as something that could not necessarily stand independently. On the other hand, from twenty-one years on, he was using multiplication only, with the addition functioning merely as mathematical proof.
2. To begin with he had not completely mastered multiplication and thus made mistakes, hence there were corrections to be found in his workings. However, later on, once he came to understand multiplication fully, the corrections gradually disappeared.

He carried on multiplying one year at a time until he reached forty, and then there was a sudden leap to eighty-nine, which by his dot method of calculation he worked out to be 32,485 days, a figure from which he then subtracted 253 days to reach a final total of 32,232 days, exactly as before. He had drawn a circle around this number, to make sure that it caught the eye and stood out from all the other figures.

There was one final page of workings, which appeared very confused, but Young Lillie realized at first glance that Duckling was trying to work out the principles of multiplication. At the very bottom of the page, the rules were clearly set out. As the old man looked at this page, he could not stop himself from reciting it out loud –

Once one is one.
Once two is two.

Once three is three . . .
Two twos are four.
Two threes are six.
Two fours are eight . . .
Three threes are nine.
Three fours are twelve.
Three fives are fifteen.
Three sixes are eighteen . . .

What he was reading was indubitably multiplication.

When he had finished, Young Lillie looked silently at the child, as he was enveloped by a very strange and unfamiliar sense of uncertainty. The quiet little room still seemed to resound with the echoes of his chanting; as he concentrated, he felt warmed and comforted. It was at that moment he decided that he had to take the child away. He said to himself, the war has gone on for years now and there is no end in sight; at any moment, with the very best motives at heart, an unconsidered action might bring disaster down upon me and those dearest to me. But this child is a genius and if I don't take him away with me right now, I am going to regret it for the rest of my life.

Before the end of the summer holidays, Young Lillie received a telegram from the provincial capital to say that the university would begin classes again in the autumn. They hoped that he would return as soon as possible to prepare to begin teaching. Once he received this telegram, Young Lillie thought that he might well not return to take charge, but that he would have to bring back a new student for them. He called out to the major-domo and told him that he was leaving. When he finished, he gave the man a fistful of notes. The major-domo thanked him, imagining that this was a tip.

Young Lillie said, 'This is not a tip. I want you to do something for me.'

'What is it?' asked the major-domo.

'Take Duckling into the village and buy him two sets of clothes.'

The major-domo just stood there, thinking that he must have misheard.

'Once you have done that, I will give you your tip,' said Young Lillie.

A couple of days later, when the major-domo came for his tip, Young Lillie said, 'You had better help Duckling to pack: we are leaving tomorrow.'

As you might imagine, yet again the major-domo just stood there, thinking that he must have misheard.

Young Lillie had to repeat what he had said all over again.

The following morning, just as the sky was getting light, all the dogs in the Rong family mansion suddenly started barking. First one started barking and then the next joined in, until the cacophony was indescribable and wrenched every member of the household — masters and servants — out of bed, to peer at what was going on outside through the cracks in the doors. Thanks to the lamp that the major-domo held, the residents of the Rong mansion were treated to such an amazing sight that they were hardly able to believe their eyes. They saw Duckling in a new suit of clothes, carrying the ox-hide suitcase that Mr Auslander had arrived with all those years before, walking silently in Young Lillie's wake, trying desperately to keep up. He seemed scared, and moved like a bewildered little ghost. Because it was so amazing, they none of them dared believe their own eyes. When the major-domo got back from the docks, they learned from him that it was only too true.

There were many questions. Where was Young Lillie taking him? Why was he taking him away? Would Duckling ever come back? Why was Young Lillie so kind to Duckling? And so on and so forth. The major-domo had two answers to all these questions.

To his masters he said: 'I don't know.'

To the junior servants he said: 'Who the fuck knows!'

4

If the horse made the world smaller and boat travel made the world larger, then the internal combustion engine made the world magical. A couple of months later, when the Japanese Army advanced from the provincial capital in the direction of Tongzhen, the advance motorbike division arrived within a couple of hours. They were the very first motors ever to be seen on the road between the provincial capital and Tongzhen and their speed made people wonder whether Heaven might not have finally taken pity on the Foolish Old Man who wanted to move a mountain and shifted the entire mountain range that lay between them out of the way. Up until that moment, the quickest way to go between the city and Tongzhen was to travel by horse. If you could find a horse with a good turn of speed and applied the whip when necessary, it was possible to make the journey in about seven or eight hours. Some decades earlier, Young Lillie had always made this journey by horse-drawn carriage. though this was of course slower than going on horseback, nevertheless, providing the driver pressed on, it was quite possible to reach your destination by dusk if you set out at dawn. However, now that he was getting on, Young Lillie could no longer cope with the jolting that entailed and so he had to travel by boat. The journey to Tongzhen took two days and two nights, but that was moving against the current. Coming back wouldn't take nearly so long, but it would still be at least one day and one night.

Sitting on the boat, Young Lillie started to worry about the boy's name. Even when the boat travelled the final stretch before the provincial capital, he still hadn't come to any decision. Once he had started thinking about it, he discovered what a tricky problem this was. The fact is, Young Lillie was confronted with exactly the same problems that old Mr Auslander had faced when he was asked to pick a name for the baby: this was not a difficulty that had resolved itself with time. Having thought about it carefully, Young Lillie decided to put all other considerations on one side and give the boy a name suitable for someone who had been born in Tongzhen and grown up in Tongzhen, and that way he came up with two names, both of which seemed to him a little forced: Jinzhen, meaning 'Golden Sincerity', and Tongzhen, meaning 'Childlike Sincerity'. He decided to let the boy decide for himself which one of the two he would prefer.

'I don't care,' said Duckling.

'In that case,' said Young Lillie, 'I will pick for you. Do you think that Jinzhen would be all right?'

'Fine,' replied Duckling. 'In that case I'll be called Jinzhen.'

'I hope that you live up to your name in future,' said Young Lillie.

'Fine,' Duckling replied, 'I will try to live up to my name.'

'That means I hope that in the future you will shine like gold,' said Young Lillie.

'Fine,' Duckling replied, 'I will try to shine like gold.'

After a moment, Young Lillie asked another question: 'Do you like your name?'

'Yes,' said Duckling.

'I would like to change one of the characters in your name,' said Young Lillie. 'Would that be okay by you?'

'Okay,' said Duckling.

'I haven't even told you which character I want to change,' said Young Lillie, 'so why do you just agree?'

'Which character?' Duckling asked.

'I want to change the character *zhen* meaning "sincerity" to the *zhen* that means "pearl",' said Young Lillie. 'Is that okay with you?'

'Okay,' replied Duckling. 'The *zhen* that means "pearl".'

'Do you know why I have changed that character in your name?' Young Lillie asked.

'No,' said Duckling.

'Would you like to know?'

'Well . . . I don't know . . .'

To tell the truth, the reason that Young Lillie wanted to change the character in his name was purely out of superstition. In Tongzhen, just like in the rest of the Jiangnan region, there was a popular saying: 'Even the devil is scared of a feminine man.' That means that when a man has some feminine quality, he has both *yin* and *yang* in his nature and the two complement each other. Strength is complemented by pliability. They thought that this was the way to produce the very best kind of man – a truly outstanding individual. It was because of this that local customs developed a million ways to balance *yin* and *yang*, including the names that they gave to their sons. A father who hoped for great things from his son would often deliberately pick a girl's name for him, in the hope that this would guarantee him a sterling future. Young Lillie wanted to tell Duckling this, but then he decided that it would not be quite appropriate. After hesitating a bit, he realized it would be best if he kept his reasoning to himself. So in the end he just said: 'Right, that's decided then. You are going to be called Jinzhen, the *zhen* that means "pearl".'

By that time, the skyline of C City was just emerging on the horizon.

Once they had arrived at the docks, Young Lillie called for a rickshaw, but he did not go home. Instead he went straight to a very well-respected primary school near the West Gate, to find the headmaster. The headmaster was a man named Cheng. This man had once been a pupil at the high school associated with N University, and when Young Lillie was a student – and later as a junior instructor at the university – he would often teach classes at the high school. Cheng had a remarkably lively character and was much admired by his fellow students; he had made a deep impression on Young Lillie. When he finished high school, his grades were such that he could easily have gone on to university, but by that time he had been bewitched by the uniforms of the National Revolutionary Army. When he came to say goodbye to Young Lillie, he was already shouldering a gun. In the depths of winter two years later, Cheng came back to see Young Lillie again. He was still wearing the uniform of the National Revolutionary Army, but this time he did not carry a gun. Looking more closely, Young Lillie realized that it was not only the rifle that was missing, the arm that was needed to hold it was also gone, leaving an empty sleeve. As Cheng manoeuvred himself awkwardly into place, Young Lillie felt more than a little uncomfortable. He gingerly took hold of his remaining hand – the left one – and realized that it was just as strong as normal. He asked whether he could write with that hand and Cheng said that he could. Young Lillie then provided him with a letter of introduction to a newly established primary school near the West Gate, where he could train as a teacher. This gave the wretched man a new lease of life. Because of his handicap, when he first became a teacher, everyone called him One-Arm. Now that he was the headmaster, people still called him One-Arm, because he had single-handedly made the school what it was.

A couple of months earlier, Young Lillie and his wife had hidden out at the school when the battle raging around the city was at its height – they had lived in the shed attached to the carpentry workshop. Today, the moment that Young Lillie clapped eyes on One-Arm, he said, 'Is the shed where I used to live still empty?'

'It is,' replied One-Arm. 'There are just a couple of basketballs and footballs in there.'

'I'd like it if this young man could stay there,' said Young Lillie. He pointed to Duckling.

'Who is he?' asked One-Arm.

'Jinzhen, your new student,' said Young Lillie.

From that day onwards, no one called him Duckling any more; everyone called him Jinzhen.

'Jinzhen!'

'Jinzhen!'

This new name marked the beginning of Duckling's life in the city and everything that happened to him after that; it was also the end of his connection with Tongzhen.

As for what happened over the course of the next couple of years, the most reliable witness is Young Lillie's oldest daughter, Rong Yinyi.

Everyone at N University called Miss Rong the Master, Master Rong, but I do not know whether this was the result of their fond memories of her father, or out of respect for her unusual position. She never married, but that is not because she never fell in love. Rather, it is because she fell in love too deeply, too painfully. The story goes that when she was young she had a boyfriend, a brilliant student from the physics department of N University, specializing in wireless technology. Supposedly he could make a triple waveband radio for you from scratch in the space of a couple of hours. Once the War of Resistance broke out, given that N University was a hotbed of patriotism in C City, it is hardly surprising that every month there were students abandoning their studies to join the army, rushing headlong for the front line. One of the students who left was Master Rong's boyfriend. For the first couple of years after he joined the army, he and Master Rong were able to keep in touch, but later on they gradually lost contact. The last letter she ever received from him was sent from the city of Changsha in Hunan province in the spring of 1941. It explained that he was now engaged in top-secret research work for the military and that he would temporarily have to break off contact with his family and friends. He wrote over and over again about how much he loved her and how he hoped that she would wait for him. The last line was the most moving: 'Darling, wait for me to come back to you. The day that the Japanese are defeated will be our wedding day!' Master Rong waited until the Japanese were defeated and then she waited until the Liberation, but still he did not come back – there wasn't even word that he had died. She heard nothing until 1953 when someone returned from Hong Kong bringing a message for her, saying that he had gone to Taiwan many years earlier and was now married with children. He told her to find someone else.

That was the end result of all Master Rong's decades of devotion and waiting. It goes without saying that it was a terrible shock to her and she never really got over it. Ten years ago, when I went to N University to meet her, she had just retired from the position of Head of the Department of Mathematics. Our conversation began with a discussion of a family photograph hanging in her living room. There were five people in the photograph. Young Lillie and his wife were in the front row, sitting down, and standing behind them was Master Rong, then in her twenties, with her hair in a shoulder-length bob. Standing to her left was her younger brother, wearing glasses, and on her right was her younger sister with her hair in pigtails, aged maybe seven or eight. This photograph was taken in the summer of 1936, just as Master Rong's younger brother was getting ready to go abroad to study. The picture was taken to commemorate the occasion. Because of the war, her younger brother did not come back home until 1945; during that time the family lost and then gained a member. The person they lost was the little sister, who had died in the epidemic the year before; the person they gained was Jinzhen, who joined the family that summer, just a few weeks after she died. As Master Rong explained:

[Transcript of the interview with Master Rong]

My little sister died during the summer holidays, when she was just seventeen.

My mother and I didn't even know of Jinzhen's existence until after she was dead. Daddy had him hidden in the house of Mr Cheng, the headmaster of a primary school near the West Gate. We didn't have much to do with Mr Cheng, so even though Daddy was hoping to keep this all a secret from us, he didn't bother to specifically warn him not to mention it to us. One day, Mr Cheng came to the house. I don't know where he had heard that my sister had died, but he came to pay a visit of condolence. My father and I happened to be away from home that day, so only my mother was there to greet him and, as they talked, Daddy's secret came out. When he came back, Mummy asked him what was going on, and he told her everything he knew about all the misfortunes this boy had already suffered in his short life, his remarkable intelligence, and the old foreign gentleman's request. Perhaps it was because Mummy had been so deeply affected by my sister's death that she just burst into tears when she heard about his unhappiness. She said to Daddy: 'Yinzhi (that was my little sister's name) has gone and this boy needs a family. Bring him to live here.'

That was how my little brother Zhendi joined us – Zhendi was Jinzhen's nickname, you see.

My mother and I both called him Zhendi, only Daddy called him Jinzhen. Zhendi called Mother 'Mummy', but he called Daddy 'Professor' and me 'Sis', so everything was kind of topsy-turvy. Of course, if you looked at the family tree, I would be one generation senior to him, so by rights he should have called me 'Auntie'.

To tell the truth, I didn't like Zhendi one little bit when he first turned up. He didn't smile at all and wouldn't speak to anyone. He moved round the house in absolute silence, like a ghost. He turned out to have all sorts of disgusting habits, like belching while eating. His hygiene was also appalling: he didn't wash his feet at night and he would just take his shoes off and throw them down by the stairs, filling the dining room and the corridor with a foul stench. We were living in the house that my father had inherited from Grandpa, a kind of Western-style villa. There was a kitchen and dining room on the ground floor and all the bedrooms were upstairs. Every time I came down the stairs from my bedroom for meals, I would see his rotten and stinking old shoes and think about the way that he belched over his food, and I would find myself not really wanting anything to eat at all. Of course the problem with his shoes was sorted out almost immediately: Mummy told him that he ought pay attention to this and make sure that he washed his feet and put on clean socks every day – after that his socks were cleaner than anyone's. He was a very capable boy: he knew how to cook, wash his clothes, build a fire out of coal-dust briquettes; he even knew how to sew – in fact he was much better at that kind of thing than I was. Of course, this was all to do with the way that he had been brought up: he had learned how to do all sorts of things. The belching and farting turned out to be much more difficult habits to break him of. Habits can be broken eventually, but in this case it turned out that he had very serious stomach problems, which were also the reason why he was so thin. Daddy told me that his stomach problems were the results of drinking the pear-blossom tea that Mr Auslander was so fond of day in and day out: that kind of thing was all very well for an old man, but how could it possibly be considered suitable for a growing child! To tell the truth, once we found out about his stomach problems, he ate more medicine than food in our house. He could only eat one little bowl of rice per meal, less than a cat, and even so after just a mouthful or two he would start belching.

One day, Zhendi forgot to lock the door of the lavatory and I walked in, not realizing that it was already occupied. That really wasn't acceptable. As far as I was concerned, that was the last straw and now I wanted him out of our house. I told Mummy and Daddy that I couldn't stand it any longer and I wanted him to start boarding at school. I told them that, even though he was a relative, that was no reason for him to be living in our home and that lots of other boys lived as boarders at the school. Daddy didn't say a word – he let Mummy do the talking. Mummy said that it wouldn't be right to make him leave when he had only just arrived; she said that once term had started, then it might be all right for him to become a boarder. Daddy then chipped in and said, 'Okay, once term has started he can stay at school as a boarder.'

Mummy said, 'We will go and fetch him so that he can spend every weekend here, because he ought to feel that this is still his home.'

Daddy agreed to that. So everything was decided.

However, that is not at all what happened in the end . . .

[To be continued]

One evening, towards the end of the summer holidays, Master Rong happened to mention at the dinner table something that she had read in the newspapers earlier that day: the previous summer many parts of the country had suffered one of the worst droughts since records began, with the result that in some cities there were more beggars than there were troops. Her mother sighed and said that the previous year had been a double leap year – those years always saw terrible natural disasters. In the final analysis it was always the peasants that suffered the most. Jinzhen did not often open his mouth and so Mrs Lillie always did her best to bring him into the conversation. It was for this reason that she made a point of asking him if he knew what a double leap year was. When he shook his head, Mrs Lillie explained that it came about when a leap year in the solar calendar coincided with one in the lunar calendar; when the two leap years came together. Seeing that he didn't really understand what she was talking about, Mrs Lillie asked him, 'Do you know what a leap year is?'

He shook his head again, without making a sound. He was that sort of person: if it was possible to express something by any other means, he would not open his mouth. Immediately Mrs Lillie began to explain to him what a leap year was and how it was dealt with in first the solar calendar and then the lunar calendar, and so on and so forth. When she had finished, he just stared at Young Lillie as if he had been pole-axed, waiting for him to confirm what his wife had just said.

Young Lillie said, 'Exactly. That is how it works.'

'You mean my calculations were wrong?' Jinzhen went bright red in the face and looked as if he was about to burst into tears.

'Your calculations?' Young Lillie did not know what he was talking about.

'Daddy's age – I thought that every year was 365 days long.'

'That is not quite right . . . ' Before Young Lillie had finished speaking, Jinzhen broke down into floods of tears.

It proved impossible to console him. Whatever people said to him to try to cheer him up, it did not make the blindest bit of difference. In the end Young Lillie had simply had enough and angrily thumped his fist down on the dining table, shouting at him to control himself. Although he did stop crying at that point, it was clear that he was still terribly upset. He was holding onto his thighs, digging his nails in, as if his life depended on it. Young Lillie ordered him to keep his hands above the table. Afterwards, he spoke to him very sternly, though he was clearly intending his words to console the boy. He said, 'What are you making that kind of racket for? I still haven't finished speaking. When I have, then you can see if you still want to cry.'

He continued, 'When I said that you were wrong just now, I was speaking theoretically – the fact is that you ignored the existence of leap years. On the other hand, if you look at it from the point of view of mathematics, it would be impossible to say that you were wrong, because there are acceptable errors in any calculation.

'According to my knowledge, the time it takes the earth to complete one orbit of the sun is three hundred and sixty-five days, five hours, forty-eight minutes and forty-six seconds. So why do we need leap years? There is a simple reason: according to the solar calendar, every year there are five extra hours, whereby every four years you need a leap year which consists of three hundred and sixty-six days. However, as I am sure you will realize if you think about it, if you calculate that ordinary years consist of three hundred and sixty-five days and that each leap year contains three hundred and sixty-six days, you are still not going to obtain a completely accurate calculation. It is convenient for most ordinary purposes to let the mistake go by; in fact, it would be impossible to work the solar calendar without this acceptable error. What I am trying to tell you is that even if you had allowed for leap years, your calculation would still be wrong.

'Now you can go away and work out how many leap years Mr Auslander lived through during his eighty-nine years and then add that number of days to your original calculation. Then you can work out how big the difference is between your original calculation and the new one. In a calculation involving figures of more than four places of decimals, the acceptable margin for error is normally set at 0.01 per cent; any more than that and you have made a mistake in your calculations. Right: now you tell me, is your mistake within the acceptable margin for error?'

Mr Auslander died in a leap year at the age of eighty-nine, thus he had lived through twenty-two leap years: that does not sound many, but it is also not a few. Adding one day for every leap year means that twenty-two leap years is equivalent to twenty-two days. Adding that to the more than 30,000 days that Mr Auslander had spent on this earth meant that it was a mistake well within the acceptable margin of error. The reason why Young Lillie made such a point of this is that he wanted Jinzhen to find a way to forgive himself for the mistake that he had made. Thanks to the way that Young Lillie first shouted at him and then cajoled him, Jinzhen finally calmed down.

[Transcript of the interview with Master Rong]
Later on, Daddy explained to us how Mr Auslander had asked Zhendi to work out his age. Thinking of how upset he had been, I

suddenly found myself feeling moved by his obvious affection for the old foreign gentleman. On the other hand, I also realized that he had an obsessive streak in his character – not to mention an inability to cope with his own mistakes. Later on we realized more and more clearly that Zhendi could on occasion be really stubborn and fiery-tempered; most of the time he was so quiet and kept himself to himself. He could put up with all sorts of things and simply carry on as if nothing had happened – in fact he could tolerate things that most people would find absolutely unendurable. But once an invisible line was crossed, once something had touched the most delicate part of his psyche, he would lose control very easily. This loss of control was always expressed by some extreme act. I could give you lots of examples of this kind of thing. For instance, he really loved my mother and so one day he wrote a message in his own blood, completely in secret. What he said was: 'Daddy is dead. The rest of my life is going to be devoted to looking after Mummy.'

When he was seventeen, he got terribly sick and spent a long time in hospital. Mummy discovered this note then, because she was forever popping into his room to look for something or other that he wanted. It was slipped inside the binding of his diary and written in large characters. It looked as though he had used the tip of a finger to write it, but there was no date on it, so we didn't know when it had been written. It was clear that it was not recent, so I reckon that he probably wrote it during the first year or two that he was living with us. The foxing on the paper and the fading of the characters certainly suggested that it had been there for some time.

My mother was a very kind and gentle woman, friendly with everyone. She remained the same throughout her long life. When you think about her relationship with Zhendi, it really seemed as though they were destined to be friends, because the two of them got along amazingly well right from the very beginning. They had the kind of silent rapport that you normally only see among close family members. From the very first day that he came to live with us, Mummy called him Zhendi. I don't know why she called him that; maybe it was because my little sister had only just passed away and she was transferring all her affection to him. After my sister died, Mummy didn't set foot outside the house for the longest time; she just sat at home and mourned. Many nights she had nightmares, and during the day she often imagined that she saw my dead sister. Once Zhendi arrived, Mummy gradually recovered. Maybe you don't know this, but Zhendi knew how to interpret people's dreams. He was wonderfully good at it, just like visiting a professional shaman. He was a Christian though and read a little English-language Bible every day, even though he knew lots of passages completely off by heart. I think that the reason Mummy recovered so quickly and with so few setbacks along the way was entirely thanks to the fact that Zhendi was there interpreting her dreams for her and telling her stories out of the Bible. It is hard to explain exactly why they got on so well together. Of course, Mummy loved Zhendi; she always thought of him as one of the family and respected and cared about him. What nobody knew at the time was how deeply Zhendi was affected by this and how he became determined to repay her for everything that she did for him. That is why he secretly wrote that message in his own blood. In my opinion, Zhendi had lacked affection in his earlier life; in particular he had never experienced mother-love. Everything that Mummy did for him – cooking him three meals a day, making his clothes, asking him if he was too hot or too cold – this was all new to him and he felt it deeply. As time went on and more and more things were done for him, he wasn't able to deal with his emotions any more and found this way of expressing his gratitude. Of course, the way that he chose was more than a little melodramatic, but that is the kind of boy he was. If I may be allowed the benefit of hindsight, I think that nowadays we would say that Zhendi was autistic.

I could cite lots of other examples of similar kinds of behaviour, and perhaps I will tell you about them later on. However, right now we need to go back to the evening when he had hysterics, because the matter is not yet over . . .

[*To be continued*]

The following evening, again at suppertime, Jinzhen returned to the matter that had been under discussion the previous day. He said that Mr Auslander had lived through twenty-two leap years and hence it might appear that he had got his figures out by twenty-two days, but that in fact he was wrong by only twenty-one days. That seemed completely stupid! If you have lived through twenty-two leap years then that adds one day for every year – it should be twenty-two days. Why did he say that it was twenty-one? Everyone, including Mrs Lillie, thought that he must have gone off his head. But when Jinzhen explained what he meant, those present realized that he had a point.

You see, Young Lillie had explained that leap years were introduced because in fact each year is 365 days, 5 hours, 48 minutes and 46 seconds long, and thus every four years they add another 24 hours. But obviously it is not precisely 24 hours that needs making up, because that would require the earth to take 365 days and 6 hours to travel once around the sun. How much is the error introduced? Every year it is 11 minutes and 14 seconds, so in other words over the course of four years, an error of 44 minutes and 56 seconds is introduced. This means that in every leap year cycle, a certain amount of time is added: 44 minutes and 56 seconds. Mankind steals that time from the earth. Mr Auslander lived through twenty-two leap years, so for him, a total of 16 hours, 28 minutes and 32 seconds of non-existent time had been added to his life.

However, as Jinzhen pointed out, according to the original figure Mr Auslander had lived for 32,232 days, a number that he obtained not by working out how many days there were in eighty-eight years, but how many days there were in eighty-eight years plus 112 days. While it was perfectly true that when he was calculating the 112 extra days he ignored the existence of leap years, it is also a fact that a day is not precisely twenty-four hours long. In actual fact a day is twenty-four hours plus almost a minute long – over the course of 112 days that would add up to 6,421 seconds, or in other words one hour and forty-seven minutes. So you have to deduct that one hour and forty-seven minutes from the original figure of 16 hours, 28 minutes and 32 seconds, which gives you a new total of 14 hours, 41 minutes and 32 seconds. That gives you the real figure for the non-existent time added to Mr Auslander's life by the modern calendar.

Jinzhen went on to say that, according to his information, Mr Auslander had been born at noon and he died at nine o'clock in the evening, so at the beginning and end of his life, there were at least ten hours of non-existent time being factored in, not to mention the 14 hours, 41 minutes and 32 seconds that he had accumulated during his lifetime. No matter how you worked it out, Mr Auslander had one whole day's worth of non-existent time added to his lifespan. Jinzhen had clearly spent a lot of time thinking about what a leap year meant. You could say that since the existence of leap years had put his calculation of the number of days that Mr Auslander spent upon this earth out by twenty-two days, now he had got his own back by cutting down his mistake by twenty-four hours.

According to Master Rong, she and her father were both amazed at this development. They both felt impressed and moved by this evidence of the boy's crystal-clear intellect. However, the most amazing thing was yet to come. A couple of days later, when Master Rong had just arrived back home in the afternoon, her mother (who was cooking downstairs) told her that her father was in Zhendi's room and that she was to go and join them. When Master Rong asked why, her mother said that Zhendi seemed to have come up with some kind of mathematical theorem and that her father had been absolutely stunned.

As mentioned before, since the last 112 days of old Mr Auslander's life had originally not been calibrated to take account of the existence of leap years, if you insist that each day consists only of twenty-four hours, in fact you are leaving 1 hour and 47 minutes, or 6,421 seconds, unaccounted for each year. The error introduced annually is 6,421 seconds. In the cycle of one leap year, you can deduct the uncounted time from the non-existent time: $-6,421 + 2,696$ seconds, where 2,696 represents the number of seconds in 44 minutes and 56 seconds. In the second leap year cycle, the amount of non-existent time is $(-6,421 + 2 \times 2,696)$ seconds, and so on and so forth until you arrive at the calculation for the last leap year: $(-6,421 + 22 \times 2,696)$ seconds. Jinzhen had calculated the missing time, unaccounted for in his original figure for how many days Mr Auslander had lived, which he worked out as 88 years and 112 days, or 32,232 days, into twenty-three lines of elegant calculations, to wit:

$$(-6,421)$$
$$(-6,421 + 2,696)$$
$$(-6,421 + 2 \times 2,696)$$

$$(-6,421 + 3 \times 2,696)$$
$$(-6,421 + 4 \times 2,696)$$
$$(-6,421 + 5 \times 2,696)$$
$$(-6,421 + 6 \times 2,696)$$
$$\cdots$$
$$(-6,421 + 22 \times 2,696)$$

Based upon this, and without any instruction from anyone, he had gone on to work out a mathematical formula:

$$X = [(\text{first value} + \text{last value}) \times \text{number}] / 2\star$$

He had managed to work out a mathematical formula completely unaided.

[Transcript of the interview with Master Rong]

Mathematical formulae are not such bizarre and abstruse things that ordinary people cannot work them out. The fact is that anyone with a good knowledge of mathematics could reframe their knowledge in the shape of a formula – provided they know that formulae exist in the first place. I could shut you up in a dark room, having told you in considerable detail about its contents. If I then demanded that you find me a particular object, even though the room was pitch-dark, you might well still be able to find it. If you used your intelligence, if you moved your feet carefully and felt with your hands, gradually working out what things have been put where, you ought to be able to find what I have asked you to look for. On the other hand if I had not told you what was in the room in the first place and then demanded that you go and find me a particular object, the chances are that you would not be able to do it.

Well, if he had been faced with a simple list of numbers, like say 1, 3, 5, 7, 9, 11 (not something complicated and irregular), and he had worked out a mathematical formula for that, it would have been much more easy to understand and we wouldn't have been quite so amazed. You could compare this to someone making a piece of furniture from scratch without a single lesson from a carpenter. It doesn't matter that other people have made the same piece many times before:

$\star$ Conventionally, this formula would be given as: $S = [(A_1 + A_n) \times n] / 2$.

we would still be impressed at your abilities. If the tools and material at your disposal were of poor quality, if the tools were rusty and the wood rough, and yet you still managed to produce a decent piece of furniture, we would all be doubly impressed. That is what Zhendi had done: he had effectively taken a stone hand-axe and a tree standing in the forest and turned them into a beautiful piece of furniture. We were that amazed, we could hardly believe the evidence of our own eyes. It was completely unbelievable!

After this, we felt that it would not be a good idea to keep him on at primary school, so Daddy decided to enrol him in the middle school attached to N University. The school was only a couple of doors down from our house, so if he went there as a boarder, it would quite possibly be even more damaging to Zhendi's fragile psyche than if we had just thrown him out onto the streets. So, at the same time as Daddy decided to enrol Zhendi in the first year at middle school, he also decided that he would have to continue living with us. The fact is that after Zhendi came to live with us that summer, he never left until he got his first job . . .

[*To be continued*]

Children like giving each other nicknames; any child in the least bit peculiar will find himself being given a nickname by his classmates. When the other pupils at the school first caught sight of Jinzhen's huge head, they called him 'Big-head'. Later on they realized that he had all sorts of peculiar habits – like he really enjoyed counting the hordes of ants that marched backwards and forwards across the playground and was completely oblivious to anything else while he was doing it, or that in the winter he would always wear a tatty old scarf trimmed with dog-fur (apparently this had been a present from old Mr Auslander), or that he would fart and belch in class, without the least sign of restraint, just letting it all hang out, as it were. People really did not know how to take him. Another thing: he always wrote his homework in duplicate – once in Chinese and once in English. What with one thing and another, people felt that there was something wrong with him, that he must be stupid. But at the same time his grades were fantastic, really impressive, better than what the rest of the class could achieve put together. So they came up with a

new nickname for him, 'Idiot-savvy', by which they meant 'idiot sa-
vant'. This nickname was particularly apposite because it encompassed
his behaviour both inside and outside the classroom. Like many nicknames it seemed to denigrate its possessor, but at the same time it had
an element of praise – a perfect mix of contempt and respect: everyone felt it was the right name for him. Everyone called him that.

'Idiot-savvy!'

'Idiot-savvy!'

Fifty years later, when I went to visit the university, there were
plenty of people who had no idea who I was talking about when I
mentioned Jinzhen, but the moment I said 'the Idiot-savvy', it was
like putting a match to the train of their memories – this nickname
brought a whole host of stories to mind. One of the people I talked
to, an old gentleman who had once been Jinzhen's class teacher, was
happy to share the following memories with me.

> I remember one interesting thing. During break in class, one of the
> other pupils noticed a line of ants crawling along the corridor and
> called him over. He said to Jinzhen, 'You like counting ants, don't
> you, so why don't you come and count how many ants we have here?'
> I saw it with my own eyes – he came over and counted a couple of
> hundred ants walking along – just like that. There was another time
> that he borrowed a book off me, a dictionary of proverbs and apho-
> risms, and he gave it back to me a few days later. I said he could keep
> it but he said that he didn't need it, since he had already memorized
> the whole thing. Later on, I found out that he could recite the whole
> damn thing from memory! I can tell you, of all the many, many
> pupils that I have taught during my career, there was no one else who
> came even close in terms of basic intelligence or academic ability. His
> memory, creative ability, comprehension, his ability to calculate, to
> extrapolate from the evidence, to make a summary, to come to a deci-
> sion . . . in many, many ways his abilities were truly amazing; ordinary
> people could not even begin to imagine what he could do. In my
> opinion, he did not need to waste his time in high school and could
> have gone straight on to university, but the Headmaster refused – he
> said that old Mr Rong didn't want it that way.

The old Mr Rong that this gentleman was talking about was Young Lillie.

Young Lillie had two reasons for his refusal. First, he was worried about the fact that Jinzhen had spent much of his childhood entirely cut off from other people, so he now needed to learn how to build normal social relations, spending time with other children of his own age, growing up in the ordinary way. Putting him in a situation where he would be entirely surrounded by people many years older than himself would be extremely damaging to a difficult and inward-looking personality. Secondly, he had discovered that Jinzhen would often do stupid things: he would try to conceal from Young Lillie and his teachers that he was trying to prove things that they had already explained to him had been demonstrated conclusively by other people – maybe it was just that he was too clever. Young Lillie thought that someone with no experience of the world, but with such great intelligence, needed to proceed one step at a time, otherwise he might end up wasting his genius on finding out things that other people already knew.

Later on it became clear that they would have to let him skip whole grades or the teachers simply would not be able to carry on themselves: he was treating his high-school teachers to barrages of obscure questions that they simply could not answer. There was nothing that could be done: Young Lillie had to listen to the advice of the boy's teachers and let him skip a grade. Having created a precedent, he skipped one grade after the other and so by the time that his fellow classmates from the first year of high school had reached the last, he was already long gone. He passed the university entrance exams with flying colours: 100 per cent in mathematics and seventh place in the entire province. Naturally he ended up in the mathematics department of N University.

6.

The mathematics department at N University was famous; in fact it was often said to be the cradle of the best mathematicians in the country. About fifteen years ago, a famous author from C City happened to overhear some people making derogatory remarks about his home town. His response was really remarkable. He said, 'Even if C City was twice as run-down and backward than it is, we would still have the outstanding N University. If N University also started to fail, they would still have a mathematics department that ranks among the best in the world. How dare you make derogatory remarks about us!'

He meant it as a joke, but the fact is that the mathematics department of N University has always been very highly regarded.

On Jinzhen's first day at university, Young Lillie gave him a diary. He had written a message on the fly-leaf, which ran as follows:

> If you want to become a mathematician, you have come to the very best place in the country to foster your talents. If you do not want to become a mathematician, then you do not need to attend this university, for you already know enough mathematics to last you for the rest of your life.

Perhaps there was no one more aware than Young Lillie of the rare and amazing mathematical genius concealed beneath Jinzhen's impassive exterior. Because of that, there was no one who hoped that Jinzhen would become a mathematician more than Young Lillie. As you will have realized, the note that he wrote in the front of Jinzhen's diary is proof of that. Young Lillie was quite sure that in the future there would be a long train of other people who followed in his footsteps in realizing that Jinzhen had a remarkable genius for mathematics. However, at the same time he was worried that if that recognition came now it would be damaging – he was trying to hold it off for a year or two, to let Jinzhen concentrate on his studies, for he was sure that Jinzhen's mysterious mathematical genius would sooner or later shine through.

As things turned out, Young Lillie was perhaps a bit too conservative. After just two weeks of class, Professor Jan Liseiwicz joined him on the list of people who had noticed the boy's talents. As the professor said, 'I can see that N University has produced yet another fine mathematician, and perhaps he will be one of the great mathematicians of our time. At the very least he will be the best that you and I will ever see.'

He was talking about Jinzhen.

Jan Liseiwicz was almost the same age as the century. He was born into a Polish aristocratic family in 1901. His mother was Jewish, and she bequeathed him what people in those days thought of as a typical Jewish face: a strong forehead, a hawk-like nose and dark curly hair. He was also remarkably intelligent: his memory amazed people; on the Binet-Simon tests he registered practically off the scale. At the age of four, the young Liseiwicz was already obsessed by games in which the competitors pitted their intelligence against each other – it was at this stage that he started playing chess and learning set variations. By the time he was six, none of his family or their friends would dare to play against him. Everyone who saw him play chess said the same thing: he was a genius such as comes along maybe once in a century. Others complimented his mother: 'Another great Jewish mathematician has been born!'

At the age of fourteen, Jan Liseiwicz accompanied his parents to a party to celebrate a wedding in another local aristocratic family; also present on this occasion were the family of Michael Steinroder, at that time one of the most famous mathematicians in the world. At the time of this unexpected meeting, Michael Steinroder was the Director of the Institute of Mathematics at Cambridge University and a chess grandmaster. Mr Liseiwicz senior explained to the mathematician that he hoped that one day his son would be able to study at Cambridge University. Steinroder said arrogantly, 'There are two ways to gratify that ambition. Either he has to pass the standard entrance examinations held every year for Cambridge University or he has to win the Newtonian Prize in Mathematics or Physics offered every two years by the

Royal Society.' (The prize was awarded in mathematics in odd-numbered years and for physics in even-numbered years. The first five highly commended individuals could attend Cambridge University without having to pass the entrance examinations and for free.)

The young Jan Liseiwicz then piped up: 'I have heard that you are regarded as the world's finest amateur chess player. How about we play a game? If I win, surely I should be allowed to attend the university without having to take the entrance examinations?'

Steinroder replied sternly, 'I am happy to play a game with you, but let me make it clear – you have demanded a great favour from me if you win. I am happy to oblige, but in return I am going to ask something of you if you lose. In this way the game will be fair. If you do not agree, then I decline to play.'

'Tell me what you want me to do,' Jan responded.

'If you lose,' the mathematician said, 'you can never apply to attend Cambridge University.'

He was hoping to scare Jan off, but the only person who got frightened was the boy's father. A storm of protest from Mr Liseiwicz senior made his son somewhat hesitant, but in the end he said confidently, 'Fine!'

Surrounded by onlookers, the pair of them began to move their chess pieces, but within less than half an hour, Steinroder got up from the table and said with a laugh to Mr Liseiwicz: 'Bring your son to Cambridge next year.'

Mr Liseiwicz said, 'You haven't finished the game yet.'

The mathematician said, 'Do you really think I can't tell when I am beaten?' Turning back, he asked young Jan: 'Do you think you can beat me?'

The boy replied, 'Right now I only have a thirty per cent chance of victory; you have a seventy per cent chance.'

The mathematician said, 'You are absolutely right. On the other hand, because you have realized that, there is at least a sixty to seventy per cent chance that you could force me to make a mistake. You have done very well and I hope to play many more games of chess with you when you come to Cambridge.'

Ten years later, Jan Liseiwicz (then aged just twenty-four) was listed

by the Austrian journal *Monatshefte für Mathematik* as one of the rising
stars in the world of mathematics. The following year he won the
highest prize offered in international mathematics: the Fields Medal.
People call this the equivalent of the Nobel Prize in Mathematics, but
in fact it is much harder to achieve, for the Nobel Prize is offered every
single year while the Fields Medal is only awarded once every four
years.

One of Liseiwicz's fellow students at Cambridge was a young
woman who belonged to one of the junior branches of the Austrian
imperial family. She fell madly in love with this young winner of the
Fields Medal, but he remained completely indifferent to her. One day,
the young woman's father came to see Liseiwicz – naturally this was
not in the hope that he would marry his daughter, but because he
wanted to discuss his ideas for improving the state of mathematical
knowledge in Austria. He asked the young man if he was prepared to
help him achieve this ambition. Liseiwicz asked him what exactly he
had in mind, and he said, 'I will put up the money. You find suitable
people. We ought to be able to put together a nice research institute.'

'How much money are you prepared to invest in this?' Liseiwicz
asked.

'Tell me how much you need.'

Liseiwicz thought about it for two weeks and worked out a mathematical formula for calculating the benefits to his own future career
and for the field as a whole. The result was that going to Austria won
over staying in Cambridge, no matter what number he looked at.

So he went to Austria.

A lot of people thought that he went to Austria at the behest of two
people – one was the rich father and the other the besotted daughter.
Some people imagined that this lucky young man would marry the
girl and massively advance his career at one fell swoop. However, in
practice the only thing that happened was that he advanced his career.
He used the Hapsburg prince's inexhaustible resources to create the
finest mathematical research institute in Austria and gathered many
excellent mathematicians under his banner – eventually the young
woman who had been so desperate to marry him found a replacement
from among their number. There was much gossip at the time that he

was homosexual, and some of his actions did indeed seem to give cre-
dence to the rumours: for example, he never employed a woman in his
research institute – even the secretaries and support staff were all male.
Furthermore, when newspapers required an interview with him, they
quickly learned to send a male reporter. As a matter of fact, more
women reporters went to interview him than men, but they came back
empty-handed; although this was probably more the result of his
secretive nature than anything else.

[Transcript of the interview with Master Rong]

Jan Liseiwicz came to N University as a visiting scholar in the
spring of 1938 – I imagine that he was headhunting. Of course, he was
not expecting that such earth-shattering events would occur over the
next couple of weeks. When he heard that Hitler had invaded Austria, he had no choice but to stay on at N University, at least until the
situation in Europe became clearer. While he was waiting, he received
a letter from a friend in the United States, informing him that the
situation in Europe was truly appalling. The Nazi flag was already on
the march through Austria, Czechoslovakia, Hungary and Poland,
and Jewish people were being forced to flee. Those who did not leave
in time were being rounded up and placed in camps. It was then that
he realized that there was now nowhere to go and that he was stuck
with us for the foreseeable future. He took up the position of professor of mathematics here, but he was still waiting for an opportunity
to get to America. It was during this time that his personality (or
perhaps it was his body) underwent a mysterious and unexpected
change – almost overnight he began to experience an overwhelming
attraction to the young women at the university. This was apparently
something that had never happened to him before. He seemed like a
strange tree that puts out different flowers when it is planted in different places, which then mature into different kinds of fruit. His
decision to go to the United States was swamped by this new interest
in the opposite sex, and two years later he married a young instructor
from the physics department – he was forty years old at the time and
she was a good fourteen years younger. This delayed his plan of going
to the United States yet again, and he did not come back to the idea
for another decade.

Everyone involved in the world of mathematics realized that after Jan Liseiwicz went to China he changed a great deal, becoming a wonderful husband and father, but less and less of an original and creative mathematician. Perhaps his remarkable talents were intrinsically bound up in his undomesticated existence; and thus once he married his genius deserted him. The fact is that if anyone had thought to ask him, he would have been hard put to answer whether his actions had destroyed his talent, or whether it had just vanished of its own accord. As any mathematician could tell you, before Jan Liseiwicz went to China, he wrote twenty-seven papers which were greeted with international acclaim, but afterwards he did not write even one. On the other hand, it was during this time that his sons and daughters were born. It was as if his genius vanished in a woman's embrace, only to transform itself into a succession of adorable babies. Looking at what happened to him, people came to believe that there might be something in the old adage about how east is east and west is west and never the twain shall meet. For such a strange man to change in such a mysterious way, in such a profound way, was really quite unbelievable. At the time no one realized quite what was going on, but we all saw the results.

Of course, though he might have lost one part of his genius, Jan Liseiwicz remained a truly remarkable teacher. You could say that while he became less and less of an original, creative mathematician, he had transformed himself into a professional and highly respected instructor. Liseiwicz taught at the mathematics department in N University for eleven years, and the chance to become one of his students was unquestionably a great honour and a wonderful beginning to any mathematician's career. To give you just one example: of the handful of students of N University who have achieved international recognition in their field, more than half were his students during his eleven years there. Of course, being one of his students was no sinecure. First, you had to be able to speak English (after Hitler's invasion of Austria he refused to speak German ever again). Secondly, he would not allow anyone to take notes in his classes. Furthermore, when setting out a problem he would often give only half of it, or he would deliberately set out part of it incorrectly. Having set it out wrongly he would not correct it, or at least not on the same occasion. If he happened to remember it a few days later, he might give you the problem correctly, but if not, he didn't care. It was that little trick more than any of the others which made many of his less intelligent students give up halfway or transfer to another department. His whole educational theory could be summed up in a single sentence: An interesting but wrong theory is always better than a boring but perfect proof. If you get right down to it, the reason he used these tricks was to force his students to think, to develop their imaginations and their creative abilities. At the start of every new academic year, facing his new students, he would begin his first class with the same message, couched in a strange mélange of Chinese and English: 'I am a wild animal, not an animal trainer. I am going to chase you deep into the mountains and forests and you are going to have to do your damnedest to run ahead of me. The faster you run, the faster I will chase you. If you run slowly, I will chase you slowly. Whatever happens, you must run, you must never stop, whatever difficulties you face. The day that you stop running, our relationship is over. The day that you run deep into the woods and disappear from sight, our relationship is also over. In the first instance, I have given up on you; in the second, you have set yourself free. Right: now it is time to start running and see who can get away from whom.'

Of course, it was very difficult to set yourself free from him, but the means of doing so was extremely simple. At the start of every term, in the very first class, Liseiwicz would begin by writing a tricky equation in the top right-hand corner of the blackboard. Whenever someone worked out the answer, he would be given 100 per cent as his grade, and for the rest of the term he would have to attend class only if he wished to do so. You could say that you had set yourself free for the rest of that term. Once that had happened, he would write a new equation in the same place on the blackboard and wait for a second person to get the answer right. If you solved three equations in a row, he would set a new problem for you alone, which would function as your graduation thesis. If you solved that too, whenever it happened, even if you had attended the university only for a couple of days, you would graduate with top marks, thereby completing your studies. Of course, in the nearly ten years that he had been teaching by then, there had never been anyone who had achieved anything close – even being able to solve one or two of his equations was a remarkable achievement.

[*To be continued*]

Jinzhen was now sitting in Liseiwicz's class, and because he was so short (being still only sixteen), he sat in the very front row. He could see the sharp flash and sparkle of Jan Liseiwicz's pale blue eyes much more clearly than any of his fellows. Liseiwicz was a tall man and, standing by the teacher's podium, he seemed even taller. His eyes were fixed on the very back row of seats. Jinzhen felt the occasional fall of drops of spittle when the professor became excited and the sudden exhalation of breath when he raised his voice. He talked about these dry, abstract mathematical notations in a voice filled with intense emotion. Sometimes he waved his arms and shouted; sometimes he walked slowly up and down, reciting. Liseiwicz, when he stood in front of the teacher's podium, seemed like a poet, or maybe like a general. At the end of the class, he walked out without a further word. However, on this occasion, just as he was stomping out, Jan Liseiwicz's gaze happened to fall on the thin young man seated in the front row. He had his head bent over the sheet of paper where he was working out a calculation. He seemed entirely intent upon his work, like a student in an exam hall. Two days later, Liseiwicz held his second class. When he took his place at the podium, he asked a general question: 'Is there someone here called Jinzhen? If so, could you please raise your hand?'

Liseiwicz realized that the student who raised his hand was the young man in the front row that he had noticed when he left after his first class. He waved the couple of sheets of paper that he was holding in his hand, and asked, 'Did you put these under my door?'

Jinzhen nodded.

Liseiwicz said, 'Let me tell you, this term you don't need to attend class.'

There was a sudden uproar.

Liseiwicz seemed to be enjoying something, for he waited for the hubbub to subside with a smile on his face. Once everyone was quiet again, he wrote the equation out on the blackboard again – not in the top right-hand corner this time, but on the top left-hand side – and then he said, 'Let us have a look at how Jinzhen solved this problem. This isn't an extracurricular novelty. His solution is going to be the subject of our class today.'

He began by writing out Jinzhen's answer on the board in full and explained it from start to finish. Then he used different methods to produce three alternative solutions, so that those sitting in class felt that they were learning something through the comparison, tasting the strange joy of reaching the same goal by travelling different routes. The topic of this new class was developed step-by-step as he explained each method. When he had finished, he wrote a new question at the top right-hand corner of the blackboard and said: 'I would be really pleased if someone can answer this before the beginning of the next class. That is the way to go: I give you a question in one class and you answer it in the next.'

That was what he said, but Liseiwicz was well aware that the chances of that happening were vanishingly small. If you were going to express it mathematically, you would need to use a very small fraction of a per cent, and even then you would be rounding the number up. Calculation often proves a slipshod method of determining the future – it shows the possible as being impossible. People often do not work as tidily as calculations: they can make the impossible possible; they can turn earth into heaven. That means that in actual fact there is no great gulf between heaven and earth: one fraction more and earth becomes heaven, one fraction less and heaven will change into earth. Liseiwicz really had no idea that this silent and impassive boy would be someone who could confuse him as to the nature of what he was looking at – having decided that it was earth, he could come up with a result demonstrating that in fact it was heaven. In other words Jinzhen solved the second problem that Professor Liseiwicz set him right away!

This problem having been solved, of course a new one had to be set. When Liseiwicz wrote this third question up on the top right-hand corner of the blackboard, he turned round and, rather than speaking to the class as a whole, he directed his comments to Jinzhen alone: 'If you can answer this problem too, then I am going to set you your personal question.' He was talking about the question that would be the basis of his graduation thesis.

Jinzhen went to three of Professor Liseiwicz's classes in total, lasting just over a week.

In the case of this third question, Jinzhen was not able to solve it as quickly as the previous two, so when the next class came around, he did not yet have a solution to offer. When Professor Liseiwicz finished the third class of that term, he stepped down from the teacher's podium and spoke to Jinzhen: 'I have already thought of the question for your graduation thesis. You can come and pick it up whenever you finish the previous one.' Having said that, he walked out.

After he married, Jan Liseiwicz rented a house in Sanyuan Lane, just near the university. That was officially where he lived, but in fact he still spent a lot of time in the rooms he had occupied when he was a bachelor, living in faculty accommodation. His set was up on the third floor, a suite of rooms with a bathroom attached. He would read there, or do research – it was his library-cum-office. That afternoon, having had his siesta, Professor Liseiwicz was listening to the radio. The clumping sound of feet coming upstairs interrupted his listening. The heavy footsteps stopped right by his door, but instead of being fol- lowed by the sound of a knock, there was a susurrating noise, like a snake moving through dry leaves, as something was pushed under the door. It was a couple of sheets of paper. Liseiwicz went over and picked them up, recognizing immediately a familiar handwriting: Jinzhen. He flipped through the pages until he got to the answer: it was correct. As if he had just been flicked by a whip, he wanted to throw open the door and shout for Jinzhen to come back. However, when he got as far as the door, he hesitated for a moment and then went back to sit on the sofa. He began looking at the first page of calculations. When he had read the whole thing through carefully, Liseiwicz felt the same impulse that had propelled him towards the door. This time he rushed to the window, from which he could see Jinzhen walking slowly away. Throwing open the window, Liseiwicz bellowed at the retreating back, far in the distance. Jinzhen turned round, to discover that the foreign professor was pointing at him and yelling to come upstairs.

Jinzhen sat down opposite the foreign professor.

'Who are you?'

'Jinzhen.'

'No,' Liseiwicz was smiling, 'I mean what family are you from? Where do you come from? Where did you go to school? I can't help feeling that I have met you somewhere before – who are your parents?'

Jinzhen hesitated. He hardly knew how to reply.

Suddenly Liseiwicz exclaimed: 'Ah! I remember. You look just like the woman whose statue stands in front of the main building – Miss Lillie – yes, Rong "Abacus" Lillie, that's it! Tell me, are you related to her? A son . . . no, a grandson?'

Jinzhen pointed to the papers lying on the sofa and asked, as if Liseiwicz had not spoken: 'Did I get it right?'

Liseiwicz said, 'You still haven't answered my question. Are you related to Miss Lillie?'

Jinzhen didn't admit it, but he also didn't deny it. He just said woodenly, 'You will have to talk to Professor Rong – he's my guardian. I don't know anything about my parents.'

Jinzhen was simply trying to avoid discussing his relationship with Miss Lillie, which was a subject he found very difficult to deal with; but he was not expecting that this would start Liseiwicz down an even worse line of enquiry. Staring at Jinzhen suspiciously, he said: 'Oh, really . . . So tell me, did you come up with the answer to my equations all on your own, or did someone help you?'

Jinzhen drew himself up: 'Of course I did it myself!'

That evening, Jan Liseiwicz went in person to visit Young Lillie. When Jinzhen saw him, he imagined that the foreign professor was still concerned that he might have received help with his work. In fact, although Liseiwicz had indeed expressed such a possibility earlier in the day, he had immediately dismissed it. His reasoning for this was that if either the professor or his daughter had suggested a solution, they would never have expressed it in those terms. After Jinzhen left, Liseiwicz had reviewed his papers and was impressed all over again by his method of working. He discovered that the method of proof used was most unusual and impressive: at once naïve and yet clearly demonstrating both the grasp of logic and the intelligence of the young student who had worked it out. Liseiwicz found it hard to put his feelings into words. It was only in talking to Young Lillie that he gradually found a way to express what he thought.

Liseiwicz said, 'The way that I think about it is this: it is as if we were asking him to go somewhere and pick up something which is located inside a maze of tunnels so dark that you cannot see the five fingers right in front of your face, and furthermore, the maze is full of crossroads, forks and traps. If you don't have a source of light, you can't move even one step from your starting position. If you want to find your way through this maze of tunnels, you first need to prepare a source of light. There are lots of possible sources. You might use a torch, or an oil lamp, or a brand, or even a heap of firewood. This kid is so ignorant that he does not know about these tools and even if he did, he could not find them. So he does not go near them – he uses a mirror instead, setting it at just the right angle so that it will bend the sunlight into the tunnel that he is digging. When he comes to a bend in the tunnel, he sets up another mirror to light his path. He carries on his way, thanks to that one feeble beam of light, past all the traps and dangers. The thing that I find most mysterious is that every time he reaches a fork in the road, some kind of sixth sense seems to be telling him which is the right path to take.'

In almost a decade as colleagues, Young Lillie had never heard Jan Liseiwicz say anything so complimentary about anyone. It was very difficult to get someone like Liseiwicz to admit anyone else's mathematical abilities, but here he was praising Jinzhen to the skies without the slightest hesitation. It was a pleasant surprise for Young Lillie, but also made him feel very strange. He thought to himself: 'I was the very first person to discover that the boy has remarkable mathematical abilities and Liseiwicz is the second, but all he is doing is confirming my initial discovery.' On the other hand, what could be better than confirmation of his discovery from a man like Liseiwicz? The two men talked together more and more happily.

However, on the subject of Jinzhen's future studies, the two men were diametrically opposed. In Liseiwicz's opinion, the boy already knew quite enough and had shown signs of such remarkable ability that he did not need any further classes on the basics. He thought that he could skip all of that and move straight on to completing his graduation thesis.

Young Lillie did not agree.

As we know, Jinzhen treated other people with an unusual degree of coldness – he liked spending time on his own. He had very little experience of interacting with his peers. This was a weak point in his character and something that would endanger him greatly in the future. Young Lillie was doing his very best to repair the damage caused by his early upbringing. In many ways, Jinzhen's social problems and his unstable character, not to mention his unspoken animosity towards other people, would be obviated if he spent more time with other children – it would be more relaxing for him. He was by far the youngest of the students in the mathematics department and Young Lillie felt that the boy was already dangerously alienated from people of his own age. If he were forced to expand his social circle to an even larger number of adults, it could have a devastating effect on his future development. Young Lillie didn't feel able to explain this right now; it really wasn't the kind of thing that he wanted to talk about. It was all so complicated and the boy had the right to some privacy. All he could do was to say that he disagreed with the professor's point of view: 'In China we have an expression, "Iron needs time and effort to become steel." The boy is unusually clever, it is true, but he also lacks basic ordinary knowledge. As you just said yourself, there are lots of tools that you can use to light your way and they are lying all around you, but he won't pick up any of them – he will find some weird and unusual way to achieve something perfectly simple. In my opinion, he is not doing this on purpose; it is because he has no choice – his lack of basic knowledge forces him to become inventive. It is wonderful that in such circumstances he can still think of using a mirror to light his way, but if he spends the rest of his life using his genius in the same way, wasting his time on finding weird ways to achieve something that could perfectly well be done by simple means, he may be able to satisfy his own intellectual curiosity, but what is the point of it all? So, for the sake of his education, I think it is very important that Jinzhen spends more time studying, learning the things that other people have already done. It is only when he has a good grasp of the basics that have already been laid down that he can go on to research genuinely worthwhile unknowns. I have heard that when you came back from your travels last year, you brought back a very fine library. Last time I visited your house, I was hoping to be able to borrow a couple of your books. However, when I saw the notice pinned to the shelf saying "Don't even bother asking," I decided that there was no point. But I was thinking, if you would be prepared to make an exception, I would very much appreciate it if you would let Jinzhen read your books. I am sure that would be a very great help to him. As the saying goes, golden mansions are to be found in books.'

Now it was Jan Liseiwicz's turn not to agree.

The fact is that at that time there was a lot of talk about the two weirdos of the mathematics department. One weirdo was Professor Rong Yinyi (that is, Master Rong), who treasured a heap of letters, sticking to them when she could have been getting married to any one of her admirers. The other weirdo was the foreign professor, Jan Liseiwicz, who cared more for a couple of shelves of mathematics books than for his wife – certainly he would not let anyone other than himself look at them. Young Lillie could say whatever he liked, but he didn't hold out much hope that Liseiwicz was going to change his mind. He was well aware that the chances of that happening were vanishingly small. If you were going to express it mathematically, you would need to use a very small fraction of a per cent and even there you would be rounding the number up. However, calculation often proves a slipshod method of determining the future – it shows the possible as being impossible.

That evening, when Jinzhen mentioned at the supper table that Professor Liseiwicz had lent him a couple of books and agreed that in the future he could borrow whatever books he wanted whenever he liked, Young Lillie suddenly felt his heart thud. He now realized that in spite of his assurance that he was ahead of the rest, in fact Liseiwicz had already left him far behind. More than anything else, it was this that made Young Lillie realize quite how important Jinzhen was in Liseiwicz's eyes: he was irreplaceable. Liseiwicz was hoping for great things from Jinzhen, much greater than Young Lillie could even begin to imagine.

7

Of the two weirdos of the mathematics department, Master Rong's story was very sad and people felt a great deal of respect for her. Professor Liseiwicz on the other hand seemed to be making a mountain out of a molehill, and it caused a lot of talk. Under normal circumstances, where there is a lot of talk, you end up with endless gossip. Hence, of the two weirdos, there were a lot more rumours about Professor Liseiwicz than there ever were about Master Rong. Pretty much everyone at the university had some sort of story to tell. Because everyone had heard about him refusing to lend anyone his books, they also heard about the fact that he was now lending books to one person — this is the effect you get when some little thing is done by someone famous. This is like the mathematical conversion of mass into energy. People gossiped constantly, asking why Professor Liseiwicz was so kind to Jinzhen, and only to him. It was practically as if he were letting him sleep with his wife. One explanation was that the foreign professor appreciated his student's intelligence and hoped for great things from him — but the theory that he was doing it purely out of friendly motives was not particularly popular. Eventually those who said that Professor Liseiwicz was taking advantage of Jinzhen's genius out-shouted the rest.

Even Master Rong mentioned this in my interview with her.

[Transcript of the interview with Master Rong]

The very first winter after the end of the Second World War, Jan Liseiwicz went back to Europe. The weather was terribly cold, but I guess that it was even worse in Europe, because he didn't take any of his family with him — he just went on his own. When he came back, Daddy borrowed a Ford car from the university and told me to go down to the docks to collect him. When I got there I was stunned to see that Professor Liseiwicz was sitting on an enormous wooden packing case, about the same size as a coffin, with his name and address at N University written on it in both Chinese and English. The size and the weight of his packing case made it impossible to get into the car. I had to get a cart and four brawny men to transport it back to the department. On the way, I asked Liseiwicz why on earth he had brought so many books back with him and he said excitedly, 'I have a new research interest and I need these books!'

Apparently on this trip to Europe, Liseiwicz had recovered the interest in research that had been dormant in recent years: he was feeling inspired and was going to make a new start. He had determined to begin research on an enormous new topic: artificial intelligence. Nowadays, everyone has heard of the subject, but at that time the world's first computer had only just been built.* That was what had given him the idea – he was way ahead of most people in realizing the potentials of the field. Given the massive scope of the research project that he had in mind, the books that he brought back were just a tiny part of the whole; but it is not surprising that he was not prepared to lend them to other people.

The problem is that the blanket ban applied to everyone except Zhendi, and so people started making wild guesses about what was going on. There were all sorts of stories circulating in the mathematics department anyway about what a genius Zhendi was – how he completed four years of study in the space of two weeks, how cold sweat broke out on Professor Liseiwicz's face at the mere sight of him; and before you knew it, some people who didn't understand the first thing about how these things work were saying that the foreign professor was using Zhendi's intelligence to advance his own research. That kind of gossip breaks out all the time in academia – it makes professors look bad and people enjoy the idea that they get where they are by stealing someone else's work – that is just the way it is. When I heard this story, I went right round to Zhendi to ask him about it and he said it was a pack of lies. Daddy asked him about it too and he still said it was all rubbish.

Daddy said, 'I hear that you spend every afternoon round at his house, is that right?'

'Yes,' said Zhendi.

* The world's first computer, ENIAC, was built in 1946.

'What are you doing there?' asked Daddy.

'Sometimes I read books, sometimes we play chess,' said Zhendi.

Zhendi was very definite, but we still felt that where there is smoke, there must also be fire – we were worried that he was lying. After all, he was still only sixteen years old and knew nothing about how complicated the world can be; it was quite possible that he was being deceived. Well, I made excuses several times to go round to Liseiwicz's house and find out what they were doing, and every time I saw that they were indeed playing chess: the standard international game. Zhendi often played Go at home with my father, and he was a fine player – the two of them were pretty evenly matched. Sometimes he also played tiddlywinks with Mummy, but that was just for fun. When I saw the two of them playing chess together, I thought that Liseiwicz was just doing it to keep him company, because everyone knew that he played at grandmaster level.

In fact, something completely different was going on.

According to what Zhendi told me himself, he and Liseiwicz had played all sorts of different kinds of chess together – the standard kind, Go, elephant chess, battle chess and so on. Occasionally he could win at battle chess, but he never beat Liseiwicz at any of the others. Zhendi said that Liseiwicz played all these games to an amazingly high level, so the only reason that he could occasionally win at battle chess was because ultimately victory in that game is not dependent entirely upon the player's skill; at least half the time the outcome is determined by sheer luck. If you think about it, even though tiddlywinks is a much simpler game than battle chess, it is a much better determinant of the player's skill, because the element of luck is so much smaller. In Zhendi's opinion, battle chess should strictly speaking not be considered a type of chess at all; at the very least, it should not be regarded as a chess game for adults.

You may well be wondering, given that Zhendi was so far from being able to give Liseiwicz a good game, why did they keep on playing together time after time?

Let me explain. As a game, all types of chess are easy to learn to play, in the sense that they do not require the player to develop any special skills: you can just learn the basic rules and get stuck in. The problem is that once you have started playing, chess calls upon completely different attributes from any game requiring physical skill, where as you practise you just get better and better; from a rank beginner you become a practised player, then a skilled one, and finally an excellent one. The more you play chess the more complicated it gets. The reason for this is that, as you improve, you learn more of the set variations and that then opens up more avenues for you to explore – it is like walking into a maze. At the entrance, there is only one way to go, but the further you penetrate, the more crossroads you encounter; the more options you are faced with. That is one reason that the game is so complex; the other is that, as you might imagine, if two opponents are walking through the maze at the same time, as one proceeds he is also trying to block the other's advance, and he is trying to do the same – advance and block, advance and block – well, that is adding another level of difficulty to an already extremely complex game. That is what chess is like: you have standard openings and endgames, attacking and defensive moves, obvious and secret manoeuvres, pieces that you move close at hand and those you send to the other side of the board, enveloping your opponent in a fog of mystery. Under normal circumstances, whoever knows the most set variations has the most room to manoeuvre, and can create the most mystery about his moves. Once his opponent has become confused and can no longer determine the direction of attack, he has created the most favourable circumstances to win the game. If you wish to play a good game of chess, you have to learn the set variations, but that is not enough. The whole point about set variations is that everybody knows about them.

What is a set variation?

A set variation can best be compared to a path beaten through the jungle by many passing feet – on the one hand you can be sure that it is a route that goes from A to B, on the other hand it is also available for anyone to use. You can travel this path, but so can everyone else. Or to take another example: set variations are like conventional weapons. If you are fighting against people who have no weapons at all, your weapons will kill them dead in an instant. On the other hand if your opponent has exactly the same conventional weapons, you may be out there laying mines but he just sends in the mine-sweepers to clear them up, so you have been wasting your time; you send up your planes but he can see them bright and clear on his radar and he can blow you out of the sky. In those circumstances, you need secret weapons to win on the battlefield. Chess has many secret weapons.

The reason that Liseiwicz was prepared to carry on playing chess with Zhendi was because he realized that he had many secret weapons. He seemed to be able to conjure up an endless series of bizarre and tricky moves, apparently from thin air, giving his opponent the feeling that, as he was walking along, someone was tunnelling through the ground beneath his feet. He could really confuse you, because a piece that you thought was dead would – in his hands – suddenly turn out to be crucial for his next move. Zhendi had been playing chess for such a short time, he had so little experience, and he knew so few of the set variations that it was easy to confuse him with your conventional weapons. Or to put it another way, because he did not know any but the most basic set variations, your standard moves were deeply mysterious to him. Of course each of these moves had been used by tens of thousands of people – they are reliable, they have been proved time and time again – so whatever peculiar and tricky move he had thought up was not able to stand up against the tried and tested, and in the end he would lose the game yet again.

Liseiwicz once told me himself that Zhendi was losing not on the basis of intelligence, but on experience, knowledge of the set variations, and playing skill. Liseiwicz said, 'I have played all sorts of different kinds of chess, starting at the age of four, and over the course of the months and years I got to learn the set variations for each type of game like the back of my hand. Of course it is difficult for Jinzhen to beat me. The fact is that there is no one in my immediate circle who can beat me at chess – I can say without fear of contradiction that at chess I am a genius. Furthermore, having played for such a long time, I have honed my skills. Unless Zhendi were to spend the next few years concentrating solely on improving his chess-playing abilities, he is never going to be able to beat me. However, when we range our forces against each other, I often feel a refreshing sense of surprise, which I enjoy enormously – that is why I have carried on playing with him.'

That is what he said.

Another game of chess!

And another game of chess!

Because they were playing chess together, Zhendi and Liseiwicz became close friends – they quickly moved beyond the normal teacher–pupil relationship to become really good friends, going out for walks together and eating together. Because they were playing chess, Zhendi spent less and less time at home. Up until then, during the summer and winter holidays, Zhendi would hardly put his nose out of doors – Mummy would often have to practically throw him out of the house in order to get him to spend some time in the fresh air. However, that winter Zhendi was hardly ever at home during the day; to begin with we thought he was playing chess with Liseiwicz but later on we found out that this was not the case. They weren't playing chess – they were developing a new kind of board game.

I am sure that you will find it difficult to believe they were inventing their own variant of chess – Zhendi called it 'mathematical chess'. Later on, I got to see them play on many occasions and it was really weird – the board was about the same size as a desktop, and there were two military encampments on it – one was a kind of hatch # shape, the other the shape of a Coptic cross. They played this game with mahjong tiles rather than chess pieces. There were four routes across the board and each player held two of them, stretching out from the hatch and the Coptic cross encampments. The pieces that started in the hatch encampment had a set arrangement, somewhat like that seen in elephant chess, where each piece has a particular starting position, but the pieces in the Coptic cross encampment could begin in any position – the arrangement was determined by your opponent. When your opponent arranged your pieces, he was of course thinking entirely of his own plan of campaign, placing them in the most favourable positions for his own purposes. Once the game began, you took over control of these pieces and it was up to you to move them. Naturally, your priority was to move these pieces from a position advantageous to the enemy to one favourable to yourself at the earliest possible opportunity. During the course of a game, a piece could move between the hatch and the Coptic cross encampments, and in principle, the fewer impediments you faced in advancing your pieces into the enemy encampment, the greater your chances of victory. However, the rules governing the circumstances in which you could simultaneously move a piece into the opposition camp were very strict and needed careful planning and preparation. Furthermore, once a piece had entered the enemy encampment, the way in which it could move changed. The biggest difference in the types of movement possible was that pieces in the hatch encampment could not move on the diagonal nor could they jump over other pieces. Both of these types of moves were allowed in the Coptic cross encampment. Compared to standard chess, the biggest difference was that, when you were playing, you had to be thinking about how you would advance your own pieces along the two routes under your control, making sure that you had them arranged for the moves you intended to carry out, while at the same time making sure that at the earliest possible moment the disadvantageous pieces were moved into better positions and that, when the time came, both you and your opponent could simultaneously move a piece into the enemy camp. You could say that you were playing chess against your opponent, but also against yourself – it felt as though you were playing against two different opponents at one and the same time. It was one game, but it was also three, for each of the two players had the game going on against themselves, as well as the one against their opponent.

It was a very complicated, strange game. The best comparison I can think of is to say that it is like the two of us joining battle, only to discover that my troops are under your command and your troops are under my command. Just think how bizarre and complicated it would be to fight a battle with only the opposing army at your command – bizarreness can in some cases be a kind of complexity. Because this game was so very complicated, most people simply could not play it. Liseiwicz said that it was designed solely for mathematicians to play and that is why it was called mathematical chess. There was one occasion when Liseiwicz was chatting to me about this game and he said triumphantly: 'This game is the result of much research into pure mathematics: given the level of mathematical knowledge required to deal with its complexities, not to mention its intricate rules, the subtle way in which the subjective role of the player transforms the structural organization – really only human intelligence can compare. Inventing this chess game was a way of challenging the limits of our intelligence.'

The minute he said this, I was immediately reminded of his current research topic – artificial intelligence. I suddenly felt alarmed and uncomfortable, because I started to wonder whether this mathematical chess might not be part and parcel of his research. If that was the case, then Zhendi was clearly being used – he was covering up what he was doing by pretending that it was all about developing this game. I then made a special point of asking Zhendi why they had decided to develop mathematical chess and how they had gone about it.

Zhendi said that they had both enjoyed playing chess together but that Liseiwicz was so strong a player that he simply had no hope of ever being able to beat him, which in turn made him depressed and unwilling to play. Afterwards the pair had started thinking about developing a new kind of chess game, whereby the two of them would both start at the same level, without one having the advantage of knowing all the set variations. This game was to be structured so that victory would be determined purely by intelligence. When they were designing the game, Zhendi said that he was primarily responsible for designing the board, while Liseiwicz worked out the rules for how the pieces would be allowed to move. In Zhendi's opinion, if you wanted him to work out how much of the game was his own work, he would say that it was around ten per cent. If this game was indeed part of Liseiwicz's research, then Zhendi had made a significant contribution and he deserved some credit for it. So I asked about Liseiwicz's work on artificial intelligence. Zhendi said that he knew nothing about it and that, so far as he was aware, Liseiwicz was not working on anything of the kind.

I asked him, 'Why do you think that he is not working on anything of the kind?'

Zhendi said, 'He has never mentioned it to me.'

It was all most strange.

I thought to myself, the moment Liseiwicz caught sight of me he was bubbling over with news of this new research plan, but now Zhendi spends pretty much every day with him and he doesn't say a word about it? I was sure that something was up here. Later on, I asked Liseiwicz about it myself, and the only reply was that we did not have the facilities, he could not continue, and so he gave up.

Gave up?

Had he really given up or was this just something that he was saying?

To tell the truth, I was very unhappy about the whole thing. I don't need to tell you, if he was just pretending to have given up on this research then we had a serious problem, because only someone who is engaged in unethical (if not downright criminal) activities feels the need to hide from other people's eyes like that. The way that I thought about it, if Liseiwicz was indeed involved in something unethical, there was only one person he could be using, and that was poor little Zhendi. The whole department was buzzing with rumours, which had already forced me to think seriously about the unusual relationship that had developed between Lisciwicz and Zhendi – I was really worried that he was being cheated, being used. He was really still only a child at the time, completely unaware of how nasty other people can be, very emotionally immature and naïve. If someone is looking for a patsy, that is the kind of person that they would pick: innocent, isolated, timorous; the kind of person where if you bully them they keep quiet about it; the kind that suffers in silence.

Fortunately it was not long after this that Liseiwicz did something truly unexpected, which completely put all my fears to rest.

[To be continued]

8.

Jan Liseiwicz and Jinzhen finalized the rules for mathematical chess in the spring of 1949. Not long afterwards, which was also not long before the provincial capital, C City, was liberated, Liseiwicz received an invitation from the journal, the *Annals of Mathematics*, to attend an event to be held at UCLA. In order to facilitate the travel arrangements for attendees from Asia there was a contact address in Hong Kong. Everyone was to meet there and then fly to California on the final leg of their journey. Liseiwicz did not spend very long in the States, maybe a month and a half in total, and he was back at work at the university so quickly that people found it hard to believe that he could really have been to America and back in that time. However, he had plenty of proof: job offers from universities and research institutions in Poland, Austria and the US; photographs of himself in the company of John von Neumann, Lloyd Shapley, Irvin Cohen and other famous mathematicians. In addition, he had brought back the question paper for that year's Putnam Mathematical Competition.

[Transcript of the interview with Master Rong]

Putnam is the name of a mathematician: his full name was William Lowell Putnam and he was an American — people called him 'the second Gauss'. In 1921 the Society of American Mathematicians, in concert with a number of universities, established the annual Putnam Mathematical Competition — the focus of considerable interest in universities and mathematical societies and an important way to discover new talent at undergraduate level in mathematics departments and institutes. The competition is designed to test basic principles learned by university students, but the questions are so difficult that they require a very high level of mathematical ability. Although every year the students who take part in the competition are the very best from each university, due to the unbelievable difficulty of the questions set the majority of people who take part will score around zero.

The top thirty competitors in any one year will be picked up by the finest universities in America and indeed the world – for example Harvard offers the top three highest-scoring competitors the most generous scholarships available at the entire university. That year there were fifteen questions, whereby full marks in the competition would be 150, with forty-five minutes to complete the entire paper. The highest mark awarded was 76.5, and to get into the top ten you had to score over 37.55.

Liseiwicz had brought back the competition questions because he wanted to test Zhendi. The only person he wanted to test was Zhendi – everyone else (including the other professors at the university) would just be put to unnecessary trouble and distress by being made to sit these questions, so it was much better for all concerned if they were left in peace. Before he tested Zhendi, he shut himself up in his own office for forty-five minutes and tested himself. Afterwards he graded his own paper. He decided that his final mark should be less than the highest awarded that year, because he had only correctly answered the first eight questions – the ninth was unfinished. Of course, if he had had just a couple of minutes more he would have been able to answer this question correctly as well: the time-constraints were ferocious. But then the purpose of the Putman Mathematical Competition was to emphasize two important points:

1. Mathematics is the most scientific of sciences.
2. Mathematics is the science of time.

Robert Oppenheimer, who is often called the father of the atom bomb, famously said: 'In science, time is the real obstacle. Given unlimited time, everyone can learn all the secrets of the universe.' Some people say that, by building the world's first atom bomb, he came up with the best way to solve the problem of how to put an end to the Second World War. But if you think about it, if it had been Hitler who had succeeded in developing the atom bomb, wouldn't the result have been that mankind would have been facing an even worse problem?

Zhendi succeeded in answering six questions in the forty-five minutes allotted to him. In the solution that he offered for one of the

questions, Liseiwicz decided that he had made the mistake of tamper-
ing with the original question and hence he received no marks. The
last question was a logic problem and he had only had a minute and a
half left to look at it. There was no time to even begin working out
this problem, so he had written nothing, he had just thought about it
and, in the very last seconds of the examination, he had scribbled
down the correct answer. It was a remarkable achievement and yet
again demonstrated that Zhendi had a most unusual intelligence.
Grading this kind of question is up to the individual examiner – one
person might give him full marks, on the other hand someone else
might deduct some points: it depended entirely on the examiner's
perspective on the student's abilities. At worst, he would still have to
be given 2.5 points for this answer, so, after some thought, Liseiwicz
decided to be harsh and give him this mark. Zhendi's total was 42.5
points, in a year when to reach the top ten in the Putnam Mathematical Competition you had to get over 37.55 points.

That would mean that if Zhendi had really been able to take part in
the competition, he would have been ranked in the top ten, giving
him the opportunity to study in an Ivy League university, with a full
scholarship and all the fame accorded to a Putnam Fellow in the
world of mathematics. But because Zhendi hadn't formally taken
part, if you took his papers and showed them to someone, they would
just laugh in your face. No one would have believed that this little kid
from somewhere in China that nobody had ever heard of could get
such a high mark – they would have thought you were having them
on. A stupid attempt to take them in. Even Liseiwicz, looking at the
answer papers in front of him, felt that in some way he must be being
deceived. It was only a feeling, of course. Because Liseiwicz knew
that it was true – he knew that Zhendi had not cheated in any way –
and so he turned something that started out as just a game into
something very serious indeed.

[To be continued]

The first thing that Liseiwicz did was to go and find Young Lillie, to
explain the manner in which he had tested Jinzhen on the Putnam
Mathematical Competition questions. Afterwards he gave his considered opinion on the matter: 'I tell you that Jinzhen is the best student

the university has ever had, and in the future he could likewise become the best student at Harvard, MIT, Princeton, Stanford or any other world-class university. That is why I am telling you that he really ought to go abroad to study. Harvard, MIT, wherever.'

Young Lillie was silent for a moment.

Liseiwicz pursued the matter: 'You should believe in his abilities and give him this opportunity.'

Young Lillie shook his head. 'I am afraid it is impossible.'

'Why?' Liseiwicz's eyes were completely round.

'We don't have the money,' Young Lillie said frankly.

'You would only need to pay for one semester,' Liseiwicz said. 'I am sure that by the time the second semester started he would be on a scholarship.'

'The problem isn't the first semester,' Young Lillie said with a bitter smile. 'With the situation we are in right now we could not even pay for his fare.'

Liseiwicz left disappointed.

Part of Liseiwicz's disappointment was due to a natural feeling of sadness that his dream for his student had not worked out, but the remainder was darkened by suspicion. He and Young Lillie had never agreed about Jinzhen's academic future. Now he did not know whether Young Lillie was telling the truth, or whether it was simply an excuse because he did not want to go along with the plan. He thought that the latter possibility was very likely correct, for he found it hard to believe that a family as wealthy as the Rongs could really be in financial trouble.

Everything that Young Lillie had said was perfectly true, however. Jan Liseiwicz did not know that, a couple of months earlier, the remnants of the family property at Tongzhen had been seized in the Land Reform, and the only thing that was left in their possession was a few ramshackle buildings in the old mansion. One commercial property remained in the provincial capital, but a few days earlier at the welcome ceremony for the new mayor, Young Lillie (as a member of a well-known patriotic family) presented it to the People's Government of C City as a sign of his support for the newly established People's Republic of China. The decision to select such a public occasion for making the gift might seem like he was currying favour but in fact this was not the case – it was the recipients who decided it should be done this way. Furthermore, he agreed with their reasoning that it would set an example encouraging other members of wealthy and socially prominent families to support the new government. I can say categorically that the Rong family were great patriots and that Young Lillie was no exception – he beggared himself in order to demonstrate his loyal support for the People's Republic. His support was determined by both his appreciation of the bigger picture and his personal experience of unfair treatment at the hands of the KMT government. Anyway, of the property that Old Lillie had inherited from his ancestors, when it reached the hands of himself and his son, some had been given away, some had been spent, some had been ruined and some had been divided, to the point where it was now all gone. Young Lillie's own personal savings had gone in the battle to save his daughter's life. His salary had not risen to cover the rising cost of living and he had lost all other possible sources of income. Now Jinzhen wanted to go and study abroad, but even though Young Lillie supported him wholeheartedly, there was nothing that he could do to help.

Eventually Liseiwicz realized what had happened. That came about just a couple of months later, when Liseiwicz received a letter from Dr Gábor Szegő, then the Head of the Department of Mathematics at Stanford University, which accepted Jinzhen as a scholarship student and included a money order of $110 for travel expenses. This had been extracted from department funds purely thanks to Liseiwicz's persuasive lobbying. He had written a 3,000-word letter to Dr Szegő, and now those 3,000 words had returned, metamorphosed into a fully funded PhD place at Stanford and a ticket for the boat. When he told Young Lillie the news, Liseiwicz was delighted to see how happy the old man was.

Just as Jinzhen was getting ready to spend his last summer at the university before heading off to Stanford, he became terribly sick. It was this that determined he would spend the rest of his life in China.

[Transcript of the interview with Master Rong]
    He had renal failure!
    Zhendi almost died!

When he first became sick, the doctor told us that he was going to die – at best, he would live for another six months. During that time, death was near him all the time; we watched a young man who had always been slim swell up until he looked vast, though his actual body weight continued to drop.

He was suffering from oedema. The renal failure affected him so badly that it was as if Zhendi's body was made of dough, constantly fermenting, constantly swelling, making him as light and soft as a cotton-ball; it seemed as though he would burst if you poked him with a finger. The doctors said it was a miracle that Zhendi survived – in fact, in his case he did practically rise from the dead. He was in hospital for close on two years and the whole of that time he was not allowed to eat any salt; it was poison to him. The struggle to live wore him out. The money that the people at Stanford had sent to pay for his journey ended up going on his medical expenses, and his scholarship to study there, his diploma, his life as a student, his very future were all swallowed up by the appalling present, becoming a vaguer and vaguer dream. All of Liseiwicz's hard work went for nothing – he had wanted to create a brilliant future for his very best student but now he had to face two unpalatable facts: One, the money was gone and there was no way that the state of the Rong family finances would ever allow us to be able to replace that $110. Two, the people Liseiwicz relied on for his own future security (including me) had suspected him of the worst possible motives.

Liseiwicz's actions had demonstrated the purity of his intentions and proved beyond any reasonable doubt that he was genuinely fond of Zhendi. Just think about it – if Liseiwicz was really using Zhendi to get results for his own research, there is no way that he would encourage him to go to Stanford. There are no true secrets in this world – over time the truth is always revealed. Liseiwicz's secret was that he – more than anyone else – had become convinced that Zhendi was a truly rare mathematical genius. Maybe he saw in Zhendi some kind of reflection of himself as a boy – he loved him in the same kind of selfless way as he loved his own childhood – he was completely serious and totally innocent in this.

If Liseiwicz was ever unfair to Zhendi, it came much later and came about as a result of the mathematical chess game that they had developed together. It ended up being very influential in mathematical circles in Europe and America – lots of mathematicians played it. It wasn't called mathematical chess though, because it was named after Jan Liseiwicz: Liseiwicz chess. I got to read a number of articles on Liseiwicz chess over the years and people clearly thought very highly of it. Sometimes its significance was even compared to that of von Neumann's theory of chess as a two-person zero-sum game. It was said that, while von Neumann's concept was of particular importance in economic theory, Liseiwicz chess had great significance in military strategy. Although the practical applications of the two games had yet to be demonstrated, their theoretical importance was supposed to be enormous. People pointed to Liseiwicz, the youngest ever recipient of the Fields Medal, and said that he was an ornament to the world of mathematics – however, after he went to China, he had really done no original research of any importance with the exception of Liseiwicz chess – the last great achievement of his later career.

As I said before, Liseiwicz chess was originally known as mathematical chess and it was developed by Jan Liseiwicz and Zhendi together – Zhendi deserves some of the credit. Once Liseiwicz called the game after himself, there was no chance that Zhendi's role would be recognized: he was eliminated from the story and Jan Liseiwicz took all the credit himself. You could say that he was unfair to Zhendi, but you could also say that the pair were really fond of each other and that Liseiwicz really did do his best for the boy . . .

[To be continued]

9.

Early in the summer of 1950, it began pouring with rain one evening and just continued through the night without a break. Enormous raindrops fell against the tiles, sometimes with a noise almost like that of hammering, at other times with a duller thudding. From the sound of the rain lashing against the roof, you might have imagined that there was some kind of giant centipede up there, running for its life. The changes in the noise were the result of the wind getting up – when it blew strongly the sound became sharper. At the same time you could hear the tug of the wind on the window frames. Thanks to all this racket, Young Lillie hadn't slept at all well. The sleepless night had given him a headache and his eyes were somewhat swollen. He listened to the sound of the wind and rain, realizing that he and his house were both getting old. He finally fell asleep just before dawn. However, he woke up again pretty quickly – something seemed to have woken him. Mrs Lillie said it was the sound of a motor-car.

'It sounds as though a car has stopped downstairs,' she said. 'It will be gone in a moment.'

He knew that he was not going to fall asleep again, but Young Lillie stayed in bed. Once it was dawn, he got up the way that an old man does get out of bed, feeling his way, moving so gently that he made almost no noise, like a shadow. After he got up, he didn't even go to the bathroom – he went straight downstairs. His wife asked him why he was going downstairs. He didn't know. He just carried on going, fumbling in the dark, and once he got there, he opened the front door. There were two parts to the front door. The inner door opened into the house; the outer door opened out into the court-yard. The outer door seemed to be being blocked by something, because you could only open it a crack, maybe 30 degrees. Since it was summertime, the outer door was in use – a piece of cloth had been hung over the frame so that during the daytime you could leave it open but people couldn't see into the house. The old man couldn't see what was blocking the door, so he had to turn sideways and slide out through the crack. He discovered that two enormous cardboard boxes were filling the tiny courtyard. The first one was blocking the door, stopping him from getting in and out; the second one had already become sodden in the wind and rain. The old man tried to push the second box somewhere out of the rain but he simply couldn't move it — the contents couldn't have been heavier if they had been paving slabs. He inched his way back into the house and found a couple of pieces of oiled paper to cover it with. Once he had done that, he noticed that there was a letter on top of the box, held down by the stone they normally used to prop open the front door.

The old man picked up the letter — it was from Jan Liseiwicz. This is what he had to say:

Dear Lillie,

I am leaving and since I do not want to put anyone to any trouble, I have decided to say goodbye in this letter — I hope you can forgive me.

I need to talk to you about Jinzhen — in fact, I can't be happy until I have told you what I want to say. The first thing is that I hope he gets well soon. The second is that I hope you will make the best possible arrangements for his future, so that we (by which I mean humanity as a whole) can gain the greatest benefit from his genius.

To tell you the truth, in my opinion, letting Jinzhen immerse himself in an enormous and complex mathematics research topic would be the most suitable use for his remarkable talents. That in its turn creates a further problem. The world has changed, people are becoming more and more short-sighted and profit-orientated; they want to see some immediate and concrete benefit and are less and less interested in topics of purely theoretical application. This is completely stupid. It is no less stupid than entirely subordinating pleasures of the mind to those of the body. However, we cannot change this fact, any more than we can guarantee that the scourge of war has been completely eliminated from our society. It was because of this that I started to wonder whether it might not be better to encourage him to become immersed in a technical topic which would be of some concrete practical benefit. The good point of that kind of research is that you get great encouragement from it: each result pushes you on to the next one – it can be deeply fulfilling. The downside is that once you have finished you have also lost control of your project – your own personal wishes on the subject will be ignored. Your creation may bring great benefits to the world, or it may bring great harm – either way, you have no choice but to stand aside. It is said that Oppenheimer now really regrets his work on the first nuclear bomb and that he would like to rescind his creation – if he could destroy it with a blow from a hammer, like a statue, I am sure that he would. But is that kind of thing possible? Once the genie is out of the bottle, you cannot put it back in again.

If you decide that you want him to try to undertake a scientific research topic, let me suggest that he work on artificial intelligence. Once we have solved that particular mystery, we will be able to create a machine that in some way mimics the human mind, and the next step will be the development of robots – inanimate human beings. Science has already begun to unlock the secrets of other organs – eyes, noses, ears – we are now even in a position where we can create artificial wings. Why cannot we begin to work on artificial intelligence? The fact is, the development of the computer involves the creation of a kind of artificial intelligence, though it is solely concerned with calculations. Since we can already create a machine that can carry out that kind of function, surely other aspects cannot be too far behind? Think about it for a moment: if we have this kind of inanimate human beings – creatures made of metal, robots powered by electricity – how many uses they could be put to! In this generation we have suffered so much warfare – in the space of less than half a century we have been forced to go through two world wars. What is more, I suspect (indeed I have already seen some proof) that soon we will have another war – what a terrible thing that is! In my opinion, humanity can now make warfare even more appalling, even more frightening, even more terrible than at any point in history. It is now possible to kill a truly enormous number of people on the same field of battle, to have them die at the same time, to have them die instantly, to have them die the moment the bomb explodes. It seems that we will never be rid of warfare, and yet the hope that one day we can rid the world of this scourge has been handed down from one generation to the next. Mankind is faced with many terrible problems of this kind, which require enormous labour; which require exploration in dangerous circumstances . . . Mankind seems unable to extract itself from the difficulties that beset it.

If scientists were to succeed in creating an artificial human being – a robot, a creature made of metal, a being without flesh or blood – we could allow them to do work that is at present carried out by people working in genuinely inhuman conditions, fulfilling some of our more perverse requirements. I am sure that no one could object to that. That means that this branch of scientific endeavour, once fully publicized, would have an immeasurable practical value and a wonderful future. The first step is to solve the mystery of intelligence. It is only in this way, by creating artificial intelligence, that you have any chance of making the next step and creating a robot that can undertake some of the tasks at present carried out by humans. At one time I decided that the rest of my life would be devoted to cracking the problems connected with artificial intelligence but before I had even properly begun I was forced to give up this idea. I have never told anyone why I gave up – let me just say that it was not because of any particular problem or lack of ability, but at the express command of the Jewish people. The last few years I have been working on something very important on their behalf – the troubles that they have faced and their hopes for the future have moved me deeply; for their sake I have given up a long-cherished ambition. I have said this much in the hope of piquing your interest.

Let me remind you: without Jinzhen, you cannot do this. What I mean is that if Jinzhen does eventually die from this terrible disease, you had better give up the idea of developing this project, because you are too old for it. If Jinzhen survives, perhaps within your lifetime you will see one of the last great mysteries to confront humankind solved through the creation of artificial intelligence. Believe me, Jinzhen is the best person to find a solution to this problem – this is what he was born to do; God has chosen him. As you have mentioned to me before, dreams are the most mysterious manifestation of the human spirit, and this is something he has confronted day and night since the time he was a tiny child. Over the course of time, he has built up truly remarkable skills at interpreting the meaning of dreams. Although he did not realize it, right from the beginning of his conscious life, he began preparations for researching the mysteries of human intelligence. This is what he is meant to do!

Let me end by saying that if you and God are both in agreement that Jinzhen is here to develop the science of artificial intelligence, then this letter may prove helpful. Otherwise, if either you or God is determined to prevent him from pursuing this line of inquiry, then give this letter to the university library, that it may serve as a memento of the twelve happy years that I have spent working there.

I hope that Jinzhen will recover soon!

Jan Liseiwicz.
Written on the eve of departure.

Young Lillie read this letter straight through, sitting on the cardboard box. The wind ruffled the pages; raindrops caught and tossed in the breeze spattered down, as if they too wanted to read the contents of this letter. Maybe it was because he had not slept well the night before; maybe it was because the letter had touched some hidden corner of his mind: the old man sat quiet for a long time after he had finished reading. He sat quietly, looking up into space. After a very long time, he finally seemed to come to. Turning into the wind and rain, he suddenly spoke the following words: 'Goodbye, Jan. I hope that you have a good journey . . . '

[Transcript of the interview with Master Rong]

Jan Liseiwicz decided to leave after his father-in-law was almost executed as a war criminal.

As I am sure you are well aware, Liseiwicz was offered many opportunities to leave, particularly in the wake of the end of the Second World War. There were all sorts of universities and research institutes in the West that wanted him to join them, and his drawers were stuffed with invitations of one kind or another. However, it was quite clear that he had no intention of going anywhere – for example, he brought back that huge wooden case of books and then a little bit later on he bought not only the house in Sanyuan Lane that he had been living in for years, but the whole courtyard. He was working hard at his Chinese and spoke the language better than ever. In the end he announced that he was going to apply for Chinese citizenship (this was never followed up). I believe that Liseiwicz and his father-in-law were very close. This man was the son of a Provincial Graduate and a member of a very wealthy family – by far the most important gentry family in the region. When his daughter announced that she wanted to marry a foreigner he was extremely opposed to the idea. When she told him that she was getting married anyway, he placed very strict demands on the couple. Liseiwicz was told that he would never be allowed to take his wife to live abroad, that he would not be allowed to divorce her, that he would have to learn to speak Chinese, that any children would take their mother's surname, and so on. From all of this you can see that, while the man was a member of a prominent gentry family, he was neither educated nor gentlemanly. He was the kind of unpleasant person who would take advantage of his wealth and power to bully everyone else. When someone with that kind of personality finds themselves in an exalted position, it is easy to imagine that they will build up a lot of resentment against themselves. Furthermore, during the time of the puppet government, he occupied an important office in the county administration and was involved in some very dubious dealings with the Japanese. After the Liberation, the People's Government was determined to deal with him and he was arrested, tried and sentenced to death. At the time of which I am speaking, he was in prison awaiting execution.

In the run-up to the appointed date, Liseiwicz went the rounds of every professor and student that he could think of, including Daddy and me, in the hope that we would write a joint letter to the government and thereby save his father-in-law's life. Everyone refused. I am sure this wounded Liseiwicz deeply, but we really didn't have a choice. To tell the truth, it is not that we did not want to help; there was genuinely nothing we could do. The situation in those days was not such that a couple of people making a fuss or a small demonstration was going to change anything. Daddy did actually go to speak to the mayor on his behalf, but the only answer he got was: 'Only

Chairman Mao himself can save the man now.' What he meant was that Liseiwicz's father-in-law was doomed!

The fact is that in those days the People's Government was targeting men like him – bullies who had used their position to make the lives of the local people miserable. This was a matter of state policy and there was nothing that anyone could do about it. Liseiwicz didn't understand that: he was far too naïve about the whole situation. There was nothing that we could do and so we simply ended up hurting him.

What no one could have imagined was that Liseiwicz was in the end able to use the government of X country to save his father-in-law from the firing squad. It was quite unbelievable! Particularly when you consider that, at that time, our two countries were open enemies – you can imagine how difficult it was to achieve what he did. Apparently X country sent a special envoy to Beijing to discuss the matter with our government – in the end the whole matter did end up on Chairman Mao's plate – either his or Zhou Enlai's! The final decision must have been made by someone right at the top of the Politburo. It really was quite unbelievable!

The end result of their discussions was that Liseiwicz's father-in-law was released, and in return X country allowed two of our scientists whom they had barred from leaving to come home. It seemed almost as if this horrible old man – who deserved everything that he had coming to him – had suddenly become a national treasure. Of course, he was nothing to X country; they wanted Liseiwicz. It seems as though they had decided that no price was too high to pay for him. So the question was, why was X country so determined to get Liseiwicz? Was it simply because he was a world-famous mathematician? It seemed that there must be more to it, but as to what on earth that could be, I did not have the faintest idea.

Shortly after his father-in-law was released from prison, Liseiwicz and his entire family departed for X country.

[To be continued]

When Liseiwicz left the country, Jinzhen was still hospitalized, though it seemed that he was now out of danger. The hospital, concerned about the mounting medical bills, accepted the patient's request to be transferred to his home to recover. The day that he left hospital, Master Rong and her mother went to collect him. The doctor who was waiting to meet them naturally mistook one of them for the patient's mother. However, judging by their ages, one was a bit old and the other a bit too young, so he had to ask a rather bold question: 'Which of you is the patient's mother?'

Master Rong was just about to explain, but her mother had already answered loud and clear: 'Me!'

The doctor explained to Mrs Rong that Jinzhen's illness was now under control and his condition was stable, but he would require more than a year of special treatment to make a full recovery. 'During the course of the next twelve months, you are going to have to look after him like a baby, or he might well still suffer a relapse.'

When the doctor took her through the detailed list of what she would have to do, Mrs Rong realized that his comparison was entirely justified. There were however three key points to the treatment:

1. His food would be subject to extremely severe restrictions.
2. During the night he would have to be woken up at set intervals to empty his bladder.
3. Every day he would have to be given his medication, which would include injections, at certain set times.

Mrs Rong put on her spectacles and made notes of everything the doctor said; then she checked through them and asked questions to make sure that she had entirely understood every point. When she got back home, she asked her daughter to bring a blackboard and some chalk from the university and wrote out everything that the doctor had said. She then placed the blackboard in the stairwell so that she would see it every time she went up or down the stairs during the day. Since she had to get up regularly during the night to wake up Jinzhen to empty his bladder, she and Young Lillie started sleeping in separate bedrooms. She had two alarm clocks placed by the head of the bed, one set to ring just after midnight, the other in the early hours of the morning. After the early morning call to empty his bladder, Jinzhen would go back to sleep, but Mrs Rong would remain up so that she could prepare the first of the five meals that he had to eat during the course of the day. Although she was a fine cook, this was now by far the most difficult and time-consuming thing that she had to do. By comparison, having spent a lifetime punching holes in thick layers of felt to make cloth shoes, giving an injection was not a particularly difficult thing to learn to do – it was just the first couple of days that she was nervous and hesitant. But when it came to making food, how to prevent it from becoming tasteless and bland was a constant source of worry. The basic principle was simple: at that time Jinzhen was abnormally sensitive to salt and yet his life depended upon it: give him too much and he would suffer a relapse; give him too little and he would take much longer to recover than was strictly necessary. The doctor's instructions on this point were extremely precise: during the patient's period of convalescence, he would start by being allowed merely micrograms of salt, but as time went by the amount could be gradually increased.

Of course, if a person's daily intake of salt could be measured in grams or ounces, this is not a particularly difficult problem to solve – you just buy a good pair of scales. The problem the Rong family was faced with was not nearly so easy to solve, because Mrs Rong found it impossible to lay hands on an accurate enough set of scales, so to begin with she just had to use her own careful and patient judgement. Later on Mrs Rong took a whole load of different dishes into the hospital and got the doctors to pronounce on whether they were suitable. She had already made a note of how much salt she had put in each one – having counted every single grain – and once the doctors had decided which ones were suitably unsalty, five times a day she would put on her spectacles and dole out the white and glossy grains of salt, counting them one by one as if they were the pills that would save Jinzhen's life.

She was enormously careful when she put salt in his food.

She put the salt in as if conducting a scientific experiment.

Thus as one day followed another, as one night followed another, as one month followed another, her diligence and patience were as tested as if she had indeed been looking after a baby. Sometimes, in a moment of rest between bouts of this exhausting labour, she would take out the letter that Jinzhen had written in his own blood and look at it — it had been Jinzhen's secret but having discovered it by accident, she kept it without being entirely sure why. Now, every time she looked at this slip of paper, she was even more sure that everything she was doing was worth it: it encouraged her to go back to work with redoubled energy. More than anything else, it was this that dragged Jinzhen from the brink of the grave.

The following spring, Jinzhen was back in the classroom.

Liseiwicz was gone, but part of him had remained behind.

While Jinzhen was being coddled like a newborn baby, Liseiwicz was in contact with Young Lillie on three occasions. The first was not long after he arrived in X country: he sent a picture postcard with a beautiful landscape – on the back there was a simple greeting and a return address. It was his home address so there was no way of knowing where he was working. The second communication arrived not long after the first. It was a letter in response to Young Lillie's reply. He said that he was very happy to know that Jinzhen was better. He gave a vague reply concerning Young Lillie's questions about his work; he said that he was working in a research institute but said nothing about which one or what he was doing there – it was almost as if he wasn't allowed to tell us about it. The third letter addressed to Young Lillie arrived just before Chinese New Year – Liseiwicz wrote it on Christmas Eve. The stamp on the envelope showed a Christmas tree. In his letter, Liseiwicz mentioned that he had recently received amazing news from a friend: Princeton University had amalgamated several independent research units to create an institute dedicated to the issue of artificial intelligence – their work would be directed by the famous mathematician Paul Samuelson. He wrote: 'This means that it is not just me that has realized the value and importance of this field of research . . . As far as I am aware, this is the first group working on this subject anywhere in the world.'

Supposing that Jinzhen was really better (and in fact he had pretty much recovered completely by this time), he was hoping that he too would start work on the field. He made it clear that if Jinzhen could not carry out research into artificial intelligence in China, he thought he should leave and find somewhere better to work. He told Young Lillie that he should not let short-term benefits or problems prevent Jinzhen from achieving the great things of which he was capable.

Perhaps it was because he was afraid that Young Lillie would insist on making Jinzhen stay with him and work on this problem that he even lugged a Chinese proverb into his argument: 'A fine sword should not be used for chopping firewood.'

'Anyway,' he wrote, 'the reason why I insisted that Jinzhen should study in America in the past, the reason why I want him to do so now, is because here he has the facilities to support his work – if he comes here, he will find everything much easier.'

He concluded with the following paragraph:

> As I have said before, Jinzhen was sent to us by God to research this subject. In the past I have been worried that we would be unable to provide him with quite the surroundings that he needs, not to mention the support that would carry him through all the difficulties that he will face. However, I now believe we can give him the right circumstances in which to carry on his work and space in which to breathe: Princeton University. There is a joke in your country about the girl who sews a wedding gown for another bride to wear – maybe one day people will discover that all the work Paul Samuelson's group has put in has achieved nothing but cutting the cloth for a Chinese bride . . .

Young Lillie read this letter in a break between undergraduate classes. While he was reading it, the loudspeaker just outside the window was playing a popular song at top volume:

> With heads held high,
> Grinning in the teeth of danger,
> We cross the Yalu River.

The newspaper he had just been looking at was lying on the table in front of him – the headline was one of the political slogans of the day: 'American Imperialism is a Paper Tiger'. Listening to the rousing words of the song, looking at the heavy black ink of the headline, he felt completely helpless. He had no idea what he should say to his faraway correspondent – he was also more than a little frightened, as if there was some other person, hidden in the shadows, who was waiting for him to write back. At that time he was the vice-chancellor of N University, but he was also the deputy mayor of C City. That was the reward the People's Republic of China had given the Rong family for their many years of devotion to science, learning and patriotism over the course of several generations. This was the happiest time of his life – he wasn't the kind of person to care for nothing but personal aggrandizement, but he wouldn't have been human if he didn't enjoy it. The Rong family had been going through a long period of decline, but now the good days were back again – he was treasuring every minute of it. It was only the fact that he had very much the air of an ivory-tower intellectual that made people imagine that he did not appreciate his present good fortune.

In the end, Young Lillie did not write back to Jan Liseiwicz. He took Liseiwicz's letter and two newspapers full of coverage of the bloody battles between the American Army and the Chinese People's Volunteer Army in Korea to Jinzhen, and told him to write back to the man.

He said, 'Thank him, but tell him that you can't leave, because of the Korean War. I am sure that he will be very sad that things ended like this: I am too, but the person who has lost the most here is you. I think that God wasn't on your side here.'

Later on, when Jinzhen handed him the draft of the letter and asked him to have a look, the old man seemed to have forgotten his earlier advice. He struck through about half of the text, which expressed regret and disappointment – the remainder was given back to Jinzhen with further instructions: 'You had better clip some of the newspaper reports and send them to him along with your letter.'

That was in the spring of 1951.

After Chinese New Year, Jinzhen went back to class. Of course, he didn't go to Stanford, or to Princeton, but back to N University. When Jinzhen dropped his carefully worded letter and a couple of newspaper reports that he had clipped into the postbox, he was confining one of the paths that his life might have taken to history. As Master Rong said, some letters record history while others make it: this was a letter that changed one person's entire life.

Before Zhendi went back to class, Daddy discussed with me whether he should go back to rejoin his original class or whether he should start again as a freshman. I knew that Zhendi had fantastic grades as a student, but he had spent a total of only three weeks in class; what is more he had just recovered from a life-threatening illness – he could not possibly cope with a heavy workload. I was afraid that sending him to join the third-year classes would put too much pressure on him so I suggested that he re-enrol as a freshman. However, in the end he did not have to start again from the beginning; the university allowed him to rejoin his original classmates. Zhendi wanted it that way himself. To this day, I remember what he said: 'God wanted me to become sick so that I would be forced to spend some time away from science books – He was worried that I might become their prisoner and lose my way creatively – in which case I would never have achieved anything.'

A weird thing to say, don't you think? So bizarre as to almost seem a bit mad?

The fact is that Zhendi had previously suffered from very low self-esteem, but getting so sick seemed to have changed him. In actual fact, the thing that really changed him was the books that he read, a huge number of books that were nothing to do with mathematics. While he was at home recovering, he read all my books and all Daddy's books, particularly the fiction. He read them very quickly and in a very strange way – some books he would pick up, flick through a few pages and then put them straight back again. Some people imagined that he was actually reading the books from cover to cover in that time and so they called him Little Tuk, after the H. C. Anderson character who learns his lessons by putting his schoolbooks under his pillow at night. That was ridiculous, of course. He did read very quickly, it is true – the majority of books that he took from our shelves were back within twenty-four hours. The fact is that reading quickly is related to reading a lot; the more you read, the more you know and then the quicker you read the next thing. As he read more and more books related to topics beyond the subject he was studying at university, the less interested he was in the things written in his textbooks. That is why he started to cut classes – sometimes he even cut my classes. At the end of the first term after his resumption of study, both his grades and the number of classes that he had missed were quite eye-opening: he was the top of the class and by a very long way. Another thing that he was way ahead of his classmates in was the number of books he borrowed from the university library – in one term he had borrowed more than two hundred books in subjects ranging from philosophy to literature, economics, art, military science – there was all kinds of stuff in there. It was for this reason that during the summer holidays Daddy took him up to the attic and opened up our storeroom. Pointing to the two cases of books that Liseiwicz had left behind, he said: 'These aren't ordinary textbooks. Liseiwicz left them. In the future when you don't have anything else to do, why don't you read them? I am afraid though that you may not understand them.'

Another term passed and then in about March or April of the following academic year, Zhendi's classmates all started working on their graduation theses. It was at around this time that a couple of the other professors in the same department came to see me, because they thought that there was a problem with the subject that Zhendi had chosen. They were hoping that I would speak to him, that I would find a way to persuade him to pick another topic. Otherwise it was going to be impossible for any of them to supervise his graduation thesis. I asked what topic he had picked and they said it was a political problem.

Zhendi had decided that he wanted to write his thesis based on a theory propounded by the famous mathematician Georg Weinacht concerning the binary nature of certain constants. The topic was to be structured around coming up with a mathematical proof for this theory. The thing is that Georg Weinacht was famous at that time in the mathematical community for his anti-communist stance – it was said that he had a notice pinned to the door of his office saying, 'No Communists or Fellow Travellers Beyond This Point'. At the time of the most appalling carnage during the Korean War, he went on record encouraging the American Army to cross the Yalu River. I know that science is international and knows no borders, and that it is not affected by any 'ism', but Weinacht's powerfully anti-communist stance did overshadow his mathematical theories and give them a political dimension. At that time, there were a number of communist countries, led by the Soviet Union, where the validity of his theories was not admitted and his work was not even mentioned – if it did come under discussion, it was the subject of much criticism. If Zhendi was hoping to prove one of his theories, that would very much run counter to the tide. It was a very sensitive topic and would be seen as having dangerous political implications.

Well, I don't know what kind of intellectual maggot Daddy got in his head – maybe he was persuaded by Zhendi's cast-iron proofs – but at a time when everyone else was either avoiding the issue or hoping that he would talk to Zhendi and get him to change his topic, he not only did nothing of the kind, he even went so far as to weigh in on Zhendi's side and take over as his thesis supervisor. Daddy consistently encouraged Zhendi to continue with his chosen subject.

In the end, the title of Zhendi's graduation thesis was: 'The Constant π as a Definable yet Irrational Number'. This was a subject far from anything that he had ever studied in class – it was much more the kind of topic that you would expect for an MA thesis. There is absolutely no doubt that his choice was heavily influenced by the books that he was reading in the attic . . .

[*To be continued*]

When he read the first draft of Jinzhen's graduation thesis, Young Lillie was more enthusiastic than ever. He was transfixed by the beautifully incisive and logical thinking recorded therein, but some of the mathematical proofs he felt to be unnecessarily complicated and in need of improvement. The improvements were aimed at simplifying the presentation and removing unnecessary elements to the proofs. However, in order to develop the basic proofs (which in some cases were extremely elaborate), he had to use comparatively sophisticated and direct means, showing an understanding that was far from simply being confined to the field of mathematics. The first draft of Zhendi's thesis came to 20,000 characters. After a couple of revisions, the final version came in at just over 10,000 characters. Later on it was published in the magazine *Popular Mathematics* – and made not a small splash in Chinese mathematical circles. However, there seemed to be no one who was prepared to believe that Zhendi had done it all on his own because, having been revised a couple of times, the quality had also been significantly improved. It really didn't look like an undergraduate student's thesis, but the groundbreaking essay of an established academic.

Having said that, the good points and the failings of Zhendi's thesis were both perfectly clear: when you talk about the good points, beginning from a single mathematical constant, Zhendi had developed Georg Weinacht's binary theory into a pure mathematics solution for one of the major problems facing scholars working on the issue of artificial intelligence. This gave the reader something of the feeling of having seen the invisible wind caught and held in the human hand. The failing of this thesis is that it was all built upon a supposition, whereby π is treated as a constant – all the proofs that he had developed were based upon this theory and so it was impossible for the reader not to feel that this particular castle had been built entirely upon sand. If you wanted the castle to be built upon firmer foundations, if you wanted to demonstrate the academic value of this thesis, then you would first have to prove that π is indeed a genuine constant. As to the problem of whether or not π is actually a constant, even though this issue was first raised by mathematicians many centuries ago, it still has not been conclusively proved. Today most mathematicians do believe that it is a constant, but the fact remains that, as long as proof is lacking, it remains in the realm of supposition – you cannot ask that everyone else agree with you. In the same way, until Newton noticed that an apple will always naturally fall to the earth and expressed this in terms of his theory of universal gravity, everyone had the right to express their own doubts as to gravity's existence.

Of course, if you don't believe that π is indeed a constant, then Jinzhen's thesis was completely useless – the theory upon which it was based falls through. On the other hand, if you accept that π is a constant, then you would be amazed by what he had managed to achieve – it was somewhat like bending an iron bar into the shape of a flower. In his thesis Jinzhen suggested that human intelligence should be regarded as a mathematical constant and an irrational number, one that never comes to an end. If you accept this concept, then the second part of Georg Weinacht's binary theory comes into play, which could serve to resolve one of the major problems with developing artificial intelligence. Human intelligence also includes an element of confusion. Confusion is indefinable: it represents something that you cannot know completely; it is also something that you cannot replicate. Therefore he suggested that, under present conditions, it is impossible to be very optimistic about the prospect of entirely replicating human intelligence by artificial means, since the closest you were going to get was a near approximation.

I should mention that there are plenty of mathematicians who entirely agree with Zhendi's position, including many working today. You could say that there was nothing new about his conclusion: the interesting thing is that starting from a daring hypothesis about the binary nature of the mathematical constant π, he went on to develop a proof for this derived from pure mathematics. At least he was trying to develop a proof; the problem is that the materials he was using (the foundations of his house) had not been proved themselves.

To put it another way, if one day someone does succeed in proving that π is a constant, then the value of this thesis is clear. The problem is that this day still has not dawned, so, strictly speaking, his work remains completely pointless — its only success lies in demonstrating his own intelligence and daring. But thanks to his connection with Young Lillie, many people found it difficult to believe that it was entirely his own work and hence his genius remained under question. The fact is that this thesis brought nothing good to Jinzhen: it did not change his life in any way, but it did change the very last years of Young Lillie's life . . .

[*Transcript of the interview with Master Rong*]

I can be absolutely categorical: Zhendi wrote that thesis all on his own. Daddy told me that apart from recommending a couple of reference books and writing the introduction, he had nothing to do with any of the contents — it was all Zhendi's hard work. I remember what Daddy wrote in the introduction. He said, 'The best way to deal with our demons is to go out and fight them – let the devils see how strong we are. Georg Weinacht is a demon infesting the sacred halls of scientific research, and for a long time he has been able to get away with murder. Now is the time for us to lay this demon to rest. This thesis will serve to set Weinacht's pernicious theories in their place for ever; although some of the notes that it strikes are dull and muffled, the rest ring true.'

Not long after the thesis was published, Daddy went on a trip to Beijing. No one knew what he was up to; he left quite suddenly one day without telling anyone what he was doing. About a month later, when someone came to N University with three decisions from the central authorities, we finally realized that this must have been the motive for Daddy's earlier trip to Beijing. The three decisions were:

1. They gave permission for Daddy to resign as chancellor.
2. The government gave the necessary money to found a computer research unit at the university.
3. Daddy was going to be responsible for setting up this research facility.

At that time there were a lot of people who were hoping to be recruited by this new research facility, but after Daddy interviewed them, he decided in the end that none of them came up to Zhendi's standard. Zhendi was the very first person recruited for the research facility and as things turned out he was the only person who could have done it – the remainder of the people hired were basically just his assistants, helping out with day-to-day tasks. This gave people a very bad impression, suggesting that this international standard research unit had basically been monopolized by members of the Rong family, and there was a lot of gossip about it.

The fact is that when Daddy was a government official, he was determined to demonstrate how impartial he was, particularly when it came to hiring new staff – he avoided giving a job to anyone with even the remotest connection to the family, to the point where he seemed positively heartless. We in the Rong family founded N University, and if you gathered together all the members of the clan who had worked there over the generations, at the very least you would have had enough people to fill a couple of dinner tables. When Grandpa (Old Lillie) was alive, he looked after the family, finding them jobs in the government and giving those in academia the opportunity to develop their talents, visit other institutions and learn something from them . . . But when it came to Daddy, to begin with he had an official position but no real power, so even if he had wanted to help out he would not have been able to. Later on, when he had both the official position and the power, he could have helped out but he didn't choose to. During the years that Daddy was the chancellor of the university, he did not give a job to one single member of the Rong family, no matter how well qualified they were. Even in my case, the department recommended me for promotion a couple of times, wanting to make me assistant dean, but each time he turned it down. He put a cross down just like you would when finding a mistake on an examination paper. What happened to my brother was even more infuriating – he had come back to the country from abroad with a PhD in physics and he really should have been recruited by N University, but Daddy told him to go elsewhere. Just think about it: in C City, where else could he go? He ended up at the Normal University, but the working conditions and the level of the students were both significantly inferior – he took a job in a university in Shanghai the following year. Mummy was really furious with Daddy about this. She said that he was intentionally forcing our family to split up.

Well, when it came to recruiting Zhendi for the new research facility, all Daddy's principles about not giving jobs to members of the family went out of the window. He ignored all the gossip and just did what he wanted – he seemed to have become completely obsessed. Nobody understood what could possibly have changed Daddy's mind; but I knew, because one day he showed me the letter Jan Liseiwicz wrote just before he left. He said, 'Liseiwicz's letter did tempt me, but the real clincher was when I saw Jinzhen's graduation thesis. Up until that moment I thought the whole thing was going to be impossible, but when I saw that I decided to give it a go. When I was young, I really hoped that one day I would be able to make some concrete contribution to science. Maybe it really is too late to start now, but Jinzhen has given me the confidence to try. You know, Liseiwicz is absolutely right: without Jinzhen, I would not stand a hope in hell; but with Jinzhen, who knows what we might not achieve? In the past, I have always underestimated the kid's genius; now I am going to give him a real chance to show what he can do . . . '

[To be continued]

That is how it all happened. As Master Rong said, her father was inspired to work on this project by Jinzhen – how could he possibly give the job to anyone else? She went on to explain that Jinzhen not only changed the last years of her father's life, he also changed one of his long-standing principles – you could even say he changed his faith in humankind. In the very last years of his life, the old gentleman went back to the dreams of his youth – he decided to make a real contribution to the development of the field, to the point where he was prepared to discount as worthless everything he had done during most of his working life; everything he had done during his public career. It has always been one of the problems that Chinese intellectuals face: that they regard an academic career as fundamentally incompatible with an official position. Now the old gentleman was effectively starting his working life over again; whether this was a tragedy or a source of great delight, only time will tell.

Over the course of the next couple of years, the pair of them were completely immersed in their work for this research facility – they had very little to do with what was going on in the outside world. They attended the occasional mathematics conference and published a few papers; that was it. From the six papers that they co-authored which appeared in academic journals, it was clear that their work was progressing one step at a time – certainly their research was much further advanced than any other facility in the country, and they were not far behind the international cutting edge. After their first two papers were published in China, they were reprinted in three different international journals – indicating the importance of the results that they had achieved. It was around this time that the chief editor of *Time* magazine in the US, Roy Alexander, warned the American government: the next computer is going to be built by the Chinese! Jinzhen's name was now news.

Of course, this was all media scaremongering. The fact is that if you read this pair of papers closely, ignoring all the hype, you would immediately notice that they had encountered some very real problems in the course of their research. That was perfectly normal – after all a computer is not like a human brain; with people all you need is to have a man sleep with a woman and lo and behold! You have a new example of human intelligence created. Of course, in some cases once the new intelligence is created things go wrong – the result is someone with a mental handicap. In many ways, in the creation of artificial intelligence, what you were trying to do could be compared to turning a mentally handicapped person into a clever one – a very, very difficult task. Given the difficult nature of the task, frustration and setbacks are only to be expected – there is nothing to be surprised at there. In fact, it would not be surprising if these frustrations and setbacks made you give up. Later on, when Young Lillie decided to let Jinzhen go, nobody believed a word of his explanation. He said, 'We have encountered enormous problems in our research, and if we carry on like this I really cannot see any prospect of success. I don't want to see such a talented and clever young man follow me down this questionable path, running the risk of ruining his own future. I want to make sure that he gets to do something meaningful.'

That was in the summer of 1956.

That same summer, everyone in the university was talking about the man who came to take Jinzhen away. People thought that the whole thing was most mysterious. Why Young Lillie was prepared to let Jinzhen go was much discussed, but without anyone coming up with a good answer – that was part of the mystery.

The man walked with a limp.

That was also part of the mystery.

The First Turn

This man's surname was Zheng, and he walked with a limp. Perhaps because of this striking characteristic, it seemed as though he did not need a personal name — that it was an unnecessary ornament, like wearing a piece of jewellery. He will appear at various crucial junctures in this narrative — some of the time he will be anonymous and some of the time he will be referred to by the name Zheng the Gimp.

'Zheng the Gimp!'

'Zheng the Gimp!'

The mere fact that people were happy to call him that tells you one important fact about the man — his life was not defined by his physical disability. If you think about it, there are two possible reasons for such a reaction: One, that Zheng the Gimp got that way as the result of an honourable wound — it was the proof that he had once carried a gun and fought side-by-side with his comrades. Two, that Zheng the Gimp's leg wasn't that bad — it was just that his left leg was a little bit shorter than his right. When he was younger, such a difference could have been corrected by wearing a shoe with a thicker sole on the relevant foot, but once he got past fifty, he was reduced to walking with a cane. When I met him, he walked with a stick, but he was not the kind of old man that you can possibly overlook. This was in the early 1990s.

That summer, the summer of 1956, Zheng the Gimp was still in his thirties — a strong and healthy young man. Thanks to the built-up soles of the shoes he wore on his left foot, nobody realized his physical problems — his limp disappeared and, to the outside observer, he looked pretty much like anyone else. It was purely by chance that the people at the university discovered what was wrong with him.

This is how it all came about. The afternoon of the day that Zheng the Gimp came to the university, the entire student body was in the main auditorium, listening to a report about the amazing feats of valour achieved by the heroes of the Chinese People's Volunteer Army. The campus was very quiet and the weather was lovely. It was not roasting hot, that day, and there was a light breeze blowing, fluttering the leaves of the avenue of French plane trees growing on either side of the road. That light susurration made the university seem even quieter than it actually was. He found the peace of the place so striking that he decided to order his jeep to stop – telling the driver to come back three days later to collect him from the university guest house. He got out of the car and started walking through the grounds alone. Some fifteen years earlier, he had spent three years at the attached high school, followed by the freshman year at the university. After such a long absence, he was keenly aware of the changes that had overtaken his alma mater and he was overtaken by a strange sense of nostalgia – many memories from the past seemed to press around him as he walked slowly along, as if called to life by his footsteps. When the presentation for the students finished, he was standing just outside the auditorium. The crowd poured out of the hall, spreading out like a flood. In an instant, he found himself engulfed, surrounded on all sides. He followed the crowd nervously, worried that someone might bump into him; because thanks to his gammy leg, if he fell it would be impossible for him to get up. The students continued coming and he found himself being moved to the back of the crowd, but these stragglers picked him up and marched along, shoulder to shoulder. The young people around him were careful, though; every time it seemed as though someone were just about to knock him down, they moved away just in time to prevent a collision. Nobody looked back, nobody seemed to have so much as noticed him; clearly his special shoe hid his condition from all casual observers. Maybe knowing this gave him confidence; anyway, he started to feel a sudden affection for this band of students, male and female, so bright and lively, chatting with each other; like a bubbling stream carrying him along. He felt himself rejuvenated – time had rolled back fifteen years.

When they arrived at the playing field, the crowd broke up the way a wave does when it hits the sand. He was now in no danger of being knocked off his feet. It was just at that moment that he suddenly felt something fall against the back of his neck. Before he had time to react, the crowd were already beginning to shout: 'Rain!' 'It's raining!' When this cry first went up, people didn't move, they just looked up at the sky. A moment later, the first drops were followed by a huge bolt of lightning, and then the rain really did begin to hammer down, as if someone had turned on a high-pressure hose. Immediately the crowd began to scatter like a flock of frightened hens – some were running forward, others had turned back towards the auditorium, some were rushing towards nearby buildings, some were heading for the bike sheds. As people ran around shouting at each other, the playing field was reduced to chaos. He was now in a real fix – he couldn't run and he couldn't not run: if he ran people would realize that he had a gammy leg; if he didn't run he was going to get soaked. Maybe he didn't even particularly want to run – he had faced the full force of enemy fire so why should he be scared of rain? Of course he wasn't bothered by the prospect of getting wet. But his feet were obeying commands from some other part of his brain – he was starting to hop forward, one foot striking out, the other dragging behind. That was the way he had to run, the way a lame man runs, one leap at a time, as if there was a shard of glass stuck in the bottom of his shoe.

When he first started, everyone else was too busy running themselves to pay any attention to him. Later on, when they had found sanctuary in nearby buildings, he was still in the middle of the playing field. He hadn't wanted to run in the first place, he was hampered by his gammy leg, he was still carrying his suitcase – no wonder he was so slow! No wonder everyone else had vanished! Now, in the whole of that massive playing field, he was the only person to be seen – he stuck out like a sore thumb. Once he realized that, he decided to get away from the playing field as quickly as possible, but that meant having to hop even faster. It was valiant, it was comical; to the people watching, it seemed like this was all part of the spectacle. Some people even started to shout encouragement at him.

'Faster!'

'Faster!'

Once the cry of 'Faster!' went up, it attracted the attention of even more people. It seemed as if all eyes were fixed on him – he felt almost nailed in place by their stares. He immediately decided to stop, cheerfully waving his hands in the air: a gesture of appreciation for the people who had shouted encouragement to him. Afterwards he began to walk forward, a smile on his face, like an actor leaving the stage. At that moment, seeing him walk normally, it looked as if his hopping run had been put on: a performance. In reality, something that he tried to cover up had been glaringly revealed to everyone. You could say that this sudden rainstorm forced him to play a role which disclosed the secret of his gammy leg – on the one hand this embarrassed him, and on the other, it made sure that everyone recognized him as . . . a gimp! An amusing and friendly gimp. The fact is that when he left this place fifteen years earlier, having spent four years there, nobody noticed that he had gone. However, this time, in the space of just a couple of minutes, he had become famous throughout the university. A couple of days later, when he took Jinzhen away on his mysterious mission, everyone said, 'It was the cripple who danced in the rain that took him away.'

2

He had come to take someone away.

Someone like him came to N University every year in the summer, wanting to take people away. Whoever came in any particular year had certain distinguishing features, no matter what they looked like. They seemed to be able to call on considerable resources; they were very mysterious; and the minute they arrived, they would go straight to the office of the chancellor of the university. On this occasion the chancellor's office was empty, so he left and went to the office next door, which belonged to the registrar. As it happened, that was where the chancellor was, discussing something with the registrar. The moment he entered, he announced that he was looking for the chancellor. The registrar asked who he was. He said with a laugh, 'I am a coper, looking for horses.'

The registrar said, 'Then you ought to go to the Student Centre: it's on the first floor.'

'I need to talk to the chancellor first,' he said.

'Why?' asked the registrar.

'I have something here that the chancellor needs to see.'

'What is it? Give it to me.'

'Are you the chancellor? It is for his eyes only,' he said aggressively.

The registrar looked at the chancellor. The chancellor said, 'Let me have a look at whatever it is.'

Once he was sure that the person he was speaking to was indeed the chancellor of the university, he opened his briefcase and took out a file. The file was perfectly ordinary, the kind made out of card – somewhat like the kind of thing that schoolteachers use. He took a single-page document out of the file and handed it to the chancellor, asking him to read it.

Having taken the document, the chancellor stepped back a pace or two and read it. The registrar could only see the back. As far as he could see, the paper was not particularly large, nor was it particularly thick, nor were there any special seals or stamps attached to it. It seemed like a perfectly ordinary letter of introduction. However, judging by the chancellor's reaction, there was clearly more to it. He noticed particularly that the chancellor seemed to just run his eye over the paper – maybe he looked only at the letterhead at the top – before immediately becoming much more serious and concerned.

'Are you Section Chief Zheng?'

'I am.'

'I do apologize for your reception, sir.' The chancellor was all smiles as he invited the man into his own office.

Nobody had the first idea as to what kind of organization could produce a letter that would have quite that kind of result, making the chancellor so very obsequious. The registrar thought that he would be able to find out: according to the rules of the university, all letters of introduction from external work units had to be filed with his office. Later on, when he realized that the chancellor had not handed over the document as he should have done, he went to the trouble of putting in a request for it. He was not expecting the chancellor to say that he had burnt it. The chancellor went on to explain that the very first sentence in the letter was that it should be destroyed immediately after it was read. The registrar was startled into an exclamation: 'Top secret!' The chancellor told him sternly that he was to forget all that had happened and not to mention it to anyone.

In actual fact, when the chancellor was showing the man into his office, he already had a box of matches ready in his hand. When the chancellor had finished reading the letter, he struck a match and said, 'Shall I burn it?'

'Why not?'

So the letter was burnt.

The two men stood there in silence, neither saying a word, as the paper went up in flames.

Afterwards, the chancellor asked, 'How many people do you want?'

He held up a finger: 'One.'

Then the chancellor asked, 'What field?'

He opened up the file again and took out another piece of paper. He said: 'This is my list of the requirements that whoever it is must fulfil – it is probably not complete but there is enough to give you an idea.'

The paper that he held out was exactly the same size as the previous letter, sextodecimo. There was no letterhead printed on this sheet though, and the words on it were written by hand, rather than being typed. The chancellor ran his eye down the list and then asked, 'Is this another one where it has to be burnt as soon as I have read it?'

'No,' he laughed. 'You think this is also top secret?'

'I haven't read it properly yet,' the chancellor said, 'so I don't know whether it is top secret or not.'

'It isn't,' he said. 'You can show it to anyone you like, even to students. Anyone who thinks that they fit this set of requirements can come and find me. I will be staying in Room 302 in the guest house attached to your university – you are welcome to turn up whenever you like.'

That evening, the chancellor of the university took two final-year students with particularly high grades to Room 302. Afterwards a constant stream of visitors arrived. By the afternoon of the third day twenty-two students had gone to Room 302 to meet the mysterious man with a limp: some were brought by their professors; some came under their own steam. The vast majority were students in the mathematics department. There were nine undergraduates and seven graduate students from that one department; the people who came from other departments were all taking specials in mathematics. Mathematical ability was the first requirement that Zheng the Gimp had set down for the person that he wanted – in fact, it was virtually the only condition. The thing is that the people who had gone in to see him had a very different story to tell once they came out again – they said it was a totally bizarre experience. They were inclined to think that it was all a joke of some kind, or at the very least not as serious as they had been led to believe. As for Zheng the Gimp – if you had listened to them you would have thought he was a lunatic, a psycho with a gammy leg! Some of them said that when they went into the room, he paid no attention to them at all. They stood there or sat there for a bit, feeling like complete fools, and then Zheng the Gimp waved them away, telling them to leave. Some of the professors in the mathematics department were so upset at what their students were telling them that they rushed round to the university guest house to complain to the lame man in person, asking him what on earth he thought he was doing. Why was he sending people away without asking them any questions? The only answer they got was that it was his way of doing things.

What Zheng the Gimp said was, 'Every discipline has its own requirements, right? In physical education they pick athletes by feeling their bones. The person I am looking for has to have an independent mind-set. Some people were really uncomfortable about the fact that I didn't pay any attention to them – they couldn't even sit still, nor could they stand up straight and not fidget. They found the whole experience extremely unsettling. That is not the kind of personality I am looking for.'

That sounds very fine, but only Zheng the Gimp knew whether he was telling the truth or not.

On the afternoon of the third day of his stay, Zheng the Gimp invited the chancellor of the university to visit him at the guest house, to discuss his search. He wasn't very happy, but he had got something out of it. He gave the chancellor five names from the list of the twenty-two people he had interviewed and requested permission to see their personal dossiers – he thought that the person he was looking for would most likely be one of these five. When the chancellor realized that the whole thing was in its final phase and that Zheng the Gimp was proposing to leave the following day, he stayed behind at the guest house to eat a simple dinner with him. While they were still at table Zheng the Gimp seemed to suddenly remember something. He asked the chancellor about what had happened to Young Lillie, and the chancellor explained. He said, 'If you would like to see the retired chancellor, I will tell him to come.'

Zheng said with a smile, 'How could I possibly ask him to come and see me? I should go and visit him!'

And just as he had said, that very evening, Zheng the Gimp went to see Young Lillie . . .

[Transcript of the interview with Master Rong]

It was I who went and opened the door for him. I didn't recognize him and I didn't know that he was the mysterious man who had been the subject of so much gossip in the department over recent days. To begin with, Daddy didn't know anything about what was going on, but some of the people in the department had been dragging people off to meet the mystery man at a rate of knots, and I had happened to mention this to him. When Daddy realized that Zheng was one and the same as the mysterious man that everyone was talking about, he called me over and introduced me. I was very curious and asked what exactly it was that he wanted someone for. He didn't answer my question directly; he just said it was important work. When I asked what kind of important we were talking about – for humanity or the development of the country or what – he said it was a matter of national security. I asked him how the selection process had gone, but he didn't seem very satisfied – he muttered something about picking the tallest out of a group of dwarves.

He must have discussed the whole thing with Daddy at some point in the past, because Daddy seemed to know exactly what kind of person he was looking for. Seeing him so unhappy with the results of his search, Daddy said in a joking kind of voice, 'The fact is that I know of someone very suitable.'

'Who?' He immediately pricked up his ears.

Daddy, still in a joking tone of voice, said, 'Someone suitable might be the other side of the globe; on the other hand they might also be right here with you . . . '

He thought that Daddy was talking about me and immediately started asking about my work. Daddy just pointed to a photo of Zhendi pushed into the frame of the mirror on the wall and said: 'Him.'

'Who is he?' he asked.

Daddy pointed to the photograph of my aunt, Rong Lillie, and said, 'Don't they look alike?'

He went over to the mirror and had a good look; then he said: 'They do.'

'That's her grandson,' Daddy said.

As far as I can remember, Daddy didn't often introduce Zhendi to
people like that – in fact it was practically the first time. I don't know
why he spoke to the man in that way; perhaps it was because he wasn't
local – he didn't know more than the bare outlines of the story so it
did not matter so much. On the other hand he was a graduate of our
university, so he would know who my aunt was. After Daddy had
said that, he started asking us excited questions about Zhendi. Daddy
was perfectly happy to tell him all sorts of things about Zhendi, all
about how clever he was. Nevertheless, right at the end of their conversation, Daddy still told him not to think about trying to take
Zhendi away. When he asked why, Daddy said: 'The research institute needs him.'

He smiled and said nothing. He didn't return to the subject again,
so we had the impression that he had put the matter of Zhendi aside.

The following morning, Zhendi came home for breakfast. He told
us that someone had come to find him really late the previous night.
Because the facilities at the research institute were so excellent,
Zhendi often spent the entire night there, sleeping in his office, coming home only for meals. The moment he spoke up, Daddy knew
exactly who had gone to find him. He burst out laughing and said,
'Clearly he hasn't given up yet.'

'Who is he?' Zhendi asked.

'Don't pay any attention to him,' said Daddy.

'I think he wants me to go and join his work unit,' Zhendi said.

'Do you want to go?' asked Daddy.

'That is up to you,' said Zhendi.

'Then ignore him,' Daddy said.

Just as they were talking, there was a knock on the door and Zheng
walked in. When Daddy caught sight of him, he began by asking very
politely if he had had breakfast already – he said he had eaten at the
guest house. Daddy asked him to go upstairs and wait, that he would
be finished soon. When he had finished eating, Daddy told Zhendi to
go away. He said exactly the same thing as he had said before: 'Don't
pay any attention to him.'

After Zhendi left, Daddy and I walked upstairs together. Zheng was waiting in the sitting room, smoking a cigarette. Daddy might have looked very courteous and polite, but his meaning was quite plain. Daddy asked him if he was here to say goodbye or because he wanted someone. 'If you are here because you want him, then I am afraid I can't help you. As I told you last night, I don't want you taking him away from me – there is no point.'

'If you can't help then you can't help,' he said. 'I will just say goodbye.'

Daddy asked him to go into his study.

I had a class that afternoon, so after a few pleasantries, I went to my room to collect the things I needed. On my way out, a little bit later, I thought I should go and say goodbye. However, the door to Daddy's study was closed, something that very rarely happened. I decided not to disturb them and went off. When I got back after my class, Mummy told me sadly that Zhendi would be leaving us. I asked where he was going and Mummy had to wipe away her tears before she could reply. 'He is going with that man. Your father has agreed . . .'

[To be continued]

Nobody knows what Zheng the Gimp said to Young Lillie in his study that day, behind closed doors. Master Rong told me that until the day he died, her father refused to answer questions on the subject – if anyone mentioned it, he would get angry. He was clearly determined to take this secret to the grave. One thing is perfectly clear and that is that Zheng the Gimp managed to change Young Lillie's mind in the space of just over half an hour. Whatever it was that he said, when Young Lillie walked out of his study, he went straight to tell his wife that Jinzhen was leaving.

These events made Zheng the Gimp even more mysterious, and now an atmosphere of secrecy began to envelop Jinzhen too.

3

Jinzhen began to become mysterious that very afternoon – the afternoon that Zheng the Gimp and Young Lillie shut the door to his
study to talk in private. It was that afternoon that Zheng the Gimp
collected him in the jeep and took him away – he did not return
home until the evening. He was brought back in an ordinary car.
Once he got home, there was already a secretive look in his eyes.
Faced with the questioning glances of his family, it was a long time
before he opened his mouth. Everything he did now seemed to be
touched with mystery. Having gone away with Zheng the Gimp for
just a couple of hours, it seemed as though a wedge had already been
driven between him and his family. After a very long time, and
repeated questioning from Young Lillie, he sighed deeply and then
said hesitantly, using the same respectful term of address as usual,
'Professor, you have sent me somewhere that really doesn't suit me.'
He spoke lightly but the words had underlying implications that horrified everyone present: Young Lillie, his wife and Master Rong.
They had no idea what to say next.

Mrs Lillie said, 'If you don't want to go then don't – it's not as if
you have to.'

'I have to go,' Jinzhen said.

'What are you talking about? He –' she pointed to Young Lillie
' – is he and you are you: if he wants you to do something it does not
automatically mean that you have to agree. Listen to me. Decide
what you want to do for yourself. If you want to go then go; if you
don't want to go then don't – I will talk to them for you.'

'That won't work,' said Jinzhen.

'What do you mean it won't work?'

'If they want me to go, I don't have the right to refuse.'

'What kind of work unit is that? Who has such powers?'

'I am not allowed to tell you.'

'You are not allowed to tell your own mother?'

'I am not allowed to tell anyone. I had to swear . . . '

Just then, Young Lillie clapped his hands and stood up. He said seriously, 'Right, in that case you must not say another word. When are you leaving? Has it been decided yet? We need to pack your things.'

'I am leaving before dawn tomorrow morning,' Jinzhen said.

Nobody got any sleep that night, because everyone was busy packing Zhendi's belongings. At around four o'clock in the morning, his stuff was pretty much packed – his books and his winter clothes had been corded into two cardboard boxes. After that it only remained to collect some daily necessities: even though Jinzhen and Young Lillie both said he could buy whatever he needed when he got there, the two women were both in packing mode and rushed up and down the stairs, racking their brains for anything that he could possibly need. First they put in a radio and some packets of cigarettes, then tea leaves and a first-aid kit – they managed to fill a leather suitcase with the fruit of their labours. At about five o'clock in the morning, everyone met downstairs. Mrs Lillie was almost hysterical – she could not possibly make breakfast for Jinzhen that morning, so she had to ask her daughter to do it for her. She went with her to the kitchen and sat there, explaining exactly what it was that she had to do. That was not because Master Rong couldn't cook, but because this was to be a very special meal – they were saying goodbye to Jinzhen. Mrs Lillie was determined that this meal had to comprise four important elements.

1. The main dish was going to be a bowl of noodles, just like the kind that people eat on their birthdays to symbolize many happy returns of the day.

2. The noodles had to be made of buckwheat. Buckwheat noodles are softer than the ordinary kind. This would symbolize that people have to be more forgiving and flexible when they are among strangers.

3. The flavourings for this noodle soup should include vinegar, chilli peppers and walnuts. Walnuts are bitter. This would symbolize that, of the four flavours, bitterness, sourness and

spiciness would be left behind at home; once he left everything would be sweet.

4. Not too much soup was to be made, because when the time
came, Jinzhen was supposed to drink every last drop, to
symbolize completeness and success.

It was just a bowl of soup, but it represented all the old lady's
fondest hopes and wishes for him. When this meaningful bowl of
soup was brought bubbling into the dining room, Mrs Lillie called
Jinzhen to table. She took a jade pendant, in the shape of a crouching
tiger, out of her pocket and put it in Jinzhen's hands, telling him to
eat up and then tie this to his belt, where it would bring him good
luck. Just then, they heard the sound of a car pulling up outside.
Shortly afterwards, Zheng the Gimp came in with his chauffeur.
He said hello to everyone and told the chauffeur to put the boxes in
the car.

Jinzhen sat there quietly eating his noodles. Once he started eating, he did not say anything, but it was the kind of silence that you
get when someone has a great deal that they want to say but no idea
where to start. Even when he had finished his noodles, he sat there
without a word. He clearly had no intention of getting up.

Zheng the Gimp came in and clapped him on the back, as if he
were in complete charge of the situation. He said, 'It is time to say
goodbye. I will be waiting for you in the car.' He said goodbye to
Young Lillie, his wife and Master Rong, and then left.

The room fell silent. The people present looked quietly at one
another; their gaze became concentrated, fixed. Jinzhen was still
holding onto his jade. He was stroking it with one hand. That was
the only movement in the room.

Mrs Lillie said: 'Tie it onto your belt. It will bring you good luck.'

Jinzhen put the jade up to his lips and kissed it, after which he
started to tie it onto his belt.

It was just at that moment that Young Lillie took the jade out of
his hands and said: 'Only a fool would expect something to bring
him good luck. You are a genius and you are going to make your own
luck.' He took out the Waterman pen that he had used for nearly half
a century and put it in Jinzhen's hands, saying: 'You will find this

much more useful. You can use it to make a note of your ideas. If you don't let them run away from you, you will find that no one can even come close to you.'

Jinzhen did exactly the same thing. He kissed the pen in silence and then put it in his breast-pocket. At that moment, they heard the brief blast of a car horn coming from outside – very short. Jinzhen didn't seem to have noticed it; he sat there without moving.

Young Lillie said, 'They are trying to hurry you up. Off you go.'

Jinzhen sat there, without moving.

Young Lillie said, 'You are going to be working for the nation – you should be happy.'

Jinzhen continued to sit there without moving.

Young Lillie said, 'This house is your home. When you leave this house, you are in your country. If you have no country you can have no home. Go on. They are waiting for you.'

Jinzhen sat there, unmoving. It was as if the sorrow of parting had nailed him to his chair. He couldn't move!

There was another blast from the horn of the waiting car. This time it was much longer. Young Lillie realized that Jinzhen was still showing no signs of going, so he glanced at his wife, wanting her to say something.

Mrs Lillie stepped forward, resting her two hands lightly on Jinzhen's shoulders. She said, 'Off you go, Zhendi. You have to go. I will be waiting for your letters.'

It seemed as though the touch of the old lady's hands had woken Jinzhen from his sleep. With a curious stumbling motion, he rose to his feet, moving as if in a trance. When he got to the door, he suddenly turned round and fell to his knees with a thud. He kowtowed to the old couple with resounding knocks of the head. In a voice choked with tears, he said, 'Mum, I am leaving now. But even if I go to the ends of the earth, I am still your son . . . '

It was five o'clock in the morning, on 11 June 1956. Jinzhen, the star of the mathematics department for the last ten years, a man who had quietly become a fixture at N University, upped and left on a mysterious journey from which he never returned. Before he left, he requested permission from the old couple to change his name – in

future he wanted to be called Rong Jinzhen. He said goodbye to his
family and embarked upon a new life with a new name – an already
tear-soaked parting was now rendered even more upsetting, as if
both sides were aware that this was no ordinary separation. The fact
is that, when he left, no one knew where Rong Jinzhen went. He got
into the jeep just as dawn was breaking and it took him away – he
disappeared into another world. He simply vanished. It was as if his
new name and his new identity fell like an axe, separating his past
from his future, marking his departure from the mundane world. All
that anyone knew was that he had gone somewhere else – the only
contact address that they had was right there in the provincial capital:
Box No. 36.

It seemed that he was really close by, right beside them.

But in fact no one knew where he had gone . . .

[Transcript of the interview with Master Rong]

I asked a couple of my former students who had ended up working
for the post office what work unit had Box No. 36 and where was it?
They all said that they did not know – it seemed to be an address for
somewhere beyond human ken. To begin with we all thought it was
a box associated with an address somewhere in the city, but when we
got the first letter that Zhendi posted to us, the amount of time it had
taken since posting told us that the local address was just a fake,
designed to mislead people. He might well be a very long way away
from us, maybe even further than we could imagine.

The first letter that he wrote to us was written three days after he
left, but we received it twelve days later. There was no indication on
the envelope of a sender's address – where that would normally have
been written there was one of Chairman Mao's slogans: 'Who Dares
to Make the Sun and Moon Shine in New Skies?' It was printed in
Chairman Mao's calligraphy, in red ink. The strangest thing was that
there was no frank from the post office from which the letter was
sent, just a frank from the receiving sorting office. All the letters
we received afterwards were the same: the same kind of envelope,
the same lack of a post office frank, and roughly the same amount of
time spent en route – around eight or nine days. At the beginning
of the Cultural Revolution, the quotation from Chairman Mao was

exchanged for a line from a really popular song of the era: 'Sailing Across the Ocean, We Rely on the Helmsman'. Everything else stayed the same.

What does it mean, working for National Security? I got to know at least a little bit about it from the letters that Zhendi sent home.

In the winter of the year that Zhendi left us, in December, there was a terrible storm one evening and the temperature simply plummeted. After supper, Daddy told us that he had a bit of a headache – probably because of the change in the weather – and so after taking a couple of aspirin, he went upstairs to go to bed even though it was still early. A couple of hours later, when Mummy went to bed, she found that he had stopped breathing, though his body was still warm. The way that Daddy died . . . it seemed as though the couple of aspirins he took before bedtime might as well have been arsenic; now that Zhendi was gone he knew that his research institute working on artificial intelligence was going to collapse, so he took this way out.

Of course, that is not what happened at all – the fact is that Daddy died of a brain haemorrhage.

We debated whether or not we should ask Zhendi to come back – after all he had not been gone for long and he was now attached to a very mysterious and powerful work unit – not to mention the fact that he was so far away – we had already discovered by that time that Zhendi was not in the provincial capital. In the end Mummy decided to call him back. She said, 'Since his surname is Rong, since he calls me "Mother", he is our son – his father is dead so of course we ought to call him back.' So we sent Zhendi a telegram asking him to come back for the funeral.

The person who came was a complete stranger. He brought an enormous wreath of flowers with him, which he laid on behalf of Rong Jinzhen. It was the largest of any of the wreaths at the funeral, not that that was much consolation. The whole thing upset us very much. You see, given what we knew of Zhendi, if it was at all possible he would have wanted to be there in person. He was a very highly principled person: if it was something that he thought was right he would find a way to do it – he was not the sort of person to be put off by inconvenience or difficulty. We thought a lot about why it was that he had not been able to come for the funeral. I don't know why – maybe it was because the man who came spoke so very evasively – I got the impression that it was most unlikely that Zhendi would ever come back, no matter what happened to the rest of us. He said something about how he was a very close friend of Zhendi's and was here on his behalf. On the other hand there was also a lot about how he couldn't answer that question, or that this subject was something he couldn't discuss, and so on and so forth. The whole thing was very odd; I sometimes even found myself wondering if something had happened to Zhendi – maybe he was dead. Particularly given that afterwards the letters that he sent were so much shorter and came at much longer intervals. It went on year after year – letters came but we never got to see him. I was becoming more and more certain that he was dead. Working in a secret organization dedicated to preserving the security of the nation is a great honour, a great glory, but it would be perfectly possible for them to give the family of a dead person the impression that he was still alive – that would be one way of showing how powerful they are, how special the work that they do. Anyway, given that Zhendi didn't come home from one year to the next, given that we never got to see him, never got to hear his voice – I became more and more certain that he was never coming back. The letters did nothing to convince me otherwise.

In 1966, the Cultural Revolution broke out. At the same time, the landmine that fate had planted under my feet some decades earlier exploded. There was a big-character poster put up to criticize me, saying that I was still in love with him [this referred to Master Rong's ex-boyfriend], and after that there were a number of absolutely outrageous suggestions made. It was said that the reason I never married was because I was waiting for him, that loving him meant that I loved the KMT, that I was a KMT whore, that I was a KMT spy. They said all sorts of horrible things about me, and they were all presented in a very bald way, as incontrovertible facts.

On the afternoon of the day that the big-character poster went up, a couple of dozen students made a confused attempt to surround the house. Maybe thanks to Daddy's reputation, they did a lot of shouting but they did not break in and drag me away – eventually the chancellor arrived just at the right moment to get them to leave. That was the first time I had ever been in any kind of trouble. I thought that this would be the end of it. They hadn't behaved too badly, after all.

They came back a little over a month later. This time there were a couple of hundred people. They had a lot of important figures from the university, including the chancellor, under arrest. They burst into the house, grabbed hold of me and dragged me out. They put a dunce's cap on my head with the words 'KMT Whore' written on it and I was thrust into the group who were there to be 'struggled against'. They were going to start by parading us about the place like criminals, as an example to the populace. When that was over, I was imprisoned in a women's lavatory, together with a woman professor from the chemistry department who was accused of immoral practices and bourgeois corruption. During the daytime they would take us out and beat us up, at night we were returned to our prison to write self-criticisms. After a while they shaved one half of our heads in the *yin-yang* style, making us look like nothing on earth. One day, Mummy saw me being struggled against and she was so horrified that she fainted dead away, right then and there.

Mummy was in hospital – I didn't know if she was alive or dead. I was just one step away from death myself. That evening, I wrote a secret message to Zhendi – just one line: 'If you are still alive, come back and rescue me!' I signed it with my mother's name. The next day, one of my students who felt sorry for me helped me to send it. Once the telegram had gone, I thought out the various possible options. It seemed most likely that I simply wouldn't hear any response. The next most likely result was – like when Daddy died – that a stranger would come. I couldn't imagine that Zhendi would be in a position to be able to come himself, not to mention that he would turn up quite so quickly . . .

[To be continued]

That day Master Rong and her colleague were being 'struggled against' in front of the chemistry department building. The two of them were standing on the steps in front of the main building, wearing tall dunce's caps on their heads, with heavy placards hung round their necks. There were red flags and posters hung to either side, while massed in front of them were students from the chemistry department and other professors – about two hundred people in all. They were sitting on mats on the ground. The people who had been selected to speak stood up. The whole thing looked to have been very carefully organized.

Starting at ten o'clock in the morning, they alternated exposés of the pair's evil actions with interrogations. At midday, they ate lunch on site (it was brought in). Master Rong and the other professor were ordered to recite sayings of Chairman Mao. By the time it got to four o'clock in the afternoon, neither of them could stand up any more. *Faute de mieux*, they were kneeling on the ground. It was then that a jeep with military number-plates drove up. It stopped in front of the chemistry department building, drawing all eyes. Three men got out. Two of them were very tall and they walked on either side of a short man, bracketing him. They marched right into the middle of this 'struggle session'. When they approached the steps, a couple of the Red Guards on duty that day tried to stop them, asking them who they were. The short man in the middle said aggressively, 'We have come to take Rong Yinyi away!'

'Who are you?'

'The people who are going to take her away!'

One of the Red Guards, incensed by his casual attitude, warned him in a loud voice: 'She is a KMT whore, you can't take her away!'

The little man glared at him. Suddenly he spat on the ground and cursed: 'Fuck you! If she is KMT, then what does that make me? Do you know who you are talking to? I am telling you, she is coming with me! Out of my way!'

As he spoke, he pushed the people blocking his path out of the way and marched up to the platform.

It was just at that moment that someone shouted from the back: 'How dare he curse us Red Guards! Let's beat him up!'

In the blink of an eye everyone was on their feet, pressing in, punching the man wildly. If no one had intervened, he would have been killed. Fortunately the people who had come with him moved in to protect him. They were both tall and strong – you could tell at a glance that they had had martial arts training. Pushing and pulling, the pair of them fought back against the attackers. The man was now standing in the middle of a circle, the other two protecting him on either side like bodyguards. They shouted in unison, 'We work for Chairman Mao — anyone who hits us is anti-Chairman Mao, anti-Red Guards! We are Chairman Mao's guards — stand back! Stand back!'

Thanks to their courage and persistence, they were able to extract the little man from the crowd. One of them protected him as he ran. The other was running too, but then suddenly he turned round and whipped out a gun. Pointing it into the air, he fired a single shot. He shouted, 'Do not move! Chairman Mao sent us here!'

Everyone was paralysed by the sound of the shot. They looked at him in amazement. At the back you could hear people shouting that Red Guards were not afraid to die, that there was nothing to be frightened of. It seemed like the situation was just about take a turn for the worse again when he took out his credentials — there was a bright red letterhead and a huge state seal on the envelope. Taking out the document inside, he held it up high so that everyone could see. 'Look, we come from Chairman Mao! We have been entrusted with a mission by the Chairman himself! If anyone dares cause any more trouble, Chairman Mao will send someone to arrest him! Given that we are all working for the Chairman, can't we sit down and discuss the matter properly? Let the comrades in charge here stand forward, so you can hear the orders we have been given by Chairman Mao!'

Two people stepped forward out of the scrum. The man put his gun away and took them off to one side to speak in private. Clearly they accepted whatever he said to them, since when they came back, they said that he was indeed working for Chairman Mao and that everyone should sit down in their seats. A little bit later, once calm had been restored, the other two came back again, having run a good long way. One of the Red Guard leaders went so far as to walk out to meet them and shake the little man's hand. The other Red Guard leader introduced him to the assembled company as a Hero of the Revolution and asked them to give him a round of applause. Sporadic and lacklustre handclapping was heard, indicating that people had not been much impressed by this hero. Perhaps because he was afraid of further trouble, the man who had opened fire with his gun decided not to let the hero come over. He went to meet him and whispered a couple of words in his ear, telling him to get in the car. He shouted at the driver to take him away, while he himself stayed behind.

Just as the car drove away, the hero stuck his head out of the window and shouted, 'Sis, don't be scared. I am going to get someone to save you!'

It was Jinzhen!

Rong Jinzhen!

The sound of Rong Jinzhen's voice rolled over the crowd. While the last notes were still hanging in the air, another jeep with military number-plates drove up with screeching tyres, coming to a halt just in front of Rong Jinzhen's car.

Three men got out of the jeep. Two of them were wearing PLA uniform, indicating that they were military cadres. They walked straight over to the man with the gun and spoke a couple of words in his ear, then they introduced the third man. He was the head of the Red Guards at the university – people called him Marshal Yang.

They held a quiet conference next to the cars. Afterwards Marshal Yang walked over to the other Red Guards alone, a very serious expression on his face. He didn't say anything to them – he just raised his fist and shouted, 'Long Live Chairman Mao!' Other people took up the chant, shouting it so that the very buildings reverberated. Once that was over he turned round and jumped up the steps to remove Master Rong's dunce's cap and placard. He told the assembled company, 'I swear by Chairman Mao, this woman is not a KMT whore but the sister of a national hero, a revolutionary comrade.' He raised his fist and shouted over and over again: 'Long live Chairman Mao! Long live the Red Guards! Long live our revolutionary comrades!'

Having repeated each slogan a couple of times, he took the Red Guard armband off his own arm and tied it onto Master Rong's. As he did so, other people started shouting out the same slogans, as if it was a gesture of respect to Master Rong or something. Maybe they were trying to protect her; maybe by shouting out slogans like that they were hoping to distract people's attention. Whatever the reason, Master Rong came to the end of her career as a counter-revolutionary to the sound of wave after wave of shouting . . .

[Transcript of the interview with Master Rong]

To tell you the truth, I didn't recognize Zhendi when I saw him – he had been gone for ten years. He was much thinner than he had been before and he was wearing a pair of old-fashioned spectacles with lenses as thick as bottle glass – he looked like an old man. I didn't believe that it could be him, right up until he called me 'Sis', and then I suddenly seemed to come to my senses. It still seems more than a little unreal to me. Even today, I sometimes wonder if what happened that day was not all a dream.

He arrived the day after my telegram was sent. To be able to get here so quickly, he must have been in the provincial capital anyway. Once he came back, it was clear in all sorts of different ways that he was both very powerful and extremely mysterious: he must have become a very important person. When he visited our house, the man with the gun didn't leave his side for so much as a moment – it seemed like he was a bodyguard, or maybe just a guard. Zhendi didn't seem to be allowed to do anything without his permission. When we were talking, he was butting in every five minutes – we weren't allowed to ask such-and-such, or this topic was out of bounds. In the evening, the car brought dinner to our house – they said this was to save us the trouble of cooking but it looked to me like they were worried we were going to put something in the food. After dinner, he started chivvying Zhendi into leaving and it was only when Mummy and Zhendi both made a real fuss that he finally agreed that he could stay overnight. It must have seemed a most dangerous proceeding to him, because he called up two jeeps which parked right in front of our house, with seven or eight men inside. Some of them were in military uniform; some in plain clothes. He slept overnight in the same room as Zhendi, but before the pair of them went to bed he searched the whole house from top to bottom. The next day, when Zhendi asked to be allowed to go to Daddy's tomb, he flatly refused.

The whole thing seemed completely unreal – Zhendi arrived, stayed the night and left again – all as if in a dream.

Even though he was able to come and visit us on this one occasion, Zhendi's life over the last decade remained a complete mystery to us – it was even more mysterious when we were able to see him in the flesh. Really, the only two things we found out were that he was still alive and had got married. Apparently, he had not been married for long – his wife was part of the same work unit. Although we had no idea what she did or where she lived, we did find out that her surname was Di and that she came from somewhere in the north. Looking at the couple of photographs he had brought with him, we could see that she was a good bit taller than Zhendi, a nice-looking woman – but the expression in her eyes was sad. Just like Zhendi, it seemed that she was not good at expressing her emotions. Just before he left, Zhendi gave Mother a really fat envelope, which he said was from his wife. He asked that we wait until after he had left before looking at it. When we opened it, there were 200 yuan and a letter from his wife inside. The letter explained that the Party had refused permission for her to go with Zhendi on this visit and that she was really sorry about that. She called Mummy 'Mother', 'Dear Mother'.

Three days after Zhendi left, a man representing his work unit turned up. He had been to our house before, representing Zhendi at the ceremonies for the anniversary of Daddy's death. He gave us a document from the PLA Military Region headquarters and the Provincial Revolutionary Committee, written out on paper with a fat red letterhead. It said that Rong Jinzhen had been recognized as a Hero of the Revolution by the Central Politburo, the State Council and the Central Military Commission and thus by extension, we had become a revolutionary family. In the future, no work unit, no member of the Communist Party and no private individual would be able to enter our house without our permission. More importantly, in the future no one would be allowed to cast aspersions on the revolutionary credentials of a hero's family. At the very top there was a hand-written comment – 'Anyone disobeying this order will be treated as a counter-revolutionary and punished accordingly!' That was written by the commander of the local Military Region himself.

We treasured that letter! Thanks to it, we never had any trouble afterwards. Thanks to it, my brother was able to return to N University from Shanghai and later on, when he decided that he wanted to go abroad, it was that letter that got him permission. My brother was working on research into superconductors; at that time there was no way he could continue his work in this country! He had to leave. But think about it – think how difficult it was in those days if you wanted to go abroad. In many ways, that was a very special time, and yet Zhendi was able to ensure that we could live and work normally.

We had absolutely no idea though what enormous task Zhendi must have accomplished for his country that he would be granted such remarkable powers in return; that he would effectively be able to transform our lives with a clap of his hands. Later on, not long after Zhendi came back to save my life, people in the chemistry department started a rumour that Zhendi had played a key role in our nuclear weapons programme. They made a good story of it. When I heard what they were saying, I suddenly thought that it might very well be true, because the dates dovetailed nicely – China started its own nuclear weapons programme in 1954, not long before Zhendi left. What is more it would make sense: if you want to build a nuclear device you would definitely need mathematicians. The way I thought of it, that was the only kind of job that would be quite so secretive, quite so important, and would give him the kind of status that he so clearly had. But in the 1980s, the state published a list of the scientists who worked on the first and second generations of the Chinese nuclear weapons programme and Zhendi's name wasn't there. Maybe he changed his name, or maybe the whole thing was just a rumour in the first place . . .

[To be continued]

4

Just like Master Rong, Zheng the Gimp played an important role in making it possible for me to write this book. I interviewed him long before I interviewed Master Rong, and we became good friends. At that time he was already more than sixty years old, and the loss of elasticity in his skin meant that the bones showed through clearly. Likewise, the problems with his gammy leg had only got worse with age – he could no longer conceal the problem by having a raised sole in one shoe; he was now reduced to walking with a stick. People said that he looked very grand, walking along leaning on his stick, but in fact I think that it was the man himself who was impressive and it was nothing at all to do with the stick. When I got to know him, he was the most important member of Unit 701 – the director of the whole place. Given his position, no one would dare call him Zheng the Gimp – even if he asked you to call him that you would not dare obey. Given his rank, given his age, there were a lot of ways to refer to him: 'Director'; 'Boss'; 'Sir'.

Those were the kinds of terms of address that people used for him, all very respectful. The thing is that he often referred to himself as 'the Crippled Director'. To tell you the truth, even now I don't know his full name, because there were too many other ways to refer to him, some vulgar, some respectful: his job title, cover-names, his code name – there were loads! It seemed like his real name was superfluous and apparently he hadn't used it for ages – it almost seemed as though he had decided to get rid of it as unnecessary. Of course, given my position, I always used a respectful term of address for him. I called him 'Director Zheng'.

Director Zheng.

Director Zheng . . .

Let me tell you one of Director Zheng's secrets – he had seven phone numbers. He had as many phone numbers as he had names! He gave me two of his numbers, which to be quite frank was more than enough – one was the number for his secretary and that phone was always answered immediately. Basically this meant that I could always let Director Zheng know that I wanted to talk to him, but he would not necessarily be able to pick up the phone and answer – that was very much a matter of luck.

After I had interviewed Master Rong, I rang both of the numbers that Director Zheng had given me. No one picked up on the first number and when I phoned the second, they told me to wait for a moment – that meant I was in luck that day. When Director Zheng came to the phone he asked me what I wanted. I told him that even today, people at the university thought that Rong Jinzhen had played a key role in building our first nuclear bomb. He asked me what on earth I was talking about. I said that I was talking about the fact that although Rong Jinzhen had achieved great things in the service of our country, because his work was secret, he was doomed to remain an unknown hero. However, it was because his work was secret that people imagined that he had done even greater things than were actually the case – he was being accorded a crucial role in our nuclear programme. I was interrupted at this stage by a bellow of rage down the phone line. 'What on earth do you think you are talking about?' he shouted. 'Do you really think that you can win a war with nothing other than a nuclear weapon? With Rong Jinzhen we could have won pretty much any war we cared to fight! The nuclear programme was a way to show off our strength; like putting a flower in your hair to attract other people's attention. What Rong Jinzhen was doing was to watch other people – he could hear the sound of other people's heartbeat in the wind, he could see other people's most treasured secrets. If you know the enemy and you know yourself, you will win every battle that you fight. That is why I tell you that from a military perspective, Rong Jinzhen's work was of much more practical importance to us than any nuclear weapon.'

Rong Jinzhen was a cryptographer.

[Transcript of the interview with Director Zheng]

Cryptography involves one genius trying to work out what another genius has done – it results in the most appalling carnage. To succeed in this mysterious and dangerous process, you call together the finest minds at your disposal. What you are trying to do is apparently very simple: you are trying to read the secrets hidden in a string of Arabic numerals. That sounds kind of fun, like a game; but this particular game has ruined the lives of many men and women of truly remarkable intelligence ... that's the most impressive thing about cryptography.

It's also the tragedy of cryptography. In the history of human endeavour, the majority of geniuses have been buried within the borders of cryptography. To put it another way: having destroyed one genius after another, having destroyed one generation of geniuses after another, all that we have left are the ciphers. They have brought so many great minds together – not to show what it is that they can do, but to make them suffer, to put them to death. No wonder people say that cryptography is the most heartbreaking profession in the world.

[To be continued]

As Rong Jinzhen was bundled half-asleep into the car and driven away from the university at dawn on that summer's day in 1956, he had no idea that the arrogant man sitting next to him would force him to spend the rest of his life working in the heartbreakingly difficult and secretive world of cryptography. He also did not know that his companion, whom his fellow students laughingly referred to as the gimp who had danced in the rain, was in fact a very important (if mysterious) individual, the head of the cryptography section of Special Unit 701. Or to put it another way, from here on in he was going to be Rong Jinzhen's immediate superior. After the car had been driving for a while, the boss decided that he would like to talk to his new subordinate; but perhaps because of the sorrow of parting, he could not get a word out of him. The clear light of the car headlights shone into the darkness ahead of them and lit up the road; a strange and unlucky feeling enveloped them.

Just as dawn was breaking, the car drove out of the city limits and came out on National Highway XX. This alarmed Rong Jinzhen very much, and his head whipped from side to side. He thought, 'Aren't I supposed to be staying in the same city – the address was a

local post-box, No. 36 – why are we going on a national highway?'
When Zheng the Gimp had taken him yesterday afternoon to complete the paperwork to do with his hiring, the car had turned again
and again – not to mention the fact that for fully ten minutes they
had insisted that he wear dark glasses so he could not see where they
were going – but he could have sworn that at no time did they leave
the city limits. Now the car was whizzing along the highway, he realized that they must be going somewhere very far away. Puzzled, he
asked, 'Where are we going?'

'To the unit.'

'Where is that?'

'I don't know.'

'Is it far?'

'I don't know.'

'Aren't we going to the same place as yesterday?'

'Do you know where you went yesterday?'

'I am sure it was somewhere in the city.'

'You have already infringed the oath you swore . . . '

'But . . . '

'No buts. Repeat the first part of the oath you swore!'

'Everywhere I go, everything I see and hear is accounted classified
information and I am not allowed to mention it to anyone.'

'In future you had better remember it! From here on in, everything you see and hear is top secret . . . '

At nightfall, the car was still en route. Scattered lights could be
seen in the distance, suggesting a medium-sized town. Rong Jinzhen
was keeping his eyes peeled – he wanted to know where he was.
Zheng the Gimp demanded that he put dark glasses on. By the time
he was allowed to take them off again, the car was moving along a
mountain road with numerous hairpin bends. On both sides of the
road there was forest and mountain scenery, but there was not a
single road-sign or even any kind of marker to indicate where they
were. There were many twists in this mountain road; it was narrow
and pitch-black. The car headlights lit up the darkness – the beam of
light seemed concentrated, fixed upon the road – as clear and bright
as a searchlight. Sometimes he felt as though the car were not being

propelled forward by its engine, but as if the light were pulling it along. They proceeded like this for about another hour. Far in the distance, Rong Jinzhen could see a couple of spots of light on the side of the dark mountain – that was their destination.

There was no sign on the gate. The man who opened the gate was missing one arm and sported a livid scar across his face, starting at his left ear and proceeding across the bridge of his nose, until it finally came to an end on his right cheekbone. When Rong Jinzhen caught sight of him, he was instantly reminded of the pirate stories he had read as a child. The surrounding buildings were completely silent, looming out of the darkness. This too reminded him of the medieval castles that figured so prominently in the foreign fairy stories he had read. Two people walked out of the gloom – they looked like ghosts. As they came closer, it became apparent that one of them was a woman. She came over to shake hands with Zheng the Gimp, while the man got into the car and started lifting Rong Jinzhen's luggage out.

Zheng the Gimp introduced Rong Jinzhen to the woman. In his scared and unhappy mood, Rong Jinzhen didn't catch her name – he just heard that she was Department Head Something-or-other and that she was the director here. Zheng the Gimp told him that this was Unit 701's training base. All new comrades had to come here to receive political education and professional training when they joined Unit 701. He said, 'When you have finished your basic training, I will send someone to collect you. I hope you will finish soon and become a fully-fledged member of Unit 701.' When he had finished speaking he clambered back into the car and drove off. It was almost as if he were a human trafficker – having collected his wares in some other part of the country and delivered them to the purchaser, he now washed his hands of the whole situation without the slightest hesitation.

One morning, some three months later, just as Rong Jinzhen was getting out of bed, he heard the sound of a motorbike pulling up outside his bedroom. A short time later he heard someone knocking on his door. Opening the door, he saw that a young man stood outside. The man said, 'Section Chief Zheng sent me to come and collect you. You'd better get ready.'

The motorbike took him away, but it did not drive in the direction of the main gate. Instead it headed deeper into the complex, right into a mountain cave. There was in fact a huge cave complex there, spreading out in all directions; one opening out into the next, like a maze. The motorbike continued on and after about another ten minutes they stopped at a round-topped steel door. The driver got off the bike, went in and then came out again shortly afterwards; then they proceeded on the bike. After a further short space of time, the bike emerged on the far side of the underground complex and a series of buildings many times larger than the training centre unfurled before Rong Jinzhen's eyes. This was where the mysterious and secretive Special Unit 701 was based, and this was where Rong Jinzhen would spend the rest of his life. His work would be conducted on the far side of the round-topped steel door that the motorbike had stopped next to just a few minutes before. The people here called this series of buildings the Northern Complex; the training centre was known as the Southern Complex. The Southern Complex was the gateway to the Northern Complex – not to mention being its checkpoint: there was something of the feel of a moated citadel accessible only by a single drawbridge to the whole thing. A person who did not pass the inspections at the Southern Complex would never be able to so much as gain a glimpse of the Northern Complex – that drawbridge was never going to be lowered for him.

The motorbike proceeded on its way, before finally coming to a halt in front of a redbrick building entirely covered in creepers. The delicious smell of cooking that came wafting out informed Rong Jinzhen that this must be a canteen. Zheng the Gimp happened to be eating inside and when he spotted Jinzhen through the window, he got up and came outside, still clutching a bun in his hand. He invited him in.

He still hadn't had breakfast.

The dining hall was full of all sorts of people – there were both men and women; young and old. There were some people wearing military uniform, some in plain clothes; and there were even some wearing police uniform. During his time at the training centre, Rong Jinzhen had been trying to work out what kind of unit this was.

How was it organized? Was it military or was it attached to the local government? Now, looking at the scene before him, he was completely confused. He thought to himself, 'This must be one of the special features of a Special Unit. In fact, in any Special Unit, in any secret organization, there are naturally going to be many unusual features. Secrecy is at its very core. It is ever-present, like a note of music humming through the air.'

Zheng the Gimp took him through the main dining hall and into a separate room. The table there was already laid for breakfast. There was milk, eggs, stuffed buns, plain buns, and a number of little side dishes.

'Sit down,' said Zheng the Gimp.

Jinzhen sat down and started eating.

'Look outside,' said Zheng the Gimp. 'They aren't getting the kind of quality of food that you are eating; and they only have rice gruel to drink.'

Jinzhen raised his head and looked over. The people outside were all holding bowls, but he had been given a cup. There was milk in his cup.

'Do you know why?' asked Zheng the Gimp.

'Is this some kind of special welcome?'

'No. It is because your work is much more important than theirs.'

When he had finished breakfast, Rong Jinzhen began the work that he would devote the rest of his life to: cryptography. However, right up until that moment, he did not know that he was going to be assigned to this secret and heartbreaking profession. At the training centre, he had received unusual instruction – for example, his teachers had required him to familiarize himself with the history, geography, foreign relations, holders of key government offices, military might, military installations, defensive capabilities and so on of X country – he even had to read background material on a number of important government and military figures. This had made him very curious about what his future work was going to be. His first thought was that he was going to be researching some secret weapon that X country had developed for some special military objective. Later on he thought that maybe he would be joining some kind of PLA think-tank, say as a secretary to a senior military officer. After that, he thought that maybe he was supposed to become a military expert. After that, he thought of a number of other professions, all unpalatable in the extreme: a military instructor who would be sent overseas; a military attaché at an embassy; a spy; etc. He thought of all sorts of important and unusual professions that they could be intending for him, but he never even considered the possibility of becoming a cryptographer.

That really isn't a job, it is a conspiracy: a trap within a conspiracy.

5

To tell the truth, to begin with the people of Unit 701, then based in a mountain valley outside the suburbs of a certain city in China, did not realize quite what a great future Rong Jinzhen had ahead of him. Or at least you could say that they were not impressed by his work. He was engaged in lonely and difficult work – decrypting ciphers, for which, in addition to training, experience and genius, you need a luck that comes from far beyond the stars. People in Unit 701 said it was perfectly possible to catch that luck that comes from far beyond the stars, but it requires that you raise your hands up high every morning and every evening at exactly the same time as black smoke comes curling out of your ancestors' tombs.

When he first arrived, Rong Jinzhen did not understand this; or perhaps he simply did not care. But he spent the whole day reading a bunch of books that had nothing to do with anything – for example he would often have his nose in an English-language copy of the *Complete Book of Mathematical Puzzles* or a bunch of tatty old books stitched together with thread, their titles invisible. He seemed to fritter away each and every day in complete silence. He was obviously solitary (not snobbish or arrogant), but he did not say anything suggestive of particularly remarkable intelligence (in fact, he said very little to anyone), and he did not show signs of either great genius or great creative powers. People really did start to question his abilities and his luck. What was worse, no one was in any doubt as to his lack of interest in the work – as mentioned above, he was usually to be seen with his nose in a book totally unrelated to what he was supposed to be doing.

That was just the beginning. That was the first sign that he wasn't working hard at his job, and the second was not far behind. One afternoon, Rong Jinzhen left the dining hall after lunch and, as was his wont, took a book and went for a walk in the woods. He didn't have a siesta in the afternoons but he also didn't do overtime — any spare time he had was usually spent reading in a quiet, out-of-the-way corner.

The north wing of the complex had been constructed on the mountain slopes. There were patches of natural woodland through-out the complex and he often went to one particular stretch of pine woods which was most conveniently located right by the main entrance to the caves where he worked. Apart from that, his other reason for selecting this particular woodland as his favourite walk was that he liked the particular piny smell of the trees, somewhat like medicated soap. Some people don't like that resinous smell, but he enjoyed it. His love of this smell seemed closely related to his tobacco addiction, since after he took up walking regularly through the woods, he smoked a lot less.

That day, just as he walked into the wood, he heard the crunching sound of someone approaching. It was a man of about fifty. He seemed very modest and unassuming as he asked if he could play elephant chess, a sincere and ingratiating smile spreading across his face. Rong Jinzhen nodded his head and the other man happily whipped out a set and asked if he would like to play a game. Rong Jinzhen didn't want to play — he wanted to read his book — but he felt bad saying so to the man's face; it would have been rude to refuse, so he nodded again. Although it was now many years since he had last played, he had some experience of this game gained against Jan Lisei-wicz — most people would not be able to beat him. This man wasn't most people — the two men quickly realized that the other was a fine player in his own right and it would be very difficult for either of them to defeat the other. After that, the man often came to find him to play chess. He would come in the afternoon, he would come in the evening — sometimes he would even have the chess set waiting by the entrance to the cave or the door of the dining hall, to be sure of catching him when he went past. It was almost as if he was being stalked. This ensured that everyone knew he was playing chess with the lunatic.

Everyone in Unit 701 knew about the lunatic who liked to play chess. Before the Liberation, he had been an honours student at the

mathematics department of Sun Yat-sen University, then after graduation he had been specially recruited by the KMT military and sent
to Indo-China to work in their cryptography unit there. He had succeeded in cracking a high-level Japanese military cipher, making him
famous in the world of cryptography. Later on, unhappy at Chiang
Kai-shek's decision to take the country into a second civil war, he
managed to leave the military secretly and went to work as a foreman
in a Shanghai electricity company under a different name. After the
Liberation, Unit 701 went to a lot of trouble to find out what had
happened to him; they invited him to come back. He had managed to
crack a number of mid-level American ciphers, making him by far
the most successful cryptographer they had. Two years ago, he had
unfortunately developed schizophrenia — overnight he turned from a
hero that everyone admired into a lunatic that they were all afraid of.
If he saw someone he would curse at them, yelling and screaming;
sometimes he would even hit people. Apparently this kind of acute
schizophrenia, particularly when it is accompanied by a violent reaction on the part of the patient (what is commonly called paranoid
schizophrenia), has a comparatively high rate of successful treatment.
But because he knew too many important secrets, nobody dared to
be the one that signed the order to send him to hospital. Instead, he
was treated at the clinic attached to Unit 701. The doctors there were
surgeons; they were quickly instructed in a handful of therapeutic
methods by experts brought in from outside, and the whole thing
did not go at all well. They managed to get him calmed down, but it
all went far too far — other than his obsession with playing chess, he
did not seem to think about anything else at all. In fact, he could not
think about anything else. He had gone from being a paranoid schizophrenic to being a catatonic schizophrenic.

    In actual fact, he did not know how to play elephant chess until he
got sick, but by the time he left hospital he had become a very fine
player. He had learned the game from one of the doctors. According
to what the experts said later on, the whole problem developed as a
result of the fact that the doctor taught him to play elephant chess at
too early a stage in his recovery. As the expert said, when someone is
starving, you can't give them a full meal straight away. In this kind of

case, when the patient begins his recovery you do not want him to concentrate his intelligence upon one object – if that happens, it may well be the case that later he finds it impossible to detach his concentration from that object. Of course, there is no reason why a surgeon should know anything about the treatment of psychological problems; what is more he was a fan of elephant chess and often played the game with his patients. One day, when he realized that the schizophrenic seemed to be able to understand the movements of the pieces on the board, he thought that this was a sign that he was beginning to recover, so he started playing the game with him too. He thought that this was consolidating the man's recovery, but in fact it all ended in disaster; he turned a great cryptographer, who might well have made a full recovery from his breakdown, into a chess-playing lunatic.

In a nutshell, this was a failure of medical care at Unit 701, but what choice did they have? As it is, people have to muddle through life – if things go well it is because you are lucky; if things go badly who are you going to blame? You can't blame anyone. If you want to find something to blame here, then blame the wretched man's job; blame the fact that he knew too many secrets. It was the fact that he knew so much top-secret information that decreed that he would spend the rest of his life confined in this mountain valley, crippled in mind. People said that when he played elephant chess, you could still see how clever he must have been before he got so sick, but the rest of the time his IQ was about the same level as that of a dog. If you shouted at him he would run away; if you smiled at him he would obediently obey your commands. Because he had nothing to do, he would wander around inside Unit 701 all day every day, like a poor little lost soul.

Now this lost soul had found Rong Jinzhen.

Rong Jinzhen didn't try to make him go away, like other people did.

It was very easy to get him to leave you alone: all you had to do was shout at him sternly a couple of times. Rong Jinzhen did not do that; he didn't avoid him, he didn't shout at him, he didn't even glare at him. He treated him just the same as he treated everyone else – neither warm nor cold; quite simply as if he really didn't care. Because of this the lunatic kept on coming to find him, he wouldn't leave him alone; he wanted him to play another game of chess.

Another game of chess!

And another game of chess!

People were not sure if Rong Jinzhen felt sorry for the lunatic and that is why they played chess together, or whether it was because he admired the other man's skill. Which it was did not really matter – the point is that a cryptographer does not have time to play chess. The fact is that the lunatic got that way in the first place because he became too obsessed with his ciphers – they drove him mad in the same way that a balloon that you carry on pumping air into will eventually explode. When people saw Rong Jinzhen wasting time playing chess when he should have been concentrating on his cryptography, they decided that either he really didn't want to do this kind of work, or he was another lunatic, who imagined that he would decrypt all the ciphers in the world by moving his pieces across the board.

Was it that he didn't want to do the work, or that he couldn't? Very soon, they would get what seemed to be cast-iron proof that Rong Jinzhen was in the former category. It came in the form of a letter from Jan Liseiwicz.

6.

Seven years earlier, when Professor Jan Liseiwicz scooped up his family and relatives by marriage and took them to X country to live, he certainly had no idea that one day he would have to bring these bloody people back again. The fact is, he had no choice: bargaining his way out was not an option. Originally, his mother-in-law had been a very healthy woman, but thanks to her transplantation to an entirely alien country and an ever-growing homesickness, her health was quickly undermined. When she realized that she might very well be facing the prospect of dying far from home, she demanded with as much force as ever an old Chinese person did to go home to die.

Where was home?

In China!

Half the guns in X country were trained against China!

As you will have gathered, it was not going to be easy to satisfy his mother-in-law's demands. In fact, it was so difficult that Jan Liseiwicz simply refused to even consider the idea. However, his father-in-law revealed a thuggish streak in his character – belied by his family's respectable reputation – by putting a knife against his neck and threatening to commit suicide. It was at that moment that Liseiwicz realized that he was caught in a horrible trap; he had no choice but to obey the old brute's demands. It was also perfectly clear that the reason his father-in-law proceeded to this extreme – where he was prepared to risk his own life – was because his wife's demands now were exactly the same as those he was planning to make one day. The knife that he put to his neck was there to tell his son-in-law that if it turned out that survival meant that he was doomed to die abroad, he would rather kill himself immediately so he could be buried with his wife back in China!

To tell the truth, Jan Liseiwicz found it very difficult to understand this old Chinese gentleman's strange determination, but the fact that he did not understand did not matter in the least. When the knife was at the neck and a scene of carnage looked likely to unfold at any moment, what does it matter whether you understand or not? You have no choice but to do what he wants; if you don't understand it you still have to do it; if you find it horrible you still have to do it; and what is more, you have to do it in person. Given the constant barrage of exaggerated propaganda that they were all living under, his family (including his wife) were very worried that he would not be able to come back alive. Nevertheless, that spring Jan Liseiwicz took his failing mother-in-law back to her old home town by plane, train, and finally by car.

The story goes that when his old mother-in-law was lifted into the car that had been hired to take her to her home town, she opened her eyes wide when she heard the driver speak in familiar accents, then she peacefully closed her eyes for ever. What does it mean when they say that a life is hanging by a thread? That is a life hanging by a thread. The voice of the driver speaking in the dialect of her home town was like a knife. The knife descended and the thread that was her life blew away in the wind.

On his journey, Jan Liseiwicz had to travel through C City. That did not mean that he was able to visit N University. He was under strict restrictions the whole way – I do not know if these restrictions were imposed by the Chinese or by X country, but either way he was followed everywhere by two minders: one was Chinese and the other came from X country. The trio seemed to be roped together – they dragged him along between them. Where he went and how fast he got there was entirely up to them – it was as if he were a robot, or perhaps some kind of national treasure. The fact is that he was only a mathematician, or at least that is what it said in his passport. These conditions were, to hear Master Rong tell it, imposed by the historical circumstances . . .

[Transcript of the interview with Master Rong]
You know what the relationship between our country and X was like in those days: there was no good faith to speak of – we were enemies. The slightest movement on either side was treated as evidence of aggressive intent. I could never have imagined that Jan

Liseiwicz would be able to come back, let alone that he would arrive at C City only to discover that he would not be allowed anywhere near N University. That meant that I had to go and see him at his hotel. When we met, I might as well have been visiting a criminal in his prison cell – the two of us were sitting there talking and we each had two further people, one on either side of us, listening and making a recording of everything we said – each sentence had to be enunciated clearly so that all four of them could hear. Thank goodness all four of them were completely bilingual or it would have been impossible for us to so much as open our mouths – we would immediately have been condemned as spies or secret agents; anything we said would have been taken as intelligence. It was a very special time – in those days when Chinese people met anyone from X country they were not treated as other human beings: they were devils, our most hated enemies – the least little thing could be evidence of evil intent, shooting out venom, sending the other to their deaths.

In actual fact, Jan Liseiwicz didn't want to see me, but Zhendi. As you know, by that time Zhendi had left N University to go who knows where. I couldn't see him, let alone Professor Liseiwicz. When he found this out, Liseiwicz decided that he wanted to see me; I had no doubt that this was because he was hoping to get information about what had happened to Zhendi. When I had received permission from my guards, I told him what I could about what had happened to Zhendi. It was very simple and obvious: he had stopped working on artificial intelligence and had gone on to do something else. I was surprised by Liseiwicz's reaction to my words – he looked completely horrified. To begin with he clearly couldn't think of anything to say, then after a long silence he spat out one word: 'Appalling!' He was so angry that his face went bright red; he simply could not sit still in his seat. He started pacing up and down the room, going on and on about how remarkable the results of Zhendi's research into artificial intelligence had been and how he would achieve even greater breakthroughs if he were allowed to continue.

He said, 'I have seen a couple of the papers that he co-authored. I can tell you that, in this field, they are already achieving international-standard research. To give the whole thing up midway . . . how dreadful!'

'Sometimes things don't work out the way that one might wish . . . '

'Was Jinzhen recruited by a government unit?'

'Pretty much.'

'To do what?'

'I don't know.'

He kept on asking, and I kept on saying that I didn't know. In the end he said, 'If my guess is right, Jinzhen is working for a top-secret unit now?'

I just repeated what I had already said: 'I don't know.' It was true – I didn't know.

The fact is that even today I don't know what unit Zhendi was working for, where he was, or what he was doing. Maybe you know, but I am not expecting you to tell me. To my mind, that is Zhendi's secret, but above and beyond that, it is our country's secret. Every country, every army has its own secrets: secret organizations, secret weapons, secret agents, secret . . . too many to name. How could a country survive without its secrets? Maybe it couldn't. Like an iceberg, if it didn't have the part that is hidden under the water, how would it be able to survive?

Sometimes I think that it is very unfair to ask someone to keep something secret from his own closest relatives for decades – or maybe even for his whole lifetime. But if it were not like that, maybe your country wouldn't survive, or at the very least would be in serious danger. That would also be unfair. The one seems to me to outweigh the other. I have thought this way for many years. It is only by thinking in this way that I feel I can understand the decisions that Zhendi made. Otherwise, my life with Zhendi would seem to have been a dream, a daydream, a waking dream, a dream within a dream, a long and strange dream that even he, who was so good at interpreting what other people saw in the still watches of the night, would have difficulty in understanding . . .

[The end]

During his meeting with Master Rong, Jan Liseiwicz repeated over and over again that she should tell Zhendi that if it were at all possible he should ignore all other temptations and come back to continue his work on artificial intelligence. After they said goodbye, Liseiwicz watched Master Rong walking away. Suddenly he decided to write to Jinzhen himself. He realized that he had no way of getting in touch with Jinzhen, so he shouted to Master Rong and asked for his address. Master Rong asked her companion whether she could tell him or not, and the latter indicated that she could, so she told him what it was. That evening, Liseiwicz wrote a short letter to Jinzhen. Having shown it first to his own guard and then to the Chinese one and received permission from both of them to send it, he dropped it in the letterbox.

The letter arrived at Unit 701 according to the normal route. As to whether Jinzhen would be allowed to read it or not, that would depend entirely upon the contents. Given that this was a top-secret unit, the Party inspected even personal mail – that was just one of the many ways in which this unit was special. Anyway, when the people in the surveillance team opened Liseiwicz's letter, they were initially completely baffled because the letter was written in English. That was quite enough to put them on guard and make them take this missive very seriously. It was immediately reported to the head of the team, who demanded a translation from the relevant authorities.

The original text covered an entire sheet of paper but when it was translated into Chinese, it worked out as just a couple of lines. The text ran as follows:

Dear Jinzhen,

I have returned to China at my mother-in-law's behest and so at the moment I am staying at the provincial capital. I have been told that you have left the university and are now engaged in some other kind of work. I don't know what it is that you are doing, but from the level of secrecy surrounding it (including the address that I have been given) I am sure that you are engaged in important work for some top-secret unit, just as I was some ten years ago. Out of sympathy and love for my people, I made a terrible mistake ten years ago and accepted a mission entrusted to me by a particular country [given that Liseiwicz was Jewish, this must probably refer to the state of Israel]. That mission can be said to have ruined my life. Given my own experience and my knowledge of you, I am very worried about your present situation. Your intelligence is extremely acute, but it is also fragile; it would be disastrous for you to be placed in circumstances where you are subject to external pressure and control. You have already achieved deeply impressive results in your researches into artificial intelligence; if you carry on, I am sure that great fame and glory awaits you! You should not let yourself be diverted onto another path. If at all possible, I hope that you will listen to my advice and go back to your original work!

Jan Liseiwicz

13 March 1957

The Friendship Hotel at the provincial capital

It was very clear that the contents of this letter were related to the way in which Rong Jinzhen had reacted to being recruited to Unit 701. Right then, people (at least the relevant project directors) had no difficulty at all in understanding why Rong Jinzhen seemed to be so work-shy; there was someone telling him to go back to his original field. The foreign professor, Jan Liseiwicz!

7

As it turned out, due to the 'unhealthy contents' of this letter, Rong Jinzhen was not allowed to read it. There was a rule in Unit 701: don't ask forbidden questions, don't discuss forbidden topics, don't try to find out about forbidden things. As far as the Party was concerned, the fewer letters of that type that turned up the better – it just caused trouble. The Party was having to keep far too many things secret from its own people already.

As it turned out, this simple method of trying to get rid of the problem didn't work where Rong Jinzhen was concerned. A month later the surveillance team received another letter for him. This time it had come all the way from X country. X country – how sensitive was that! When they opened it up, it was written in English. Looking at the signature, it was another missive from Jan Liseiwicz. This letter was much longer than the first one. Yet again, Liseiwicz was trying to persuade Jinzhen to go back to his original research, and expressed even greater regret that he had given it up midway. He began the letter by discussing various articles he had read in mathematics journals concerning the most recent advances in research into artificial intelligence, but then (as if turning to the main subject of the communication) he wrote:

It was a dream that decided me to write this letter to you. To tell you the truth, the last couple of days I have been wondering what you are doing now and what reward you were offered (or what pressure you were placed under) that resulted in you making such a startling decision. Last night, you appeared in my dreams to tell me that you were working for a top-secret unit in your country and that you have become a cryptographer. I do not know why I have had this dream; I have neither the knowledge nor the experience to be able to interpret what I experience in my dreams and relate it to real events – maybe it was just a dream and does not mean anything at all. I hope that is all it was; just a dream! However, I believe that this dream represents my hopes and fears for you – I am worried that your genius has attracted the wrong kind of attention and they are going to force you into this kind of work. Whatever happens, you must not agree. Why do I say that? There are two reasons:

I. THE NATURE OF CRYPTOGRAPHY

Nowadays many mathematicians are involved in the world of cryptography and so some people have begun to claim that it is a science in its own right; as a result many people have been attracted into the field and some of them have even ended up sacrificing their lives. Nothing that they have done has succeeded in changing my opinion of ciphers; in my experience, regardless of whether you are talking about the construction of ciphers or their decryption, they are fundamentally anti-scientific, anti-intellectual; they are a poison that mankind has developed to destroy science and a conspiracy against the people that work with them. You need intelligence to work in cryptography, but it is a devilish intelligence; every success that you achieve in this field forces other people to become more inventively evil, more fiercely cunning. Ciphers are a kind of concealed warfare, but it is pointless to win this kind of battle, because it achieves nothing.

II. YOUR CHARACTER

As I have said before, you have a very acute but also fragile intelligence, as well as an obsessive character – these are the classic signs of an excellent scientist, but they also mean that you are fundamentally unsuited to cryptography. Top-secret work involves a lot of pressure; it means that you have to subordinate your own personality and demands to that of your work – do you think you can do that? I am quite sure that you can't, because you are at once too fragile and too stubborn – you are simply not resilient enough. If you are not very careful, this work will break you! You ought to know for yourself under what circumstances people develop their ideas. It is when they are relaxed, when they are free to let their thoughts roam, when no demands are placed upon them. But from the moment you first take up cryptography, you are heavily circumscribed; your actions are controlled on all sides in the interests of national security – you are under pressure. It is crucial here to think about what your country is. I often ask myself, what is my country? Is it Poland? Is it Israel? Is it England? Is it Switzerland? Is it China? Or is it X?

Now I have finally come to understand that when people talk about 'their country' they mean their relatives, their friends, their language, the bridge they cross when they go to work, the little stream that runs past their house, the woods, the paths, the gentle wind blowing from the west, the chirping of the cicadas, the fireflies at night, and so on and so forth – not a particular piece of land confined within set borders, nor the object of a nationalist party or demagogue's veneration. To tell you the truth, I have a great deal of respect for the country in which you are living, because I spent the happiest years of my life there. I can speak Chinese; I have many family and friends there, including some now sadly dead. Thanks to my family and friends there – living and dead – I have a host of memories that are inextricably linked with that country. In many ways you could say that your country – China – is also my country, but that doesn't mean that I want to deceive myself, nor that I want to lie you. If I didn't say these things to you, if I didn't point out the constraints of your present position and the dangers that you will have to face, then I would indeed be lying to you . . .

It seems as though Liseiwicz felt with this letter that he had burnt his boats, because less than a month later, a third letter arrived. This time he was very angry and he complained vociferously because Jinzhen had not written back. He clearly had his own opinion about why not –

If you don't reply, it means that you are involved in this work – decrypting ciphers!

His reasoning was simple enough to understand: silence = agreement = admission.

Afterwards, trying hard to control his emotions, he went into considerable detail about his reasoning. This is what he wrote:

I do not know why, but every time I think about you, I feel as though my heart is being run through a wringer – I feel completely helpless. Everyone has some regrets in their life; maybe you are mine. Jinzhen, dear Jinzhen, what has happened to make me so worried about you? Please tell me that you are not involved in cryptography – I have been so worried that it is giving me nightmares. With your genius, with the research subjects that you have picked, with your long silence – I am more and more worried that my dream is correct. Ciphers are accursed things! They are very sensitive, they take the people that touch them and enfold them in a close embrace – it is a prison sentence; they might as well drop you at the bottom of a dark pit and forget about you! Dear Jinzhen, if this is true, then you must listen to me; if you have an opportunity to go back, take it! If you are offered even the slightest chance, do not hesitate: take it! If you have no opportunity to go back, then you must remember the following advice. You can work on any cipher they need you to decrypt, but you must never, ever work on PURPLE!

PURPLE was the most difficult cipher that Unit 701 had ever been charged with breaking. Rumour had it that some religious organization had spent a lot of money (not to mention resorting to gangster methods) to cajole and threaten a mathematician into creating this cipher for them. After he had developed it, because it involved so many procedural steps, because it was so difficult, because there were further internal ciphers contained within the main encryption method, because it was so damn complicated, because it was so mysterious and arcane, the new owners had no idea how to use it, so in the end they sold it to X country. At the moment, it was the highest-level cipher used by the military in X country and hence of course it was also the cipher that Unit 701 most wanted to decrypt. For the last couple of years, the geniuses in Unit 701's cryptography division had been wracking their brains over it; they had worked so hard, suffered so much, thought about it day and night, waking and sleeping; apparently the only result was that people were getting more and more scared to even touch it. The fact is that the lunatic went mad as a result of working on PURPLE. Or to put it another way, the lunatic was driven mad by the anonymous mathematician who originally developed PURPLE. Those who had escaped this fate had done so not because they were so much mentally stronger, but because they were too cowardly – or maybe that should be too clever – to even touch PURPLE. They were clever enough to know what the result would be of beginning to work on it, so you could say that refusing to even touch it was a sign of their good sense. This was a trap, a black hole; anyone sensible would avoid it like the plague. The only person foolhardy enough to give it a go had been driven mad and that made people even more cautious, even more determined to give it a wide berth. Given what Unit 701 had already been through to try to decrypt PURPLE, they were at one and the same time both desperate to crack it and completely incapable of doing so.

Now here was Jan Liseiwicz specifically warning Rong Jinzhen not to touch PURPLE. On the one hand that demonstrated that PURPLE would indeed be very difficult to decrypt and that if he tried, he would not get anything out of it; but on the other hand it also made it clear that Liseiwicz must know something about how PURPLE worked. From the letters that he had sent to date, it was clear that he and Jinzhen were unusually close. If they were able to make use of that affection, they might find a way to make him disgorge some useful information. So a letter was sent back to Jan Liseiwicz, signed with Jinzhen's name.

The letter was typed; only the signature at the bottom was handwritten. It looked like Rong Jinzhen's signature, but it was forged. To put it bluntly – at least in this matter, Rong Jinzhen was being used by the Party. The aim of writing back to Liseiwicz was to help with the decryption of PURPLE – why did they have to let Jinzhen know what was going on when he spent all day reading his novels and playing chess with a lunatic rather than getting on with his work? Besides which, if they had let him write the letter himself, he would not necessarily have come up with anything as good as what they did – the first draft was prepared by five experts and it was approved by three of the directors before it was sent. The burden of the message, couched in the most sincere and respectful terms was simple: 'Why can't I decrypt PURPLE?'

Apparently all this sincerity and respect had its effect since Liseiwicz wrote back extremely quickly; a letter filled with sincere advice.
He began by bewailing the fact that his dream was correct and
upbraiding Jinzhen for being so stupid as to take this path. He seemed
to see it as a sign of the unfairness of fate. After that, he went on to
write:

> I feel an irresistible impulse to tell you my secret – I really don't
> understand why. Maybe when I have written this letter and posted it,
> I will regret what I have done. I swore an oath that I would never tell
> anyone this secret, but for your sake, I have to speak . . .

What secret?

In the letter, Liseiwicz explained that in the winter of the year that
he brought the two packing cases of books back to the university, he
was originally planning to start work researching artificial intelligence. However, the following spring, an important personage in the
newly established state of Israel came to visit him. This person said,
'It has long been the dream of all Jewish people to have our own
homeland. However, we are now faced with enormous problems.
Are you prepared to see your own people suffer any more than they
have already?'

Liseiwicz replied, 'Of course not.'

'Then I hope that you are going to do something for us,' his visitor
said.

'What?'

Liseiwicz explained in his letter: 'They wanted me, on behalf of
the Israeli government, to decrypt a couple of the military ciphers in
use among neighbouring countries. I did this kind of work for the
next couple of years.' That must have been what Liseiwicz was referring to in the letter he left for Young Lillie when he and his family
departed for X country: 'The last few years I have been working on
something very important on their behalf – the troubles that they
have faced and their hopes for the future have moved me deeply; for
their sake I have given up a long cherished ambition.' Liseiwicz went
on to write: 'I was very lucky. After they began employing me in this
work, I was able to decrypt quite a few mid-level and a couple of

high-level ciphers being used by neighbouring countries without too
many problems. Pretty quickly I was just as famous in the world of
cryptography as I had ever been in the world of mathematics.'

That made what happened next so much clearer. It explained why
X country was so determined to help him at all costs, why they took
him and his family away – it was because they were hoping to be able
to make use of his cryptographic abilities. But after he arrived in X
country, things had worked out completely differently from anything Liseiwicz could have imagined. As he wrote:

> I could never in my wildest dreams have imagined that they wanted
> me to come not because they were hoping that I would be able to
> decrypt enemy ciphers but because they wanted me to decrypt one of
> their own: PURPLE! I am sure that I do not need to tell you that the
> moment I can decrypt it – maybe even the moment I get close – it is
> going to be rendered obsolete. My job is to decide whether PURPLE
> lives or dies. I am effectively a signal, informing X country of when
> the enemy is likely to have got close to cracking PURPLE. Maybe I
> ought to feel proud of this; they clearly think that if I can't decrypt
> PURPLE then no one can. I don't know why; maybe it is because I
> don't like the role in which I have been cast, maybe it is because I don't
> like people claiming that PURPLE can never be broken – anyway,
> for whatever reason I have become particularly determined to decrypt
> it. But up to the present moment I have not even begun to feel my
> way towards a method for doing so – that is why I am telling you not
> to even think about touching PURPLE yourself . . .

The people reading this missive noticed a couple of striking things
about it – the handwriting and sender's address were completely different from previous letters, which meant that Liseiwicz was well
aware of how dangerous his actions were – in sending this letter he
could easily have been accused of treason. It also demonstrated how
genuinely fond of Jinzhen he was. It seemed entirely possible that
this affection could be used and so another letter signed with Jinzhen's name was sent to Liseiwicz in X country. In this letter, the
false Jinzhen was clearly trying to use the professor's fondness for his
former student to force him into making some kind of disclosure:

I have lost my freedom. If I wish to recover it, I have to decrypt PURPLE . . . I am sure that after working on PURPLE all these years you can offer me a few pointers to guide me through the maze . . . I have no experience in this kind of work, I need advice; any advice would be useful . . . Dear Professor Liseiwicz, curse me if you like, spit at me, hit me, I feel like a Judas . . .

It was of course impossible to post a letter with this kind of content straight to Jan Liseiwicz. In the end it was decided to send it first to some of our comrades in X country, who would arrange for it to be privately delivered. Even though they could be quite sure that it would arrive safely, as to whether Liseiwicz would reply, the people at Unit 701 were far from feeling confident. After all, this Jinzhen – the false Jinzhen – really was a Judas; most professors would not pay the blindest bit of attention to a student like that. To put it another way, this false Jinzhen was nicely poised between being pitiful and being despicable. Getting someone like Liseiwicz to ignore the despicable features and concentrate on the pitiable ones was going to be quite as difficult as cracking PURPLE. Sending this letter really was just trying their luck; it tells you that the cryptography division at Unit 701 was so desperate at this point that they would try anything.

Well, the miracle happened and Liseiwicz wrote back!

During the next six months, Liseiwicz repeatedly risked a traitor's death to contact our comrades, giving 'dear Jinzhen' a mass of material about PURPLE and suggesting ways to proceed in decrypting it. As a result, Headquarters decided to temporarily create a PURPLE decryption working group, providing the majority of the cryptographers themselves. They were told to crack this difficult nut as quickly as they could. No one had any idea that Rong Jinzhen would be ahead of them all! In actual fact, by this time Liseiwicz had been patiently writing to Jinzhen for the best part of a year, without Rong Jinzhen having received a single letter – he didn't even know the first thing about what was going on. That means that these letters meant nothing to him – if they affected him at all, it was by lifting the pressure a little bit. After all, when the directors realized that Jinzhen wasn't working hard at his ciphers (in fact, if anything he was even worse than before) they could easily have got rid of him as a complete waste of space – but the fact is that the Party decided to leave him alone. They did not need his input. He was going to be the bait that would allow them to decrypt PURPLE.

When people said that he was even worse than before, they were complaining about the fact that he was wasting more and more of his time in playing chess and reading novels; later on he also got into trouble for interpreting people's dreams. Once they realized that he could interpret dreams, he attracted a horde of curious people, tracking him down so that they could tell him about the weird things that had popped into their heads overnight and wanting to know what it all meant. As with playing chess, Rong Jinzhen really didn't know very much about the subject, but he found it difficult to say no to people's faces. Maybe it is simply that he did not have the savoir-faire to be able to turn them down politely. Anyway, he had no choice but to agree. He would take their tangled night-time thoughts and straighten them out into something that seemed to make good sense.

Every Thursday afternoon there was a political meeting for all the people working at Unit 701. They did different things at this meeting: sometimes a new policy would be explained, sometimes there would be a reading from the newspapers, sometimes there would be free discussion. When it was the latter, people would often drag Rong Jinzhen off into a corner and get him to interpret their dreams. There was one time where just as he was in the middle of explaining someone's dream, he happened to come to the attention of the deputy division chief (one of the cadres in charge of raising political awareness) who was overseeing this particular meeting. This deputy division chief was very left-wing, and liked making a mountain out of a molehill – he was the sort of person that always leaps to the very worst conclusions. He decided that what Rong Jinzhen was doing was feudal superstition. Jinzhen was criticized in pretty severe terms and told to write a self-criticism.

The deputy division chief did not have many friends among his subordinates. The people in the cryptography division loathed him and so they all told Rong Jinzhen not to pay any attention to the man – just write a couple of lines and draw a line under the whole thing.

Rong Jinzhen tried to follow this advice but his idea of how to draw a line under the whole thing and anyone else's really did not coincide. When he handed in his self-criticism, it consisted of just one line: 'All the secrets in the world are hidden in dreams and that includes ciphers.'

This is not the kind of thing that gets you out of trouble. He was clearly trying to prevaricate, as if interpreting other people's dreams were in some way related to cryptography. There was even an arrogant overtone to the statement, suggesting that he was the only person who understood this crucial point. Even though the deputy division chief understood nothing about cryptography, he found the idea that something as individualistic as a dream could be allowed to go unchecked profoundly disgusting. He looked at the self-criticism and felt as though each word were pulling faces at him, sneering at him, humiliating him, running wild, throwing stones . . . how could this possibly be acceptable? He was not going to stand for this! Jumping up, he grabbed hold of the self-criticism and rushed furiously out of his office. Leaping onto the back of a motorbike, he drove straight for the mountain cave. He kicked open the steel door to the cryptography division and right there in front of everyone he swore at Rong Jinzhen, using the tone of voice of a much-tried superior. Pointing at Jinzhen, he fired off his final shot: 'You have expressed your opinion; now let me tell you mine: every ugly toad thinks that sooner or later he is going to get to eat the meat of a swan!'

The deputy division chief had no idea that he would have to pay a horrible price for what he said on this occasion; in fact, he ended up being so humiliated over it that he had to leave Unit 701. The fact is that while the deputy division chief was maybe a little hasty, it was the kind of thing that everyone in the cryptography unit was also saying – they found nothing wrong with it at the time; in fact, as far as they could see he had it absolutely right. As I have said before, in order to succeed in this solitary, difficult and dangerous profession, quite apart from great intelligence and the necessary knowledge and experience, you also need a luck that comes from far beyond the stars. The impression that Rong Jinzhen had given everybody was that he simply did not have the natural intelligence required.

Furthermore, he had shown no signs of being either lucky or of creating his own luck. It seemed more than likely that the deputy section chief was right.

There is a proverb in China which these people should have remembered: 'You cannot measure the ocean with a ladle; you cannot tell what someone can do just by looking at him.'

Of course, the ultimate reply to his detractors was that one year later Rong Jinzhen cracked PURPLE.

One year!

He decrypted PURPLE!

Who would have guessed that at a time when everyone was avoiding PURPLE like the plague, this so-called ugly toad was just squaring up to the task! If anyone had realized what he was up to, they would have laughed at him. Sometimes people say that the ignorant are fearless. Well in this case, as it turned out, the facts demonstrated that this particular ugly toad was not only a genius, he also had the luck of one. He had the luck that comes from far beyond the stars. He had the luck that you see when you raise your hands at exactly the same moment as smoke appears above your ancestors' graves.

Rong Jinzhen's luck was unbelievable. You cannot ask for that kind of thing. Some people said that he decrypted PURPLE in his sleep – or perhaps it was as a result of interpreting someone else's dream. Some people said that he found inspiration in the chess games that he played with the lunatic. Some people said that he got the key to the whole thing when reading one of his novels. Whatever the truth of the matter, it seemed as though he had managed to decrypt PURPLE with hardly any effort – that really amazed people, as well as making them jealous and excited! Everyone was excited. Jealousy was left to the experts who had been sent by Headquarters. They really thought that with the pointers Liseiwicz was sending them, they would be the ones who would be lucky enough to decrypt PURPLE.

This was the winter of 1957. Rong Jinzhen had spent just over a year at Unit 701.

8.

Thirty-five years later, the crippled director of Unit 701 sat in the middle of his very plainly appointed living room and told me that when everyone else was using a ladle to measure the potential of Rong Jinzhen's sea, he was one of the few people who still held out any hope that he might ever achieve something. To hear him tell it, no one else at that time really understood Jinzhen in the slightest. I don't know whether this is all hindsight, or whether the thing really did happen the way that he said. All I can tell you is what he told me:

[Transcript of the interview with Director Zheng]
To tell the truth, I have spent my entire life working in cryptography and I have never seen anyone with such a remarkable sixth sense where ciphers were concerned as [Rong Jinzhen] had. He seemed to find a kind of connection with the ciphers he worked on, an umbilical connection such as you see between a mother and baby – whereby a great deal of information seemed to pass directly between them, through the blood as it were. That was one impressive thing about the way he approached a cipher. The other impressive thing was his remarkable powers of concentration and his cold and calm intelligence – the more other people gave the thing up as hopeless, the more determined he was to push it. He really didn't care what other people thought about him. His creative abilities were fully the equal of his intelligence – they were a key part of his personality. In both cases they were easily double that of an ordinary person. When you discovered just how magnificent his quiet achievements were, it was inspirational; but also made you realize how puny and incapable you were in comparison.

I remember particularly, not long after he had joined the cryptography division I went to Y country to participate in a three-month professional assignment – it was also to do with PURPLE. At that time Y country was also working on decrypting PURPLE and they had got a lot further with it than we had – Headquarters decided to send us there specially to see what we could learn. Three people were selected to go, me and one of the cryptographers from my section, plus a deputy division chief from Headquarters – the man who oversaw our work on behalf of the central authorities.

When I got back I heard a lot of complaints about Jinzhen from the directors of our division and my co-workers; they said that he wasn't concentrating on his work, that he wasn't really getting into the spirit of the thing, that he didn't make demands of himself, and so on. I was very upset to hear this, of course, because it was I who had brought him here – I was supposed to be bringing back an expert and apparently all I had managed to recruit was a clown. The following evening I went to his rooms to find him. The door was ajar. I knocked and there was no answer, so I went in. There was no one in the main room, so I went through to the bedroom. I could see that he was curled up on the bed fast asleep. I coughed and walked into the bedroom, switching on the light. When it clicked on, I was amazed to discover that the walls were plastered with diagrams. Some were like logarithmic tables, covered with lines twisting and turning across each sheet of paper; others were more like trigonometric tables, and their numbers, written in all the colours of the rainbow, seemed to quiver like soap bubbles caught in a beam of light. The whole room seemed as magical as a castle in the air.

When I looked at the annotations he had made to each of the diagrams, I immediately understood that he had rewritten the *History of Cryptography* in a more concise form – if it hadn't been for those notes, I simply wouldn't have understood what it was all about. The *History of Cryptography* was this massive fat book – three million Chinese characters – and he had managed to condense it down to these simple annotations using just a few lines of numbers – that really did impress me very much. To be able to look at a body and see the bones beneath the skin, to represent them exactly upon paper – that is the work of a genius. But he didn't even need the skeleton – he had just taken a single finger bone away! Just think about it: think what it means to be able to recreate the whole living organism if all you have is one finger bone!

The fact is that Rong Jinzhen was a genius – there were many things about him that an ordinary person simply could not understand. He could go for months, maybe as long as a year, without saying a word to anyone – it really didn't seem to bother him – but when he did finally open his mouth, he would say something that quite possibly was more important than everything you have said in your entire life put together. Whatever he did, it seemed as though he did not care about the process at all, the only thing that mattered was the result. The results of what he did were always perfect – it was amazing! He seemed to have an uncanny ability to get to the crux of the matter, but the way that he went about it was unique, peculiar; something that you would never have thought of in a million years. To put the *History of Cryptography* up in his own room – who would have thought it? Nobody else behaved like that. Let me make a comparison. If we say that a cipher is like a mountain and that decrypting that cipher is like finding the secret hidden in the mountain, then the first thing that most people would do would be to find a way to climb the mountain and when they got to the top, they would start looking for the secret. He wouldn't do anything of the kind. He would go and climb a completely different mountain and then when he got to the top, he would fire up a searchlight and start looking for that mountain's secret using a telescope. He was a very strange person, with truly remarkable gifts.

There can be no doubt that when he decided to move the *History of Cryptography* into his room in this strange way, he was ensuring that his every move, waking and sleeping, was in some way linked with decryption – you can imagine that each cipher recorded in that book seemed to be breathed into his lungs like oxygen, passing through his blood until it reached his very heart . . .

. . . The first shock I got was from what I saw. However, I immediately received a second shock from what he said to me.

I asked him why he was wasting his time with history. In my opinion, cryptographers are not historians; for a cryptographer to get involved in the history of the subject is stupidly dangerous. Do you know what he said?

He said, 'I think all ciphers are like living organisms – because they are alive, there is an invisible connection between the ciphers in use in history and those that we use today; furthermore, all the ciphers developed at the same period in time have an intimate relationship. Whatever the cipher is that we want to decrypt now, the answer may well be hidden in an earlier one.'

'When people create ciphers,' I said, 'they have to eliminate every sign of their history; otherwise when you cracked one message you'd crack them all.'

'That doesn't affect my basic contention,' he said. 'If you are trying to eliminate history from all your ciphers, that also creates a connection between them.'

That really did open my eyes!

He continued, 'Changing a cipher can be compared to changing a face – it is shaped by trends in evolution. The difference is that the changes of a human face are always predicated upon the same basis – no matter what you do it is still a face, though you may have changed it to make it even more face-like, even more perfect. The changes that you can introduce to a cipher are completely different – today it is a human face, but tomorrow you can make it change into something else – a horse's face or a dog's face, or maybe the face of something else entirely. It has no fixed parameters. But no matter how much you change it, the internal features are simply refined, clarified, advanced, rendered even more perfect – that is an evolutionary development that you cannot escape. It is a given that every effort is made to change the face, but it is also a given that you try to make the internal structure more refined – these two givens create a twin path that goes right to the heart of any new cipher. If you can find those two paths in the forest that is the history of cryptography, then they will help you in decryption.'

While he was explaining this, he was pointing to the columns of figures written up around the room like a hoard of ants. Sometimes his finger moved, sometimes it was still, as if he were gradually working his way through to the very heart of the matter.

To tell you the truth, I was astounded by his idea of the twin paths. I understood immediately that although in principle these two paths had to exist, in actual fact they might well not exist at all. Maybe nobody else realized, but if you treated those paths as strings and pulled on them, the person tugging would in the end find himself garrotted . . .

Of course I will explain what I mean. Tell me, what does it feel like when you walk closer and closer to a bonfire?

Exactly. You will feel a hot, burning sensation. After that, you do not dare to get too close; you want to preserve a certain distance, so that you won't get burnt again. The same principles apply when you get close to a person – the influence that a particular person exerts over you depends on their individual attractiveness, character and capacities. I can tell you categorically, regardless of whether you are talking about a person who creates ciphers or a person who decrypts them, cryptographers are the most remarkable people, with really unusual capacities – their minds are like black holes. Any one of them is capable of exerting an enormous influence upon their fellows. When you walk into the forest that is a cipher, it is like walking through a jungle in which there are countless traps – at every step you run the risk of falling into one and not being able to get out again. That is why those who create ciphers (just like those who unlock them) don't dare think too much about the history of encryption, because each concept, each theory in the history of this field can attract you like a magnet; can destroy you. The minute your attention has been distracted by one of these concepts, you are worthless as a cryptographer, because ciphers cannot have any intrinsic similarity to one another, to prevent them from being cracked too easily. Any similarity would make the two ciphers so much rubbish – ciphers are indeed heartless, mysterious things.

Well, now you can see why I was so amazed – the two-paths theory that Rong Jinzhen had developed resulted in him disobeying one of the cardinal rules in cryptography. I don't know whether he was ignorant of it, or whether he knew and decided to go ahead anyway. Given the first shock that he had caused me, I think that it is most likely that he knew and had decided to go ahead regardless – he was intentionally breaking one of our cardinal rules. When he hung the diagrams he had worked out from the history of cryptography up on his walls, he was demonstrating that he was of no mean intelligence.

He was breaking the rules not because he was stupid and ignorant, but because he knew exactly what he was doing and was brave enough to go ahead with it.

When I heard his two-paths theory, I didn't criticize him the way that maybe I ought to have – I was struck with a kind of silent admiration, not unmixed with jealousy, because he was clearly way ahead of the rest of us.

At that time, he had not even spent six months in the cryptography unit.

I was very worried about him, because it seemed to me that he was in a very perilous situation. As you will now realize, Rong Jinzhen wanted to tug on the two strings that he had found – that meant that he was proposing to become entrenched behind every concept and theory in the history of cryptography, cutting his way through each of the countless layers of evolution to reach to the underlying principles. Every single layer would represent endlessly attractive theories and concepts, any one of which might lay its dead hand upon his mind and turn everything that he had done into worthless rubbish. That is why for so many years there had been one unwritten rule in cryptography: Avoid history! Everyone was perfectly well aware of the fact that – in the history of the subject – there was no doubt any number of opportunities and pointers to help decrypt modern ciphers. But the fear of going in and not being able to find a way out overcame all other considerations – that was more important than any information to be found therein.

If I may put it in these terms, the forest that is the history of cryptography is very silent and very lonely. There are no people there to ask the way from; nobody would dare to ask for directions! This is one of the tragedies of cryptography – they have lost the mirror of history, they have lost the sense of community that comes from planting the same seeds and harvesting the same fruit. Their work is that difficult and mysterious; their souls are that lonely and alienated – they cannot even climb on the bodies of those who went on ahead. At every stage they are faced with closed doors, with mantraps, forcing them to travel by side roads, to avoid any open path. For history to have become a troublesome burden to later generations . . . what an unhappy state of affairs! That is the reason why so many geniuses have been buried within the borders of cryptography – the number is appallingly high! . . .

. . . Okay, let me explain this in simple terms. The usual way that cryptography proceeds is by a slow process of elimination: the first thing that happens is that intelligence agents collect a load of relevant information and you then try to use this information to develop hypotheses – this feels very much like using a limitless number of keys to open a limitless number of doors. You have to design and make the keys and doors yourself – how endless the task is in practice is determined by how much material you have to work with; it is also determined by how sensitive you are to the cipher you are working with. I should explain that this is a very simple and stupid way of proceeding, but it is also the safest, the most secure, and the most effective. This is particularly the case when you are trying to decrypt a high-level cipher. Given the comparatively high success rate, this method is still in use today.

But Rong Jinzhen, as you understand, was not interested in doing it the traditional way. He had gone rushing straight into forbidden territory – in spite of the fact that he was a cryptographer he was immersing himself in the history of the field, standing on the shoulders of the giants of previous generations, and the only result to be expected from this was a terrible, frightening one. Of course if it worked, if he was able to come and go through every trap set by cryptographers of old, that would be a genuinely unbelievably impressive achievement. At the very least he would be able to narrow the focus of his search. Say for example that if there were 10,000 little byroads, he might be able to eliminate one half by this process – maybe less. The number that he would be able to eliminate would determine the prospect of success for his approach. That would decide how feasible it would be to put his two-paths theory into practice. To tell the truth, the success rate for such a thing was so low that very few people tried it and the ones that had succeeded were as rare as morning stars. In the world of cryptography, there would only be two types of people prepared to run so great a risk. One would be a genius, a real genius, and the other would be a lunatic. A lunatic is afraid of nothing, because he does not understand that the thing is genuinely frightening. A genius is afraid of nothing, because he knows he is armed with unusual weapons. Once he has made up his mind to the task, any difficult or dangerous obstacle can be overcome.

To tell you the truth, at that time I was not sure if Rong Jinzhen was a genius or a lunatic, but there was one thing that I was absolutely certain of – I was not going to be surprised if he turned out to do amazing things or did nothing at all; whether he became a hero or the whole thing ended in tragedy. So when he decrypted PURPLE without a word to anyone, I was not surprised at all – I just felt a great relief on his behalf. At the same time I was so impressed I really felt like getting down on my knees and kowtowing to him.

I should also explain that after Jinzhen cracked PURPLE, we discovered that all the suggestions that Jan Liseiwicz had been sending him for how to decrypt it were completely wrong. That means that we were very lucky that right from the beginning, the team working on deciphering PURPLE had decided not to let him know what was going on – otherwise he might well have ended up taking completely the wrong path, in which case he would never have been able to decrypt it. There are all sorts of things where it is very difficult to sort out the rights and wrongs; originally it seemed terribly unfair that he should not be allowed to see the letters Lisciwicz was sending him, but as it turned out, it was all for the best – kind of like dropping a sesame seed and picking up a pearl. As to why Liseiwicz's suggestions were so wrong, there seemed to be two possibilities. One is that it was intentional: he was trying to ruin our work. The other is that it was unintentional: he was making the same mistakes in his own attempts to decrypt PURPLE. Given the situation as we understood it then, it seemed like the second option was the most likely, because he kept telling us that PURPLE was impossible to decrypt . . .

[To be continued]

PURPLE had been cracked!

Rong Jinzhen did it!

It goes without saying that in the weeks and months that followed, this mysterious young man reaped enormous rewards for what he had achieved. It did not matter that he was as solitary as before – living alone, working alone; it did not matter that he carried on reading his novels, playing chess with people, interpreting their dreams, saying little, impassive in company, not caring who he was speaking to – he was absolutely the same as he had always been. The difference was how everyone else felt about him, which had undergone a complete revolution – now everyone believed in his genius, his abilities and his luck.

There was not a man or woman in the whole of Unit 701 who did not know him and respect him. As he walked back and forward, alone as usual, even the dogs seemed to recognize him. Everyone understood that even if all the stars in the heavens dropped from the sky, his star would still be shining there for ever – he had achieved more glory than anyone could use up in the course of a lifetime. As year followed year, people watched his promotion: team leader, deputy group leader, group leader, deputy section chief . . . he accepted it all calmly, with perfect modesty. As they say, still waters run deep.

That was how people felt about it – they admired him without jealousy, they sighed but without sadness. They had all come to accept that he was unique, that there was no one else like him, that there was no point in trying to compete. Ten years later, in 1966, he became chief of the cryptography section – a position that would have taken anyone else twice as long or more to achieve. However, everyone seemed to have been expecting it of him; there was no sense of amazement at his early promotion. Everyone seemed convinced that sooner or later he would end up taking over management of the whole of Unit 701 – the title of director was just waiting until the right moment before it settled down upon this silent young man's head.

It would have been perfectly easy for the thing that everyone was expecting and waiting for to happen, because in Unit 701, as in any secret organization, it would not be easy for the vast majority of the senior managers to take on the heavy responsibilities of the job. Furthermore Rong Jinzhen's impassive and adamantine personality seemed to make him a very suitable choice for the role of head of a secret unit.

However, in the space of just a couple of days at the end of 1969, something happened. Even today, very few people know what occurred in those crucial hours, and so explaining the course of events is the subject of the next section of this book.

Another Turn

I.

It all began with the research symposium on BLACK.

BLACK, as the name perhaps implies, was the sister of PURPLE, but much more advanced, sophisticated and profound, just as the colour black is deeper than purple. Three years before — Rong Jinzhen would always remember that terrifying day, it was 1 September 1966 (not long before he had gone and rescued Master Rong) — the first traces of BLACK had made themselves known. It was akin to a bird somehow comprehending that lurking within a mass of cloud there is a mountain of snow cutting off access to what lies beyond. From his first engagement with BLACK, Rong Jinzhen had a premonition that his attempt to crack it would bring him perilously close to annihilation.

What happened later was exactly that: the tentacles of BLACK spread continuously throughout PURPLE, expanding, growing, just like rays of darkness engulfing the light, thoroughly consuming it. According to members of Unit 701, the dark days of ten years ago had come again, and nearly everyone put their hopes for a resolution square upon the shoulders of Rong Jinzhen, Unit 701's star cryptographer. Three years on, and day after day and night after night Jinzhen was still searching for even the smallest ray of light, but none was to be found: the darkness was overwhelming. It was in the midst of this situation that Unit 701 and the General Headquarters jointly organized a research symposium on BLACK — a low-key and yet grand conference.

The conference was held at Headquarters.

Much like many other government divisions, Unit 701's General Headquarters was located in Beijing. Travelling from A City by train required three days and two nights; there were also flights between A City and the capital, but it was not possible to take these as aeroplanes always made people think of hijackings. Quite honestly, the chances

of an aeroplane being hijacked were slim, but if such a plane were to
have on board a cryptographer from Unit 701, then the likelihood of
a hijacking would increase dramatically, perhaps even a hundredfold.
And if that cryptographer was Rong Jinzhen, the man responsible
for cracking PURPLE, and who was in the midst of deciphering
BLACK, then the chances of an attempted hijacking would increase
beyond measure. You could even say that if Rong Jinzhen was aboard,
it would be best for all concerned if the flight never took off. This
was because if the intelligence agency of X country had managed to
get wind that Rong Jinzhen was on board, then their agents would
have already infiltrated the aeroplane and be waiting anxiously for it
to take off to carry out their insane and brazen actions. This was no
joke, but something that had been learned the hard way. Everyone at
Unit 701 knew of the spring of 1958. It was just after Rong Jinzhen
had cracked PURPLE: a low-ranking cryptographer from Y country had been abducted in just this manner by agents from X country.
Zheng the Gimp was familiar with this case; he had learned of it almost
immediately; he had even had a few dinners with the cryptographer
in question. But now, who knows where this person is, who knows
whether he is dead or alive? This is perhaps one aspect of the cruelty
of the cryptographer's profession.

In contrast, boarding a train or a car is a much more reliable and
safer method of travel – even though unexpected incidents can happen, there are also always countermeasures at hand; there are always
escape routes. Needless to say then, while in a car – unlike on an
aeroplane – one needn't sit and wait to be kidnapped. That said, driving such a long way is rather difficult to endure, and so Rong Jinzhen
settled on the only choice left: train. Because of his special status and
because he carried top-secret documents, he was able to book a soft
sleeper car for the trip; all that was required was for them to ensure
upon departure that a station security official had cleared them a
berth. Of course, carrying out such an action was an extremely rare
occurrence which couldn't help but make Rong Jinzhen feel a little
uneasy.

Accompanying Rong Jinzhen was a man of an incredibly serious
demeanour, rather tall, with a dark complexion, a somewhat big

mouth and triangular eyes. Adorning his upper lip was a longish mous-tache which stubbornly curled up on itself, rather like hog bristles. His stiff mode of conduct made people think of steel wire, and his determined approach suffused everything he did. In many ways, he gave off what seemed to be an aura of death. Saying that this man projected a lethal spirit, a ferocious appearance, is perhaps not saying enough. The fact is that throughout Unit 701, this rather serious man was held in very high respect; he had always possessed a certain power and prestige. But, as people also said, his power was not the same as that of Rong Jinzhen, whose importance lay in his intelligence. However, the man had a very special role to play: whenever a senior member of Unit 701 needed to travel beyond the complex, they would always want him along for the ride. Because of this, everyone called him Vasili, after Lenin's bodyguard in the 1939 Russian film *Lenin in 1918*. He was Unit 701's Vasili.

Most people would say that they had never seen Vasili wearing anything other than his fashionably large windbreaker. His hands would always be stuffed in its pockets. He walked with long strides, full of energy – an awe-inspiring figure, just what you would expect in a bodyguard. Among Unit 701's younger members, there were none who did not harbour a mixture of envy and respect for Vasili. They would often gather together and talk about him enthusiasti-cally – his vigour, his various demonstrations of bravery. Even though his hands were always in his pockets, this only made people speculate fantastically on what lay therein, saying that in his right-hand pocket was a German-made B7 pistol, ready to be drawn at a moment's notice. In his left, a special permit, handwritten and given to him by the Head of the Intelligence Service – some famous high-ranking military officer: all he had to do was take it out and wherever he needed to go, he went; not even the prince of heaven would dare to obstruct him.

Others swore that under his left arm he also had another pistol. But to tell the truth, no one had ever seen it. Still, not seeing it doesn't mean it wasn't there. After all, who was able to look casually under his arm? Even if one was to see that there was no gun there, the young members of Unit 701 would never concede the issue, saying instead with great gravity that he only carried his pistol when he was on assignment.

Of course, that is quite likely.

Most professional bodyguards carry more than one pistol, as well as an assortment of concealed weapons, just like Rong Jinzhen would sport more than one pencil or pen, and more than one book. Put simply, there is nothing odd about this; it is rather quite as it should be, just like people needing to eat.

Nevertheless, even though Rong Jinzhen had this man of extraordinary capabilities accompanying him, he still did not feel safe or at ease. Upon departure from the complex, he couldn't help but sense some indescribable foreboding. He felt as though everyone on the train were staring at him, as if he were the Emperor without his clothes. He was sweating profusely; he was nervous, uneasy, terribly out of sorts, and he had no idea as to what he should do, and certainly no clue as to what would make him feel better. Actually, his state of mind was due in large part to the fact that he was overly concerned with his own personal welfare and the importance of his task –

[Transcript of the interview with Director Zheng]

I've already said this, but the low-level cryptographer from Y country who was abducted by X country's agents could not compare to Rong Jinzhen: the difference between the two was like that between heaven and earth. It wasn't that we were being overly cautious, and it wasn't that Rong Jinzhen was just frightening himself. The mission they were on involved quite a bit of risk. Even at the beginning, we felt that something was a little strange. After Rong Jinzhen had cracked PURPLE, despite everything being kept quiet about his accomplishment, the levels of secrecy on the part of X country were maintained intact, as if they already knew the cipher had been broken. Of course, they would learn sooner or later that PURPLE had been cracked; things of such magnitude cannot be kept silent for long even if we hadn't used any of their secret files. But they *knew*, even though they shouldn't have. In fact, not only did they know that it was Rong Jinzhen who had broken PURPLE, they were also intimately familiar with much of his work. Realizing the situation, all relevant sections and specialists set about investigating the breach, arriving at certain suspicions and threads in the story. All these threads led to Jan Liseiwicz. This was the initial reason for us to begin to suspect his actual identity, but at that time, they remained only suspicions – there was no concrete proof.

One year later, we received an extraordinary report detailing how Jan Liseiwicz and that notorious anti-communist Georg Weinacht were one and the same. It was then that we understood Liseiwicz's truly repulsive nature. We wondered how was it that Liseiwicz had gone from being a scientist to a virulent anti-communist and why he was attacking communism in such a roundabout fashion (even changing his name). That, I guess, is a secret he will carry to his grave. But once the veil was drawn from his true face, his attempts to conspire against us became all too obvious. Perhaps there was no one other than Liseiwicz who truly understood Rong Jinzhen's formidable talent – after all, he had also worked in cryptography, and had feigned attempts to crack PURPLE. Liseiwicz seemed to guess that Rong Jinzhen would follow the same path towards cryptography, sensing that he would most assuredly become an expert. The decryption of PURPLE was, in a sense, inevitable. Knowing this, Liseiwicz had initially made great efforts to prevent Rong Jinzhen from moving into this field, but upon discovering that Jinzhen was indeed a cryptographer, he shifted his efforts towards hindering the cracking of PURPLE. Once he learned that it had been broken, he tried misdirection once again, launching a covert stratagem aimed at ensnaring Rong Jinzhen. I think much of what Liseiwicz did was at the behest of political interests, something he had little choice about. Consider, for instance, that had Rong Jinzhen broken PURPLE right at the beginning, Liseiwicz would have become a disgrace – it would have been worse than having all of his possessions stolen. But the alarm never sounded. At that time, his role was as an early-warning system. How else could it have been discovered that Rong Jinzhen was the man responsible for cracking PURPLE? It had to have been Liseiwicz that put two and two together. He got it right! However, there is one thing that he could not have thought of and that was that his scheme to ensnare Rong Jinzhen would have no effect! You could say that in this matter, God was on Rong Jinzhen's side.

What is more, the enemy's JOG radio station propaganda broadcasts over the next few days spoke evasively on the subject, offering huge amounts of money to 'buy' our cryptographers; such and such a person for such and such a price. I clearly remember that the bounty they first put on Rong Jinzhen was over ten times that for a pilot: 100,000 yuan.

Can you believe it!? One hundred thousand!

According to Rong Jinzhen's reckoning, such a bounty put him up in the heavens and, simultaneously, put him one step away from hell. He realized that since such an amount had been placed on his head, those seeking to harm him would have sufficient cause and incentive; it would attract not a few people. All this left him feeling helpless. This was his mistake, as our security preparations to ensure his safety far exceeded any danger that he might run into. Besides the faithful Vasili, there were any number of plain-clothes protectors accompanying him every step of the way, including those trained in advanced combat techniques. They were all ready for the unexpected. He didn't know about any of this, so feeling himself being jostled by the hordes of people coming and going along the train made him feel really nervous.

Rong Jinzhen certainly seemed to possess a quality that forced him to waste time on insignificant matters. And yet, his remarkable intelligence and divine luck perhaps all relied upon this indomitable spirit to keep at it, no matter how many times he might have to bang his head against the wall. What's more, it was this spirit that seemingly gifted him with a sublime deliberateness. This was simply Rong Jinzhen. Although he had read a countless number of books and possessed an unparalleled breadth of knowledge, when it came to daily life he was completely clueless, unaware of what was happening around him; which made him overly cautious and stupid at the same time. It was truly beyond belief. During all those years, he had only left the complex once, and that was to rescue his sister, Master Rong. His trip to Beijing was only his second time away. In all honesty, in the years that had followed his decryption of PURPLE, his life was not especially stressful and he had the time to go home for a visit, if he so desired. Indeed, we would have made arrangements immediately

should he have asked. But he always flatly refused any suggestion that
he leave the unit. It was as though he were a criminal being watched
by a prison guard: his speech was circumspect; his movements, too.
The thought of doing simply as he pleased had no meaning for him.
But perhaps more to the point, he was afraid that something would
happen if he were to leave even for a short period of time. Just like a
person who fears being locked at home alone and divorced from
human contact, he feared stepping outside his door; feared meeting
people. His reputation and his job were like a sheet of glass to him,
transparent and fragile. There is nothing that can be done for this
kind of person, and he himself made matters worse by nursing these
reclusive emotions, painstakingly cultivating them inside him. There
was simply nothing we could do . . .

[To be continued]

Due to his profession and his overly cautious nature, to say nothing
of his fear that something might happen, Rong Jinzhen was trapped
within a valley of secrets. Days and nights passed in this fashion; from
beginning to end he was like a fenced-in animal. His approach to life
at Unit 701 soon became familiar to everyone: he had a singular attitude – stiff, almost suffocating. His only joy was to pass the time in a
world of the imagination. But now he was on his way to Beijing. It
was only his second time away from the complex and it would also be
his last.

As his habits dictated, Vasili was once more wearing his windbreaker – a crisp beige jacket, very stylish, with the collar turned up.
He looked terribly mysterious. Today, however, his left hand was
not buried in his pocket; instead it grasped a leather suitcase. The
suitcase was neither big nor small. Brown in colour, it was made of
cowhide with a hard shell; a perfectly common travelling safety-
deposit box. Inside, however, were the files on BLACK, a veritable
ticking time-bomb. Vasili's right hand, Rong Jinzhen noticed, was
constantly twitching inside his pocket as if he had some nervous tic
that he was self-conscious about. Rong Jinzhen of course understood that Vasili had no nervous tic; his pistol was in his pocket.
Jinzhen had once inadvertently caught a glimpse of the weapon and
he had overheard what people said about it. Rong Jinzhen couldn't

help but feel somewhat aghast: holding tight onto that firearm had become a habit, a need for Vasili; something he couldn't do without. Taking this thought further, Rong Jinzhen felt a sense of enmity, of terror. A sentence came into his mind – 'A pistol is like money in one's pocket; it can be taken out and used at any moment.'

Thinking that there was a weapon next to him, perhaps even two, Rong Jinzhen felt anxious. They might be pulled out suddenly to deal with trouble, like water is used to douse flames. But sometimes water can't put a fire out. If that were to happen . . . he could dwell on it no further. Meanwhile, the muffled sound of gunshots rang in his ears.

Of course Rong Jinzhen understood that if anything happened, if they were hopelessly outnumbered and outgunned, Vasili would not hesitate to turn the pistol on him and fire. 'Death before divulging secrets.' Rong Jinzhen repeated this maxim in silence. The sound of gunshots that had begun to fade once more echoed in his ears.

This sense of impending failure, a sense that catastrophe was just waiting to happen, accompanied Rong Jinzhen throughout his trip to the capital. No matter how he tried to beat it back, to resist it, he couldn't help but think that the way was long and the train moved ever so slowly. It was not until he arrived safely at Headquarters that his mood began to change and the dread in his heart subsided to be replaced by a warm and relaxed feeling. At that moment, he bravely thought that there was no need for him to frighten himself so in future.

'What could possibly happen? Nothing. After all, no one knows who you are; no one knows that you carry top-secret information,' he mumbled, as though berating himself for his earlier silliness.

2

The conference began the day after he arrived.

It had a grand inauguration, with four deputy heads of the Intelligence Service in attendance. An elderly, grey-haired senior official acted as host. According to the introduction provided, the elderly man was the first director of the research section. Privately, however, many said he was the first secretary and military adviser for official XX. Of course, Rong Jinzhen cared little about titles. The only thing he was thinking about was what the senior director had said – 'We must decipher BLACK; our country's security depends upon it.'

'What we are talking about here,' he said, 'is decryption; but not all attempts at decipherment have the same objective or significance. Some ciphers are broken to ensure victory on a battlefield; others are cracked to demonstrate military superiority; still others are decrypted to guarantee the safety and security of a nation's leader; and others for diplomatic reasons. Some are even broken simply to satisfy professional pride. There are of course numerous other reasons for decryption, and yet, out of all of those many reasons, none truly involve the very security and safety of the nation as a whole. To speak frankly, this extremely sophisticated cipher now being deployed by X country threatens the very integrity of our nation. There is only one means by which we can resolve this precarious situation and that is by swiftly decrypting BLACK. Some people say, give me a place to stand and I will move the earth; decrypting BLACK is where we take our stand. If we say that at present the security of our nation is in a critical situation, that we are being pressured, then decrypting BLACK will be the key to fighting against this threat.'

The emotional and yet stately inaugural address delivered by this solemn and respected elderly official brought forth a resounding chorus of applause. When he spoke, his silver hair moved in unison with his excited gestures, as if it too were speaking.

In the afternoon, it was time for the professionals to give their lectures. Rong Jinzhen was ordered to take the lead, giving a report that lasted well over an hour on his progress towards deciphering BLACK. Unfortunately he had made no progress whatsoever. Later, on the way back to Unit 701, he regretted having publicly shared his own bewilderment at the conference. Over the course of the next few days, he spent countless hours listening to the opinions of other cryptographers as well as attending the two final closing addresses. Taken as a whole, Rong Jinzhen felt that the entire conference had been more of a discussion and not a rigorous research symposium. It had all been rather frivolous and shallow. The lectures had been more flowery speech and clichéd slogans than anything of substance. There had been no meaty debates, nor any cold, detached contemplation. From beginning to end the conference seemed as though it had been floating on a calm sea and all that Rong Jinzhen could do was to blow bubbles – the tranquillity and monotony had been suffocating.

It could perhaps be said that deep down Rong Jinzhen despised this symposium and everyone who attended it. Later, however, he felt that feeling this way was uncalled for; and what's more, it was useless. BLACK, he had come to realize, was a cancer eating at his body. For years he had tried to get at it, and still he was no closer to it. Death now shadowed him, sinisterly threatening him. Those who had attempted to help were neither geniuses nor sages, only gossipers. To think that they could find a cure for this cancer, that they could be the Saviour, was completely absurd, a dream, complete nonsense.

[Transcript of the interview with Director Zheng]

A lonely and exhausted man, Rong Jinzhen would spend his days absorbed in thought, or perhaps we should say fantasy. Every night he would purposefully dream. As I understand things, he encouraged himself to dream every night for the following reasons: first, he had previously grasped that a certain lucidness came with his dreams (some said that it was while dreaming that he found the means to decipher PURPLE). Secondly, he began to suspect that the creator of BLACK was a monster gifted with a form of intelligence completely alien to humankind, and since he himself was human, the only way to get close to it would be in his dreams.

When he first came upon this idea it boosted his morale; it was as if he had found a way out. I heard that he was now instructing himself to dream every night. Dreaming had become one of his responsibilities. His deliberate excessiveness, however, only resulted in bringing him to the verge of mental collapse. One look at him and you could see that all manner of dreams were coming upon him thick and fast, never-ending. The dreams were disorderly, without coherent thought; the only thing they accomplished was to disrupt his normal sleep. In order to restore some normality to his nights, he had no choice but to dismantle the dream patterns he had become entangled in. He took to reading novels and going for walks before heading to bed. The former helped put him at ease, especially considering the stresses of the day. The latter would tire him out. The results were positive. To use his words: reading and walking before bed were his two sleeping pills.

Still, Rong Jinzhen dreamed a great deal. He had taken everything from this world and experienced it in his dreams. In a sense, he had two worlds of existence: one real, the other a dream. People say that everything on land is also in the sea, but not everything in the sea is on land. Rong Jinzhen's situation paralleled this: the things he had in his dreams did not necessarily exist in the real world, but everything from the real world was most certainly to be found in his dreams. I guess you could say that for Rong Jinzhen everything possessed a duality: on the one hand was reality – the realness of things, the living world; on the other, the dream, virtuality, chaos. As the idiom 'baseless gossip' suggests, we only accept the real world on evidence. But for Rong Jinzhen, there was always a duality: the real and the dream, and only he knew of the latter. It goes without saying that his dream world was more absurd, more incoherent, than reality . . .

[*To be continued*]

Now, a more tranquil Rong Jinzhen realized that to hope for someone else to offer advice on how to decipher BLACK, to hope that someone else could put him on the correct path – that was just nonsense from his dreams, an absurdity within an absurdity. To console himself he reiterated, 'Don't count on anyone but yourself, don't hope for someone else to help; they cannot tell you the right path, it's not possible, not possible . . . ' He repeated this to himself, believing perhaps that such a mantra might make him forget the disappointment of the conference.

As it turned out, reciting this mantra did in fact make him feel better; it was not entirely without benefit. Rong Jinzhen was able to find some reassurances in it; four in fact:

1. Attendance at the conference allowed him to see that the Head of the Intelligence Service was immensely concerned about the progress made towards deciphering BLACK and the future thereafter. This made Rong Jinzhen feel somewhat stressed, but it also encouraged him, urging him on in his attempt to decrypt the cipher.

2. Attendance at the conference also allowed him to witness how nearly everyone in his profession fawned over him, either in speech or by deed (say for instance by shaking his hand overly affectionately, or by bowing at the waist instead of just a nod, or by politely smiling at everything he said, and so on). Rong Jinzhen had discovered that in their secretive world, he was a celebrity, loved by all. Before, he had had some awareness of this but had never really been sure. Now that he knew, he couldn't help but be a little cheered by it.

3. At the first drinks reception of the conference, the elderly statesman had made an impromptu promise to provide Rong Jinzhen with an incredibly sophisticated calculator, capable of over 40,000 calculations. Such a gift would be tantamount to providing Jinzhen with an internationally top-ranked assistant!

4. Before leaving, he had bought from the Yesterday Bookstore two books he had long desired, one being *The Riddle* (a translation of *The Writing of the Gods* by the famous cryptanalyst Klaus Johannes).

In sum, then, what makes a trip worthwhile?

For Rong Jinzhen, it was getting these particular items. With these in hand, Rong could happily head back to Unit 701. The train ride home would be free of incident, and free too of men hiding in shadows. Vasili would have no difficulty in booking a soft sleeper car for the journey. Once on board, Rong Jinzhen felt at ease, in total contrast to the journey six days before.

He really was quite happy to be departing the capital. Another reason for this happiness was that the night before leaving, the city had received its first winter snowfall, almost as though it had been arranged as a special send-off for this man from the south. The snow had fallen intensely, blanketing the ground, brightening the darkness. In this wintry setting, Rong Jinzhen waited for the train to depart. The silence of the falling snow and the scent of moisture it carried in the air filled his heart with peace; it was a splendid daydream.

Such a start would have satisfied even the fussiest of people, making Rong Jinzhen feel quite confident that this would be a relaxing journey home.

But what happened was anything but.

3

The trip home was completely different. For one thing, it was two days and three nights, whereas the train to Beijing took three days and two nights. Two of the nights had already passed, and the second day was in the midst of dying away. Except for sleeping, Rong Jinzhen spent his time reading his newly purchased books. It was quite obvious that he felt nothing of the anxiety or fear that had marred his previous train ride. The fact that he could sleep well and enjoy reading was proof enough. A journey home has certain advantages. For their party this was especially so since they had been able to get a sleeper car that had its own independent heating unit, which somewhat separated their berth from the rest, making it a more secure location. Rong Jinzhen couldn't help but feel rather pleased and happy about their good fortune in getting such a car.

No one can deny that for a man who lacks courage, who is overly sensitive and rather cold and detached, to be removed from close proximity to others is a most pressing desire, an overriding concern. At Unit 701, Rong Jinzhen was always taciturn and uncommunicative, always aloof from the world around him. This was how he maintained his distance from people, how he separated himself from the crowd. Whichever way you looked at it, his motivation for befriending the chess-playing lunatic must have been to ensure his own ostracism from everyone else. To associate with the lunatic was the best means to make sure that he was left alone. He had no friends and no one tried to be his friend: they respected him, they admired him, but they weren't affectionate towards him. He lived a solitary life (and even the chess-playing lunatic left Unit 701 when his dementia began to come under control). Most people said that he was untouched by the world around him: he never got close to people, and was always alone and rather depressed-looking. But loneliness and depression did not bother him; the greater torment was enduring the myriad idiosyncrasies of other people. From this point of view, he did not much fancy the rank of section chief, or even the title of husband . . .

[Transcript of the interview with Director Zheng]

Rong Jinzhen got married on the first of August in 1966. His wife's surname was Di, an orphan who had come to work for us quite early, initially as a telephone switchboard operator. In 1964 she was transferred to the cryptography section as a security officer. She was a northerner, rather tall – half a head above Rong Jinzhen – and she had quite large eyes. She spoke a most proper Mandarin Chinese, although she never said very much. When she did, it was in a low tone of voice. Perhaps that was due in large part to her position as a keeper of secrets.

To speak of Rong Jinzhen's wedding – well, I've always felt that it was exceptionally odd, as if fate were teasing him in some way. Why do I say that? It's because I know that in the beginning there were a great many people who were concerned about his marrying someone. Some even thought that they should propose to him, in an effort to somehow bask in his glory I suppose. And yet maybe not, perhaps it was his own indecisiveness, or some other reason. But whatever the cause, whenever the possibility of marriage arose, he always shut the door. It seemed as though he simply lacked interest in women and marriage. But then later, I don't know how, and with very little fanfare, he married Miss Di. He was thirty-four at the time. Of course, his age was not an issue; I mean, he was a little old, but if someone was willing to marry him, then what's the problem? None. The problem came after they were married: BLACK came and stole him away. It goes without saying that if he hadn't married Miss Di at that time, he would probably never have got married: BLACK would have prevented that. Their wedding gave people an odd feeling, just like when you are about to close a window and a bird abruptly flutters into the room: it's a little strange and yet it seems almost like fate, and you don't really know what to do – is it a good or bad omen, something right or wrong?

To tell you the truth, he was a terrible husband, completely unreasonable. He would often not return home for days, sometimes staying away for the best part of a couple of weeks; and then when he did go home, he would hardly say a word to his wife: he would just eat then leave again, or eat, sleep, and then leave when he got up. That was their married life. They lived together but she rarely saw him, and spoke with him even less. As section chief, an administrative leader, Rong Jinzhen was not up to the task. Generally, he would show up at his office an hour before the day ended; the rest of the time he was squirrelled away in the cryptography room. He would even unplug the telephone to ensure that he would not be disturbed. It was in this fashion that he shirked the responsibilities and pains of being a section chief as well as a husband. He seemed to preserve his customary habits and longed-for style of life: a solitary existence – living alone, working alone, not wanting anyone to trouble him or to help. What's more, things only became more extreme after BLACK entered the picture. It was as if he had to hide himself away, that doing so was the only means by which he could find the hidden secrets of this cipher . . .

[*To be continued*]

Rong Jinzhen was reclining in a rather cosy soft sleeper bunk, feeling as though he had finally found a safe place to take refuge in. It had been indeed rather fortunate that Vasili had secured two berths in a soft sleeper car. Their travelling companions were a retired professor and his nine-year-old granddaughter. The professor must have been around sixty years old. He had previously served as vice-chancellor at G University, but because of an eye disease he had resigned not long before. He carried himself with authority, and liked to drink and to smoke Pegasus cigarettes – this was how he whiled away his time on the journey. His granddaughter, who aspired to be a singer when she grew up, spent the time singing, using the carriage as a stage. The two of them, one old, one young, served as a tranquillizer for Rong Jinzhen, putting him at ease. In this simple and unsophisticated space, he felt devoid of any sense of foreboding. Or to put it another way, he was able to forget his own timidity, and he devoted his time to his two most important endeavours: sleeping and reading. Sleep compressed the long dark nights into a dream; reading dispatched the boredom of the days. Sometimes he would lie in the dark, unable to sleep, unable to read, and instead passed the time by letting his imagination run wild. This was how he spent the journey home – engaged in sleeping, reading and flights of fancy. The hours slipped by one after another, as he gradually drew ever closer to the last leg of the trip and home, back to Unit 701.

The second day of the trip was coming to a close. The train was briskly making its way through a wide open field. At the far end, the setting sun was flushed red; its last rays of crimson light had a beautiful, benevolent hue. The remaining sunshine bathed the train in a warming, tranquil light, much like a dreamscape or a gentle landscape painting.

During dinner, Vasili and the professor struck up a conversation which Rong Jinzhen listened to with only half an ear. That was until the professor said in an envious tone of voice, 'Ah, we've just entered G province – by tomorrow morning you two will be home.'

Hearing this was music to Rong Jinzhen's ears, and he asked, 'When will you arrive at your destination?'

'Tomorrow, at three in the afternoon.'

That would be the terminus for the train. Rong Jinzhen joked, 'You two are certainly faithful passengers: you've accompanied this train from beginning to end.'

'While you are a deserter . . . ' The professor laughed heartily. It was quite evident that he was happy to have found people to talk to on the train. But his happiness was fleeting. After a couple of chuckles, Rong Jinzhen once more turned his attention to Johannes' *The Riddle*, paying the professor little heed. All the latter could do was stare at him curiously, wondering whether or not he might be unwell.

Rong Jinzhen was not ill, of course; this was simply his customary manner. Once he had finished what he wanted to say, then he was finished. He didn't drag things out, he didn't switch topics, he wasn't polite; there was no preface, no postscript: he spoke when he had something to say, he was silent when there was nothing to say – like talking in one's sleep, he made his interlocutors feel as if they too were dreaming.

Speaking of Johannes' *The Riddle*, it had been published by the China Publishing House before the Revolution, translated by the Eurasian author Han Suyin. It was a rather slim volume, more a pamphlet than a book. On the title page it had the following epigraph:

> A genius is the spirit of this world, there are few but they are the finest of humankind, they are noble, they are to be treasured. Like any other treasure in this world, they are delicate, fragile as a newly planted bud; once hit they crack; once cracked they fracture.

These words hit Rong Jinzhen like a bullet . . .

[Transcript of the interview with Director Zheng]

Genius is easily broken. This was not news to Rong Jinzhen, nor was it a topic he was uncomfortable with; many times before, he had discussed it with me. He said, 'This fragility is what makes a genius a genius. It is what allows them to transcend all limits, to become ever more refined, like gossamer silk; to become almost transparent, but to be unable to bear any knock.' In a sense, a person's intelligence can exceed any frontier, and from a certain perspective knowledge can easily be seen as limitless. But in another sense, we could say that erudition is achieved by sacrificing a broad knowledge of the world for the particular. Therefore, on the one hand, the great majority of geniuses are incredibly sensitive and learned, but on the other, they are stupid and clumsy, incorrigibly obstinate, very unlike ordinary people. The exemplar of this sort of person was Professor Klaus Johannes, a legend in the field of cryptography, and Rong Jinzhen's personal hero. *The Riddle* was his work.

No one would deny that there was something almost godlike about Johannes' ability; he was beyond reach, a god himself really. Nothing could disturb him. He knew the ciphers behind the ciphers! But in the real world, in life, he was a fool, a fool who didn't even know his way home. He was like a house pet – if he was let out without a collar, he mightn't return. The story goes that he was like this because his mother had been so afraid of losing him that she wouldn't let him out of her sight, shadowing his every movement and making sure he always returned home.

It goes without saying that from his mother's perspective, he was, without a doubt, an abysmal child.

Nevertheless, in the first half of this century, in the fascist camp, this man – this thoroughly sheltered and socially inept child – was known as the Grim Reaper: he could make Hitler piss in his pants at the mere mention of his name. Johannes was actually from the same place as Hitler, born on an island named Tars (known for its gold deposits). If it's true that every man needs to have an ancestral homeland then his was Germany, and Hitler at that time was the commander-in-chief. You could say he should have been serving Germany, serving Hitler's Reich. But he didn't, at least not from start to finish (he had at one time). He was the enemy of no country, of no individual – his only enemies were ciphers. At any given time he might become the enemy of a certain nation, a certain person, but at any other time he might become the enemy of some other country, some other person: it all depended on who – which country, which person – had created and used the most complicated secret cipher. Whoever possessed such a thing was his adversary.

In the 1940s, after documents encrypted using EAGLE appeared on Hitler's desk, Johannes chose to betray his homeland, to desert the German military and switch sides, joining up with the Allied forces. His betrayal had nothing to do with political beliefs, nor with money. His only reason for leaving was EAGLE, a cipher that caused every cryptographer to fall into despair.

It was said that EAGLE was developed by an Irish mathematical genius who had once been resident in Berlin. The story was that during a visit to a Jewish synagogue he had been helped by God to create it: a cipher so sophisticated that it was reckoned secure for thirty years. EAGLE outstripped other ciphers of the time ninefold – this was incredible, unheard of; indeed, it was downright unbelievable.

We could say that the fate that awaits all cryptographers everywhere is that whatever they strive after will always remain just out of reach, always on the other side of the glass. Like the chance of a particular grain of sand from the sea colliding with a particular grain on the shore, the odds are millions upon millions to one: completely impossible. Even so, cryptographers still chase after this gargantuan impossibility. In the process of writing ciphers, the cryptographers, or the ciphers themselves, will invariably encounter certain unavoidable mishaps – akin to people randomly and instinctively sneezing:

it's bound to happen but there is really no way to calculate the numerical probability of when it will actually take place. The problem is that when pinning one's hopes on the possible mistakes of others, one cannot but help feel this is at once absurd and terribly sad. This layering of absurdity upon absurdity, sorrow upon sorrow, has become the fate of many cryptographers: so many – all of them the elite – have passed their lives in this fashion, obscure and unknown, living dark and tragic lives.

Whether it was thanks to his genius or his luck, Professor Klaus Johannes needed only seven months to crack EAGLE. In the history of cryptography it could be said that his accomplishment was unique and never to be repeated: an unbelievable occurrence, like the sun rising in the west, or a single raindrop deciding to fall upwards in a downpour . . .

[*To be continued*]

Every time he thought about his fate, Rong Jinzhen had an inexplicable sensation of shame and uneasiness, a dreadful feeling of unreality. He would frequently gaze at Johannes' photo and repeat to himself: 'Everyone has a hero, and you're mine: all my knowledge and power come from your example and your encouragement. You're my sun: my brilliance can never be separated from yours, never outshine yours . . . '

This type of self-deprecation wasn't due to Rong Jinzhen feeling dissatisfied within himself; no, it was due to the enormous respect he had for Professor Johannes.

In truth, besides Klaus Johannes, there was no one else that he admired other than himself; he didn't believe that anyone else in Unit 701 could break BLACK if he couldn't. He didn't have confidence in his colleagues; or at least his reason for feeling this way was completely straightforward: no one else at Unit 701 showed any sincere admiration for Klaus Johannes. Amid the clattering of the train along the tracks, he clearly heard himself speak to his hero. 'They cannot see your intellectual magnificence, and if they did, they would only be afraid of it. But I cannot understand nor trust their reasoning. To appreciate something that is truly beautiful requires courage and talent; without this, beauty can only terrify.'

Rong Jinzhen believed that only in the eyes of other geniuses could one's own genius be valued. In the eyes of the common man, geniuses were quite likely to be seen as freaks or fools. This was because those with superior intellect had left the common man behind, had marched far off into new frontiers, so far that even if the commoner raised his eyes to look, he could not see them, thus thinking erroneously that the genius had fallen behind. This was the plebeian way of thinking. All it took for them to exclude – to fear – a genius was for the latter to be uncommunicative; they would never realize that the genius's silence issued from his fear and not from contempt.

It was here that Rong Jinzhen believed the reasons for his distance from his colleagues lay: he could appreciate and thus respect Johannes' abilities. He could bask in this giant's intellectual brilliance – it shone over him and through him as if he were glass – but no one else was able to see; they were like stone and Johannes' brilliance could not shine through them.

Continuing this train of thought, Rong Jinzhen felt that comparing geniuses to glass and commoners to rock was particularly apposite. Geniuses after all had many of the qualities of glass: they were delicate, easily broken, very fragile; not at all like stone. Even if a stone were to be cracked, it wouldn't shatter like glass; perhaps a corner or a face would be broken off, but it would still remain a stone, and could still be used as a stone. Glass, however, did not have this resilience: its innate quality was vulnerability; to be cracked meant to be shattered, each shard becoming useless. Geniuses were just like this: all it took was for you to snap off their outstretched head, like breaking a lever in two. The remaining bits would be worthless. He again thought of his hero: if there were no ciphers in need of decryption, what would be his worth? Nothing!

Outside the window, night was slowly turning into day.

4.

Everything that happened after this was totally unreal, because it was too real.

That's how it goes: when things seem too real they become unreal; people have trouble believing them – just like most people can't believe that in any mountainous area in Guangxi you can take a sewing needle and exchange it for a cow, or even for one pure silver broadsword. No one can deny, however, that it was ten years ago, while dreaming of Dmitri Ivanovich Mendeleev (1834–1907) – who had himself been given the idea of creating the periodic table in a dream – that the secret to cracking PURPLE had come to Rong Jinzhen. This was of course an extraordinary story, but what happened next far exceeded it.

In the middle of the night, Rong Jinzhen had been woken by the sound of the train pulling into a station. As was his habit, upon waking he immediately reached out his hand to touch the safety-deposit box that was under his bunk.

It was there! Still chained to the leg of the tea table. Feeling at ease, he lay back down, trying to differentiate between the scattered sound of footsteps and the blare of the train station's public address system.

The public address system informed him that they had arrived in B City.

The next stop would be A City.

'Still three hours to go . . . And then home . . . Home . . . Only a hundred and eighty minutes left . . . Sleep a little more, home . . . ' In a daze, he fell back to sleep.

Before a moment passed, however, the train whistle blew sharply, signalling its departure from the station, waking him up once more. The clacking upon the tracks grew ever more intense, and just as music gradually increases a person's level of excitement, it prevented him from falling asleep. He never slept soundly in any case; how could he endure such auditory violence? The sounds of the train rolled over him, thoroughly waking him up. Light from the moon flitted into the cabin, shining directly upon his berth. The shadows tossed about, fluctuating sharply, tempting his drowsy eyes. Just then, he noticed something unusual out of the corner of his eye. What was it, what was wrong? Making a lazy attempt to ascertain what had happened, rolling it over in his mind, he finally realized that his leather attaché case, which had been hanging on a hook on the wall – a bag very much like a teacher's black briefcase – was gone. He got up abruptly, searching in his berth for it. It wasn't there. Then he got down and looked round the floor, the tea table, under his pillow. It was nowhere to be found!

He noisily roused Vasili and the professor, the latter telling him that about an hour before when he had got up to use the toilet (please remember that it was an hour ago), he had seen a young man in military plain clothes on the connecting platform, leaning against the door-frame smoking a cigarette. On his way out, however, the young man had disappeared without a trace. In his hand he had been holding an attaché case very much like the one Rong Jinzhen had just described.

The professor said, 'At the time, I gave it little thought, thinking that it must have been his case because he was just standing there, smoking; I never really paid much attention to what was in his hands, it seemed as though he were in no hurry, would just finish his smoke and leave, but now – ah, I should have been more attentive.' The professor's voice was full of empathy.

Rong Jinzhen thought it most likely that it had been that man in the military clothes who had stolen his case. Even though it seemed as though he had just been standing there, in truth he had been deciding upon his mark. The professor's trip to the bathroom gave him his opportunity, like seeing tracks in the snow – following them would lead you to the tiger's cave. You could speculate that while the professor was in the lavatory, the man had made his move, he had 'made use of every second and every inch'.

Mulling this over in his head, Rong Jinzhen couldn't help but laugh bitterly.

In truth, cryptography is very much like having to make good use of every second and every inch.

Ciphers are very much like an enormous, seamless net, thus seemingly unreal. But once a cipher is used, they are like anyone's mouth: it is very hard to avoid slips of the tongue. These slips are like rivulets of blood, splitting open a gash, providing a glimmer of hope for those attempting to crack the cipher. Just as lightning splits open the sky, a sharp mind squirrels itself into the gaps, passes into the inner labyrinth of a cipher as if it was a normal corridor, and sometimes even finds access to heaven. These last few years, Rong Jinzhen had used an enormous amount of patience in waiting for the gaps in the sky to open, he had waited through a countless number of days and nights, and yet he still had not succeeded in deciphering BLACK.

This was highly irregular. It was downright strange.

In trying to find a cause for this state of affairs, we at Unit 701 thought about two things:

1. Cracking PURPLE had forced our adversary to grit his teeth and bear the pain, to be ever more cautious when opening his mouth, to be circumspect and deliberate, to ensure that not one drop of water was spilt. It made us feel invulnerable.

2. Rong Jinzhen had failed to detect any errors within BLACK. The drops of water fell right through his hands. And what's more, the chances of this happening were rather high. Think about it: Liseiwicz truly understood Rong Jinzhen; he could easily have warned the creators of BLACK of Rong Jinzhen's skill at decryption and assisted them in developing countermeasures. Quite honestly, they were once like father and son, but now, because of their respective political positions and beliefs, the spiritual gulf between them was greater than any geographical distance. I still remember to this day the moment we learned that Liseiwicz was in fact Weinacht — everyone in our organization wanted to come clean to Rong Jinzhen, to tell him of Liseiwicz's clever ruse, to beg him to be wary. And guess what he said upon

learning about this? He said, 'Tell him to go to hell, this devil in the temple of science!'*

To reiterate, our adversary was increasingly cautious, making fewer and fewer mistakes; thus making it easier for us to miss things. Even if we were less than diligent, it would still have been obvious that our opponent had begun to make fewer errors. We were like an uneven mortise and tenon, echoing each other, nipping at each other, but never quite linking up; there was a heretofore unseen perfection in the network of lies we wove. But this perfection was strange and frightening. For Rong Jinzhen, each day and each night was greeted with a feeling of cold terror. No one but his wife knew what he was going through; for he had told her everything about the problems he was experiencing in his dreams: on the path to breaking a cipher, he was already too tired to be on his guard. His faith, his inner tranquillity had already met with the threat of despair; he was sick and tired of making his moves and sending off countermoves . . .

[To be continued]

Now, thinking of what had happened, thinking of how the thief had kept watch on them, thinking of his stolen leather attaché case, Rong Jinzhen's thoughts became focused on his own vigilance and desperation. He mocked himself: 'I thought of other people – the cryptographers who had constructed BLACK as well as those who had used it – and how difficult it was to get close to them, close to it. Yet it was so terribly easy for me to have my bag stolen, a task that took all of half a cigarette.' He laughed to himself and smiled a bitter smile once again.

In truth, at this time Rong Jinzhen had yet to realize the gravity of the situation, had yet to think about the seriousness of his predicament. Thinking about what was inside, all he could remember was the return train ticket and the receipt for his lodgings, as well as 200 yuan or more worth of food stamps and an assortment of credentials. Johannes' book was in there as well; he had put it in there last night before heading to bed. Realizing that he had lost a prized possession

* This recalls the introduction written by Young Lillie for Jinzhen's thesis.

sent a pang through his heart. Still, comparing these things to what was still safely locked away in the safety-deposit box made him appreciate his good fortune, to be glad he had just narrowly escaped calamity.

It goes without saying that what the thief had desired to take was the safety-deposit box. That would have been a disaster. Now it seemed as though there was nothing to be worried about: what had happened was regrettable and that's all; a pity, but not something to dread.

Ten minutes later, the carriage had become peaceful once again. Vasili and the professor had done much to console him and the emotional upheaval of losing his case had gradually receded. He felt calm. However, once he settled back into the dark of his berth, the peace of just minutes ago seemed to be swallowed by the night, shattered by the clacking of the train upon the tracks. It made him sink into a sea of regret.

Regret is a frame of mind; to recollect means to use one's brain, to mentally exert oneself.

Was there anything else in the leather attaché case?

He turned it over in his mind.

Since all he now had was an imaginary briefcase, he needed to use his imagination to pull open the zipper. But as soon as he began this train of thought, his mind was invaded and harassed by feelings of regret and pity, turning his mind blank, making it impossible to open the zipper. All that was in front of his eyes was a large, dizzying expanse of gloom. This was the outside of his leather attaché case, not the inside. Gradually, the feeling of regret began to subside and his thoughts returned to what was inside. His thinking was urgent, focused; much like the forcefulness of water running off melting snow – rising, pooling together, rising again, and again pooling together. Finally, he tore open the zipper and there was a blast of blue light that blazed in front of his eyes. It was as if an assassin's hand had just flashed before him, making him stumble backwards into his bunk. He screamed, 'My god, Vasili!'

'What is it?' Vasili had jumped up out of his berth; in the dark he could see Rong Jinzhen shivering.

'My notebook! My notebook! . . . ' Rong Jinzhen's voice trailed off.

As it turned out, he had put his notebook in his briefcase.

[Transcript of the interview with Director Zheng]

Think about it: as a solitary person, a man generally sunk in deep contemplation of something or other, Rong Jinzhen gave the impression that he often heard fantastic, astonishing sounds. These reverberations would seem as if they had drifted in from somewhere far, far away, as if emanating from some spiritual realm. But they would never fully manifest themselves, they wouldn't wait for him, they would always fall short of what was hoped for, and yet, without warning, he would encounter them on the fringes of perception. They would come uninvited, appear within his dreams, in the dreams within dreams, behind the words in a book he was reading – cryptic, always in new forms, mysterious in nature. What I would like to say is that these sounds – inspirations, really – would seem to spring from somewhere between heaven and earth, but in truth they came from Rong Jinzhen; they were ejected from his soul, they radiated out from his being, flickering once and then disappearing. He had to write them down immediately or they would be lost. As fast as they came, they left, even their shadows vanished. Because of this, Rong Jinzhen had got into the habit of always carrying a notebook on his person, everywhere he went, at all times; the notebook seemed as if it were his shadow, quietly striding alongside him.

I know it was a 64-page blue leather notebook; the title page contained a top-secret number as well as Rong Jinzhen's personal serial number; inside were his notes and scribblings made over the last few years when he was working on BLACK. Normally, Rong Jinzhen would put the notebook in his top left-hand pocket, but this time, since he had to carry along any number of official credentials and papers, he decided to bring a leather attaché case with him, placing the notebook in with them. The leather case was one that had been given to him by our director upon his return from a trip overseas. It was made of very fine calf's skin, very delicate and lightweight, with a wide elastic strap that you could carry in your hand and hoop around your waist, making it into an extension of your clothes. His notebook was inside. Certainly, Rong Jinzhen never suspected that anything would happen – he didn't believe he could lose it, he most likely felt as though it would always be there . . .

[*To be continued*]

Over the past few days, Rong Jinzhen had gone through two note-books.

He used up the first one four days ago. On that day, he had left the conference early and returned to his room feeling rather angry because of a particularly idiotic and dim-witted presentation. Pant-ing with rage he reclined on his bed and stared out the window. From the outset, he noticed that the sky outside was slanted; he blinked, and yet it still spun. He began to realize that his line of sight was becoming blurred: the window, the sky, the city, the setting sun, everything was quietly slipping away, and in its place there emerged a flowing atmosphere and the sound of the setting sun scorching the sky – he saw the firmament as a formless and swirling mass with hot embers drifting through space on into nothingness. The heavens burnt and darkness swelled up, eventually engulfing him. At that moment he understood, and he felt his body transform into an elec-tric current. He glimmered, his entire body began to float; he had become some form of energy. Like a blazing flame he began to burn, to swirl, to evaporate, to drift into nothingness. Then at that instant, a clear sound rang out, like the graceful resonance of a butterfly flap-ping its wings . . . this was the sound of his fate, the sound of nature, the flash, the blaze, the spritely imp – he had to record it.

This was the moment he had used up an entire notebook, and later he felt rather pleased about what he had written. It was the wrath he had felt that had ignited him, the ire towards that mindless presenta-tion that had inspired him. The second notebook he had filled out in the wee hours of the previous morning. While dreaming and sway-ing back and forth in unison with the train's movements, Rong Jinzhen had dreamed of Professor Johannes. They had spoken at length in his dream, and, upon waking, Rong Jinzhen immediately reached for his notebook to record their conversation.

You could say that on the trail to deciphering some secret cipher or other, passing through the narrow passageways of genius, Rong Jinzhen never cried out in distress, nor did he exert himself praying for assistance. Instead, from beginning to end, he made his way on crutches: one was diligence, the other was solitude. His loneliness hardened his mind and soul, his diligence made it possible for him to reach out to the stars and take hold of good fortune. Luck is crafty: you cannot see it, you cannot touch it, nor can you say for sure what it is. You cannot understand it, nor does it wait for you. If you pray for it, it will not come. Luck is sublime and mysterious, perhaps the most mysterious thing in this world. But Rong Jinzhen's good fortune was not mysterious, it was very real, it was hidden away between the lines in his notebook . . .

But now his notebook had been spirited away!

Realizing what had happened, Vasili became agitated, nervously moving about. He went first to see the head of the train's security, to alert him and his staff to prevent anyone from disembarking; then he used the train's telegraph machine to wire Unit 701 and report the situation. Unit 701 in turn reported to General Headquarters, who then reported to their superiors – on up the chain of command it went until reaching the most senior director. He issued forth the following directive: 'The missing documents involve national security; all departments are instructed to provide whatever assistance is necessary. The files in question must be recovered as quickly as possible!'

How had Rong Jinzhen's notebook been lost? It involved sensitive institutional secrets and it contained explicit information on the problems they had encountered in their attempts to decipher BLACK. Rong Jinzhen had used it to record his thoughts – these most important ruminations on the intricacies of BLACK. How could it have been lost?

Lost!

It had to be recovered!

The train had picked up speed. It was hurrying to the next station.

Everyone knew that the next stop was A City. You could say that Rong Jinzhen had met with calamity just outside his front door, as if it had been long predestined, set in stone. No one would have imagined that so many days could have gone by without anything happening – and now this! It was terribly unexpected, to get all the way home only to have a leather briefcase go missing (not even the safety-deposit box). The culprit behind all of this could not be considered to be someone especially villainous, rather just a damnable thief. It was all like a dream. Rong Jinzhen felt weak and confused; a pathetic, hollow web of intrigue had entangled him, was torturing him. As the train roared ahead, he felt worse and worse. The train wasn't heading for A City, it was heading to hell.

Once it reached its destination, the train doors were all locked. The orders had been given an hour ago by the Intelligence Service. But common sense told everyone that the thief in question had already left the train. He had disembarked once he had taken the briefcase, and that was in B City.

It is well known that if you want to conceal a leaf, the best place to do so is in a forest. If a person wants to conceal himself, the best place is in a crowd, in a city. Solving this case was not going to be easy. Establishing the particulars was going to be harder than hard. To give you an example, to give you a general idea of the features of this case, consider the following.

According to the records of the 'Special Investigative Team' at the time, this case involved, directly and indirectly, the following departments:

1. Unit 701.
2. A City's police force.
3. A City's PLA detachment and military reserves.
4. A City's railway authorities.
5. All of A City's affiliated government ministries.
6. B City's police force.
7. B City's PLA detachment and military reserves.
8. B City's railway authorities.
9. B City's health authorities.
10. B City's Administrative Bureau.
11. B City's Construction Administrative Bureau.
12. B City's Communications Bureau.
13. B City's Reporters Club.
14. B City's Postal Authorities.
15. All of B City's affiliated departments; and a countless number of other small work units and departments.

The terrain to be covered included:

1. A City's train station.
2. B City's train station.
3. The 220 kilometres of track between A City and B City.
4. B City's seventy-two registered guest houses.
5. B City's 637 dustbins.
6. B City's 56 public toilets.
7. B City's 43 kilometres of sewers.
8. B City's 9 rubbish tips.
9. The homes of all of B City's residents.

More than 3,700 men were directly assigned to carrying out this job, including Rong Jinzhen and Vasili.

All 2,141 passengers on board came under direct scrutiny, as well as the 43 employees working on the train and the more than 600 plain clothes military men in B City. The train was delayed for five hours and thirty minutes.

The intelligence services in B City used up 484 hours on this case, equalling ten days and four hours.

According to what people said, this was the largest and most mysterious case G province had seen: tens of thousands of people had been disturbed, whole cities were thrown into upheaval; the scale and depth of this operation had never before been seen.

5.

Returning to our main story (this is, after all, Rong Jinzhen's story, which still isn't over but rather is just entering a new phase). As soon as Rong Jinzhen stepped off the train and onto the platform in A City, he spied a delegation from Unit 701 approaching him – at the head was a rather exasperated and intimidating-looking Director (not Zheng the Gimp, who had yet to be promoted to the post, but rather the predecessor of his predecessor). This was as it should be, thought Rong Jinzhen. Walking up to him, it was clear that the Director had lost all the respect he had once had for Rong Jinzhen. He looked at him with cold, menacing eyes.

Filled with terror, Rong Jinzhen cowered away from those eyes, but he could not escape the Director's voice: 'Why didn't you place such sensitive and secret documents in the safety-deposit box?'

Everyone on the platform was fixated on the scene and saw what happened. There was a quick flash of something across Rong Jinzhen's eyes that died away almost immediately, just like a tungsten filament burning out; then everything seemed to freeze as Rong Jinzhen went rigid and collapsed to the ground.

When the early morning light shone in through the window, Rong Jinzhen returned to the conscious world, and his eyes opened upon the hazy face of his wife. For one brief moment, he had fortuitously forgotten everything. He thought he was at home, in his own bed, and his wife had just woken him from some disturbing dream, her face looking anxious (perhaps she performed this duty quite frequently). But soon the white walls and the smells of medicine brought him fully back to reality; he realized he was in hospital. The shocking memory of what had happened returned and he heard the imposing voice of his Director: 'Why didn't you place such sensitive and secret documents in the safety-deposit box?'

'Why?'

'Why?'

'Why . . . '

[Transcript of the interview with Director Zheng]

You must believe that Rong Jinzhen did not deliberately try to lose his attaché case. In fact, he was always very vigilant. Therefore if you said that this mess was the result of him lowering his guard, or because he was treating the whole thing too lightly, or that he was somehow neglecting his duty, well that would be awfully unfair. But not putting his notebook in the safety-deposit box was a lapse in judgement on his part; his vigilance had certainly left him then.

I remember clearly that before they set off on this trip, Vasili and I had repeatedly requested – had urged him over and over again – to place any secret documents (including anything that could identify him as a member of the Intelligence Service) in the safety-deposit box. And he had assured us that he would do so. On the trip back, according to Vasili, Rong Jinzhen had been very careful, he had placed all sensitive materials in the safety-deposit box, including a book of maxims written and given to him by the Director-General of the Intelligence Service, to secure anything that might expose his identity, especially his particular position, or compromise him. Virtually everything was placed in the safety-deposit box except for his notebook. As to why he left the notebook out: well, that has become an age-old and profound mystery. I believe, unconditionally, that it wasn't because he intended to write in it that he made sure to leave the notebook out; that's not possible. He didn't take risks like that; he didn't have the courage to do so. It's as though there really was no reason for him not to put the notebook away, and although he tried to figure out why after it had been stolen, he couldn't imagine a reason. What is strange, however, is that before it went missing, he didn't really seem to be conscious of having the notebook with him (and even after it disappeared, he didn't immediately think of it). Like a woman failing to notice that she has a needle slipped into the cuff of her shirt until it pricks her; normally you just wouldn't think of it.

But for Rong Jinzhen, his notebook was most certainly not an overlooked needle – there was no reason for him to think of it as being something worthless. No doubt his original intention was to remember it, to think much about it, to ensure that it was not forgotten, to enshrine it within his very being itself. This was because for Rong Jinzhen, his notebook was his most important and most valuable possession. To use his own words: his notebook was the vessel for his soul.

If this was the case, how is it that he had neglected to put away his most precious possession?

That is a most impenetrable riddle . . .

[To be continued]

Rong Jinzhen felt a profound sense of remorse about what had happened, and as though he had stumbled into a mysterious labyrinth, vainly searching for an answer to the riddle as to why he neglected to put his notebook away. At first, the darkness that lay within his mind was nearly impenetrable and brought about an acute feeling of vertigo, but gradually he adapted to it, and the darkness became his means of discovering the light. In this fashion he brought himself towards a most important thought: 'Perhaps it was because I had prized it too much, had hidden it too deeply in the heart of my heart, that I had failed to see . . . Perhaps I had subconsciously come to understand that my notebook was no longer my solitary companion, no longer a real concrete thing, just like my glasses . . . Something so necessary can so easily be lost! For so long my notebooks had been part of my life, they had become part of my blood, a bodily organ . . . I never felt them, just like a person is never truly aware of his heart or his blood . . . It is only when sick that a person becomes cognizant of his physical body; only when your glasses go missing that you discover that you need them: that's what happened with my notebook . . . '

Rong Jinzhen leapt from his bed as though he had been electrocuted. He got dressed and made haste to leave the hospital. He was like a fire consuming its fuel, a man desperately trying to flee. His wife, this young women who stood half a head taller than him, had never before seen her husband act like this: she was shocked, stupefied; all she could do was chase after him.

Because his eyes were not accustomed to the darkness of the staircase, he stumbled quickly down the steps, finally tumbling out onto the ground floor. His glasses fell with him, and although they didn't break, the delay allowed his wife to catch him up. She had just hurried over to the hospital from Unit 701 because she had been informed that due to the stresses of travel, her husband had taken ill and had been sent to hospital, and was in need of care. This was her reason for hurrying over, but she had no idea as to what had really happened. She urged her husband to return to his bed to rest but he resolutely refused.

Outside, he was pleasantly surprised to see his jeep parked in the courtyard. Rushing over to it, he saw the driver hunched over the steering wheel taking a nap. The jeep seemed to have been brought for him to use. Lying by telling the truth, he told his wife that he had left his briefcase at the station and had to go and retrieve it. But he never went to the station, going directly to B City instead.

Rong Jinzhen understood that the thief could be either on the train or in B City – there were no other possibilities. If he was still on the train, then there was nowhere for him to run. That meant that Rong Jinzhen had to make great haste to B City. A City didn't need him, but B City – B City might yet need its entire population!

Three hours later, Rong Jinzhen pulled into the courtyard of the city garrison. From there he learned that he had to go to the Special Incidents Task Force, located within the garrison guest house. The man in charge was a deputy minister dispatched from General Headquarters; but he had yet to arrive. Below him were five deputy heads whose responsibilities had been divided up between the relevant departments of the military in A City and B City. This group included one deputy head who would later become Director of Unit 701: Zheng the Gimp. Upon reaching the guest house, Assistant Director Zheng gave Rong Jinzhen some bad news: the train had been searched from top to bottom and the thief was nowhere to be found.

This could only mean that the thief had alighted in B City!

Without delay, everyone involved was dispatched to B City. In the evening, Vasili himself arrived, initially under orders from Director Feng to escort Rong Jinzhen back to the hospital; but sensing that Rong Jinzhen would most likely refuse to return, Director Feng had included supplementary instructions: if he would not relent in his desire to remain in B City, then Vasili had to accompany him everywhere and ensure his safety.

This is more or less what transpired.

No one knew that Vasili would potentially compromise the very security of Unit 701 and nearly bring ruin upon them all.

6.

Over the course of the next few days, Rong Jinzhen drifted through the streets and alleys of B City much like a wandering, displaced soul. During the long endless nights – nights that would have driven the most resolute person insane – he whiled away the hours contemplating the most far-off things. He had passed through hope and now felt the most extreme despair; the night had become torture. Every evening, his most pitiable fate nagged at him, tortured him and stole away his sleep, and yet the mornings served only to pressure him even more, like burning moxa on his body. He delved deep down into his mind in an effort to recall that day and evening, to censure himself, and to try to understand how he had committed such a terrible mistake. But in truth, it seemed as though everything he had done had been a mistake, and yet free of mistakes: it was all a dream, a fantasy. Tangled up in this bewildering, agitating and yet shameless predicament, miserably hot tears scorched his eyes, drowning him within this torture. Rong Jinzhen felt he was a withered flower, his petals in the process of falling off. He was like a lamb that had lost its way, whose mournful calls grew weaker and weaker, ever more heart-wrenching.

It was now the evening of the sixth day since the incident had occurred. This most important and yet most hurtful evening began with a torrential downpour. The rain drenched Rong Jinzhen and Vasili to the bone, giving rise to a ceaseless cough in the former, and causing them to return early from their search. Stretched out on beds that had been provided for them, the weariness in their bones was not entirely unbearable, but the endless rain outside was tormenting.

The rain made Rong Jinzhen think of a dreadful quandary . . .

[Transcript of the interview with Director Zheng]
As someone intimately involved in the situation, Rong Jinzhen had a unique point of view when compared to the other investigators

assigned to this case. For instance, he believed that the main motive for the theft had to have been money, and that once the thief had taken what was financially valuable, he would dispose of the rest, including Rong Jinzhen's most precious notebook. This perspective was not without reason, and so once Rong Jinzhen set it out, everyone working on the case paid it special attention. Consequently, men were sent out to search all the city's dustbins and landfills. Of course, Rong Jinzhen himself went out to scour through the city's rubbish, taking the lead in many instances, putting his energy into being especially meticulous, even going over the same places that someone else had already looked through.

But on the evening of the sixth day the city was immersed in a deluge of rain that showed no signs of stopping: it howled through the sky and beat against the ground, and soon the city's nooks and crannies were inundated with water. The rain made Rong Jinzhen feel even worse for all the personnel from Unit 701 who had come to search for his notebook, that most precious repository for his thoughts that the rain would now transform into an undecipherable blotch of ink. The rain had coalesced into a torrent, most likely washing the notebook away with it, making it even more difficult to find. The heavy rain drenched everyone with a feeling of acute pain and a terrible sense of anguish. But for Rong Jinzhen it must have been even worse, more dispiriting. To tell the truth, this rain was really no different from any other downpour: it harboured no ill will, and certainly had no connection to the thief's actions; but from a certain point of view, it did seem as though the rain was the far-off echo of the thief, as if the two were in silent collusion, the rain carrying on the malice of the thief, nurturing it, ensuring that this disaster became more intense, heightening its impact.

The rain drowned any remaining hope that Rong Jinzhen still held . . .

   [To be continued]

To hear other people tell it, the rain drowned any remaining hope that Rong Jinzhen still harboured.

With this torrential downpour, it was easy to see how severely this catastrophe had affected Rong Jinzhen. It was as if some unknown outside entity was manipulating the situation, bringing whatever was dreadful and unexpected all into line, to form a freak combination of events; an abhorrent situation. Because of the rainstorm, Rong Jinzhen looked back on the last twelve years, back upon its mysteries and profundities: he saw how the inspiration he received on how to decipher PURPLE, gleaned from a dream about Mendeleev, had in one night metamorphosed him into something glorious and splendid. He used to think that this type of miracle, this form of divine providence, was no longer something he possessed, because it was too extraordinary: such miraculousness meant people dare not seek it. But now he felt that this heavenly intervention had returned, but not in the same form as it once had. Now it was brightness together with darkness, a rainbow together with menacing clouds; it was the reverse of a 'thing' – as though over these many years, he had been circling round this 'thing' but had only seen the 'proper' side. Now, however, it was inevitable that he would witness the reverse.

But what was this 'thing'?

To this former student of Mr Auslander, a student whose heart had been influenced by the teachings of Jesus, this 'thing' could be nothing else but God, the omnipotent Holy Spirit. Because he felt that this 'thing' must be God, it possessed a complicated and yet absolute nature. While it possessed a beautiful side, it also and necessarily possessed an evil side; it was benevolent, but also malevolent. Though it seemed to be only a spirit, it possessed enormous power and capabilities, forever forcing you to revolve around it, spinning and spinning; allowing you to observe all: all that was happiness and pain, all that was hope and despair, all that was heaven and hell, all that was glorious and in ruin, all that was honourable and dishonourable, all that was exultation and grief, all that was good and evil, all that was day and night, all that was bright and dark, all that was proper and improper, all that was *yin* and *yang*, all that was above and below, all that was inside and out, all that was this and that, all that was everything . . .

The radiant and grand appearance of God on the scene thoroughly and decisively put Rong Jinzhen's heart at ease. He thought, 'If this is how it is, then this must be God's plan: how could I oppose it?

Resistance is futile. God's laws are just. God would not change these laws to satisfy the aspirations of any man. God's ultimate plan is to make clear to everyone the beauty of all creation.' God had shown the nature of everything to Rong Jinzhen by means of PURPLE and BLACK –

All that was happiness and pain.
All that was hope and despair.
All that was heaven and hell.
All that was glorious and in ruin.
All that was honourable and dishonourable.
All that was exultation and grief.
All that was good and evil.
All that was day and night.
All that was bright and dark.
All that was proper and improper.
All that was *yin* and *yang*.
All that was above and below.
All that was inside and out.
All that was this and that.
All that was everything . . .

Upon hearing these parallel slogans issue forth from deep inside, Rong Jinzhen calmly and serenely turned his eyes away from the downpour still raging outside. Whether it stopped raining or not seemed no longer to matter: the sound of the rain was no longer unbearable. When he lay down, the sound of the rain was amiable, so pure and unadulterated, so mild and gentle, he was entranced by it; he felt himself dissolving into it. He slept and dreamed. Within his dream he heard a far-off call – 'You still have this superstitious faith in God . . . God is a coward . . . God never gave Johannes a perfect life . . . And don't tell me that God's laws are just . . . God's laws are entirely unjust . . .'

The last phrase repeated over and over in his mind, the voice getting louder and louder; finally sounding like lightning cracking in his ears, forcing him awake – and yet he still heard the voice linger in his ears: 'Unjust – unjust – unjust . . .'

He didn't recognize who or what spoke these lines, and he certainly didn't know why it had wanted to speak these mysterious words to him – '"God's laws are unjust!" All right, let's say they are unjust, but then what?' He began to ponder. But whether it was from the pounding in his head or from some unconscious worry or unknown fear he harboured, his thoughts were uncoordinated and unfocused. Every starting point drifted out of reach, like a headless dragon not knowing which way to go. A quarrelsome cacophony raged in his head: his mind was like a pot of boiling water, bubbling and gurgling. But if you removed the lid you would discover nothing of value inside. His mind was simply going through the motions; nothing of substance was happening. A moment later, the mental undulation ceased – as if food had been put in the pot to cook. Then memories of the train ride, the thief, his leather attaché case, the rainstorm rolled over him in succession, bringing into the frame once more his own personal doom. But this time, Rong Jinzhen did not understand the significance of these memories – as if the food had yet to be fully cooked. Later, the memories pressed themselves upon him once more – like the pot beginning to slowly boil again. But now the pot was no longer empty. His mind was beginning to become excited, as a mariner is once he sees land after a long sea voyage. Moving at full throttle towards his destination, moving ever closer, Rong Jinzhen once again heard that mysterious voice speak to him: 'Allowing this accident to herald catastrophe for you, to beat you down, how is that just?'

'Noooooo – !' Rong Jinzhen roared, smashing through the door and rushing out into the downpour, assailing the darkness with invective: 'God, you have been unjust to me! God, I want to let BLACK defeat me! Only by letting BLACK defeat me can there be justice! God, only the vilest person need suffer such unfairness! God, only the vilest divinity could force me to suffer such blame! Oh wicked Lord, you shouldn't do this! Oh vicious God, I will fight you to the bitter end – !'

After this raging outburst, Rong Jinzhen felt as though the freezing rain were burning him, and his blood began to gurgle and flow forth, making him realize the rain too was gushing. As this thought flashed in his mind, he soon felt that his entire body was streaming forth, becoming one with the sky and the earth, drop by drop melting into them, like air together with cloud, like dream together with fantasy. It was then that he heard once more that faint, indiscernible voice from somewhere beyond. It was as if this most pitiable sound issued forth from his lost notebook, in the dirt and the mud, miserable and desperate, appearing and disappearing, intermittently crying out: 'Rong Jinzhen, listen . . . the rainwater is surging, turning the ground into a bubbling mass . . . even though the water may have carried your notebook away, it might also carry it back to you . . . back to you . . . after everything that has happened, why can't this also happen . . . even though the water may have carried your notebook away, it might also carry it back to you . . . back to you . . . back to you . . . back to you . . . '

This was the final strange thought Rong Jinzhen had.

It was an eerie and evil night.

Outside the window the sound of the rain was indomitable, unceasing.

7

This part of the story will make people feel both inspired and sorrowful. It is inspiring because Rong Jinzhen's notebook will finally be found, sorrowful because Rong Jinzhen will disappear without a trace. Taken altogether, this outcome is what Rong Jinzhen spoke about: God gives us happiness and also suffering; God reveals everything to us.

Rong Jinzhen disappeared the very same evening of the torrential downpour. No one really knew exactly when he stepped out of his room, whether it was early or late in the night, during the rainstorm or after. But everyone knew that he wouldn't return – like a bird that for ever leaves its mother's nest, or like a circling star for ever torn from its orbit.

Rong Jinzhen's disappearance caused the case to become more complicated and confused. One person suggested that perhaps his disappearance was the next stage in the case of the missing notebook, that the operation was a two-step procedure. The identity of the thief now became more mysterious and sinister. However, more people believed that Rong Jinzhen's disappearance was due to his lack of hope, his inability to withstand the fear and pain of what had happened. Everyone knew that ciphers were Rong Jinzhen's life, and that meant that his notebook was too. Now hope of finding his notebook was slowly but surely fading – even if it were located, it would most likely be nothing more than a water-soaked ink smudge. There was no way that he could take a lighter view of what had happened; suicide no longer seemed impossible.

What happened afterwards seemed to confirm everyone's misgivings. One afternoon, along the eastern side of the river that made its way through B City, close to an oil refinery, a leather shoe was picked up. Vasili identified it immediately as belonging to Rong Jinzhen because of its stretched mouth, caused by all the recent rushing about in search of the notebook.

It was at this time that Vasili began to believe that their efforts to find Rong Jinzhen would in truth result in nothing. Dejected, he couldn't help but feel that they would never find the notebook either. Perhaps all that they would find would be Rong Jinzhen's corpse floating down a muddy torrent.

If things turned out this way, Vasili conjectured, then it would have been better had he taken Rong Jinzhen home at the beginning. The whole situation seemed to be hanging over his head like an evil sword of Damocles.

'Fuck it all!' Holding Rong Jinzhen's dirtied shoe in his hand, he couldn't help but violently fling it as far away as possible, as if he were attempting to do away with all of the bad luck that had hung over these past days.

This all transpired on the ninth day of the investigation. No information had come to light about the missing notebook, which couldn't help but make people lose heart; the shadow of despair began to entrench itself in people's minds, growing and expanding, consuming all hope. Because of this, Headquarters agreed with the investigators and decided to publicize what had happened instead of keeping it a secret.

The following day, in the morning edition of the *B City Daily*, a lost-property notice was printed and widely circulated. The person in search of the missing item was identified as a scientist; the notebook that had been lost contained information on certain new technological innovations the nation had been working on.

We should say that carrying out this sort of action was exceptionally risky due to the fact that the thief could, upon learning of this public search, either hide the notebook away or destroy it, causing the investigators' work to reach an impasse. However, contrary to expectations, that evening at precisely 22:03, the telephone hotline at the Special Investigative Team's office rang. Three hands immediately reached out to grab the phone, but Vasili, being exceptionally nimble, took hold of it first: 'Hello, this is the Offices of the Special Investigative Division, please state your information.'

'. . .'

'Hello, hello, is anyone there? Please speak.'

'Ah, ah, ah . . .'

The telephone went dead.

Crestfallen, Vasili returned the receiver to its base, feeling as though he had been making a mountain out of a molehill.

A minute later the telephone rang again.

Yet again Vasili grabbed the receiver first. When he said hello, he immediately heard a hurried and agitated voice issuing from the phone: 'The note . . . notebook . . . is in a letterbox . . . '

'A letterbox? Where? Hello, what letterbox?'

'Ah, ah, ah . . . '

Again the phone went dead.

This vile thief; this pathetic and yet somehow adorable little thief. Because the thief was so terribly flustered, as you can imagine, he was unable to finish telling them exactly which letterbox the notebook was in. But no matter, this was enough, quite enough. B City possessed only a few hundred letterboxes, and what did this matter? Luck had finally arrived, for in the first letterbox Vasili opened he discovered –

Under the starlight, the notebook exuded a blue serene glow, a deep quiet that made you a little afraid. But that quiet was perfect, inspiring, like a frozen ocean beginning to thaw, like an ever-so-valuable sapphire.

The notebook was completely unscathed, save for a few pages torn out of the back. An official at Headquarters couldn't help but humorously remark over the phone: 'Perhaps that thief used them to wipe his dirty arse.'

Later, another senior official at Headquarters, upon hearing this, furthered the image: 'If you ever find that little prick, give him some toilet paper; you have that at Unit 701, no?'

But no one was ever assigned the task of finding the thief.

Because, after all, he wasn't a traitor.

And because Rong Jinzhen had not yet been found.

The next day, in the *B City Daily*'s main edition, a missing person's report was printed. It was for Rong Jinzhen:

Rong Jinzhen, male, thirty-seven years of age, 1.65 metres tall, thin stature, pale skin. He was last seen wearing a pair of brown near-sighted spectacles, a blue-green Sun Yat-sen jacket and light-grey trousers. His breast pocket held a fountain pen (imported). Around his wrist was a Zhongshan watch. He speaks Mandarin Chinese and English, loves to play chess, his movements are always slow and exact, and it is possible that he is missing one shoe.

On the first day after the missing person's report, there was no news; the same for the second day.

On the third day, the *G Provincial Daily* also printed the missing person's report; there was still no news on that day.

According to Vasili, no news was quite as expected: after all, expecting news from a dead person was rather optimistic. But Vasili had already sensed deep down that he would eventually bring a living Rong Jinzhen back to Unit 701 – this was his duty – it was also an already exceptionally exigent affair.

Two days later, in the afternoon, the Special Investigative Office informed him that a man from M county had just telephoned to say that they had seen a man matching Rong Jinzhen's description hanging about and that they should hurry over and see as quickly as possible.

A man matching Rong Jinzhen's description? Vasili thought that his premonition had come true. Before heading out, the normally staunch and ferocious Vasili broke down like a coward and cried.

The main town in M county was about 100 kilometres to the north of B City. How Rong Jinzhen had managed to make his way over such a distance to look for his notebook left people feeling especially strange. While on the road, Vasili took stock of all that had happened; his heart was filled with listlessness, a mournfulness that made it hard for him to know what to think.

Arriving at M county, he did not make his way directly to the man who had made the call; rather, upon passing a paper mill, Vasili spied a man in the factory's pile of waste paper who caught his interest. The man was unusually conspicuous, and upon closer inspection you could see that he had problems, that he wasn't *normal*. His body was covered in filth. His feet were bare and they had a bluish-black tinge to them. Both his hands were bloodied, but the man kept sifting through the rubbish just the same, turning over mound after mound of refuse. Each torn and frayed book he discovered went through meticulous and exacting scrutiny. His eyes blurred, he mumbled continuously, he had the look of misfortune about him, and extreme piety – like a Taoist abbot who has suffered through calamity and is now standing in the midst of the ruins of his temple solemnly and tragically searching for his holy scriptures.

This all happened in the afternoon, under a winter sun, with the rays of sunshine beating over this pitiable man –

Beating over his bloodied hands.

Beating over his bent knees.

Beating over his crooked waist.

Beating over his deformed cheeks.

His mouth.

IIis nose.

His spectacles.

His eyes.

Gazing upon this man, on his black, trembling hands, Vasili's eyes began to dilate, to expand; at the same time his feet carried him forward. He had recognized that this most pitiable man was Rong Jinzhen.

Rong Jinzhen – !

Vasili found him on the sixteenth day after the briefcase had gone missing, on 3 January 1970, at four in the afternoon.

On 14 January 1970, late in the afternoon, in the care of Vasili, Rong Jinzhen, this now broken and tormented man, was brought back to the high-walled compound of Unit 701, thus bringing to a close this part of the story.

In the End

I.

Endings are also beginnings.

For this fifth section – a follow-up report, as it were – I want to provide some supplementary details about Rong Jinzhen's life.

I feel this current section functions much like a pair of hands behind the scenes, one touching upon the past of the story, the other stretching out towards the future. Both hands have been extremely industrious; they have stretched out very far and very wide. They have been fortunate; they have touched upon something very real, very exciting – something akin to finally catching hold of a long-sought-after answer to a rather troublesome riddle. In fact, all the various mysteries and secrets included in the previous four sections, even though they might have lacked a certain splendour, will have their true brilliance revealed in what follows.

What is more, this division purposefully disregards plot and narrative conventions; it disregards literary mood. I make no attempt to present a unified, coherent story. My intention has been rather skewed and varied. It may seem that this section endeavours to challenge traditional literary norms, but in truth I am only surrendering to the vicissitudes of Rong Jinzhen's story. What's strange, however, is that after I decided to surrender to his tale, to set myself at its mercy, I felt profoundly at ease, terribly satisfied, as though I had won some victory in battle.

But surrender is not the same as giving up! Upon reading this entire section, I hope you will come to realize that the revelations presented herein were provided by the creator of BLACK. Ah, but perhaps I've said too much. Still, to be honest, this is how it is: the pages that follow pulled me this way and that – and they will do the same to you. It's as though by witnessing Rong Jinzhen fall into madness, I too have gone mad.

Back to business . . .

In fact, there have been some people who have raised suspicions about the veracity of this story. Their suspicions provoked me to write this final part.

I used to think that lulling the reader into believing that a story was actually real wasn't the most essential aim in writing fiction; it was something you could do without. But this story . . . this particular tale, well, it requires this belief, it hungers to be trusted. That's because, in the end, it is unquestionably a real story. In order to preserve this original essence, I've had to take many risks, most notably with the plot. Oh, I could have relied on my imagination and spun an elaborate tale to tie up all the loose ends, or even employed some convenient narrative sleight of hand to finish things up. But an intense desire – a passion – to protect the spirit of the story prevented me from taking this route. Therefore I can say that, if the story seems to suffer from some chronic malaise, the roots of this disease do not emanate from this lowly narrator, but rather from the characters and the lives they lived. This of course is not wholly beyond the realm of imagination. After all, logically speaking – or, let's say, to speak from experience – the possibility that one will encounter some altogether unforeseeable chronic illness is a very real one. There is really nothing one can do.

I must stress, therefore, that this story is historical; it is not some imaginary tale. What I have written has been gleaned from the taped transcripts I have obtained; the factual core remains intact. You can understand – and I hope forgive me – for adding some narrative framing and fictional elements such as personal names and places, and of course the descriptions of the skies, the landscapes. There may be some errors regarding the exact times when events took place; of course, certain parts of the story that are still classified have been omitted; at times I may have overdone things with respect to the inner thoughts of the characters. But I had no choice in this matter. After all, Rong Jinzhen was a man thoroughly absorbed in a fantasy world: he did nothing but crack various ciphers, and because this work was top secret, the general public couldn't know about it. That's how it is.

Additionally, I must admit that it wasn't Vasili who ultimately discovered Rong Jinzhen at the paper mill, or printing works, or wherever it was in M county. Rather it was the Director of Unit 701 who personally saw to the matter: he brought Rong Jinzhen home. Vasili, over the course of those few days and because of the strain of what had happened, had actually fallen dreadfully ill and could do very little. The Director, however, died ten years ago. Furthermore, even before he passed away, he would, by all accounts, refrain from raising the issue of what had happened then, almost as if he felt sorry for Rong Jinzhen. Some people said it was because he felt guilty about how he had treated Rong Jinzhen's madness, and as death drew near, he blamed himself very much. I'm not sure if he was right to feel guilty or not; all I know is that his self-recrimination made me feel even more regret for how things turned out for Rong Jinzhen.

Getting back to our story, there was one other person who had accompanied the Director on that fateful day: his chauffeur. People said that he was a very accomplished driver but functionally illiterate. Hence we can't be sure if it was a 'printing works' or a 'paper mill' where they found Rong Jinzhen. From the exterior, they both look very much the same, and for an illiterate person who had only seen things in passing, failing to distinguish between the two is quite to be expected. In my discussions with him, I was initially at great pains to help him understand that there are distinct differences between a paper mill and a printing works. For instance, the former would have several towering smokestacks whereas the latter would not. With respect to smells, a printing works would have the distinct odour of printing ink hanging in the air, whereas a paper mill would simply have turbid water spewing forth; there would be a decided lack of any pungent odour. Despite this explanation, however, the driver still could not provide me with precise details. Instead, his speech remained consistently evasive and unclear. Sometimes I thought that his equivocation was probably due to the difference between those who are educated and those who are not. For those less educated, judging what is real and what is not, what is right and what is wrong, must be fraught with difficulties and obstacles. And for this doddering, senile old man, whose love of tobacco and drink had eaten away at his memory – a decrepitude that would terrify the stoutest individual – speaking about something that had happened decades back was extremely difficult. But he was adamant that the incident took place in 1967 and not in 1969. Needless to say, this mistake made me doubt him all the more. As a result, for the ending, I decided I might as well take some liberties and have Vasili be the one who made his way to M county to find Rong Jinzhen and bring him home.

I have given you these details as I felt the episode needed clarification.

I have to accept that the ending is the most unreal part of the entire story.

I sometimes feel regret for having fabricated it so.

The second reason for me to write this final section was that some people have shown great interest in finding out about what happened to Rong Jinzhen after he returned to Unit 701. This has served as encouragement for me.

This concern also implies that you, my reader, would like me to tell you how I understand Rong Jinzhen's story. How I appreciate his tale.

I couldn't be happier to tell you.

To tell you the truth, I came to learn of this story because of my father's medical condition. In the spring of 1990, my then 75-year-old father suffered a paralysing stroke and had to be admitted to hospital. Because treatment proved ineffective, he was transferred to a nursing home in Lingshan County in Guangxi. You could say that this wasn't really a nursing home, but rather a hospice where the only concern was for the patients to quietly and peacefully wait for death.

That winter, I paid a visit to my poor father and discovered that the pain and torment of his condition over the last year had mellowed him enormously. He was much kinder and more loving towards me, and much given to entertaining conversation. It was plain to see that he was hoping that repetition would convince me of his fatherly affection. In all honesty, it wasn't necessary for him to act in this manner. Both of us already knew that the time for him to show this sort of affection had passed. When I had needed him, he wasn't there – perhaps he never thought that this day would come, or perhaps there was some other reason: whatever the case may be, I have to admit that he never really loved me as a father should. It did not matter though. I wouldn't hold it against him now and try to exact some form of revenge. I wouldn't let it influence my sense of duty concerning how I should love and respect him in his final days.

To be honest, I was greatly opposed to having him transferred to this particular nursing home in the first place, but my father had insisted on it most vociferously. I simply couldn't change his mind. I understood, too, why he was adamant about coming here. He was worried that my wife and I would soon grow to hate having to take care of him day in and day out had he remained closer to home. It was a humiliation that he could do without. Of course, the possibility of this happening was not altogether remote – long-term sickness can weaken the resolve of even the most filial son. Nevertheless, I thought that there could be other possibilities; seeing him bedridden, perhaps we would have sympathized more, become even more filial. But in all honesty, it was hard to endure listening to my father prattle on about his past embarrassments and regrets. Only when the conversation shifted to the bizarre and odd stories he had heard the other patients tell did I become attentive and eager to hear more. I was especially enthralled by the story of Rong Jinzhen. By the time I visited him, my father was quite familiar with the tale. After all, they shared the same ward – they were practically neighbours.

My father told me that Rong Jinzhen had already been a resident of the Lingshan County nursing home for several decades. Without exception, everyone knew him and understood who he was. Upon arrival, every new patient received a special welcoming gift: Rong Jinzhen's story. Discussing his great talents, the highs and lows of his life, had become the order of the day. Everyone enjoyed talking about him out of reverence and because he was so truly exceptional. I soon realized that all the patients in the nursing home had the highest regard for Rong Jinzhen. In each and every place he appeared, it didn't matter where, the people who saw him would immediately stop what they were doing, their gaze fixed upon him. If necessary, they would give way, smiling at him ever so slightly. But in spite of all of this, it is quite likely that Rong Jinzhen was completely oblivious to what happened round him. When the doctors and nurses were with him, the other patients couldn't help but notice how they would treat him as though he were a member of their own family, or perhaps some senior official. And so it was in this reverential manner that Rong Jinzhen, this clearly mentally handicapped man, lived out his days. In all my life I have never seen anything like it. Only once on television did I see something similar, and that was the care given to Einstein's British heir, Stephen Hawking.

I spent three days at the nursing home. While I was there, I discovered that during the day the patients were all given some free time to do as they pleased. Some would congregate together and play chess or cards. Some would stroll about, or just sit and chat. The doctors and nurses would eventually appear to perform check-ups or administer medicine. They would, as a rule, blow sharply on their whistles to urge the patients to return to their rooms. Only Rong Jinzhen would always remain in his room, speechless and uncommunicative. Even for meals and for exercise someone had to go and call on him, otherwise he wouldn't venture beyond his door. He behaved just as he had in those early days working in Unit 701, holed up in the cryptography room. For this reason, the day-shift nurses were given an additional responsibility: they had to be sure to go and collect Rong Jinzhen for his three daily meals and accompany him for thirty-minute walks after each repast. My father told me that in the beginning, when Rong Jinzhen first arrived at the nursing home, no one knew about his past and so some of the nurses resented giving him this special treatment. As a result, they wouldn't always perform their duties, and Rong Jinzhen would often go hungry. Later, a very senior official paid a visit to the nursing home and happened to discover the poor treatment he was receiving. He summarily called all the doctors and nurses together and warned them: 'If you have elderly parents at home, then how you would treat them is how you should treat him; if you have only children at home, then how you would treat your own children is how you should treat him; if you have no family, then treat him exactly as you would treat me.'

Afterwards, the glories and misfortunes of Rong Jinzhen's life slowly came out, and at the same time the manner in which he was cared for changed. He was now treated as someone to be treasured; no one dared to slight him – they all handled him with the utmost care and respect. My father said that he was sure that if it were not for the nature of the work that he had done, he would have already become a household name, a hero. His miraculous achievements would be eulogized for generation after generation.

I replied, 'But why should someone's former profession dictate how he is to be treated at hospital? He should receive that kind of treatment anyway, shouldn't he?'

'There is that,' my father said. 'But as his outstanding service to the nation was slowly but surely revealed, everyone began to show him greater respect. They all began to dedicate a place in their hearts to him: the man they first saw had disappeared; he was now something so much more.'

In spite of this — in spite of everyone doing as much as possible to look after him — I felt that his life was intolerably difficult, and intolerably sad. At times I would see him through the window, squatting down on a sofa, his face completely blank, his eyes without a glimmer of light — completely unmoving, like a statue. Except for his hands: they never stopped trembling, as if they were being worked upon by some unknown force. In the evenings, through the pale white tranquil walls of the home, I would often hear his old man's wheeze. It felt as though something or someone was pounding on him unremittingly. Then there were the nights when the stillness of people sleeping would occasionally be interrupted by what sounded like a Chinese oboe weeping ever so mournfully, the sound drifting through the walls. My father told me that Jinzhen made that heart-wrenching wailing noise when he dreamed.

One evening in the canteen, I unexpectedly bumped into Rong Jinzhen. He sat in the seat facing me, his back bent, his head low, completely unmoving, just like a . . . what was it . . . a heap of clothes, a rag doll? He looked rather pitiful; the expression on his face showed the unrelenting and unmerciful passage of time. Silently I stole a look at his face and thought of what my father had said, thought of this man, once young, who had shown so much promise; a special operative of Unit 701 who had distinguished himself with meritorious service, had made exceptional contributions to the Unit. But now he looked so old, so mentally infirm. The passing of time had been without compassion, it had beaten him down, had turned him into a shell of a man – all that remained were his bones. Just like water wearing down a stone, or a particular phrase becoming crystallized and refined with the passage of time. As dusk fell, he looked so incredibly ancient: a truly ghastly sight, like a centenarian who might take his leave of this world at any time.

At first, with his head bent, he didn't realize I was watching him, but after eating, as he stood up to leave, our eyes met. At that moment, a spark of something suddenly appeared in his eyes, as if life had just been returned to them. Turning towards me, he moved closer, with a kind of robotic movement; a shadow of pain clung about his face, like a beggar stumbling towards his chosen mark. Standing in front of me, he stared at me with two goldfish-like eyes, stretching out both his hands, as if begging for something. With great difficulty his trembling mouth sputtered out the following words: 'Notebook, notebook, notebook . . .'

I was scared out of my wits, at a complete loss. Fortunately the duty nurse had noticed what was happening and quickly rushed over to extricate me. Immediately she started consoling him – then, putting her arm around him, she guided him step by step out of the room and into the darkness of the corridor. He continued to look back and forth between her and me.

Afterwards, my father told me that it didn't matter who it was, but if your eyes met his, he would move towards you and ask after his long-lost notebook as though somewhere behind your eyes he had caught a glimpse of it.

'He is still searching for it then?' I asked.

'Yes, still searching,' my father replied.

'Didn't you say that they had found it?'

'Yes, it was found,' my father said. 'But how could he know that?'

I couldn't help but gasp in astonishment.

I thought that as a mentally crippled man, a man completely undone, it is perhaps no wonder that he had already lost his memory. But there was something strange about this: the memory of his lost notebook seemed to be etched in his mind, carved in stone; he seemed to be almost brooding over it. He didn't know that it had been found, he wasn't aware of how time had cruelly passed him by. Nothing remained — nothing except for this one last recollection, this notebook. As the seasons passed, he staunchly held on, continuing to search for his notebook — for more than twenty years now.

And the search continues. Even today.

What about tomorrow?

Might something unexpected happen?

Sadly, I think: maybe . . . maybe . . .

The third reason I wrote this final section has to do with the demands of my readers. There are those who are keen to believe in dark forces and evil plots. They believe in secret, clandestine meetings behind the scenes. They believe in all the conspiracies. These people, of course, hope that I will pick up my pen and write something in this fashion. The problem is that there are also many people, the majority, who are extremely practical — they like to get to the bottom of things, they want to understand everything thoroughly; they cannot help but keep turning things over and over in their minds. So they ask, what happened after BLACK? Indeed, this type of person seems to hold a grudge if they remain unsatisfied. They need to know. It was for this group that I decided to write this final section.

So, in the summer of the following year, I once again found myself paying a visit to Unit 701.

2

Just as time ate away at the colour of the gate to Unit 701's compound, it also eroded some of the mystery surrounding the entire place, and eroded some of its imposing and yet serene nature. I used to find that being granted permission to pass through those gates was a painfully tedious and complicated affair. But this time the sentinel on duty simply inspected my credentials (my national ID card and reporter's pass), instructed me to register my name in rather a nondescript logbook, and that was it. It was so easy that I couldn't help but think that something was amiss, as if the guard was neglecting his duty or something. But once I made it deeper into the compound, these misgivings soon disappeared. Before me, in the large courtyard, pedlars hawked their goods, temporary workers idled about; everyone looked rather carefree and unconcerned, as though they were in some uninhabited sector. It was a veritable picture of bucolic simplicity.

I am not especially fond of the traditional image of Unit 701, but nor do I like seeing what it has become: it made me feel as though I were stepping on something insubstantial, like air. However, after asking about, I discovered that there was yet another inner courtyard within Unit 701's complexes and I had simply stepped into the newly constructed residential area. This courtyard within a courtyard was like a cave inside a larger cave. Not only was it not easy to find, but if you did, you would not even notice that you had entered it. The sentinels on guard in this sector were like spectres. They would appear in front of you suddenly and without warning, striking a rather threatening and chilling pose, like an imposing ice sculpture towering up before you. They would forbid you to draw any closer. They seemed, in fact, almost afraid that you would come closer, as though the very warmth from your body would melt them; as if they really were made of ice and snow.

I spent ten days at Unit 701. As you can imagine, I saw Vasili, whose real name is Zhao Qirong. I also saw Rong Jinzhen's no longer young wife, whose full name is Di Li. She was still a security officer. Her tall frame had been worn down somewhat by the passing of the years but she was still much taller than most people. She had no children, no parents; all she had was Rong Jinzhen, whom she considered to be both at the same time. She told me that her greatest trouble at present was her inability to resign from active duty, given the nature of her position. However, once her resignation was accepted, she planned to make her way to the Lingshan nursing home immediately, where she would spend every day seated beside Rong Jinzhen. Until that time came, she could only spend her annual leaves with him, about a month or two in total per year. I don't know if it was because she had worked for such a long time as a security officer, or because she had spent so much time alone, but she gave me the impression of someone even more detached and reticent than Rong Jinzhen. To be frank, even though both Vasili and Di Li should be considered good people, they didn't really help me all that much; nor did anyone else, save one. It seemed as though most of the people in Unit 701 weren't really willing to drag up the tragic tale of Rong Jinzhen, and even if they did, their reminiscences would be fraught with errors and contradictions, as though the tragedy itself had made them forget that which they should have remembered. It was as though, because they didn't want to talk about it, they couldn't. That is a very effective means to leave a story buried in the past.

On one of the first evenings of my stay I paid a visit to Rong Jinzhen's wife. But because she wasn't really forthcoming, I returned to the guest house soon afterwards. Once back in my room, I began to go through the few notes I had taken when a complete stranger, who must have been about thirty years of age, burst into my room. Introducing himself as an administrator from the security office by the name of Lin, he began to badger me with questions. I must say he was really rather unpleasant towards me, even searching through my room and luggage without permission. Of course, I knew that the result of his search would only make him believe and trust me – that I was here to praise and eulogize one of their own, the hero Rong

Jinzhen – so I let him proceed with his investigation without making a fuss. The problem was that even after he searched everything, he didn't trust me. He began to interrogate me again, making things very difficult, and finally telling me that he was going to confiscate all of my credentials – my reporter's pass, my work permit, my ID card and writers' association ID – as well as my tape recordings and notebooks. He had to investigate me further was all he said. I asked when I could expect to have my documents returned, but all he told me was that it would depend upon the outcome of his investigation.

I spent a sleepless night.

During the morning of the following day, the same man, this Administrator Lin, came to find me. This time, however, his rough demeanour from the night before had disappeared. He went to great pains to apologize for his earlier presumptuousness and then politely returned my credentials and notebook. It was clear that the results of his investigation had been satisfactory, as I had expected. What caused me great surprise was that he also passed along a piece of very good news: someone higher up wished to speak with me.

With him as escort, I swaggered through three security checkpoints, ultimately entering the most secure area of the complex.

The first of the checkpoints was an armed police post with two guards on duty. Both carried pistols and truncheons. The second checkpoint was manned by the PLA. It too had two guards on duty, both armed with crow-black semi-automatic rifles. Their guard post was ringed with barbed wire and there was a small circular military pillbox made of stone adjacent to the gate. Inside were a phone and what looked to be machine guns. The third checkpoint was manned by a single guard in plain clothes who walked back and forth. He carried no weapon, only a walkie-talkie.

To tell you the truth, even today I am not entirely sure what department or sector Unit 701 belonged to: was it the military, the police or the local government? From my observations, almost everyone who worked there dressed casually, with only a few in military uniform. In the car park you could see both local licence plates and military ones, although the latter were much fewer in number. From the enquiries I made to different people I always received the same response: this was a question I shouldn't ask, and what's more, they didn't know the answer. In any case, it didn't matter whether it was a military unit or a civilian unit; all that was important was that it was a unit vital to the country's well-being – after all, the military and civilian sectors are both of the country. Of course, that was true. What more was there to say? All nations need this type of agency, just as every household has its own first-aid kit. It is essential. When all was said and done, there was nothing really strange about it at all. It would be strange, in fact, for a country not to have this type of agency. But I digress.

After passing through the three checkpoints, we came upon a perfectly straight, narrow road, hemmed in on both sides by immense trees covered in lush foliage. The incessant chirping of the birds up in the trees echoed down, giving you the feeling that you had wandered off the beaten track and into some forest reserve. Proceeding forward, it seemed as though we wouldn't encounter anyone, but then very suddenly my eyes fell upon a stunning six-floor building that towered up out of the trees. Its exterior façade was adorned with russet-coloured ceramic tiles, giving it a stately and reassuring air. In front there was a large open space, the size of half a football pitch. On either side were rectangular grassy lawns. In the middle there was a square bed of flowers brimming with colour, a stone statue placed amid the fresh flowers – a sculpture that in outline and colour was reminiscent of Rodin's *The Thinker*. At first I thought that this statue was indeed a reproduction of Rodin's work, but upon a closer inspection, you could see that the seated figure was wearing a pair of spectacles and the character for 'soul' was prominently inscribed below it. From a distance, it was *The Thinker*. Later, after thoroughly scrutinizing it, I couldn't help but feel that the statue looked vaguely familiar. I just couldn't put my finger on it. Asking Administrator Lin, I finally discovered who the statue was in honour of: Rong Jinzhen.

I stood in front of it for a long time. With the sun shining down upon it, with Rong Jinzhen's chin firmly supported by his left hand, it seemed as though the statue's eyes were fixed upon me; they shone radiantly. The statue shared some similarities with the Rong Jinzhen who now resided at the Lingshan nursing home. It was like looking at a man in the fullness of life and then seeing him in old age.

Taking leave of the statue, Administrator Lin – contrary to my expectations – led me round the back to a small two-storey Western-style structure of greenish-black brick. I soon discovered that this building contained a remarkably spartan parlour which was used to receive visitors. I was instructed to wait in the parlour, and before long I heard a distinct metallic clicking sound coming from the corridor outside. Not long afterwards an elderly man leaning on a walking stick made his way into the room. His eyes fell upon me and he said, 'Ah, hello, comrade reporter. Please, let's shake hands.'

I stood up quickly to exchange a handshake and then invited him to sit on the sofa.

Sitting down, he said, 'It should have been me going to meet you, because after all I am the one who requested to see you. But, as you can see, I don't get around as easily as I used to, so I asked you to come here.'

I replied, 'If I am right, you must be the man who went to recruit Rong Jinzhen at N University: Mr Zheng.'

He gave a roar of laughter. Pointing his cane at his lame foot, he said, 'That's what gave me away, isn't it? You reporters are not all the same, eh? Ah, not bad, not bad. I am indeed that man, so now may I ask who you might be?'

I thought to myself: surely you've seen my credentials? Do you still need to ask? But out of respect for him, I quickly introduced myself.

After listening to my introduction, he waved a number of photo-copied pages in front of me, saying, 'How is it that you came to know of this?'

What he was waving about was a copy of my notebook!

I couldn't help but ask, 'I know I did not give my consent, so how is it that you copied my notebook without permission?'

'Please don't take offence; we really had no other option. There were five people who each felt a need to examine your notebook and if we were to pass it along to each in turn, I'm afraid it would've taken much more time before we could have returned it to you.

Now, everything is fine, all the interested parties have read it and there are no issues — you could say that your notebook touches on nothing which counts as classified information and so we have returned it to you. If that had not been the case, well, it would have remained with me.' He laughed a moment and then continued, 'I do have one question that has plagued me since last night. How is it that you came to know of this? Please, comrade reporter, could you enlighten me?'

In the simplest manner possible, I related to him my first-hand experience at the Lingshan nursing home.

He listened, smiled knowingly, and said, 'Oh, so that's it. You are the child of someone in our organization.'

'That's not possible,' I replied. 'My father was a mechanical engineer.'

'How can that be? Tell me, who is your father? Perhaps I know him.'

I told him who my father was and then asked if he knew him.

'No, I don't,' he replied.

'Exactly,' I said. 'How could you know him? My father can't have been a member of your organization.'

'Ah, but each and every one of the patients in the Lingshan nursing home is one of ours,' he said.

I was truly overwhelmed by this news. My father was close to death and now suddenly I didn't even know who he was. It goes without saying that had Director Zheng not mentioned this by chance, I would never have known my father's true identity — just as Master Rong was kept in the dark about Rong Jinzhen. Now I could understand why my father had never shown my mother and me the love we needed — why my mother had wanted a divorce. It seemed as though she had treated him unjustly. But the problem wasn't there. Rather, the problem lay in the fact that Father had accepted this unfair treatment rather than trying to defend himself. What can I say about that? Was it conviction, or inflexibility? Worthy of respect or a source of sorrow? I suddenly felt a terribly suffocating feeling welling up in my heart. It would not be until six months later, in conversation with Master Rong about these events, that I would finally come to feel that my father's stoicism ought to be respected and not mourned.

Master Rong told me that to conceal the truth from those closest to you for a long time, even for a lifetime, is unfair. But if they didn't maintain such secrecy, it is possible that our country might not even exist today, or at least it would be under threat of disaster. It's unfair, but the fact is that it has to be that way.

That was how Master Rong allowed me to appreciate my father anew, to permit the love and respect I felt for him to grow.

Returning to our story: the fact that the Director was satisfied that my notebook didn't reveal any secrets left me feeling pleased, especially since had it done so, it wouldn't have been mine any longer. But his second remark made me feel as though I had been pushed into the Cold Palace – *

He said: 'I believe that more than half the details that you have learned have been acquired through hearsay. This is quite regrettable.'

'Do you mean to say the details aren't accurate?' I asked anxiously.

'No,' he shook his head, 'what's real is real, it's just that . . . hmm, how should I put it, I feel that you don't really understand Rong Jinzhen. Yes, that's it: your understanding is rather deficient.'

Having reached this point, he paused to light a cigarette. Taking a long drag, he seemed to be mulling things over; then he raised his head and intoned seriously: 'Looking at your notebook, it is rather scattered and fragmentary, with more than half of it based purely on word of mouth. But it has evoked within me many memories of Rong Jinzhen. I understood him the most, or at least – out of all of us – I understood him the best. Would you be interested in hearing me speak of him?'

I was floored. This was simply too good to be true. I couldn't have asked for better!

It was in this manner that my book received a new vitality.

I met with the Director many times while I was staying at Unit 701. My understanding and grasp of Rong Jinzhen's history expanded

* *Translator's note*: The Cold Palace refers to the area within the Forbidden City to which members of the imperial family would be confined if they displeased the emperor.

immensely, providing me with the 'Transcript of the interview with Director Zheng' sections in the earlier chapters. Of course, his purpose was not solely to provide me with material for this work; that was not his real aim. Before I got to know Director Zheng, Rong Jinzhen was something of a mystery to me, a legend. But now, after having talked with Director Zheng, he had become real, unquestionably a part of history. What is more, the man primarily responsible for putting Rong Jinzhen on this path, for changing the course of his life, was none other than Director Zheng. Not only did he not mind sharing his reminiscences with me, but he also provided me with a long list of names of people who were also familiar with Rong Jinzhen and his past, even though quite a few of them had already died.

I have only a single regret concerning my time spent at Unit 701. All the while I was there I had repeatedly referred to him as Director. I never thought to ask him his name and even now I still do not know it. As a member of a secret organization, one's name is, as a rule, of no value; it is usually hidden behind a serial number and one's official designation. For Director Zheng, his position in history was thoroughly identifiable by his lame foot. But covering up one's name doesn't mean that the name disappears; it just means that it has been buried. I truly believe that had I asked him – in a professional capacity what his name was, he would have told me, but I was too enthralled by the image he projected and so I forgot to ask. As a result, I'm still confused as to what to call him – the Gimp, Zheng the Gimp, Section Chief Zheng, the Crippled Director, Director Zheng, Sir, and so on. Most people from N University referred to him as the Gimp or as Section Chief Zheng. He usually referred to himself as the Crippled Director. I generally addressed him as Sir or Director Zheng.

3

Director Zheng told me the following –

His connection to Rong Jinzhen had begun with his maternal grandfather. In the second year after the Xinhai Revolution, his maternal grandfather had got to know Old Lillie at the theatre and the two had become quite friendly thereafter. Since Director Zheng had grown up in his maternal grandfather's residence, he had come to know Old Lillie from a very early stage. Later on, when Old Lillie died, his maternal grandfather had taken him along to N University to attend the memorial service and so he had met Young Lillie. He was fourteen at the time, in his second year of middle school, and the beauty of the campus left a deep impression on him. Once he graduated from middle school, he took his school transcripts in hand and went off to see Young Lillie to request that he be allowed to enrol in the high school attached to N University. And that was that, as they say. While a pupil at the affiliated high school, his language teacher was a member of the Communist Party, who would later recruit him. Once the War of Resistance against Japan broke out, teacher and student left the school and made their way to Yan'an. This was the beginning of his long revolutionary career.

I should say, once he set foot in N University, the foundation was laid for his path to cross that of Rong Jinzhen. But as he said himself, the sequence of events that ensured that they would meet wasn't immediately set in motion. Fifteen years would pass before he was sent to N University to recruit talent for the cryptography division in Unit 701. It was mere coincidence that in paying a visit to the former chancellor and speaking of his mission to find people of talent the latter would recommend Rong Jinzhen.

The Director said, 'Although I couldn't tell Young Lillie what kind of work I would be getting this person to do – only that they had to possess certain abilities – I was very clear about what abilities were needed. I was therefore very surprised and happy when the old man told me of Rong Jinzhen, especially since I had complete faith in his ability to discern another person's character. The former chancellor was not someone given to making wisecracks, so when he made his joke, I was sure that Rong Jinzhen was precisely the kind of person I was looking for.'

It turned out to be true. Once Director Zheng had met Rong Jinzhen, he decided he was indeed the man they needed.

'When you think about it,' the Director said, 'a mathematical genius, a man who since he was small had been in intimate contact with the interpretation of dreams, who had studied both Chinese and Western thought, who had come to explore the intricacies of the human mind – he simply must have been put on this earth to be a cryptographer. Could I have been anything but startled?'

As to how they had come to agree to letting Director Zheng take Rong Jinzhen away, he said that this would remain a secret between himself and Young Lillie, a secret he wouldn't divulge to anyone. On the whole, I thought this must be true, for at the time he must have been so eager to get the old man's consent that he most likely violated the rules of his profession and told him the truth about why he wanted Rong Jinzhen. Otherwise, why would he still be so tight-lipped about the whole affair?

Several times during our interviews he reiterated that his discovery of Rong Jinzhen was his single greatest contribution to the work done at Unit 701. But he never once thought that things would end up the way they did; he never foresaw the disaster that awaited Rong. Every time this was mentioned, he would shake his head in grief, sigh deeply, and then shout out Rong Jinzhen's name several times in succession: 'Rong Jinzhen! Rong Jinzhen! Rong Jinzhen!'

[Transcript of the interview with Director Zheng]

If we were to talk about the time before he cracked PURPLE, then the image of Rong Jinzhen in my mind would have been hazy, unclear – wavering between him being a genius and him being insane. But after he deciphered PURPLE, the image came into focus: it was graceful and yet terrifying, like a tiger silently waiting to pounce. To tell you the truth, I admired him and respected him, but I never wished to get too close to him. I was afraid that I would be scalded by him; I was fearful of him, just as you would be while watching a tiger hunting. I daresay his spirit was that of a tiger. He tore apart problems as a tiger would relish gnawing meat off the bones of a recent kill: there was an animal ferocity in him, a calculated approach – again like a tiger that stalks its prey, waiting for the precise moment at which to pounce.

A tiger!

Lord of animals!

Lord of cryptography!

To tell you the truth, although I was much older than him and was considered an old hand in the Intelligence Service (indeed, by the time he arrived I was already a section chief), in my heart, I looked on him as my senior. No matter what the trouble was, I would ask him about it. The more I understood him, the more I got close to him, the more I became a slave to his intelligence, his presence; I would kneel down before him and have no regrets about doing so . . .

. . . As I've already mentioned, the world of cryptography does not allow for the appearance of similar ciphers – such an event would result in them becoming rubbish. Consequently, the world of cryptography has an unwritten rule, practically an iron-clad law: an individual can either create ciphers or crack them. Because Rong Jinzhen possessed the ability to create *and* destroy ciphers, he was enraptured by his own mind. However, such rapture was tantamount to discarding it, to losing it, to going completely mad. In principle, Rong Jinzhen should not have assumed responsibility for deciphering BLACK. His mind already belonged to PURPLE. Such a task should be his only if he was able to re-forge the inevitable fragmentation of his mind.

But for Rong Jinzhen, for that kind of person, we didn't really believe that there were rules that applied. Rather, we trusted in his talent. To put it another way, we had faith in his ability to rebuild his mind – we believed that, for him, this was not impossible. We might not believe in ourselves, we might not believe in the impartiality of rules, but there was no way that we could refuse to believe in Rong Jinzhen. For us, his very being was built upon those things that we believed to be impossible: he made those things real; made them part of reality itself. It was in this fashion that the great burden of cracking BLACK came to fall on his shoulders.

This necessitated his return to the forbidden zone.

But unlike the first time, this time he was forced by someone else – and also by his own illustrious reputation – into the forbidden zone. It was totally unlike the situation with PURPLE. There he penetrated deep into the historical woods of cryptography; of his own initiative he stormed into this forbidden area. But one man cannot be too outstanding. Once you are too apart from your fellows, you discover that your glorious reputation is no support. In fact, it is the reverse: it brings your own destruction ever closer.

I never probed into Rong Jinzhen's frame of mind once he took on the responsibility for deciphering BLACK, but the suffering he endured as a result was unfair – that I saw clearly. If we were to talk of how he cracked PURPLE, then I could say that it was not terribly stressful for him: he was at ease going into battle; he arrived at work on time and left when the work day was over. Those around him remarked that it seemed as though it were all a game to him. But when it came to BLACK, well, his former light-heartedness had completely disappeared. The weight pressing down upon him was enormous, bowing him over. During the time he spent on BLACK, I saw at first hand how Rong Jinzhen's jet-black hair began to go grey, how his stature began to shrink: it was as though the situation had forced him into the labyrinth of BLACK; a labyrinth he couldn't escape from. As you can imagine, BLACK carried Rong Jinzhen along with it, into its deeper realms – he was obsessed with tearing it apart, as well as about smashing his own mind to pieces. The torment and pain were like the two hands of the devil pressing down upon his shoulders. This man who had originally had no connection to BLACK (because he had cracked PURPLE), now endured the full weight of it: it was his shame, his sorrow, and he even bore the pain and sorrow of the Unit itself. To speak frankly, I never doubted Rong Jinzhen's talent and diligence, but as to whether he could pull another miracle out of his hat, to decipher BLACK, to overthrow the iron-clad law of the world of cryptography, I couldn't say that I had no misgivings. I believe a genius is still a man, a man who can become confused, a man who can make mistakes; but should a man of this sort commit an error then that error must be colossal, must be shocking. In truth, in the world of cryptography there is unanimous agreement that BLACK was not some high-level cipher of exceptional rigorousness and importance. Indeed, the means by which it was cracked were shocking to everyone by their simplicity. For that reason, not long after Rong Jinzhen's mental collapse, BLACK was quickly dispatched. In terms of talent, these cryptographers simply didn't compare to Rong Jinzhen, but once the task had been undertaken, it was just like when Rong Jinzhen had cracked PURPLE: it took only three months and they did it in a completely relaxed fashion . . .

[To be continued]

Did you hear? Someone deciphered BLACK!

Who?

Was he (or she) still alive? Director Zheng told me his name: Yan Shi. What is more, he told me that he was indeed still alive. He suggested that I go and interview him, and once the interview was over, come and see him again; apparently, Director Zheng had additional information to give me. Two days later, I met with Director Zheng again and the first words out of his mouth were a question: 'So, what do you think of that old bastard?' He was referring to Yan Shi, the man responsible for deciphering BLACK. His wording left me speechless for a moment.

'Don't be offended,' he went on. 'In truth, no one around here cares much for Yan Shi.'

'Why?' I asked, feeling that this was rather odd.

'Because he has got so much out of it: too much, in fact.'

'But he cracked BLACK – doesn't he deserve to be rewarded?'

'But everyone believes that his accomplishment was only possible because he had Rong Jinzhen's notebook to work from; that his inspiration came solely from the work already carried out by Rong Jinzhen.'

'That's true; he admitted that to me,' I said.

'Really? No way – he would never have said that.'

'Eh? I heard it with my own ears.'

'What did he say, then?' Director Zheng asked.

'He told me that actually it was Rong Jinzhen who deciphered BLACK; that his own reputation was undeserved.'

'Oh, this is big news.' He stared at me in surprise. 'Previously he always skirted round the issue of Rong Jinzhen, evaded questions about how he figured out how to decipher BLACK. How is it that he didn't with you? Hmm . . . perhaps it's because you are not a member of this organization, you're somebody on the outside. I wonder.' Director Zheng paused for a moment and then continued, 'He never before so much as mentioned Rong Jinzhen, purposefully pushing him aside, trying to create the impression that he was entirely responsible for deciphering BLACK. But how could that have been possible? We've all been here together for such a long time, who doesn't know who? Yet it seemed as though he had changed into a genius overnight; now tell me, who could believe that? No one, that's who! As we saw him hog all of the glory for cracking BLACK, we really couldn't accept it. There was so much gossip and complaint – we all felt outraged by the injustice done to Rong Jinzhen.'

I fell into deep thought. I wondered if I should disclose to him everything that Yan Shi had told me. To tell you the truth, Yan Shi never explicitly told me not to share with others what he had told me, but neither did he imply that it was okay to tell other people.

A moment of silence passed. Director Zheng looked me over and then continued speaking: 'Actually, his inspiration for deciphering BLACK could only have come from Rong Jinzhen's notebook, this fact is undeniable; everyone had already come to this conclusion and you've just now said that Yan Shi himself admits to this. Then why has he never come clean with us, why hasn't he admitted it to us? It is just as I said: his only aim was to push Rong Jinzhen aside in order to obtain all the glory for deciphering BLACK himself. Everyone knew that. And because everyone knew it, he has stubbornly refused to admit it, causing everyone to loathe him even more and to not trust him at all. But I think that he was not at all clever with his selfish little machinations. Ah, but that is another topic altogether; let's leave that for now . . .

'Now, I want to ask you – and you can take your time thinking about it – how is it that he was able to discover inspiration from Rong Jinzhen's notebook when Rong Jinzhen himself couldn't? It is quite reasonable to say that whatever it was that he learned from the notebook, Rong Jinzhen should have been able to do the same and much earlier. Don't you agree? After all, it was Rong Jinzhen's notebook; his thoughts, his ideas. To use an analogy, you could say that the notebook was like a room and inside this room there was a key, the key to unlocking BLACK. Then how is it that the person whose room it was couldn't find it? How is it that someone on the outside could simply enter the room and discover it immediately? Now I ask you, is that not strange?'

His analogy was quite apropos. It laid out all of his innermost thoughts about this situation on a plate; it was all very incisive. But I wanted to say that none of what he thought was actually what really happened. That is . . . there were no problems with his analogy; rather, the problem lay in what he thought had taken place. Mulling it over while listening to him, I ultimately decided that I would tell him everything that Yan Shi had told to me; that in and of itself that should clear things up and establish for certain what actually transpired. But he never gave me the chance to get a word in edgewise; he simply continued on in the same breath: 'It was then that I came to believe that while attempting to crack BLACK, Rong Jinzhen had made a cardinal sin, and what's more, this error wound its way into his head, bludgeoning a genius into an idiot. This mistake, when all is said and done, could only have happened to someone who could transgress the iron-clad law of cryptography: it was the residual effect of his having cracked PURPLE lurking in the shadows, waiting to cause mischief.'

Having reached this point, Director Zheng stopped talking and went silent. It seemed as though he had fallen into a state of mournful melancholy. As I waited for him to speak again, it became obvious that he wasn't going to continue on with his story but rather to bid me farewell. Even though I had thought of telling him what I had learned from Yan Shi, I never had the chance. But I was happy with this. I thought, 'Since I wasn't really sure if I should tell him or not, not having been given the opportunity to do so worked in my favour; it allowed me to avoid the burden the words would have incurred.'

Before we parted, I had to remind him, 'Didn't you say that you had some additional information to give me?'

He was a bit taken aback, but then made his way over to a metal file cabinet and pulled open a drawer. Removing a single file, he asked, 'Did you know that when Rong Jinzhen was at university he was the student of a foreign professor, a man by the name of Jan Liseiwicz?'

'No, I hadn't heard that.'

'This man went to great efforts to prevent Rong Jinzhen from deciphering PURPLE. This file is the proof. Have a look, and should you need it, we can make copies for you.'

That was how I first heard of Liseiwicz.

Director Zheng admitted that he did not know Liseiwicz and what he had discovered had come by way of hearsay. He said, 'When he made contact with us here, I was overseas in Y country to learn from their experience in trying to decrypt PURPLE. Even after I returned, I did not come into contact with the Liseiwicz correspondence; only the special task force assigned to cracking PURPLE had any first-hand knowledge of these letters. At the time, Headquarters was taking direct charge of things – perhaps they feared we would fight over it, fight to see who could produce the desired outcome. As a result, they kept us in the dark about the whole affair. It was only much later on that I met a senior official from Headquarters who was prepared to let me see the letters. They are all in English, but accompanied with Chinese translations.'

Having reached this point, a thought suddenly occurred to him: the original English letters should remain in his possession. I therefore opened the file and began to separate the English originals from the translations. It was then that I saw a record of a telephone conversation on top of the file – someone named Qian Zongnan had telephoned. The note seemed to serve as a foreword to the case files. There were only a few sentences:

Liseiwicz was employed as a high-level military intelligence analyst for X country. I saw him four times, the last in the summer of 1970.

Later I discovered that Liseiwicz and Fan Lili were put under house arrest at PP military base, reason unknown. Liseiwicz died in 1978 at PP base. In 1981, the military authorities of X country released Fan [Lili] from house arrest. In 1983, Fan [Lili] arrived in Hong Kong in search of me, hoping that I would assist her in making arrangements for her to return to China. Assistance refused. In 1986, it was reported that Fan [Lili] was in her home town of Linshui county, C City, contributing funds to establish an engineering project. By all accounts, she is still resident in Linshui county.

Director Zheng told me that this person, Qian Zongnan, was at that time an informant, a comrade charged with keeping tabs on Liseiwicz in X country. Upon being handed the file, I had thought that this man would be crucial for helping me to come to a better understanding of the role played by Jan Liseiwicz in these events. I was therefore very sad to be informed that he had died the year before. Still, the record did make mention of Fan Lili, Liseiwicz's Chinese wife. If I wished to understand him, then she was without a doubt the best person to talk to.

I was ecstatic.

4.

Since I lacked a specific address, I had at first mistakenly believed that finding Fan Lili would entail a great deal of effort and be fraught with complications and setbacks; the actual experience was anything but. Making initial enquiries at the Linshui County Education Bureau, it seemed as though everyone in the building knew her. As it turned out, several years ago not only had she succeeded in establishing three primary-level Hope Schools,★ she had also donated tens of thousands of yuan worth of textbooks to the local middle schools. You could say that those on the front lines of education in Linshui, without exception, knew who she was and respected her. However, when I found her at Jinhe Hospital in C City, my original ambition went cold, for there she was, lying in bed with her larynx removed. Gauze was tied about her neck and head in a rough fashion, making it seem as though she possessed two skulls. She was suffering from throat cancer. The doctor said that even though the surgery was successful, there was no way that she could speak unless she practised making sounds through her lungs. Because the surgery had just taken place recently, her condition was still very poor. It would be impossible for me to interview her. Therefore, I said nothing and instead pretended that I was another of the numerous senior people from Linshui county who had come to pay their respects. I left her flowers and my best wishes, and took leave. Later, over the course of the next few days, I visited her in the hospital three more times. On each visit she would write her responses to my questions. Altogether, she wrote several pages and each one astonished me!

To tell you the truth, if she hadn't written these answers, no one would ever have grasped the truth about Liseiwicz. We would never

★ *Translator's note*: Hope Schools, or *xiwang xiaoxue*, refer to privately run primary and elementary schools set up in poor rural areas of China. The schools are funded primarily by wealthy Hong Kong and Taiwanese social organizations.

have realized his true identity and position, his sincere desires and
shame, his indisputable pain and sorrow. In a very real sense, Liseiwicz's departure for X country was far from being all there was to
that story. The entire tale was something truly mind-boggling, a
genuinely freakish combination of events.

To be honest with you, Fan Lili's words demand patience in order
to be appreciated and valued.

I give them to you below, word for word. The first time:

1. He [Liseiwicz] was not a code-breaker.
2. Since you already know that he wrote those letters in order
   to mystify you and put you on the wrong track, why do
   you still believe what he said? Those words were all lies –
   him a code-breaker? He created ciphers; he was the enemy
   of those who decipher them.
3. PURPLE was his creation!
4. This will take some explaining. It was the spring of 1946. A
   man had come looking for Liseiwicz, a fellow student from
   Cambridge. At that time, it seemed that this man was
   preparing to take charge of a very important post for the
   government of Israel. He took Liseiwicz to a church on
   Gulou Street, and in front of God and in the name of the
   millions of Jewish compatriots, requested him to devise a
   cipher for the state of Israel. Liseiwicz took more than a
   year to construct the cipher, but his sponsors didn't seem to
   care; they were ever so pleased. Since the time he was a
   small child, Liseiwicz had grown up surrounded with
   adulation: his ego was very strong and it wouldn't let him
   fail. But because he didn't have enough time in which to
   work on it, it was somewhat rushed – at least for him – and
   he began to feel that there were many flaws within it; so he
   took it upon himself to devise a new cipher to take its place.
   This was when he was hopelessly drawn deeper and deeper
   into the bewildering world of cryptography. Finally, after
   nearly three years of work, he succeeded in devising a
   cipher he could be satisfied with. That cipher was
   PURPLE. He then requested that the Israeli authorities

replace his previous cipher with this new one. They decided
to experiment with it, but the result was not what he
expected: PURPLE turned out to be too difficult; there
was no way that they could use it. At the time, the famous
cryptanalyst Klaus Johannes was still living. It was said that
after he saw a secret telegram encrypted with PURPLE, he
remarked: 'I would like to have three thousand similarly
encrypted telegrams come across my desk, all waiting to be
deciphered, but in the current situation,* I will probably
only see a thousand.'† The meaning of this statement was
clear – in however many years he had left, he would not be
able to crack this cipher. Once X country got wind of this,
they immediately thought of buying PURPLE, but at that
time we had not yet decided to leave N University. What is
more, considering the strained relationships between X
country and China, we decided that it was best not to
respond to this proposal. What happened later was as you
described it: in order to rescue my father, we used PURPLE
to make a deal with X country.

5. Yes, he believed that Rong Jinzhen would sooner or later
decipher PURPLE, and so he made every effort to impede
his progress.

6. In the entire world, there was only one person he admired
and that was Rong Jinzhen. He believed that concentrated
within Jinzhen was the sum of all Western knowledge and
wisdom, something only seen once every hundred years.

7. I'm tired, another day.

The second time:

1. This, using the words of a military intelligence analyst, is
for external dissemination. In fact, he [Liseiwicz] was still
engaged in the development of ciphers.

* At the time, the Second World War had ended and there was no large-scale con-
flict taking place.
† The absence of war meant that for the moment there were not as many coded
telegrams being sent back and forth.

2. A high-level cipher is like the main actor in a play: there has to be an understudy. When developing a high-level cipher, generally two are created: one for use, the other in reserve. But the essence of PURPLE was derived from Liseiwicz's very own character; it was impossible for him to simultaneously create two ciphers. Furthermore, when he was constructing PURPLE he never once thought that it would become a high-level cipher. When he created it, it was as though he had researched and developed an entirely new language, a language that itself required considerable precision. But once X country decided to use PURPLE as a high-level cipher, they immediately determined that a reserve cipher would have to be created; this understudy was none other than BLACK.

3. Correct, as soon as he set foot in X country he was immediately whisked away to participate in the development of BLACK. But to be precise, he served as an observer of the work.

4. Strictly speaking, one man can only create one high-level cipher. His participation in the development of BLACK was as an observer, meaning that he was not directly engaged in the research. His role was to highlight clearly the special characteristics of PURPLE, to work in tandem with the researchers, to guide them away from making a simple replica of PURPLE. Sort of like a navigator. For instance, if PURPLE set its gaze upon the sky, then he would ensure that BLACK directed its attention towards burrowing into the ground. How it was to in fact burrow into the ground was for the actual researchers to determine.

5. Before they learned that Jinzhen had cracked PURPLE, the underlying structure of BLACK had already been completed – the two ciphers were about the same level of difficulty. Making them difficult is the primary aim of creating high-level ciphers; why else would the field of cryptography gather in the most talented and erudite of people if not because everyone wishes to confound and

baffle their opponents? But, after learning that Jinzhen had deciphered PURPLE, he became adamant about the need to make revisions to BLACK. He had the distinct feeling that since Jinzhen had been able to crack PURPLE, he could do the same with BLACK. He knew this because he knew Jinzhen: he knew the type of person he was, and he appreciated his innate talent, a talent that only became more excited and aroused when confronted with a difficult and seemingly impenetrable problem – more determined to solve it. Nothing would stop him, not even death. If death would not stop him, then the only remaining option was to devise some means to thoroughly baffle and confuse him, to introduce manoeuvres that would challenge his entire way of thinking: this was the only way to defeat him. As a result, BLACK was revised, but not in a traditional manner. Rather, the cipher had become almost absurd; certain sections were extremely impenetrable, while others were incredibly easy: it was neither fish nor fowl but something nondescript. To use Liseiwicz's own words, it was like a man who on the outside appears absolutely refined and exquisite, but underneath is wearing neither underpants nor socks.

6. You're absolutely right,* but Jinzhen understood Liseiwicz's mind too well. You could say that cracking PURPLE was akin to him and Liseiwicz sitting down to play a game of chess; he would not be distracted by Liseiwicz. Since he couldn't be distracted, it was possible for him to go on to crack other ciphers. But BLACK was not broken in this manner.

7. I don't agree with what you said:† after all, even if such a

---

* The world of cryptography has an unwritten rule: an individual can either create ciphers or crack them! This is so because whatever path the person takes, either creating ciphers or deciphering them, that person's heart and mind have already been given over to their work. However, the world does not allow two similar ciphers to exist.

† I told her that, in the end, BLACK was not deciphered by Rong Jinzhen.

person existed there would have been no way that he could have accomplished everything himself; he must have relied upon what Jinzhen wrote in his notebook.

8. If you can, could you please tell me exactly what happened to Jinzhen?

9. I suppose what Liseiwicz said was correct.

10. He said, 'Our lives were ruined by Jinzhen, but in the end he still destroyed himself.'

11. Jinzhen – this kind of person – could perhaps only be destroyed by himself; no one else would be able to accomplish it. Actually, both of them, Liseiwicz and Rong Jinzhen, were cursed by their fates: fate killed them. The only difference was that Jinzhen's fate was not independent of itself; his fate was tied up with Liseiwicz's destiny. But from Jinzhen's perspective, Liseiwicz was simply his gifted teacher and that is all.

12. Let's talk more again another day. When you come, please bring along the letters Liseiwicz wrote to Jinzhen. I would like to see them.

The third time:

1. Yes, Liseiwicz was Weinacht.

2. This much is clear. At the time, he was a member of the Secret Service; how could he use his real name to play the role of a mathematician? A mathematician is someone in the public eye, but the nature of his real work would not allow for that. Besides which, in terms of professional ethics it would not be permitted. What kind of organization would allow you to take a high salary and then just carry on doing your own job?

3. Because he was only an observer on the team developing BLACK, he had the time and energy to engage in other research. In truth, he had always dreamed of working on artificial intelligence and I should say his theory on the binary nature of mathematical constants was of great importance in the development of computer technology.

Why did he hope to persuade Jinzhen to leave China? It wasn't because he was acting at the behest of certain people with certain political aims. No, he hoped that Jinzhen would remain overseas so that both of them could collaborate on this artificial intelligence project.

4. You will have to think about this problem yourself;* I can give you no answer. In short, Liseiwicz was a scientist: in terms of politics, he was terribly naïve and so it was very easy for him to be wounded; it was also easy for him to be used. As for what you just mentioned – that he was a virulent anti-communist – that is a complete fabrication; I am sure that he harboured no such feelings.

5. Some of the circumstances are clear.† Both of these high-level ciphers [PURPLE and BLACK] were cracked one after the other. The first, he [Liseiwicz] had created solely by himself, the second he had been a participant in. What is more, the person responsible for deciphering them both was his student. I was there. He did write so many letters – although to look at them they seemed to be an assortment of stratagems aimed at misleading their reader, in truth, who knows whether or not those riddles contained yet more secret information hidden inside them? The probability of deciphering a highly sophisticated cipher is extremely low, and now to see one person crack two of these ciphers in succession and do so incredibly quickly – well, ordinarily that would be impossible. The only way it could have happened was if someone were leaking secrets. But who? The greatest suspicion fell on him, on Liseiwicz.

6. We were put under strict house arrest after it was discovered that BLACK had been broken: that was in the second half of 1970. But even before then, starting around the time when PURPLE was cracked, we were being shadowed whenever we went out. Our telephone was also being

* This is a reference to how Liseiwicz later became involved in extremist politics.
† This is a reference to the circumstances which resulted in X country putting Liseiwicz and his wife under house arrest.

monitored, and there were so many restrictions. In truth, it was as though we were under partial house arrest already.

7. In 1979, Liseiwicz passed away due to illness.

8. Ah yes, that was while we were still under house arrest. Every day we were together, every day we had to find things to talk about. That's how I came to know so much about these things; it was during our period of house arrest that he told me everything. Before that, I knew very little.

9. I've been thinking: why has God cursed me with this disease? Perhaps it's because I know too many secrets. It's funny really – now that I have no mouth I can talk about these things. Before, when I had a mouth, I couldn't.

10. I don't wish to carry these secrets to my grave: I want to die in peace. In my next life I want to be a normal, average person. I don't want glory, I don't want secrets, I don't want friends or enemies.

11. Don't lie to me, I know how sick I am. The cancer has already spread: I have maybe a few months left.

12. You don't want to say goodbye to a person about to die, that's bad luck. Go, I wish you a happy and peaceful life!

A few months later, I heard that she underwent open skull surgery and a few months after that I heard that she had died. Supposedly, in her last will and testament she mentioned me – hoped that I wouldn't use their real names in the book I was writing; she and her husband wanted to rest in peace. In this book, the names Fan Lili and Liseiwicz are aliases. Even though this goes against the criteria I had set for writing – really, what could I do? An old person, whose fate had been full of frustrations and dashed hopes, who had loved so deeply and passionately, whose last will and testament spoke of a desire to be left in peace – because their life had been so difficult, how could I not respect their wishes!

I should talk about Yan Shi.

It was perhaps true that Yan Shi had initially attempted to push Rong Jinzhen to one side; he had deliberately tried to create estrangement between himself and everyone else in Unit 701. After his retirement, he no longer lived within the confines of the unit; instead, he had moved with his daughter to the capital of G province. The high-speed expressway had made the distance between there and A City quite short, and so I arrived in the provincial capital just three hours after leaving Unit 701. Even better, I had little difficulty in locating the daughter's home and thus seeing Yan Shi.

He was as I imagined him. Sporting a pair of thick-lensed near-sighted spectacles, he was already well over seventy; indeed, much closer to eighty. His hair was luminous silver and his eyes carried deceit and secrets within them. In short, he was completely devoid of the benevolence and grace expected of old men. As my visit was rushed, I had come upon him seated in front of a Go table; his right hand was deftly manoeuvring a set of resplendent meditation balls while his left grasped a white Go stone; he was deep in thought. But there was no opponent seated opposite him – he was playing against himself. Yes, playing against himself – like speaking to one's self; like some tragic and lonely old fool still holding onto great aspirations. His granddaughter, a fifteen-year-old high-school student, told me that since his retirement it was hard to pry him away from the game. Every day he whiled away the hours either playing Go or reading books on it. He had become quite skilled at it, so much so that it was now hard for him to find an opponent. All he could do was rely upon his Go books to satisfy his addiction.

Haven't you heard? Playing chess against one's self is actually like playing against a famous exponent.

A full table of Go was what triggered our conversations. Full of pride, he would tell me of the benefits of Go: how it could drive away loneliness, how it exercised the brain, nourished the soul and extended one's life. After relating to me the many advantages of playing Go, he summed it all up by saying that his love of the game was actually an occupational hazard. 'With respect to those working in cryptography, our collective fate is naturally tied up with the various games of chess – especially those with commonplace lives. Finally they will all be seduced by the art of chess, just like pirates and drug pushers are seduced by their own wares. It is just like how some people become interested in good works in their old age.'

That was how he explained it. His analogy allowed me to picture some form of reality, but . . . 'Why did you emphasize a commonplace life?' I asked.

Mulling it over for a moment, he said, 'In the case of very talented cryptanalysts, you could say that their passion and intellect is expressed through their work. In other words, their genius is *used* – by themselves and by their work. A soul spent in such explosive fashion tends towards the peaceful, the contemplative; it lacks the stress of having to repress oneself; it lacks anxiety about withering away. Without such pressure, naturally there is no desire to unburden one's heart. Such people do not anxiously crave a new life. Therefore, for most geniuses, their later years are filled with memories; they listen attentively to the beauty of their own voice. But for those with commonplace lives, it is different. Those of talent, members of the inner circle, would refer to us as the fairer sex. It meant that we possessed elements of genius, but could never perform such work. We spent our years searching, feeling oppressed – filled with talent but never able to truly demonstrate it, to release it. For this kind of person their later years possess no memories of glory; there is nothing to sum up. What are they to do in their so-called golden years? Only what they have done their whole lives: they continue to search in vain for something to do, unconsciously trying to find some way to put their abilities to use; enacting the ultimate and final struggle. This is the meaning of my infatuation with chess, the first meaning. The second meaning – well, if you look at it from another point of view, geniuses put in an enormous amount of time assiduously studying, pouring their hearts out, aiming to pass through an incredibly narrow path in order to reach the peak, and even if their hearts contained some other desire, a wish to do something else, they cannot: the path their minds are to traverse has been set, they cannot be torn away from it [his use of the word 'torn' filled me with a sense of horror, as if my whole spirit had been taken hold of by some unknown force]. Their minds, their mental powers, were already unable to move in a natural and unrestrained manner: they could only move forward, marching ever deeper along that same narrow path. Do you know the roots of madness? Genius and madness issue forth from the same track; both are brought about by bewitchment. Would you fancy playing a game of chess with them in their old age? Impossible, because they can't!'

In a slightly halting voice, he continued, 'I've always believed genius and madness are two sides of the same coin: they are like your left and right hands, both reaching out from this human body of ours, only they are walking different paths. In mathematics, there are positive infinities and negative infinities; in a sense, you could say that a genius is a positive infinity while a madman or a fool would represent a negative infinity. But in mathematics, both positive and negative infinities are still infinites: numbers without end. Therefore I've often thought that one day, when this human race of ours reaches a certain point of advanced development, perhaps the madman will become like the genius: a man of outstanding talent, a wise and able individual capable of making contributions to society that astound one and all. Of course, I needn't speak of anything else, just ciphers. Imagine for a moment if we were able to march the same road as the madman (which is really no road at all) and devise a cipher; then it goes without saying that there would be no one capable of deciphering it. Actually, developing ciphers is a sort of madman's work, it pulls you close to insanity and to genius. Or you could put it the other way round: in terms of composition, genius and insanity are made from the same stuff. It's really surprising! Thus, I've never discriminated against madmen. I believe that perhaps, somewhere buried in their insanity, lies something to be treasured, something that we just can't get at, at least for the moment. They are like a secret cache of mineral resources, waiting for us to extract them.'

Listening to this old man go on, I felt as though my spirit had been cleansed; my mind had never been so purified before. It was as though my mind had been encrusted with dust and grime and his words had served as a torrential flow of water scouring them away, allowing my tarnished mind to exhibit a new glow. I felt at ease, really quite happy! I listened attentively, and appreciated the subtle taste of his logic. I drank it in and became intoxicated. It seemed as though I had lost my train of thought; then at long last my eyes fell on the black and white stones on the Go board and I came to, finally asking, 'Then how is it that you have come to be infatuated by Go?'

He shifted in his rattan chair. Then, in a tone of voice at once mocking and cheerful, he said, 'I am just one of those with common-place lives.'

'No,' I retorted, 'you deciphered BLACK: how could you be common?'

His gaze became fixed, his body straightened up and the rattan chair creaked and moaned underneath him as if trying to ascertain whether his weight had increased or not. A moment of stillness passed between us and then he raised his eyes to look at me. In a serious tone he said, 'Do you know how I deciphered BLACK?'

I shook my head thoughtfully.

'Would you like to know?'

'Of course,' I replied.

'Then I shall tell you. Rong Jinzhen helped me do it!' It seemed as though he were calling out to him. 'Ah, no, no, I should say it was Rong Jinzhen who deciphered BLACK: my fame is unwarranted.'

'Rong Jinzhen . . .' I was astonished. 'Isn't he . . . didn't something happen to him?' I didn't say that he had gone mad.

'Yes, that's right. Something did happen to him: he went mad.' The old man continued, 'But you'll never guess: it was in the midst of this destruction, in his ruin, that I saw the hidden secret of BLACK.'

I felt my heart being cleaved in two. 'What do you mean?'

'Ah . . . that's a long story!' He exhaled leisurely, his gaze moved away from me, he became immersed in memories of times past . . .

6.

[Transcript of the interview with Yan Shi]

I don't remember exactly when it was – perhaps 1969, or maybe 1970 – but in any case, it was winter when Rong Jinzhen lost his mind. Prior to this, he had served as our section chief and I was his immediate subordinate. It was a big department – we were at our peak: there must've been more than X number of people in our section. Now it is smaller, much smaller. There was also another section chief there at the time, a man by the name of Zheng. He's still there; I have heard he is now the Director. He is also quite an astounding individual. He took several bullets in the leg, causing him to walk with a limp, but it never affected his rise up into the echelons of the elite. Rong Jinzhen was discovered by him; they had both studied mathematics at N University. Their relationship was good; it was said that there were even some family connections. Before him, there was another section chief, from the old National Central University; a student of some renown, who during the War of Resistance cracked many of the ciphers used by those Japs. After the Revolution, he joined Unit 701 and continued to work on special assignments. Sadly, PURPLE drove him mad. All told, we were fortunate to have had these three section chiefs; they allowed us to achieve the most glorious results. And I do mean glorious, I'm not exaggerating at all. Of course, had Rong Jinzhen not lost his mind, I daresay we would have accomplished even more; but ah, well, with what happened . . . you never know, do you? The most unexpected things happen sometimes.

Getting back to what I was saying, after Rong Jinzhen fell . . . ill, it was decided that I would assume his responsibilities, which meant deciphering BLACK. That notebook, Rong Jinzhen's notebook, was the most important piece of information we had, so naturally it came into my hands. That notebook – well, you don't know it, but that notebook was in essence the receptacle for all of his thoughts, a repository for his ruminations on BLACK; it contained all his mature reflections on the cipher as well as all his wild and crazy speculations. As I pored over each word, each sentence, each page, I began to feel that every single word meant something; every word was important. It shook me to the core: each word had a special quality to it, exciting me, provoking me. I had never discovered that kind of ability within myself, but I could admire what he had written. What is more, the notebook told me that Rong Jinzhen had already completed ninety-nine per cent of the work. All that was left was to take the last step.

That final step was related to everything that came before – namely finding the key to unlocking BLACK.

The concept behind a cryptographic key is this: say that BLACK was a house that needed to be burned down, then the first thing you would need to do is to collect the necessary kindling, enough to start the fire. Well, the amount of kindling collected by Rong Jinzhen would put a mountain to shame: enough to cover the house from top to bottom. All that remained to do was start the fire. Finding a match was the key to cracking BLACK.

From examining the notebook, you could see that Rong Jinzhen had set off down the path to finding this key a year before. This means that the other ninety-nine per cent had taken Rong Jinzhen only two years to complete, but that he couldn't take that final last step. That to me was strange. Whatever way you look at it, if it took him two years to complete ninety-nine per cent of the work, then it didn't matter how difficult that last one per cent might be, he shouldn't have needed to waste a year trying to figure it out and then still not get it. This was just too strange.

Something else was also odd, but I'm not sure whether you can understand it or not. BLACK was a high-level cipher and we had spent years working on cracking it, but without making any progress. It was as though a sane person had borrowed the words of a madman to speak. In three years, there was not a single mistake to work with; not a drop of water had escaped. In the history of cryptography, this is an extremely rare phenomenon. Rong Jinzhen had already discussed this issue with me, believing that this was exceptionally odd.

Over and over again he had raised doubts about BLACK, even suggesting that perhaps it had been plagiarized from an earlier cipher created by some agency or other. After all, once used, a cipher will invariably be modified, improved upon; this is the only way to reach perfection. Otherwise, the person creating it must be a god, possessing a genius far beyond what we can imagine.

These two strange phenomena were also the two main problems that we were forced to deal with. Looking at the notebook, I could see that Rong Jinzhen had thought extensively, profoundly, rigorously upon these two problems. The notebook brought me once more into contact with Rong Jinzhen's spirit, in contact with his majesty: a thing so beautiful that it was frightening. When I first came into possession of his notebook, I thought that I would stand upon his shoulders and use all my energies to push forward on the path laid out in it. But once I entered into it, I realized that there was no way that I could march in tandem with such genius; even the slightest contact with such a soul shook me violently – attacked me!

His mind was trying to take me over.

At any moment, it would swallow me whole!

You could say that that notebook *was* Rong Jinzhen. I was drawing closer to him (through the medium of the notebook); I was being pushed towards him; I began to feel more and more his formidable ness, his profundity, his wonder. Simultaneously, I began to feel my own weaknesses, my own insignificance – it was as though I was shrivelling up. In those days, poring over every word and sentence in the notebook, I began to realize, to comprehend, just how unique and special Rong Jinzhen was; how much talent he possessed. I began to see how crazy and bizarre his thinking was, how crafty and incisive he was. He was sharp, keen; he possessed a vigorousness about him that threatened; he was ferocious. All this implied a certain nastiness about him, an evil that lurked deep inside, ready to consume you at a moment's notice. As I read through the notebook, it was as if I were reading about all of mankind: creation and murder were lumped together in large numbers; yet, ultimately, everything had a peculiar sort of beauty about it, revealing man's remarkable intellect and passion.

To tell you the truth, the notebook had created this kind of person for me – he was like a god, he had created everything; he was also the devil, the destroyer of all things, including my own mind. Standing in front of this man, I felt devoted, awed and terrified; through and through I felt the need to prostrate myself in front of him. Three months passed and I had not stood upon his shoulders – I just couldn't do it: I couldn't stand up! All I could do was to stand meekly by his side, like a long-lost child that had finally found its mother's embrace and was loath to leave her again; like a single raindrop finally falling to the ground and burrowing itself deep inside.

As you can imagine, if this was all I could do, then the best I could hope for would be the same as Rong Jinzhen: I too would be stuck at the ninety-ninth step; that final step would remain for ever in the darkness. Perhaps time would eventually have permitted Rong Jinzhen to make that last step, but not me, because, as I just said, I was but a child walking alongside him – since he had fallen, I too would fall. It was then that I discovered that this notebook that had been given to me was filled with nothing but sorrow. It had allowed me to reach the cusp of victory, allowed me to spy it in the distance, but it kept that same victory forever beyond my grasp. How sad, how pitiful! I felt overwhelmed with horror at my plight, I felt utterly helpless.

However, just at that moment, Rong Jinzhen returned from the hospital.

It's true, he was discharged: but not because he had recuperated, rather . . . how shall I put it? It was just that there was no hope of him being cured, so remaining in the hospital was meaningless – thus he returned.

I'd like to say it was the will of heaven, but I never spoke with Rong Jinzhen again. When everything happened, I was in hospital and, by the time I was released, Rong Jinzhen had already been moved to the provincial capital to receive treatment there. Paying him a visit would have been most inconvenient and what is more, as soon as I was discharged, I was given BLACK to deal with. There was simply no time to see him. Besides which, after all, I had his notebook. The first time I laid eyes on him was after he had been released from hospital, after he had already gone mad. *But we never spoke.*

That was the will of heaven.

I should say that if I had gone to see him a month earlier, perhaps what happened later would not have taken place. Why do I say this? I have two reasons: first, while Rong Jinzhen was in hospital, I was absorbed in reading his notebook. In my mind's eye, Rong Jinzhen was metamorphosing into an ever greater, ever larger, ever more intrepid character: a veritable giant; secondly, while reading through the notebook and turning things over in my mind, the difficulties in deciphering BLACK were diminishing, tapering down to a fine point. A basis of sorts was being laid down that would serve as the foundation for everything that happened afterwards.

One afternoon I heard that Rong Jinzhen would be coming back. Upon learning this, I set off to see him, but I was a bit too early, he had not yet arrived home and so I waited in the courtyard in front of his apartment. Shortly afterwards, I saw a jeep slide into the courtyard and come to a stop. Two people leapt out, an administrator from our division by the name of Huang, and Rong Jinzhen's wife, Di Li. I went over to greet them. They looked me over, taking note of my slovenly appearance, and then turned back towards the jeep to assist Rong Jinzhen in getting out. It seemed as though he was unwilling to leave the car, as if he were something fragile, something easily broken; he could not just get out of the jeep, he had to alight carefully and slowly, ever so cautiously.

After a moment, he finally managed to get out of the vehicle. But the man I saw was not Rong Jinzhen – he bore no resemblance to the man I knew. This man was hunched over, his whole body trembling; his head seemed as though it had only been recently attached to his body – it was awkwardly placed, and seemed to be teetering off balance. His eyes were wide open, globular, filled with some unknown terror, and yet there was no glimmer of light in them; his mouth hung open like some gaping rift or breach, as though it couldn't be closed, and from time to time a line of drool slipped out . . .

Could this be Rong Jinzhen?

My heart felt as though something were squeezing it, pressing down upon it; my mind became confused, disordered. It seemed as though his notebook had drawn the strength from me, had made me afraid; and now seeing Rong Jinzhen, this shell of a man, it was the same. I stood there dumbfounded, not daring to greet him, as if this Rong Jinzhen had somehow scalded me, burnt my flesh. As his wife half carried him away, Rong Jinzhen, like some terrible thought, disappeared from in front of me. But there was no way the memory of what I had seen would ever leave me.

Once I returned to my office, I tumbled upon the sofa; my feet were heavy and devoid of energy, my mind was blank. I felt nothing, I was a corpse propped up on a couch. It goes without saying that the shock I had received was too much; in no way less than the shock I received upon reading the notebook. Slowly, gradually, my spirits began to return, but the image of Rong Jinzhen when he alighted from the jeep still danced before my eyes. It was like a rare and horrible idea rudely and unreasonably playing about in my head: I couldn't expel it, I couldn't express it – I couldn't fail but to acknowledge it. This was how I became hemmed in by the image of a deranged Rong Jinzhen. The image tortured me and the more I thought about it, the more I felt pity for him – how wretched he had become, how utterly terrifying. I asked myself: who had brought him to this pass? Who had destroyed him? Then I thought about what had happened, thought about the calamity, about the person responsible for it, the mastermind –

That bloody thief!

In all honesty, no one could have guessed that this would happen, that such a talented individual, such a formidable and frightening man (the image that came to me from reading his notebook), such an elevated and profound man, humanity's crème de la crème, a hero in the field of cryptography, could ultimately be brought so low by a common street thief; could be so utterly destroyed by a mere petty criminal. I couldn't help but feel shocked and horrified by the absurdity of it all.

All emotions possess the ability to surprise, causing you to reflect upon things. Sometimes this reflection takes place in one's unconscious and so it is quite possible that it will have no effect; you might not even be immediately aware of it. In life, we often suddenly and unexpectedly come to think of things, have ideas take shape in our minds; and we are left to marvel at them, wondering whether or not they were given to us by some divine providence. But in truth, these thoughts are already within us, they are simply buried deeply in our unconscious minds; they have only now come to the fore, like a fish that out of the blue breaches the surface of the water.

However, at that time I was completely aware of what I was thinking: the images of that wretched little thief and the amazing Rong Jinzhen – the difference between them enormous – changed the direction of my thoughts, providing me with a clear direction to follow. Without a doubt, putting these two images together and abstracting them according to their vigour or mass, what you are left with is the gap between good and evil, heaviness and weightlessness, importance and insignificance. I thought of Rong Jinzhen, this man who had not been brought down by either a high-level cipher or a clever cryptographer, but had now been felled by the inadvertent actions of a lowly thief. He had withstood all the long days of torment and pain in trying to decipher PURPLE and BLACK, but when brought face to face with the actions of an insignificant crook, he barely lasted a couple of days before collapsing.

How was it that he was felled by the first blow?

Could it be that this thief had some unknown power, some unknown strength?

Of course not.

Was it because Rong Jinzhen was weak, frail?

Exactly!

It was all because that little criminal ran off with something Rong Jinzhen considered to be sacred as well as secret: the notebook! This thing was of the greatest importance to him and yet so insubstantial: like a person's heart that can't survive any blows – even the slightest knock can bring about death.

Now I'm sure you understand this. In normal situations, your most precious and sacred belonging, the thing you value most, ought to be kept in the safest, most secure place possible. In the case of Rong Jinzhen's notebook, it should have been placed in the safety-deposit box; putting it in his leather attaché case was a mistake, a moment of negligence. But looking at it the other way round, if you think the thief was an actual enemy agent, a member of X country's secret service whose mission it was to steal Rong Jinzhen's notebook, then as a secret agent, it would be most unlikely that he would imagine that Rong Jinzhen could place that oh-so-important notebook, containing information requiring the utmost protection and vigilance, inside a completely unsecured leather briefcase. Consequently, his primary objective would not have been the attaché case; it could only have been the safety-deposit box. In essence then, if we were still to consider that the thief was some agent or other tasked with stealing the notebook, then having it placed in Rong Jinzhen's leather briefcase was an ingenious means of avoiding calamity.

Later on I hypothesized again that if Rong Jinzhen's action – placing the notebook in the leather attaché case – wasn't unintentional, but rather deliberate, and he had become entangled in an actual special operation, then he was not simply the victim of a thief. Think about it for a moment. The cunning in his placing the notebook in his briefcase couldn't be more sublime: the aim must have been to lure the special operative into a most sophisticated trap, right? This train of thought brought me back to BLACK. I thought, what if the creator of BLACK had taken the most vital means to decipher it – the key – and instead of hiding it out of the way, burying it deep within the cipher itself, had left it out in the open; had deliberately *not* put it in a safety-deposit box, but rather a leather attaché case. In that case Rong Jinzhen, this man who had searched so strenuously and persistently for the key to BLACK, was like the secret agent looking for the notebook in the wrong place.

As this thought flashed through my mind, I couldn't help but become excited.

To tell you the truth, in terms of logic, my idea was completely absurd; but its absurdity latched on precisely to the two strange phenomena I mentioned earlier. Of these two, the former seemed to suggest that BLACK was extremely abstruse – this would be the reason why Rong Jinzhen had been unable to take the last step to decipher it; the latter seemed to suggest that BLACK was extremely simple – this would explain why over the course of three years no errors in the cipher had been discerned. You see? Only the most uncomplicated of things can exercise the right of unconstrained movement; only they can seek and obtain beauty.

Of course, strictly speaking, there are two kinds of simplicity possible in these circumstances. One type is an artificial simplicity. The bastard who created BLACK possessed a rare ingenuity: he was able to create any old cipher he pleased, a cipher that was incredibly uncomplicated for him, but for me was extremely sophisticated, impenetrable. The other type of simplicity is a genuine one that uses cunning as a substitute for sophistication: it baffles you with its ultra-simplicity, it conspires against you, entraps you; it places its key right in front of you, in a leather attaché case.

You can imagine what happened afterwards. If BLACK possessed an artificial kind of simplicity, then I wouldn't be able to decipher it, because the person we were up against – the person responsible for creating it – was a genius of the kind we might not see for another thousand years. Later, I realized that Rong Jinzhen had been ensnared within this simulated and obstinate sort of simplicity; or to put it another way, he had been entrapped by this bogus minimalism, he had been bewitched and deceived by it. That said, it was actually quite logical that he would have been deceived: it was practically inevitable. On the one hand . . . how should I put it? Hmmm, like this perhaps. Imagine that you and I are involved in a boxing match and you've just knocked me to the mat. Then, from my corner, another person jumps into the ring to fight you. Now you outmatch this person in every way, but at the very least he is going to be better than me, right? Well, Rong Jinzhen was in this kind of situation. He had deciphered PURPLE, he was the winner in the ring, he had proved his formidability; in his mind he had already come out on top against a superior opponent, and he was ready for the next one. On the other hand, speaking in terms of logic, only an artificial simplicity could successfully bring together and unite the two strange phenomena found in this cipher; otherwise they would be contradictory, in opposition. It was here at this point that Rong Jinzhen committed the error that all geniuses make, because from his point of view for such a high-level cipher to exhibit such an obvious contradiction was beyond the realm of possibility; it was unthinkable. He had broken

PURPLE, he was fully aware of the deliberation and meticulousness needed in its construction. So, coming face to face with such a contradictory cipher, his mind was unable to analyse the two elements, unable to open them up; the most heroic efforts left him unable to do more than touch the fringes. That is the strength of artificial simplicity: all a genius could do was to touch its fringes.

In sum, this was where Rong Jinzhen encountered the most damage to his intellect: he had become hopelessly enthralled by this synthetic simplicity and was unable to extricate himself from it. This also demonstrates precisely Rong Jinzhen's strength and courage in challenging such a redoubtable opponent. His mind thirsted to engage with this genius in hand-to-hand combat, to fight him at close quarters!

I am not like Rong Jinzhen. For me, such artificial simplicity was frightening; it made me despair. Thus this one route for deciphering BLACK was blocked. But since one route was blocked, another one was naturally laid open at my feet. So the real simplicity – that the key to deciphering BLACK was indeed stowed away in a leather attaché case – flashed before me. I felt a supreme happiness, as though I had finally found a way out of my predicament; as if a hand had appeared from out of nowhere to lift the curtain from before my eyes and throw it upon the ground, then trample on it . . .

Yes, yes, I was so overjoyed, so excited – whenever I think of this I can't help but get extremely excited. Over the course of my life, this was my greatest moment, and because of it, my life now is calm, undisturbed, peaceful and long. It was as though heaven had gathered up all the good fortune in this world and out of pity had bestowed it upon me. I felt small; I was only half conscious; I felt that I had returned to the protection of a mother's womb. It was a real blessing, like everything being given to you by someone else: you didn't have to ask for it and you didn't have to reciprocate; like a tree that simply gives its fruit.

Ah, but the mood of that beautiful moment was fleeting – I couldn't hold onto it. I try to remember, but my mind is a blank. I can only call to mind that at the time I never even had the chance to confirm my assumption. One reason is perhaps because I feared that it would be exposed; another was perhaps because I was superstitious about the time of day: three in the morning. I had heard that after three in the morning the world belongs to both men and ghosts – this is when the soul and the spirit are at their most powerful. That's how it was: in the middle of the night, in my silent office, I was like a convict repeatedly pacing back and forth, at once listening to the excited beating of my heart while trying to calm myself down – up until that fateful time, up until three in the morning. Afterwards, I finally pulled out a calculator (the one gifted to Rong Jinzhen by Headquarters, the one capable of over 40,000 calculations) and devoted myself to confirming my absurd and bizarre assumption. I don't know how much time it took, I only remember that once I deciphered BLACK, I stormed out of the cave in a frenzy (at that time our offices were still underground in a mountain cave), fell to the ground and wailed loudly, worshipping heaven and earth. It was still dark outside, just before dawn.

Fast? Of course it was fast! Don't you see, the cryptographic key to BLACK was in a leather attaché case!

Ah, who would have imagined it: BLACK had no real lock on it!

The cryptographic key was the number zero!

It was nothing!

Absolute nothing!

Er – um – I don't know why I am explaining things in so much detail. Let me make an analogy. Let us say that BLACK is like a house concealed far, far away, high up in the vast sky. There are countless doors to this house, all of them identical down to the smallest detail and all of them locked. What is more, only one of these many doors can actually be opened. You can waste an eternity amid all of these doors, none of which you will ever be able to open and all of which look just the same as the real door. If you fancy entering this building, you must first search through the boundless universe to find where it is hidden and then you must locate the one single door that opens, out of an uncountable number of fake doors. Should you find the real door, you still have to hunt for the one key that can open it.

At that time, Rong Jinzhen had not found the key. He had found the house, he had found the one real door, but he had not found the key.

Now, when I talk about searching for the key, as I just said, this involves trying one key after another in the keyhole. Generally, to forge such keys cryptanalysts rely upon their own intellect and imagination: they create a key and try it; if it doesn't work, they create another and try that, and so on and so forth. This was how Rong Jinzhen spent the year up to the point where he lost his notebook. You can just imagine how many keys he must have gone through. Even to get to that point, you should begin to realize, a successful cryptanalyst doesn't only need genius; he also needs the luck of the gods. You could say that a talented cryptanalyst has an unlimited number of keys in his mind and there must be one that will ultimately work. The problem is you can never know for certain when you will come upon that key: will it be when you first set out, in the middle of the work, or in the final stages? It is all a matter of serendipity.

Serendipity is dangerous enough to destroy everything!

Serendipity is miraculous enough to create everything!

But in my opinion, the danger and luck supposedly attached to this type of serendipity doesn't exist, because in my mind there are no keys, I cannot manufacture them. As a result I felt none of the pain and fortune of searching them out. Now at that time, if that door was truly and firmly locked, if it had in fact required a key, then you can imagine what the result would have been – it would have been for ever impossible for me to open it. It is very incongruous, but the door did indeed appear to be locked tight when in actual fact it wasn't; it was nothing but a false façade; all I had to do was push a little and it swung open. That was all there was to it. The key to unlocking BLACK was so bizarre that people were unable to believe it; they dared not trust it, and even when the door swung open and I saw everything that was inside, I still had some difficulty believing in what I saw. I thought it must all be unreal – a mirage, an illusion, a dream.

Ah, this cipher was truly the work of the devil!

Only the devil possesses such barbarous courage and traitorous gall!

Only the devil possesses such an absurdly malicious intellect!

The devil had deftly dodged Rong Jinzhen's attack, but had no answer for mine – me, the common man, the pleb. Still, heaven knows and I know that all of this had been made possible by Rong Jinzhen; thanks to his notebook I had been carried high up into the ether, to pass through disaster and reveal the hidden secret of BLACK. Perhaps you might say that this was unintentional, but you tell me – in this world, which ciphers aren't decrypted by a mixture of hard work and luck? All of them are deciphered by this mixture, if not why do we say that decrypting ciphers calls for a luck that comes from far beyond the stars? Why do we say that they require auspicious smoke to be emanating from a person's ancestral tombs?

Indeed, in this world there is not a single cipher that has not been decrypted with equal parts of ingenuity and good fortune!

Ha ha, young fellow: you never thought that today you would discover my own secret, eh? I should explain that all the things I've told you today are my secrets, my own personal secrets: I've never told anyone else. You must be wondering why I told you these things which I have never mentioned to another person. Why should I reveal to you my own inadequacies? I'll tell you. I am nearly eighty years old now: who knows when Death will make its call, and I need no longer live with all this undeserved glory.

[End of interview]

Finally the old man told me that the reason why our enemy created BLACK – a cipher with no key – was because they had felt so dejected after PURPLE had been deciphered and they had realized that they were at a dead end with their work. They understood, after just one confrontation with Rong Jinzhen, that his was a talent to be reckoned with. If they continued to stubbornly persist in challenging him, their own destruction was assured. As a result they risked universal condemnation and in their madness brought forth this singularly freakish and malicious cipher: BLACK.

However, they never realized that Rong Jinzhen had his last countermove ready and waiting for them. To use the old man's words: Rong Jinzhen had passed through destruction – amazingly, he had already passed on to his colleagues the secret of BLACK's freakish birth by means of his notebook. In the history of cryptography he was one of a kind.

Now when I look back on everything, when I reflect on Rong Jinzhen's past and present, when I think of his mystery and genius, I cannot help but feel enormous reverence for the man and also a limitless desolation, a limitless mystery.

Rong Jinzhen's Notebook

As the name makes clear, this final section consists of one of Rong Jinzhen's notebooks, or at least excerpts from it. The following pages are like an index, completely independent of the previous five sections. These pages reveal no new information, nor do they have some secret connection to what has already been written. You can choose to read this section or not. If you do, perhaps it will add some further details to the story, but it really doesn't matter – the words that follow have no bearing on how we have come to understand Rong Jinzhen. In other words, this section is like our own appendixes: it doesn't really matter if we have them or not. For this reason – I would like to emphasize this – I consider this section an 'appendix'. Its essence is that of an afterword or coda; nothing more, nothing less.

Okay. I can tell you that according to my information, over the period of time that Rong Jinzhen worked for Unit 701 (from 1956 until 1970) he filled out twenty-five notebooks, all of which are now in the custody of his wife, Di Li. Di Li used her position as Rong Jinzhen's wife only once, to take a single notebook into her personal possession. The remaining twenty-four are in her custody because she is the security officer and they are all locked away in a rather imposing iron cabinet, secured with a double lock that requires two keys to be turned simultaneously to open it. One key she keeps on her person, the other is held by her section chief. Essentially then, although these notebooks are in her care, she is not permitted to look at them, let alone treat them as her own.

When will it be possible to see them?

According to Di Li, that's difficult to say for certain. Perhaps some will be declassified in a couple of years' time; for others it might take several decades. That is because each notebook has been classified with different degrees of secrecy vis-à-vis national security. It goes without saying, therefore, that for us it is as though

those twenty-four notebooks don't even exist; just like the man
residing in the Lingshan hospice doesn't really exist. I mean, he is
there, we can go and see him, but the real Rong Jinzhen has long
since departed; he is gone. Consequently, I was very keen to see the
single notebook in his wife's possession. From what I was able to
gather, no one has ever actually seen that particular notebook, but
everyone knows she has it. That is because when she went to get it
she had to sign it out and they keep records for that sort of thing.
So, no matter how much she might have hoped to fob me off, I
knew she had it and so in the end she had to admit it. However,
every time I mentioned that I would like to have a look at it, she
would spit out two words: 'Get out!' This was how she kicked me
out of her house each and every time. There was never any hesitation on her part, never any explanation; no room for argument. A
few months ago, once I had completed the first five sections in
manuscript, I had to visit Unit 701 one final time in order for the
authorities to inspect my work and ensure that I had not inadvertently revealed any sensitive information. Naturally, Di Li was one
of the censors in charge and upon reading it she shared her opinions
concerning the story I had written. Then she suddenly asked
whether or not I still fancied seeing the notebook? I answered, 'Yes,
of course.' She told me to come and see her the following day; but
before that day arrived, she came of her own volition to the guest
quarters and presented me with the notebook. As you would
expect, it was a photocopy of the original.

I need to explain three points:

1. THE COPY THAT DI LI PROVIDED ME WITH WAS INCOMPLETE.

Why do I say this? Well, as I understand things, each and every person
in Unit 701 uses the notebooks supplied by the Unit itself. There are
three sizes: the largest is 142 mm by 210 mm, the medium size is
130 mm by 184 mm, and the smallest is 90 mm by 100 mm. The exterior is either plastic or hard leather. Two colours are available for the
plastic covers, red or blue. Since Rong Jinzhen was partial to blue, all
the notebooks he used were the same: a blue, medium-sized notebook.

I've seen a genuine example of this kind of notebook (empty, of course), and so I know what they look like. Blazoned across the top and the bottom are the words 'Top Secret', stamped into the cover in red ink. In the middle of the cover the following is printed:

Serial No.: _____
Code No.: _____
Date: _____

The serial number gave the number in the series; the date indicated from when to when the notebook was used; the code number would tell you the agent's name. For instance, Rong Jinzhen's code number was 5603K. No one outside Unit 701 would recognize who that was, but everyone inside would: the year he began work at Unit 701 – 1956; the section he worked in – cryptography; the 03 in the middle indicating that during the aforementioned year he was the third person to have been recruited by Unit 701. Finally, each page is stamped with the words 'Top Secret' on the top right-hand side and a page number on the bottom right-hand side, all in dark red ink.

Looking at the copy given to me by Di Li I noticed immediately that it had been tampered with, because the 'Top Secret' banner on the right and the page numbers had all been removed. I thought, 'I can understand why the "Top Secret" banner was removed, since this material was no longer considered top secret. But why erase the page numbers?' At first, I couldn't figure it out. I counted the number of pages. There were seventy-two. I then began to understand. In the course of my research, I had learned that this type of notebook contained ninety-nine pages, and so it was clear that the photocopy provided by Di Li was incomplete. She offered two explanations: first, Rong Jinzhen had not used the entire notebook and thus many pages were blank and did not need to be copied; secondly, certain pages contained their personal secrets – the secrets between husband and wife – and so she did not wish me to see those. Hence they were omitted. From my point of view, those omitted pages were what I most wanted to see.

2. LOOKING AT THE DATES AND THE CONTENT, THE EARLY PAGES OF THE NOTEBOOK CONCERNED A TIME WHEN RONG JINZHEN FELL ILL.

One day in the middle of June in 1966, after he had eaten breakfast and had left the canteen, Rong Jinzhen abruptly lost consciousness and fell to the floor in the middle of the hallway. The side of his head hit the corner of a wooden bench – and the blood came gushing out. He was taken to hospital, whereupon they discovered that the blood dripping down his face was nothing compared to the bleeding in his stomach. The problem with his stomach had actually caused the fainting fit. The result of this diagnosis, coupled with the doctor believing that it was quite severe, meant that Rong Jinzhen was admitted to the hospital for treatment.

This hospital was exactly the same one as the chess-playing lunatic had been taken to all those years before – it was attached to Unit 701. Located next to the training base in the Southern Complex, the quality of its equipment and the skill of its physicians was no whit inferior to that of a big-city hospital. With respect to Rong Jinzhen's ailment – well, there was nothing really difficult about treating such a common condition, and it certainly would not give rise to the same kind of problem that the treatment of the lunatic had caused. The difficulty lay in the fact that although this hospital was attached to Unit 701, it was located in the Southern Complex and, as you can imagine, its level of secrecy could not be compared to that of the Northern Complex. To employ a rather inappropriate analogy: the relationship between the northern compound and the southern one was like the relationship between master and servant. A servant is always busy fulfilling his master's wishes, but what is the master up to? Alas, the servant is not privy to such information. Even if they were to learn of such things, they would not be permitted to talk about them, at least not openly. Strictly speaking, Rong Jinzhen's true identity was not to be disclosed even when he was in hospital. Of course, that was easier said than done, especially since he was such a well-known person; most people had already learned of him through formal or informal channels and everyone understood that he was a really important man. Of course, if your identity is made public then it is public; you could say that everyone in Unit 701 was part of the same family and so it didn't really matter one way or the other. Still, when it comes to work or other professional matters – well, those things are not to be revealed at any cost.

As we all now know, Rong Jinzhen always carried a notebook on his person. But when he got sick, when his blood was flowing down his face, he wasn't really cognizant of his own person, to say nothing of others, and so his notebook was brought along with him to the clinic. Of course, this was strictly prohibited. However, even though his personal security guard knew that he had been admitted to the hospital (in other words he was out of the Northern Complex), she didn't rush over immediately to collect it. Consequently, it wasn't until the evening of the day he took sick that Rong Jinzhen himself handed it in. Once the security bureau authorities learned of what had happened, they straight away reprimanded the guard, dismissed her from her position and began to make arrangements to appoint a new security officer to manage Rong Jinzhen's affairs. The new guard was none other than his future wife. From the looks of it, all of this must have happened three or four days after Rong Jinzhen had signed out this particular notebook – on the fourth or fifth day after he was admitted to hospital.

This notebook was most definitely not *that* notebook!

In truth, when Rong Jinzhen handed in the notebook himself, he didn't forget to make a request for a new one, because he was only too aware of his own personal habits – only too aware of his need to have a notebook always on his person. This was part of his life. You could say that this habit began on the day that Young Lillie gave him that Waterman pen; even though he was sick, a habit is a habit and they are hard to break. Of course, given his surroundings at the time, it would have been impossible for him to write anything involving work, and this is the reason why this particular notebook has been declassified and allowed to be held personally by Di Li. In my opinion, the notebook contains random thoughts and impressions about his time spent at the hospital.

3. THE PEOPLE MENTIONED IN THE NOTEBOOK ARE UNCLEAR.

The people he writes about are simply called 'you', 'he' and 'she'. It seems to me that all of these people lack any clear designation; the pronouns do not point to any single person. To use a linguist's vocabulary, the 'signifieds' are at play. That is to say, at times these pronouns seem to refer to himself, at other times to Liseiwicz, or Young Lillie, or his mother, or Master Rong. At yet other times it seems that the pronouns used refer to his wife, or the chess-playing lunatic, or the Christian God. There are times when they even seem to be referring to a tree or a dog. In any case, it's all very confusing, and perhaps he didn't really know himself who or what he was talking about, so the whole thing is quite a mess. Understanding it is something you will just have to play by ear. Why is it that I think you, my readers, can choose to read this section or not? Well, this is my reason: there is no way we can be sure we understand what is written in the notebook, no way to be certain, no way to grasp the exact meaning clearly; all we can do is rely upon our feelings and play it by ear – accept it for what it is. That being the case, reading what follows is up to you. It doesn't matter one way or the other. If you do want to continue, then to assist you in doing so, I've added numbers to each entry to help organize them, at least somewhat. Also, whatever was written in English has been translated.

01

He continues to demand that I live my life like a mushroom, to grow and flourish with the sun and earth, with the clouds and rain, and to eventually die by their hands. But it seems as though I can't do this. And now, for instance, he's changed into a house pet.

<u>A fucking house pet!</u>*

02

He feels this way: he's terrified of hospitals.

After being admitted to hospital, all the strongest men turn into pitiable creatures. Small and puny. Like children. Or old men. Other

---

* This was underlined in the original English version; as were some other passages below.

people will inevitably show concern for them . . . like the concern they show for a pet.

03

All that exists is reasonable, but not necessarily sensible – I heard him say this. Well said!

04

In the window you see the reflection of your head wrapped in a bandage; it's like a wounded soldier fresh from the front line.

05

Suppose the bleeding in my stomach is type A, the blood from my forehead is B, the serious illness is X, then it's quite obvious, the space between A and B possesses a multidirectional relationship with X, A is inside, B is outside, or perhaps A is dark, B is light. To proceed, you could also understand A as being on top, or positive, or this, B in contrast, B is on the bottom, or negative, or that, in brief it is a homologous multidirectional relationship. This type of multidirectional relationship does not need to be constructed upon a solid foundation, rather it is entirely random. But once this randomness appears, it becomes a necessity, then if there is no A there can be no B, B is the necessary counterpart of A. The concrete characteristic of this multidirectional relationship is akin to the theory of the binary nature of mathematical constants proposed by Georg Weinacht* . . . could it be that Weinacht has also experienced something similar to what you have, and took from it the inspiration to invent his theory?

06

There is an explanation for the wound on the edge of my forehead –

Paul said: 'The season prompts people to till the land, why is it that you are seated here, crying?'

The farmer said: 'Just now a donkey bucked and with one of its feet kicked out two of my front teeth.'

Paul said: 'Then you ought to be laughing, why is it that you cry?'

---

* Remember, Weinacht and Liseiwicz were one and the same. At this time, however, Rong Jinzhen did not know this.

The farmer said: 'I cry because I am in pain and feel deeply hurt, tell me, why should I laugh?'

Paul said: 'The Lord has said, for a young man to have lost his teeth and have had his forehead split is a good omen, it means that happiness will soon be upon you.'

The farmer said: 'Then please entreat the Lord to give me a son.'

In that year, the farmer indeed had a son.*

Now your forehead has also been cracked open, will happiness soon be upon you as well?

Something will indeed happen, only it is difficult for you to tell if it will be good or ill. That's because you don't know what is good for you.

07

I have seen all that is under heaven and it is all hollow, empty, all clutching at the wind. That which is crooked cannot be straightened, that which lacks cannot ever be sufficient. My heart tells me that I have obtained a formidable intelligence, surpassing all of those from my time before in Jerusalem, and my heart has experienced and possesses more knowledge and understands more of things. I have also been engrossed in open enquiries and secret searches into wisdom, egotism and ignorance, but I know that this is still only clutching at the wind. With much knowledge comes much worry and frustration; increasing knowledge only increases grief.†

08

He is very rich, ever richer.

He is destitute, ever more destitute.

He is he.

He is also he.

09

The doctor said a good stomach is smooth on the outside and rough on the inside: if you turned it inside out, with the rough side outer-

* This is a Bible story. The Apostle Paul was on the road to Jerusalem to preach. One day he met a farmer down on his knees, wailing profusely. They had the above conversation.

† This passage is derived from Ecclesiastes 5.

most, then a good stomach would look very much like a newly hatched chick, covered from top to bottom with shaggy hair. The hair would be evenly distributed. But my stomach is the reverse: it looks like someone suffering from favus of the scalp, oozing with blood and pus. The doctor also said most people assume that stomach disease is caused by the consumption of unhealthy foods, but actually, the main reason for a stomach ailment is obsessive worrying. It is not brought about by injurious drink and food, but by utopian longings and flights of fancy.

When have I consumed injurious drink and food?

My stomach seems like a foreign substance in my body, an enemy (a spy); it has never smiled at me.

10

You should loathe your stomach.

But you cannot.

The imprint of <u>Daddy</u> rests upon it.

It was that old man who had forged your stomach: it has a harmful disposition, extremely fragile, like a pear blossom. Does your stomach know how many pear blossoms it has consumed?

When your stomach hurts, you think of pear blossoms, you think of that old man.

<u>Daddy</u>, you're not dead, not only do you live in my heart, you also live on in my stomach.

11

You always exert great energy to walk forward; you don't like to look behind. Because you don't like to look behind, you make demands on yourself to exert even more energy to walk forward.

12

All that is under heaven has all been planned by God.

If you were allowed to make your own plans, you might make of yourself a hermit who has fled this world, or perhaps a prisoner. The best would be an innocent prisoner, or a prisoner who cannot be saved; in any case a man free of guilt.

At present, God's plan conforms to your wishes.

13

A shadow has caught hold of you.

Because you stopped.

14

Yet another shadow has caught hold of you!

15

Klaus Johannes said sleeping is most exhausting because you have to dream.

I say not working is most exhausting because your mind is empty. It is very much like dreaming; the past can take advantage of your weakness and burst in.

Work is the means by which the past can be forgotten, and even the reason for it can be cast off.

16

Like a bird leaving its nest. Like running away . . .

17

'You ungrateful bastard, where are you running to?'

'I'm to your west . . . in the valley a kilometre away.'

'Why haven't you returned to see us?'

'I can't . . . '

'Only a criminal cannot return home!'

'I am almost a criminal . . . '

<u>He is his own criminal!</u>

18

You gave him too much! With too much he simply won't dare to recollect, thinking makes him uncomfortable, he feels remorseful, humbled, he would think that all he has was obtained by luck and that would be depressing, as though his pitiful lot in life had been achieved by preying on your benevolence.

The ancients said, no more no less, no contentment no suffering.

God said, all under heaven is unsatisfactory . . .

19

Some people who are loved become blessed; others become cursed.

Because of such a blessing, he wanted to return.

Because of being cursed, he wanted to leave.

He did not leave because he discovered this, it was because he had left that he learned of it.

20

An ignorant person has no fear.

Fear is like a cord wound around him, pulling him back; it seemed to be hung round him telling people he was unsuitable to be confided in.

21

Mummy, how are you?

Mother, mother, my dear mother!

22

Before drifting off to sleep last night you purposely encouraged yourself to dream. But no trace remains of what you dreamed. You most likely dreamed about work because that was your objective, you wanted to free yourself of 'the worry about not working'.

23

Pointing his index finger at me, Klaus Johannes told me that in this profession he is the greatest, I'm next after him.* But he also criticized me, saying I had committed two fatal errors: first, I had become part of the system; second, I had gone about deciphering these mid- to low-level ciphers that other people could easily crack – the second mistake derived from the first.† The outcome of these two errors, Johannes told me, pushed me farther and farther away from him; it did not bring me closer. I said that now our adversary was no longer using any new high-level cipher, if I didn't do this work then what would I do? Klaus Johannes said he had recently completed writing a book, a work that represented the apex of high-level cryptography. Since comprehending the highest or the lowest level of secrets

* Karl Johannes, of German origin, was a famous cryptographer during the Second World War. He died in 1948.

† This much was certain, since after becoming section chief he participated in the deciphering of every cipher that they encountered.

was difficult, then whoever deciphered his book, whoever understood its contents, within thirty years that person could easily
decipher all of the most sophisticated ciphers in the world. He suggested that I try to decipher his book and at the same time stuck his
thumb up to me saying that if I should crack it, then his thumb
would represent me.

Contrary to what one might expect, this was actually good news.

But where is this book?

In my dream.

No, it was in the dream within my dream, in the mind of my
imaginary Klaus Johannes.

24

If this world truly had such a book, it could only have come from the
hand of Klaus Johannes.

No one else!

In all honesty, his mind was just like this book.

25

During his lifetime, Klaus Johannes did write one book; it was called
The Writing of the Gods.* Someone once said that they saw it in a
bookshop. But this is highly unlikely since I have already mobilized
all the forces at my disposal to search for the book and yet we have
not found it.

There is nothing in this world that my people can't locate, unless
there was nothing there to begin with.

26

You are a rat.

You are waiting inside a barn.

But you cannot eat the millet.

Each grain of millet has been daubed with a protective coating to
prevent your teeth from gnawing into it.

– That is cryptography.

* *The Writing of the Gods*: Chunghwa Book Company, 1945; the translation was
given the title *The Riddle*. Clearly Rong Jinzhen was angry that the secret services
had searched for this book but could not find it.

27

Ciphers on the one hand make the intelligence that you need disappear from under your eyes – you reach out and yet you cannot touch it. On the other hand they blind your eyes, so that you can see nothing.

28

When Douglas MacArthur stood on the Korean peninsula, he raised his hand into the sky and caught a handful, then he gestured to his cryptographers and said: 'this is the intelligence that I wanted, I want to know everything, things that are all around me, things that I cannot see because I am blind. It is up to you to restore my vision.'

Several years later, in his reminiscences he wrote: 'My cryptographers never once let me open my eyes, not even once. I was very lucky to come back alive.'

29

Might as well repeat MacArthur's action and extend a hand to grasp at the sky. But your purpose is not to grasp the air, but to catch a bird. There is always a bird in the sky, but the likelihood of you grabbing hold of it with your bare hands is terribly remote. This remoteness is not the same as saying it's impossible, since some people can indeed miraculously grab hold of a bird in the sky.

– That is decryption.

However, the majority of people will grab hold of only a few bird feathers, even if they work on it their whole lives.

30

What kind of person can truly grab hold of a bird?

Perhaps John Nash could.★

But Liseiwicz can't, although his genius is not necessarily inferior to that of John Nash.

★ John Nash, the American mathematician, played a key role in the development of game theory, for which he was one of the recipients of the 1994 Nobel Prize in Economics. His accomplishments in the field of pure mathematics were equally astounding: he was one of the founders of modern partial differential mathematics. Unfortunately, at the age of just thirty-four, he developed severe paranoid schizophrenia. This brought his remarkable genius to a premature conclusion.

31

Although Nash would be able to catch a bird in flight, in my mind's eye I couldn't be sure of when he might do so. However, as long as Liseiwicz paid close attention to Nash's line of sight, to the precise moment at which he began to move his hand; if he paid attention to his attitude, his nimbleness, his accuracy, his power to leap, etc.; if he were to raise his head again to scan the skies for the number of birds in it, the speed at which they were flying, their path, special characteristics and changes in their motion, etc.; then perhaps he could judge when Nash would reach out to clasp a bird in his hands.

Possessing the same level of ability, Liseiwicz's genius was more rigorous, cautious, and more beautiful, like that of an angel, like a god. Nash's genius, however, was something unfamiliar, an unfamiliarity that made it seem freakish and uncivilized, as though he was possessed by an evil spirit. Ciphers are the work of the devil; they stand as testament to the craftiness and evilness of people, to our treacherous nature, our sinister intent, our devilish aptitude, there are no steps to be added, thus Nash, a man indistinguishable from the devil, was able to draw ever so close to them.

32

Sleep and death have the same given name, but not the same surname.

Sleep prepares one for death; dreams are a kind of hell.

People say that your spirit passes through your carcass to become small, your mind passes through your corpse to become tiny, this is the fundamental characteristic of demons and hobgoblins.

People also say that since you have had dealings with the dream world since you were a child, you've been polluted by the wickedness and evil encountered there; that is why you are able to catch hold of a bird in mid-flight.

33

All the secrets of this world are held in dreams.

34

You only need to prove yourself.

When you do so, your opponent will assist you.

When you cannot, your opponent will prove himself.

35

<u>You long for some other person of talent to step forth and permit
you to keep your mouth shut. But to make this happen, you need to
continue to speak</u>.★

36

They've changed my personal security guard yet again; the reason
for this one's dismissal was her failure to come and collect my notebook.

    She's not the first to be dismissed and she won't be the last.

37

My new personal security guard will most definitely be a woman
. . . †

★ I can speculate that since English is used here, this is some quotation or other, but
I cannot find the source.
† During the mid 1970s, marriage for members of Unit 701 had to follow strict
regulations. For instance, female comrades were prohibited from having romantic
relationships with people outside the unit. If a man wished to begin a relationship
with someone from the outside (although equality between the sexes was officially promoted, in reality men were privileged over women), they needed to
report this to the relevant authorities. Once the report was made, the organization
would dispatch agents to investigate the woman's background. If consent was
given, the relationship was allowed to proceed to the next level. Later, if this person did not wish to do a particular thing, or if there was some 'problem' that was
difficult to resolve, then they could request that the Party step in and resolve it for
them. The issue of Rong Jinzhen's marriage had created quite a thorny problem
for the authorities to deal with because he was getting older and older and yet had
done nothing about getting married. He was not taking any initiative nor was he
asking the authorities for help. Once he passed thirty years of age, the Party took
it upon themselves to secretly and shrewdly arrange a marriage for him. First they
selected an appropriate person and then arranged for that person to serve as Rong
Jinzhen's personal security guard. Not only would this woman have to have the
complete trust of the Party, she also had to be determined to be by his side and
hope to marry him. If she could not do that, she would have to leave in order to
provide someone else with the opportunity – perhaps the next person would have
better luck. It was due to this intricate plan that Rong Jinzhen's personal security
guard continued to change over and over again: the current guard was already his
fourth.

38

Who is she?

Do you know her?

Do you hope it is someone you know, or not?

Did she volunteer, or was she talked into doing this kind of job?

Will she come to see me in the hospital tomorrow?

Christ! This really gives one a headache!

39

The devil continues to bear and raise children because it wants to eat them all.

40

The doctor told me that my stomach is still bleeding a bit. He felt it odd that he had administered such excellent medicine and yet still had not seen the hoped for results. I told him the reason for that: since I was in my teens I have been taking stomach medicines as if they were meals: I've simply consumed too much medicine; I've become numb to its effect. He decided to administer something new. I told him that it didn't matter, as there were no new medicines that I hadn't already tried; the crux of the matter was that the dosage needed to be increased. He told me that that was too risky, he didn't dare do it. From my point of view, I had better prepare myself to remain here a little while longer.

41

That loathsome pet!

42

She's come.

They always rush forward bravely, ready to suffer at your side.

43

When she is here, the hospital room feels practically thronged with people.

When she leaves, looking at her back, you almost forget that she is a woman.

She needed seven cakes in order to relieve her hunger.*

---

* This most likely comes from the Bible, but I cannot be sure of where.

44

She's not very good at concealing things – what a terrible cipher she would make! You couldn't help but feel that while in front of people she was not unlike you and in need of greater composure. As this is the case, why does she put herself through this? You have to realize, this is just the beginning. This has determined that every day you have to spend your time feeling bewildered and helpless; anyway, I knew that he wouldn't sympathize with someone who had taken the wrong path.

45

Trying to help me with my train of thought is a type of sickness; only bed rest can help me to fully recover.

46

Thinking too much is also a disease.

47

Blue sky, white clouds, treetops, a breeze, something swaying, a window, a bird swooping past, like a dream . . . a new day, wind just like time, water just like life . . . some memories, some sighs, some confusion, some unforgettable events, some contingencies, something laughable . . . you see two points: the first is space, the second is time, or perhaps you could say, the first is the day, the second is night . . .

48

The doctor has told me that dreaming ruins your health, it is a sickness.

49

She brought me a carton of Daqianmen cigarettes, Guoguang brand blue ink, Junshan Yellow tea, a metronome, soothing balm, a radio, a feather fan, and a copy of *Romance of the Three Kingdoms*. It seems as though she were studying me . . . but she is wrong, I wouldn't listen to a radio. My soul is my radio, every day it whispers to me non-stop; just like my metronome, the vibration caused by footsteps can cause it to swing back and forth for ever so long.

Your soul is hoisted up in mid-air, just like a pendulum.

50

It was in a dream that he first saw himself smoking and then afterwards he started to smoke.

51

Smoking Daqianmen cigarettes was a habit cultivated my Miss Jiang.* She was from Shanghai. One time, after she returned from a visit home, she brought these cigarettes back with her. She said they were good and that she was going to have her family send her a carton every month. He liked to hear her speak Shanghainese; it sounds like the chirping of a bird, melodious, sharp and clear, complex; you could imagine her tongue being pointed and thin. It seemed as though he fancied her, but there wasn't time to find out. Her problem was that when she walked there was too much noise, too much racket. Later it was as though she had horseshoes nailed to the soles of her feet, it was simply more than he could bear. In actual fact, this wasn't a noise problem; rather it implied that his soul could at any moment float away – whilst floating it is common to grasp firmly the corner of one's clothes, and then fall from up in the air.

52

If he had a choice between day and night, he would choose night.

If he had a choice between a mountain and a river, he would choose the mountain.

If he had a choice between a flower and grass, he would choose grass.

If he had a choice between a man and a ghost, he would choose the ghost.

If he had a choice between a living man and a dead man, he would choose a dead man.

If he had a choice between being blind and being deaf, he would choose deafness.

To sum up, he despised noise and anything that made it.

This is also a kind of illness, like colour blindness, there is either a greater or lesser natural disposition to suffer from it.

* Miss Jiang was his first female personal security guard.

53

A sorcerer unable to reach his goal . . .

54

What a terribly sinister-looking thing!

She said it was a chiton;* in folk legends they're said to come from the unnatural mating of a toad and a snake,† and they are peculiarly effective in treating stomach ailments. This I believe: one reason being they are used as a folk remedy to treat incurable diseases; the second being that my stomach ailment is just like this sinister-looking animal, and perhaps I can only rely on such a sinister and frightening thing to bring it under control. Supposedly, she spent an entire day trekking through the mountains to collect them, which must have been very difficult for her. <u>Until the day breaks and the shadows flee away, I will get me to the mountain of myrrh and to the hill of frankincense</u>.‡

55

The forest seems to be breathing under the moonlight, then it shrinks back, forming a thick mass, it becomes small, the treetops stand erect, then in a moment it unfolds, following the hillside, spreading out with it, becoming short, low brush, so much so that it becomes hazy, a far-off image . . . §

56

I suddenly felt that my stomach was empty, at peace, as if it weren't there – I haven't felt this way for many years! For so long now I have felt that my stomach was a septic tank, permeated with a burning, evil smell; now it seemed as though it had sprung a leak, it had deflated, gone soft, loosened up. It is said that you need twenty-four

---

* Chitons are marine molluscs: they survive between mountains and rocks and are a sort of soft-shelled turtle. Compared to other molluscs, their exterior skin is much coarser and frightening. They are extremely rare and have a multitude of medicinal properties.

† But in fact they do not; they are a type of soft-shelled turtle.

‡ Taken from the Song of Solomon 4:6.

§ Source unknown.

hours before you feel the effects of Chinese medicine, but only a few hours have passed, it is simply unbelievable!

Might this be a miracle cure?

57

It was the first time I saw her laugh.

It was an incredibly restrained laugh, very unnatural, absolutely silent and very short, over in an instant, like someone laughing in a painting.

Her laugh proved that she doesn't like to laugh.

Does she really dislike laughing? Or . . .

58

He abided by an old fisherman's proverb to handle his affairs, the primary meaning of the proverb was: the flesh of an intelligent fish is much firmer than the flesh of a stupid fish and yet they are destructive, because a stupid fish is indiscriminate about what it eats, whereas an intelligent fish chooses to eat the stupid fish . . .

59

In what seemed to be an effort to continue to provide me with treatment, the lead physician gave me a list of food to eat: hot porridge, steamed buns, soft bean curd in sauce. He made clear that this was all that I should eat, and no one was to alter the ingredients or the amounts. However, according to my experience, at this time I should eat noodles and they should be a little undercooked.

60

Our lives are full of ideas that we have created for ourselves, these are much more real than genuine ideas that have stood the test of time.

This is because our mistaken ideas appear before us, familiar and powerful.

When it comes to ciphers, you are the doctor, they are the patients.

61

You take them along the same road. The road you walk may lead to heaven but it will take them to hell. The things you have achieved are indeed fewer than those you have destroyed . . .

62

Good fortune and calamity rely upon each other, good can come from bad, bad can come from good.

63

Like a clock, she always arrives on time; she is equally punctual about leaving.

She appears with no sound, she leaves in silence.

Is she doing this because she understands you, wishes to pander to you, or was she always like this?

I thought . . . I don't know . . .

64

Unexpectedly you hope that she won't come today, but actually you worry that she won't.

65

She works more than she speaks and everything she does is done in silence, just like that metronome. But working in this way has allowed her to quietly establish authority over you.

Her silence could be smelted into gold.

66

<u>For God is in heaven, and thou upon earth: therefore let thy words be few. For a dream cometh through the multitude of business; and a fool's voice is known by the multitude of words . . . For in the multitude of dreams and many words there are also diverse vanities.</u>*

67

Has she read the Bible?

68

She is an orphan!

She's been more unfortunate than you!

She's been reared on the food of the masses!

She is a genuine orphan!

An orphan – a word you are most sensitive about!

* Taken from Ecclesiastes 5.

69

The answer to the riddle is suddenly clear.

She is an orphan, that's the answer.

What is an orphan? An orphan has its upper and lower teeth, but its tongue is incomplete. An orphan always uses its gaze to speak. An orphan is born of the earth (everyone else is born of water). An orphan's heart is for ever scarred . . .

70

Tell her, you are also an orphan . . . no, why tell her? Do you hope to draw nearer to her? Why do you want to be nearer her? Is it because she is an orphan? Or is it because . . . because . . . how is it that you suddenly have so many problems? Problems are the shadows of what one desires . . . geniuses and fools have no problems, they only have demands.

71

Hesitation is also a form of power, but it is an ordinary person's power.

Ordinary people like to complicate things; those who create ciphers have the ability to see this, but those who crack ciphers don't.

72

She stayed an extra thirty minutes today because she was reading to me about Pavel Korchagin, the main character in *How the Steel Was Tempered*. She said this was her favourite book. She carried it with her wherever she went and, whenever she had free time, she would pull it out to read. Today I scanned through it. She asked if I had read it and I answered that I hadn't; she then asked if she could read it to me. She speaks very good Mandarin. She told me that she had worked as a phone operator at Headquarters. Several years ago she actually had heard my voice over the phone . . .

73

The difference lies here: some people prepare for any eventuality while others do not; one should never criticize oneself for this.

74

In his dreams, he saw himself wading waist-deep in a river while reading a book. The book contained no words . . . then the water began to surge and swirl, he put the book on his head to prevent it from getting wet. Once the surging water passed, he realized that the water had taken his clothes with it. He was naked in the river . . .

75
In this world, every person's dream has already been dreamed by everyone else!

76/77
He dreamed two dreams simultaneously; one was above, one was below . . . *

   . . . What he experienced in his dream made him waken weary and exhausted; it seemed as though his dream had boiled him down to the dregs.

78
A terrible fall can wreck even the greatest triumph. But that's not for certain.

79
You're thinking about things you would never have imagined that you might think about.

80
There is only one method to get rid of you: to look at you with one's own eyes.

81
Listen . . . . one . . . .
you . . . .
. . . . eyes . . . .
. . . . most . . . .
. . . .
. . . . . . on . . . .
. . . . . . you . . . †

---

* This page was filled, but the subsequent page has no header: I suspect that some sections have been removed.

† Whatever he wrote here he erased; it was only possible to make out a few words.

82

Two types of sickness: the former causes mostly pain, the latter makes one dream. The former can be treated with medicine, the latter, too. But the medicine is in one's dreams. One can recover quickly from the former illness; the latter burns you up.

83

Dreams! Wake up, wake up!
  Dreams! Don't wake up!

84/85

Listen, this time he won't write something and then erase it, he . . . *
  . . . As the lily among thorns, as the apple tree among the trees of the wood!†

86

The symbol of your life is dying out, like one insect being devoured by another.

87

A cage is expecting a bird . . . ‡

88

This is one road that everyone walks, and so it is easy to recognize.

89

A bird!

90

Could it be that he hasn't struggled enough? A cage waits for a bird, although . . . §

It is easy to tell by looking at the notebook that its contents are in a jumble, and it is quite obscure at times. But you can see how Rong

---

* I suspect some sections have been removed.
† Taken from the Song of Solomon 2.
‡ Unknown source.
§ This page was completed, but the pages that followed were removed. I don't know how many are missing.

Jinzhen's love for Miss Di grew, you can see how his feelings evolved. Especially in the latter sections, his deep feelings for her become apparent. I reckon that the sections Miss Di removed were most likely expressing intimate, emotional things, and they were probably even more obscure than the rest of it. That's because I once asked her if Rong Jinzhen had expressed his love for her in a straightforward manner and she told me that he hadn't. However, she also said that perhaps he had, since some of his words had that meaning.

I asked her over and over again what those words were, but she hesitated and hesitated. Finally she told me that the words were not his own, they were quoted from the Song of Solomon, specifically song number four, the final verse. I looked this up afterwards to learn exactly what he had written. It must have been this: 'Awake, O north wind; and come, thou south; blow upon my garden, that the spices thereof may flow out. Let my beloved come into his garden, and eat his pleasant fruits.'

Since the notebook contained intimate details of their relationship, it's not really right for me to criticize her for removing those sections; it's just that from my point of view, it makes it more difficult for me to understand their relationship, because things have been held back, left behind: they are still secret. Thus, I believe you could say that this notebook serves as a sort of cipher that has encrypted their relationship, closed it off to outsiders.

I should say that, with respect to Rong Jinzhen being a man of genius and a formidable cryptanalyst, I grasp enough of the picture; I understand who he was. But in terms of emotion, of love, of the private exchanges that take place between a man and a woman, then I will for ever be left in the dark, unable to see the entire picture. The information I do possess that could shed light on this side of Rong Jinzhen is incomplete; pieces are missing. I have a feeling that there are those who do not wish to have this side of Rong Jinzhen revealed to outside people, as if this could remove some of the lustre from his image. Maybe, with respect to someone like Rong Jinzhen, personal feelings, emotions of an intimate nature, feelings of friendship – well, perhaps they shouldn't have these types of emotions. Because they shouldn't have these inner feelings, perhaps he was the one who tore them out in the first place. Even if it was difficult for him, some-one else might have thought of a means to tear them out.

According to his wife, it was on the afternoon on the third day of his discharge from the hospital that he arrived at her office to person-ally hand in the notebook. As a security guard, it was her duty to inspect all notebooks as they were turned in, to determine whether or not any pages were missing or there were any pages left over: that was her responsibility. So, after Rong Jinzhen handed her the note-book, she performed her duty and inspected it. He remarked, 'The notebook contains no work-related secrets, just my own personal ones. If you're curious about me, you might as well look through it. I hope you do; I also hope to receive your reply.'

Di Li told me that the sun had already gone down by the time she finished reading the notebook and she had to walk back to her dor-mitory room in the dark. It seemed as though some evil spirit had entered Rong Jinzhen's room. In fact, Di Li lived in building thirty-eight, whereas Rong Jinzhen lived in the specialists' building: they were in different directions. Both buildings are still there, the former is made of red brick and has three storeys; the latter is two storeys tall and constructed from a bluish-green brick. I once stood in front of this bluish-green building; now I'm looking at its photo, and in my mind I can hear her voice: 'When I arrived at my building, he was there looking at me. He didn't speak and, even though he was sitting, he didn't ask me to join him. I stood there in front of him and told him I had finished reading his notebook. He asked me to speak; he would listen. I asked him to let me be his wife. He replied: "Yes." Three days later we were married.'

How incredibly easy, like a story out of the legends – practically unbelievable!

To tell you the truth, when she said this to me she revealed no emotions, neither sadness nor happiness, neither surprise nor won-der; it seemed that even the emotional attachment people have to memories was absent, just as if she were relating the events of a dream for the umpteenth time. It made it very difficult for me to figure out how she felt at that time and how she felt when she told me this story. Perhaps presumptuously, I asked her frankly whether or not she loved Rong Jinzhen. This was her response: 'I love him as I love my country.'

Afterwards I asked her again: 'I heard that soon after you were married your adversary began using BLACK, is that right?'

'Yes.'

'And after that he rarely returned home?'

'Yes.'

'Do you think he regretted marrying you?'

'Yes.'

'And how about you, do you regret marrying him?'

I noticed then that this question took her by surprise; she opened her eyes wide, stared at me and replied excitedly: 'Regret? When you love your country, how can you regret it? No! For ever the answer will be no – !'

Her eyes immediately filled with tears and she began to sniffle as if she was about to cry.

Begun July 1991 in Beijing, Haidian, Weigongcun
Completed August 2002 in Chengdu, Qingyang, Luojianian